Dark

I sank back on my pillow. I felt as if I had a split personality. On the one hand, I was Morgan Rowlands, good daughter, honor roll student, math whiz, observant Catholic. On the other hand, I was a witch, by heritage and inclination.

I stretched, feeling the ache in my muscles. The events of the night before hovered over my head like a storm cloud. What had I done? How had I come to this? If only I knew for sure whether or not Hunter was dead. . . .

I waited until I heard the front door close behind my family. Then I got up and began pulling on my clothes. I knew what I had to do next.

. . .

SWEEP

SWEEP

Cate Tiernan

Volume II

Dark Magick
Awakening
Spellbound

speak
An Imprint of Penguin Group (USA) Inc.

For my mùirn beatha dàn

Dark Magick

SPEAK
Published by the Penguin Group
Penguin Young Readers Group, 345 Hudson Street, New York, New York 10014, U.S.A.
Penguin Group (Canada), 90 Eglinton Avenue East, Suite 700, Toronto, Ontario, Canada M4P 2Y3
(a division of Pearson Penguin Canada Inc.)
Penguin Books Ltd, 80 Strand, London WC2R 0RL, England
Penguin Ireland, 25 St Stephen's Green, Dublin 2, Ireland (a division of Penguin Books Ltd)
Penguin Group (Australia), 250 Camberwell Road, Camberwell, Victoria 3124, Australia
(a division of Pearson Australia Group Pty Ltd)
Penguin Books India Pvt Ltd, 11 Community Centre, Panchsheel Park, New Delhi - 110 017, India
Penguin Group (NZ), 67 Apollo Drive, Rosedale, North Shore 0632, New Zealand
(a division of Pearson New Zealand Ltd)
Penguin Books (South Africa) (Pty) Ltd, 24 Sturdee Avenue, Rosebank, Johannesburg 2196, South Africa

Registered Offices: Penguin Books Ltd, 80 Strand, London WC2R 0RL, England

Published by Puffin Books, a division of Penguin Young Readers Group, 2001
Published by Speak, an imprint of Penguin Group (USA) Inc., 2007
This omnibus edition published by Speak, an imprint of Penguin Group (USA) Inc., 2010

1 3 5 7 9 10 8 6 4 2

Produced by 17th Street Productions,
an Alloy company
151 West 26th Street
New York, NY 10001

17th Street Productions and associated logos
are trademarks and/or registered trademarks of Alloy, Inc.

Speak ISBN 978-0-14-240989-3
This omnibus ISBN 978-0-14-241897-0

Printed in the United States of America

BOOK FOUR

SWEEP
DARK MAGICK

1

Falling

November 1999

The council pronounced me not guilty of killing Linden. The vote of the seven elders of the Great Clans was not unanimous, though. The Vikroth representative and the Wyndenkell, my mother's own clanswoman, voted against me.

I had almost hoped they would condemn me, for then at least my life's path would be certain. And in a way, I was guilty, was I not? I filled Linden's head with my talk of vengeance, and opened his mind to the idea of calling on the darkness. If I had not actually killed my brother, then I knew he had found his way to his death along a path I had shown him.

When I was found innocent, I felt lost. I knew only that I would spend the rest of my life atoning for Linden's death.

—Giomanach

Snowflakes mixed with sleet whipped at my cheeks. I stumbled through the snow, supporting my boyfriend Cal's weight against me, my feet growing leaden and icy in my clogs. Cal stumbled, and I braced myself. In the moonlight I peered up at his face, alarmed by how white he looked, how beaten, how ill. I trudged through the dark woods, feeling like every step away from the cliff took an hour.

The cliff. In my mind, I saw Hunter Niall falling backward, his arms windmilling as he went over the edge. Bile rose in my throat, and I swallowed convulsively. Yes, Cal was a mess, but Hunter was probably dead. Dead! And Cal and I had killed him. I drew in a shuddering breath as Cal swayed against me.

Together we stumbled through the woods, accompanied only by the malevolent hiss of the sleet in the black branches around us. Where was Cal's house?

"Are we headed the right way?" I asked Cal. The freezing wind snatched the words from my throat.

Cal blinked. One eye was swollen shut and already purple. His beautiful mouth was bloody, and his lower lip was split.

"Never mind," I said, looking ahead. "I think this is it."

By the time Cal's house was in view, we were both soaked through and frozen. Anxiously I scanned the circular driveway for Selene Belltower's car, but Cal's mother was still out. Not good. I needed help.

"Tired," Cal said fuzzily as I helped him up the steps. Somehow we made it through the front door, but once inside, there was no way I could get him up to his attic room.

"There." Cal gestured with a hand swollen from punching Hunter. Feeling unbearably weary, I lurched through the parlor doors and helped Cal collapse on the blue sofa. He toppled over, curling to fit on the cushions.

He was shaking with cold, his face shocked and pale.

"Cal," I said, "we need to call 911. About Hunter. Maybe they can find him. It might not be too late."

Cal's face crinkled in a grotesque approximation of a laugh. His split lip oozed blood, and his cheek was mottled with angry bruises. "It's too late," he croaked, his teeth chattering. "I'm positive." He nodded toward the fireplace, his eyes shut. "Fire."

Was it too late for Hunter? A tiny part of me almost hoped it was—if Hunter was dead, then we couldn't help him, and I didn't even have to try.

But was he? A sob rose in my throat. Was he?

Okay, I thought, trying to calm down. Okay. Break down the situation. Make a plan. I knelt and clumsily piled newspaper and kindling on the grate. I chose three large logs and arranged them on top.

I didn't see any matches, so, closing my eyes, I tried to summon fire with my mind. But my magickal powers felt almost nonexistent. In fact, just trying to call on them made my head ache sharply. After nearly seventeen years of living without magick, to find myself bereft of it now was terrifying. I opened my eyes and looked wildly around. Finally I saw an Aim 'n' Flame on the mantel, and I grabbed it and popped its trigger.

The paper and kindling caught. I swayed toward the flames, feeling their healing warmth, then I glanced at Cal again. He looked wretched.

"Cal?" I helped him sit up enough to tug him out of his leather jacket, taking care not to scrape his wrists, which were raw and blistered where Hunter had tried to bind them with a strange magickal chain. I pulled off Cal's wet boots. Then I covered him up with a patchwork velvet throw that was draped artistically over one end of the couch. He squeezed my fingers and tried to smile at me.

"Be right back," I said, and hurried to the kitchen. I felt horribly alone as I waited for water to boil. I ran upstairs and rummaged through the first bathroom I found for bandages, then went back down and fixed a pot of herb tea. A pale face with accusing green eyes seemed to form in the steam that rose from the top of the teapot. Hunter, oh, God, Hunter.

Hunter had tried to kill Cal, I reminded myself. He might have tried to kill me, too. Still, it was Hunter who had gone over the edge of the cliff into the Hudson River, the river filled with ice chunks as big as his head. It was Hunter who had probably been swept away by the current and Hunter whose body would be found tomorrow. Or not. I clamped my lips together to keep from sobbing as I hurried back to Cal.

Slowly I got Cal to drink a whole mug of goldenseal-and-ginger tea. His color looked better when he had finished it. I gently swabbed his wrists with a damp cloth, then wrapped them with a roll of gauze I had found, but the skin was blistered, and I knew it must hurt incredibly.

After the tea Cal lay down again and slept, his breathing uneven. Should I have given him Tylenol? Should I hunt around for witch-type medicine? In the short while I had known Cal, he had been the strong one in our relationship. I had counted on him. Now he was counting on me, and I didn't know if I was ready.

The mantel clock above my head struck three slow chimes. I stared at it. Three o'clock in the morning! I set my mug down on the coffee table. I was supposed to be home by one. And I didn't even have my car—Cal had picked me up. He was clearly in no shape to drive. Selene wasn't back yet. Dammit! I said to myself. Think, think.

I could call my dad and have him come get me. Very unappealing option.

It was too late to call the only taxi service in Widow's Vale, which was in essence Ed Jinkins in his old Cutlass Supreme hanging out at the commuter station.

I could take Cal's car.

Five minutes later I let myself out of the house carefully. Cal was still asleep. I had taken the keys from his jacket, then written a note of explanation and tucked it in his jeans pocket, hoping he would understand. I stopped dead when I saw Hunter's gray sedan sitting in the driveway like an accusation. Crap! What to do about his car?

There was nothing I could do. Hunter had the keys. And he was gone. I couldn't push the car anywhere by myself and anyway, that seemed so—methodical somehow. So planned.

My head spun. What should I do? Waves of exhaustion flowed over me, almost making me weep. But I had to accept the fact that I couldn't do anything about this. Cal or Selene would have to deal with Hunter's car. Trembling, I climbed into Cal's gold Explorer, turned on the brights, and headed for home.

Cal had used spells on me tonight, spells of binding so I couldn't move. Why? So I wouldn't interfere in his battle with Hunter? So I wouldn't be hurt? Or because he didn't trust me? Well, if he hadn't trusted me before, he knew better now. I clamped my teeth together on a semihysterical giggle. It wasn't every girl who would throw a Wiccan ceremonial dagger into the neck of her boyfriend's enemy.

Hunter had tried to kill Cal, had bound his hands with spelled silver chain that had started to sizzle against Cal's flesh as soon as it touched him. That was when I'd hurled the athame at him and sent him over the cliff's edge. And probably killed him. Killed him.

I shuddered as I turned onto my street. *Had* we actually killed him? Did Hunter have a chance? Maybe the wound in his neck wasn't as horrific as it had seemed. Maybe, when he went over the cliff, he had landed on a ledge. Maybe he was found by a park ranger or someone like that.

Maybe.

I let the Explorer drift to a halt around the corner from my house. As I pocketed the keys, I noticed all the birthday gifts Cal had given me earlier, piled up on the backseat. Well, almost all. The beautiful athame was gone—Hunter had taken it over the cliff with him. With a sense of unreality I gathered up the other gifts and then ran home down the shoveled and salted walks. I let myself in silently, feeling with my senses. Again my magick was like a single match being held in a storm wind instead of the powerful wave I was used to feeling. I couldn't detect much of anything.

To my relief, my parents didn't stir as I went past their bedroom door. In my own room I sat for a moment on the edge of my bed, collecting my strength. After the nightmarish events of tonight my bedroom looked babyish, as if it belonged to a stranger. The pink-and-white-striped walls, flowered border, and frilly curtains had never been me, anyway. Mom had picked everything out and redone the room for me as a surprise while I was at camp, six years ago.

I threw off my clammy clothes and sighed with relief as I

pulled on sweats. Then I went downstairs and dialed 911.

"What is the nature of the emergency?" a crisp voice asked.

"I saw someone fall into the Hudson," I said quickly, speaking through a tissue like they did in old movies. "About two miles up from the North Bridge." This was an estimate, based on where I thought Cal's house was. "Someone fell in. He may need help." I hung up quickly, hoping I hadn't stayed on the phone long enough for the call to be traced. How did that work? Did I have to stay on for a minute? Thirty seconds? Oh, Jesus. If they tracked me down I would confess everything. I couldn't live with this burden on my soul.

My mind was racing with everything that had happened: my wonderful, romantic birthday with Cal; almost making love but then backing out; all my gifts; the magick we shared; my birth mother's athame, which I had shown Cal tonight and was now clutching like a security blanket; then the battle with Hunter, the horror as he fell. And now it was too late, Cal said. But was it? I had to try one last thing.

I put on my wet coat, went outside, and walked around the side of my house in the darkness. Holding my birth mother's athame, I leaned close to a windowsill. There, glowing faintly beneath the knife's power, shimmered a sigil. Sky Eventide and Hunter had surrounded my house with the charms; I still didn't know why. But I hoped this would work.

Once more closing my eyes, I held the athame over the sigil. I concentrated, feeling like I was about to pass out. Sky, I thought, swallowing. Sky.

I hated Sky Eventide. Everything about her filled me with loathing and distrust, just as Hunter did, though for some reason Hunter upset me more. But she was his ally, and she was the person who should be told about him. I sent my thought out toward the purplish snow clouds. Sky. Hunter is in the river, by Cal's house. Go get him. He needs your help.

What am I doing? I thought, beyond weariness. I can't even light a match. I can't feel my family sleeping inside my house. My magick is gone. But still I stood there in the cold darkness, my eyes closed, my hand turning to a frozen claw around the knife handle. Hunter is in the river. Go get him. Go get Hunter. Hunter is in the river.

Tears came without warning, shockingly warm against my chilled cheeks. Gasping, I stumbled back inside and hung up my coat. Then I slowly mounted the steps, one by one, and was dimly surprised when I made it to the top. I hid my mother's athame under my mattress and crawled into bed. My kitten, Dagda, stretched sleepily, then moved up to coil himself next to my neck. I curled one hand around him. Huddled under my comforter, I shook with cold and wept until the first blades of sunlight pierced the childish, ruffled curtains at my window.

2

Guilty

Uncle Beck, Aunt Shelagh, and Cousin Athan held a small celebration for me back at the house, after the trial. But my heart was full of pain.

I sat at the kitchen table. Aunt Shelagh and Alwyn were swooping around, arranging food on plates. Then Uncle Beck came in. He told me that I'd been cleared of the blame and I must let it go.

"How can I?" I asked. It was I who'd first tried to use dark magick to find our parents. Though Linden had acted alone in calling on the dark spectre that killed him, he wouldn't have had the idea if I hadn't put it into his head.

Then Alwyn spoke up. She said I was wrong, that Linden had always liked the dark side. She said he liked the power, and that he'd thought making herb mixtures was beneath him. Her halo of corkscrew curls, fiery red like our Mum's, seemed to quiver as she spoke.

"What are you on about?" I asked her. "Linden never mentioned any of this to me."

She said Linden had believed I wouldn't understand. He'd told her he wanted to be the most powerful witch anyone had ever seen. Her words were like needles in my heart.

Uncle Beck asked why she hadn't told us sooner, and she said she had. I saw her jut her chin in that obstinate way she has. And Aunt Shelagh thought about it, and said, "You know, she did. She did tell me. I thought she was telling stories."

Alwyn said no one had believed her because she was just a kid. Then she left the room, while Uncle Beck, Aunt Shelagh, and I sat in the kitchen and weighed our guilt.

—Giomanach

I woke up on my seventeenth birthday feeling like someone had put me in a blender and set it to chop. Sleepily I blinked and checked my clock. Nine. Dawn had come at six, so I had gotten a big three hours' sleep. Great. And then I thought—is Hunter dead? Did I kill him? My stomach roiled, and I wanted to cry.

Under the covers, I felt a small warm body creeping cautiously along my side. When Dagda poked his little gray head out from under the covers, I stroked his ears.

"Hi, little guy," I said softly. I sat up just as the door to my room opened.

"Morning, Birthday Girl!" my mom said brightly. She

crossed my room and pushed aside the curtains, filling my room with brittle sunlight.

"Morning," I said, trying to sound normal. A vision of my mom finding out about Hunter made me shudder. It would destroy her.

She sat on my bed and kissed my forehead, as if I was seven instead of seventeen. Then she peered at me. "Do you feel all right?" She pressed the back of her hand against my forehead. "Hmmm. No fever. But your eyes look a bit red and puffy."

"I'm okay. Just tired," I mumbled. Time to change the subject. I had a sudden thought. "Is today really my actual birthday?" I asked.

Mom stroked my hair back from my face with a gentle hand. "Of course it is. Morgan, you've seen your birth certificate," she reminded me.

"Oh, right." Until a few weeks ago I had always believed I was a Rowlands, like the rest of my family. But when I met Cal and began exploring Wicca, it became clear that I had magickal powers and that I was a blood witch, from a long line of blood witches—witches from one of the Seven Great Clans of Wicca. That's how I'd found out I was adopted. Since then it had been pretty much of an emotional roller-coaster ride here at home. But I loved my parents, Sean and Mary Grace Rowlands, and my sister, Mary K., who was their biological daughter. And they loved me. And they were trying to come to terms with my Wiccan heritage, my legacy. As was I.

"Now, since today is your birthday, you can do what you want, more or less," Mom said, absently tickling Dagda's batlike gray ears. "Do you want to have a big breakfast and we'll go to a later mass? Or we can go to church now and then do something special for lunch?"

I don't want to go to church at all, I thought. Lately my relationship with church had seemed like a battle of wills as I struggled to integrate Wicca into my life. I also couldn't face the idea of sitting through a Catholic mass and then having lunch with my family after what had happened the night before. "Um, is it all right if I just sleep in today?" I asked. "I am feeling a little under the weather, actually. You guys do church and lunch without me."

Mom's lips thinned, but after a moment she nodded. "All right," she said. "If that's what you want." She stood up. "Do you want us to bring you back something for lunch?"

The idea of food repulsed me. "Oh, no thanks," I said, trying to sound casual. "I'll just find something in the fridge. Thanks, anyway, though."

"Okay," Mom said, touching my forehead again. "Tonight Eileen and Paula are coming over, and we'll do dinner and cake and presents. Sound good?"

"Great," I said, and Mom closed the door behind her. I sank back on my pillow. I felt as if I had a split personality. On the one hand, I was Morgan Rowlands, good daughter, honor roll student, math whiz, observant Catholic. On the other hand, I was a witch, by heritage and inclination.

I stretched, feeling the ache in my muscles. The events of the night before hovered over my head like a storm cloud. What had I done? How had I come to this? If only I knew for sure whether or not Hunter was dead . . .

I waited until I heard the front door close behind my

family. Then I got up and began pulling on my clothes. I knew what I had to do next.

I drove my car to the back road that ran behind Cal's house and parked. Then I crunched across the snow to the cliff's rocky edge. Carefully I stretched out on my stomach and peered over. If I saw Hunter's body, I would have to climb down there, I warned myself. If he was alive, I would go for help. If he was dead . . . I wasn't sure what I would do.

Later I would go up to Cal's house and see how he was, but first I needed to do this, to look for Hunter. Had Sky gotten my message? Had 911 responded?

The ground around this area was churned and muddy, evidence of the horrific battle Hunter and Cal had fought. It was awful to think about it, to remember how helpless I had been under Cal's binding spell. Why had he done that to me?

I leaned over farther to try to see beneath a rocky ledge. The icy Hudson swept beneath me, clean and deadly. Sharp rocks jutted up from the riverbed. If Hunter had hit them, if he'd been in the water any length of time, he was surely dead. The thought made my stomach clench up again. In my mind I pictured Hunter falling in slow motion over the edge, his neck streaming blood, an expression of surprise on his face. . . .

"Looking for something?"

I turned quickly, already scrambling to my feet as I recognized the English-accented voice. Sky Eventide.

She stood fifteen feet away, hands in her pockets. Her pale face, whitish blond hair, and black eyes seemed etched against the painful blue of the sky.

"What are you doing here?" I said.

"I was about to ask the same thing," she said, stepping toward me. She was taller than me and as thin. Her black leather jacket didn't look warm enough for the cold.

I said nothing, and she went on, a razor's edge in her voice. "Hunter didn't come home last night. I felt his presence here. But now I don't feel it at all."

She hasn't found Hunter. Hunter's dead. Oh, Goddess, I thought.

"What happened here?" she went on, her face like stone in the cold, bright sun. "The ground looks like it was plowed. There's blood everywhere." She stepped closer to me, fierce and cold, like a Viking. "Tell me what you know about it."

"I don't know anything," I said, too loudly. *Hunter's dead.*

"You're lying. You're a lying Woodbane, just like Cal and Selene," Sky said bitterly, spitting out the words as if she were saying, You're filth, you're garbage.

The world shifted around me, became slightly unreal. There was snow beneath my feet, water below the cliff, trees behind Sky, but it was like a stage set.

"Cal and Selene aren't Woodbane," I said. My mouth was dry.

Sky tossed her head. "Of course they are," she said. "And you're just like them. You'll stop at nothing to keep your power."

"That's not true," I snapped.

"Last night Hunter was on his way to Cal's place, on council business. He was going to confront Cal. I think you were there, too, since you're Cal's little lapdog. Now tell me what happened." Her voice rang out like steel, actually hurting my ears, and I felt the strength of her personality pressing on me. I wanted to spill out everything I knew. All of a sudden I realized she was putting a spell on me. A flash of rage seared through me. How dare she?

I straightened up and deliberately walled off my mind.

Sky's eyes flickered. "You don't know what you're doing," she said, her words chipping away at me. "That makes you dangerous. I'll be watching you. And so will the council."

She whirled and disappeared into the woods, her short, sunlight-colored hair riffling in the breeze.

The woods were silent after she left. No birds chirped, no leaves stirred, the wind itself died. After several minutes I went back to my car and drove it up to Cal's house. Hunter's car was no longer there. I climbed the stone steps and rang the doorbell, feeling a fresh wash of fear as I wondered what I might find, what might have happened to Cal since I left.

Selene opened the door. She was wearing an apron, and the faint scent of herbs clung to her. There was a wealth of warmth and concern in her golden eyes as she reached out and hugged me to her. She had never hugged me before, and I closed my eyes, enjoying the lovely feeling of comfort and relief she offered.

Then Selene withdrew and looked deeply into my face. "I heard about last night. Morgan, you saved my son's life," she said, her voice low and melodious. "Thank you." She looped her arm through mine and drew me inside, shutting out the rest of the world. We walked down the hallway to the large, sunny kitchen at the back of the house.

"How is Cal?" I managed.

"He's better," she said. "Thanks to you. I came home and

found him in the parlor, and he managed to tell me most of what happened. I've been doing some healing work with him."

"I didn't know what to do," I said helplessly. "He fell asleep, and I had to get home. I have his car at my house," I added inanely.

Selene nodded. "We'll come get it later," she said, and I dug in my pocket and gave her the keys. She took them and pushed open the kitchen door.

I sniffed the air. "What's that?" I asked.

Now I noticed that the kitchen was ablaze with light, sound, color, scent. I paused in the doorway, trying to separate out the different stimuli. Selene walked over to the stove to stir something, and I realized she had a small, three-legged cast-iron cauldron bubbling on the burner of her range. The odd thing was how normal it looked somehow.

She caught my glance and said, "Usually I do all this outside. But this autumn has been so awful, weatherwise." She stirred slowly with a long wooden spoon, then leaned over and inhaled, the steam making her face flush slightly.

"What are you making?" I asked, moving closer.

"This is a vision potion," she explained. "When ingested by a knowledgeable witch, it aids with scrying and divination."

"Like a hallucinogen?" I asked, a little shocked. Images of LSD and mushrooms and people freaking out flashed through my mind.

Selene laughed. "No. It's just an aid, to make it easier to find your visions. I only make it every four or five years or so. I don't use it that often, and a little goes a long way."

On the gleaming granite counter I saw labeled vials and small jars and, at one end, a stack of homemade candles.

"Did you do all this?" I asked.

Selene nodded and brushed her dark hair away from her face. "I always go through a flurry of activity around this time of year. Samhain is over, Yule hasn't begun—I suppose I just itch for something to do. Years ago I started making many of my own tinctures and essential oils and infusions—they're always fresher and better than what you can buy in the store. Have you ever made candles?"

"No."

Selene looked around the kitchen, at the bustle and clutter, and said, "Things you make, cook, sew, decorate—those are all expressions of the power and homages to the Goddess." Busily she stirred the cauldron, deasil, and then tasted a tiny bit on the end of her spoon.

At any other time I would have found this impromptu lesson fascinating, but at the moment I was too keyed up to focus on it. "Will Cal be okay?" I blurted out.

"Yes," Selene said. She looked directly at me. "Do you want to talk about Hunter?"

That was all it took, and suddenly I was crying silently, my shoulders shaking, my face burning. In a moment she was beside me, holding me. A tissue appeared, and I took it.

"Selene," I said shakily, "I think he's dead."

"Shhh," she said soothingly. "Poor darling. Sit down. Let me give you some tea."

Tea? I thought wildly. I think I *killed* someone, and you're offering me *tea?*

But it was witch tea, and within seconds of my first sip I felt my emotions calm slightly, enough to get myself under control. Selene sat across the table from me, looking into my eyes.

"Hunter tried to kill Cal," she said intently. "He might

have tried to kill you, too. Anyone standing there would have done what you did. You saw a friend in danger, and you acted. No one could blame you for that."

"I didn't mean to hurt Hunter," I said, my voice wavering.

"Of course you didn't," she agreed. "You just wanted to stop him. There was no way to predict what would happen. Listen to me, my dear. If you hadn't done what you did, if you hadn't been so quick thinking and loyal, then it would be Cal now in the river, and I would be mourning him and possibly you, too. Hunter came here looking for trouble. He was on our property. He was out for blood. You and Cal both acted in self-defense."

Slowly I drank my tea. The way Selene put it, it sounded reasonable, even inevitable. "Do you—do you think we should go to the police?" I asked.

Selene cocked her head to one side, considering. "No," she said after a moment. "The difficulty is that there were no other witnesses. And that knife wound in Hunter's neck would be hard to explain as self-defense, even though you and I both know that's the truth of it."

A fresh wave of dread washed over me. She was right. To the police, it would probably look like murder.

I remembered something else. "And his car," I said. "Did you move it?"

Selene nodded. "I spelled it to start and drove it to an abandoned barn just outside of town. It sounds premeditated, I know, but it seemed the prudent thing to do." She reached out and covered my hand with her own. "I know it's hard. I know you feel that your life will never be the same. But you must try to let it go, my dear."

I swallowed miserably. "I feel so guilty," I said.

"Let me tell you about Hunter," she said, and her voice was suddenly almost harsh. I shivered.

"I've heard reports about him," Selene went on. "By all accounts he was a loose cannon, someone who could not be trusted. Even the council had their doubts about him, thought he had gone too far, too many times. He's been obsessed with Woodbanes all his life, and in the last few years this obsession had taken a deadly turn." She seemed quite serious, and I nodded.

A thought occurred to me. "Then why was he going after Cal?" I asked. "You guys don't know what clan you are, right? I heard Hunter call Cal Woodbane—did he think Cal . . . wait—" I shook my head, confused. Cal had told me that he and Hunter probably had the same father. And Sky had said Cal was Woodbane like his father. Which made both Cal and Hunter half Woodbane? I couldn't keep all this straight.

"Who knows what he thought?" said Selene. "He was clearly crazy. I mean, this is someone who killed his own brother."

My eyebrows knitted. I vaguely remembered Cal throwing that accusation at Hunter last night. "What do you mean?"

Selene shook her head, then started as her cauldron hissed and spat on the stove, almost boiling over. She hurried over to adjust the flame. For the next few minutes she was very busy, and I hesitated to interrupt her.

"Do you think I could see Cal?" I asked finally.

She looked back at me regretfully. "I'm sorry, Morgan, but I gave him a drink to make him sleep. He probably won't wake up until tonight."

"Oh." I stood up and retrieved my coat, unwilling to pursue the story about Hunter if Selene didn't want to tell me. I felt a thousand times better than I had, but I knew instinctively the pain and guilt would return.

"Thank you for coming," Selene said, straining a steaming mixture over the sink. "And remember, what you did last night was the right thing. Believe that."

I nodded awkwardly.

"Please call me if you want to talk," Selene added as I headed for the door. "Anytime."

"Thank you," I said. I pushed through the door and headed home.

3

Dread

April 2000

Scrying doesn't always mean you see a picture—it can be more like receiving impressions. I use my lueg, my scrying stone. It's a big, thick chunk of obsidian, almost four inches at its widest and tapering to a point. It was my father's. I found it under my pillow the morning he and Mum disappeared.

Luegs are more reliable than either fire or water. Fire may show you pasts and possible futures, but it's hard to work with. There's an old Wiccan saying that goes: Fire is a fragile lover, court her well, neglect her not; her faith is like a misty smoke, her anger is destructive hot. Water is easier to use but very misleading. Once I heard Mum say that water is the Wiccan whore, spilling her secrets to any, lying to most, trusting few.

Last night I took my lueg and went down to the kill that flows at the edge of my uncle's property. This was where we swam in the summer, where Linden and I caught minnows, where Alwyn used to pick gooseberries.

I sat at the water's edge and scryed, looking deep into my obsidian, weaving spells of vision.

After a long, long time, the rock's face cleared, and in its depths I saw my mother. It was my mother of all those years ago, right before she disappeared. I remember the day clearly. An eight-year-old me ran up to where she knelt in the garden, pulling weeds. She looked up, saw me, and her face lit, as if I was the sun. Giomanach, she said, and looked at me with love, the sunlight glinting off her bright hair. Seeing her in the lueg, I was almost crushed with longing and a childish need to see her, have her hold me.

When the stone went blank, I held it in my hand, then crumpled over and cried on the bank of the kill.

—Giomanach

My birthday dinner was like a movie. I felt like I was watching myself through a window, smiling, talking to people, opening presents. I was glad to see Aunt Eileen and her girlfriend, Paula Steen, again—and Mom and Mary K. had worked hard to make everything special. It would have been a great birthday, except for the horrific images that kept crashing into my brain. Hunter and Cal grappling in the churned, bloody snow. Myself, sinking to my knees under Cal's binding spell, then me looking down at the athame in my hand and looking up to see Hunter. Hunter, rivulets of blood on his neck, going over the edge of the cliff. "Hey, are you all right?" Mary K. asked me as I stood by the window, gazing out into the darkness. "You seem kind of out of it."

"Just tired," I told her. I added quickly, "But I'm having a great time. Thanks, Mary K."

"We aim to please." She flashed me a grin.

Finally Aunt Eileen and Paula left, and I went upstairs and called Cal. His voice sounded weak and scratchy.

"I'm okay," he said. "Are you okay?"

"Yes," I said. "Physically."

"I know." He sighed. "I can't believe it. I didn't mean for him to go over the edge. I just wanted to stop him." He laughed dryly, a croaking sound. "Helluva seventeenth birthday. I'm sorry, Morgan."

"It wasn't your fault," I said. "He came after you."

"I didn't want him to hurt you."

"But why did you put binding spells on me?" I asked.

"I was afraid. I didn't want you to jump into the middle of it and get hurt," Cal said.

"I wanted to help you. I hated being frozen like that. It was awful."

"I'm so sorry, Morgan," Cal breathed. "Everything was happening so fast, and I thought I was acting for the best."

"Don't ever do that to me again."

"I won't, I promise. I'm sorry."

"Okay. I called 911 when I got home," I admitted softly. "And I sent Sky an anonymous witch message, telling her where to look for Hunter."

Cal was silent for a minute. Then he said, "You did the right thing. I'm glad you did."

"It didn't help, though. I saw Sky at the river this morning. She said Hunter didn't come home last night. She was sure I knew something about it."

"What did you tell her?"

"That I didn't know what she was talking about. She said she didn't feel Hunter's presence or something like that. And she called me a lying Woodbane."

"That bitch," Cal said angrily.

"Could she find out about what happened somehow? Using magick?"

"No," said Cal. "My mom put warding spells around the whole place to block anyone from scrying and seeing what happened. Don't worry."

"I am worried," I insisted. A bubble of panic was rising in my throat again. "This is horrible. I can't stand it."

"Morgan! Try to calm down," said Cal. "It will all be okay, you'll see. I won't let anything happen to you. The only thing is, I'm afraid Sky is going to be a problem. Hunter was her cousin, and she's not going to let this rest. Tomorrow we'll spell your house and your car with wards of protection. But still—be on your guard."

"Okay." Dread settled more heavily on my shoulders as I hung up. Wherever this is going, I thought, there's no way it can end well. No way at all.

On Monday morning I got up early and grabbed the morning paper before anyone else could see it. Widow's Vale doesn't have its own daily paper, just a twice-monthly publication that's mostly pickup articles from other papers. I quickly paged through the *Albany Times Union* to see if there was any mention of a body being fished out of the Hudson. There wasn't. I gnawed my lip. What did that mean? Had his body not been found yet? Or was it just that we weren't close enough to Albany for them to cover the story?

I drove with Mary K. to school and parked outside the building, feeling like I had aged five years over the weekend.

As I turned off the engine, Bakker Blackburn, Mary K.'s boyfriend, trotted up to meet her. "Hey, babe," he said, nuzzling her neck.

Mary K. giggled and pushed him away. He took her book bag from her, and they went off to meet their friends.

Robbie Gurevitch, one of my best friends and a member of my coven, strolled up to my car. A group of freshman girls stared admiringly at him as he passed them, and I saw him blush. Being gorgeous was new to him—until I'd given him a healing potion a month ago, he'd had horrible acne. But the potion had cleared up his skin and even erased the scars.

"Are you going to fix your car?" he asked me.

I looked at my broken headlight and smashed nose and sighed. A few days ago I'd thought someone was following me, and I had skidded on a patch of ice and crunched my beloved behemoth of a car, fondly known as Das Boot, into a ditch. At the time it had seemed utterly terrifying, but since the events of Saturday night, it felt more in perspective.

"Yep," I said, scanning the area for Cal. That morning I'd noticed the Explorer was gone from my block, but I didn't know if he'd be back at school today.

"I'm guessing it'll cost at least five hundred bucks," Robbie said.

We walked toward the old, redbrick former courthouse that was now Widow's Vale High. I was striving for normalcy, trying to be old reliable Morgan. "I wanted to ask you—did you go to Bree's coven's circle on Saturday?" Bree

Warren had been my other best friend since childhood—my closest friend—until we fought over Cal. Now she hated me. And I . . . I didn't know what I felt about her. I was furious at her. I didn't trust her. I missed her fiercely.

"I did go." Robbie held the door open for me. "It was small and kind of lame. But that English witch, Sky Eventide, the one who leads their circles . . ." He whistled. "She had power coming off her in waves."

"I know Sky," I said stiffly. "I met her at Cal's. What did you guys do? Did Sky mention me or Cal?"

He looked at me. "No. We just did a circle. It was interesting because Sky does it slightly differently than Cal. Why would she mention you or Cal?"

"Different how?" I pressed, ignoring his question. "You guys didn't, um, do anything scary, did you? Like call on spirits or anything?"

Robbie stopped walking. "No. It was just a circle, Morgan. I think we can safely say that Bree and Raven are not having their souls sucked out by the devil."

I gave him an exasperated look. "Wiccans don't believe in the devil," I reminded him. "I just want to make sure that Bree isn't getting into anything dangerous or bad." *Like I did.*

We walked to the basement stairs, where our coven, Cirrus, usually hung out in the morning. Ethan Sharp was already there, doing his English homework. Jenna Ruiz sat across from him, reading, her fair, straight hair falling like a curtain across her cheek. They both looked up and greeted us.

"Bad?" Robbie repeated. "No. Sky didn't strike me as bad. Powerful, yes. Sexy—absolutely." He grinned.

"Who's this?" Jenna asked.

"Sky Eventide," Robbie reported. "She's the blood witch

that Bree and Raven have in their new coven. Oh, guess their coven's name." He laughed. "Kithic. It means 'left-handed' in Gaelic. Raven picked out that name from something she read, without knowing what it meant."

The rest of us smiled. After our fight, Bree had split off from Cirrus to start her own coven with Raven. To me it seemed both of them were just playing at being Wiccan, doing it to look cool, to get back at me for winning Cal, or just to do something different. Widow's Vale is a small town, and there aren't that many entertainment opportunities.

Or maybe I was selling them short. Maybe they were really sincere in their commitment. I sighed and rubbed my forehead, feeling like I didn't know anything anymore.

In homeroom people were already planning their Thanksgiving holidays, which would start at noon on Wednesday. It would be a relief not to have to go to school for a few days. I've always been an A student (well, mostly), but it was getting harder and harder to keep my mind on schoolwork when so many more compelling things were taking up my time and energy. Nowadays I just flashed through my physics and trig homework and did the bare minimum in other classes so I would have more time to study spells, plan my future magickal herb garden, and read about Wicca. Not only that, but just reading the Book of Shadows written by my birth mother, which I'd found in Selene's library over a week ago, was like a college course in itself. I was stretched very thin these days.

In homeroom I opened my book *Essential Oils and Their Charms* under my desk and started reading. In the spring I would try to make some of my own, the way Selene did.

When Bree came into class, I couldn't help looking up.

Her face was as familiar as my own, but nowadays she had another layer to her, a layer that didn't include me. She wore mostly black, like Raven did, and although she hadn't adopted any of Raven's gothy piercings or tattoos, I wondered if it was just a matter of time.

Bree had always been the beautiful one, the one boys flocked around, the life of the party. I had been the plain friend that people put up with because Bree loved me and was my best friend, but then Cal had come between us. Bree had even lied and told me they'd slept together. We'd quit speaking, and then Cal and I started going out.

After being like conjoined twins for eleven years, I'd found the last few Breeless weeks bizarre and uncomfortable. She still didn't know I was adopted, that I was a blood witch. She didn't know about what had happened with Hunter. At one time she had been the only person in the world I might have told.

I couldn't resist looking at her face, her eyes the color of coffee. For just a second she met my gaze, and I was startled by the mix of emotions there. We both looked away at the same time. Did she miss me? Did she hate me? What was she doing with Sky?

The bell rang, and we all stood. Bree's dark, shiny hair disappeared through the doorway, and I followed her. When she turned the corner to go to her first class, I was seized by a spontaneous desire to talk to her.

"Bree."

She turned, and when she saw it was me, she looked surprised.

"Listen—I know that Sky is leading your coven," I found myself saying.

"So?" No one looked imperious like Bree looked imperious.

"I just—it's just that Sky is dangerous," I said quickly. "She's dangerous, and you shouldn't hang out with her."

Her perfect eyebrows rose. "Do tell," she drawled.

"She has this whole dark agenda; she's caught up in this whole program that I bet she hasn't told you about. She's— she's evil, she's bad, and dangerous." I realized in despair that I sounded melodramatic and muddled.

"Really." Bree shook her head, looking like she was trying not to laugh. "You are too much, Morgan. It's like you get off on lying, raining on people's parades."

"Look, I heard you and Raven last week in the bathroom," I admitted. "You were talking about how Sky was teaching you about the dark side. That's dangerous! And I heard you saying you gave Sky some of my hair! What was that about? Is she putting spells on me?"

Bree's eyes narrowed. "You mean you were spying on me?" she exclaimed. "You're pathetic! And you have no idea what you're talking about. Cal is filling your head with ridiculous crap, and you're just sucking it up! He could be the devil himself, and you wouldn't care because he's the only boy who ever asked you out!"

Before I realized what was happening, my hand had shot out and smacked Bree hard across the face. Her head snapped sideways, and within seconds the pink outline of my palm appeared on her cheek. I gasped and stared at her as her face twisted into anger.

"You bitch!" she snarled.

Out of lifelong habit, I started to feel remorseful, and then I thought, Screw that. I took a deep breath and called on my own anger, narrowing my eyes. "You're the bitch," I snapped. "You can't stand the fact that I'm not your puppet anymore, that I'm not your charity case, your permanent audience. You're jealous of *me* for once, and it's eating you up. I have a fantastic boyfriend, I have more magickal power than you'll ever dream about, and you can't stand it. Finally I'm better than you. I'm amazed your head doesn't explode!"

Bree gaped at me, her eyes wide, her mouth open. "What are you talking about?" she practically shrieked. "You were never my audience! You make it sound like I was using you! This is what I'm talking about! Cal is brainwashing you!"

"Actually, Bree," I said coldly, "you'd be amazed at how little we talk about you. In fact, your name hardly comes up."

With that, I swept off, my teeth clenched so tight, I could feel them grinding together. I didn't think I'd ever had the last word in an argument with Bree before. But the thought didn't make me feel any better. Why had I talked to her? I had just made everything worse.

4

Haven

May 2000

I remember it rained the day Mum and Dad disappeared. When I woke up that morning they were already gone. I had no idea what was going on. Uncle Beck called late that day, and I told him I couldn't find Dad, or Mum either. Beck called around, to get a neighbor to stay overnight with us until he could get there, and he couldn't find anyone still around. In the end, I was in charge all that long day and night, and the three of us—me, Linden, and Alwyn—stayed in our house alone, not knowing what was happening to us, to our world.

Now I know that twenty-three other people besides my parents either died or disappeared that night. Years later, when I went back, I tried asking around. All I got were cautious mumbles about a dark wave, a cloud of fury and destruction.

I've heard rumors of a dark wave destroying a Wyndenkell

coven in Scotland. I'm on my way there. Goddess, give me
strength.

    —Giomanach

After my fight with Bree, I was so upset that I couldn't
concentrate on anything. My math teacher had to call my
name three times before I responded, and then I answered
his question incorrectly—which almost never happened to
me under normal circumstances. During lunch period I
sneaked off to Cirrus's hangout spot to be by myself. I
scarfed down my sandwich and a Diet Coke, then meditated
for half an hour. Finally I felt calm enough to deal with the
rest of my day.

I slogged through my afternoon classes. When the last
bell rang, I went to my locker, then followed the crush of
students outside. The snow was turning rapidly to slush, and
the sun flowed down with an Indian-summerish warmth.
After weeks of freezing weather, it felt wonderful. I raised
my face to the sun, hoping it would help heal the pain I carried inside, the guilt over what I'd done to Hunter, the terror
of being found out.

"I'm getting a ride home with Bakker, okay?" Mary K.
bounced up to me as I took out my car keys, her cheeks
flushed pink, her eyes clear and shining.

I looked at her. "Are you going home, or . . ." Don't go
anywhere with him alone, I thought. I didn't trust Bakker—
not since I'd caught him pinning Mary K. down on her bed
and practically forcing himself on her two weeks earlier. I
couldn't believe she'd forgiven him.

"We're going to get a latte first, then home," she said, her eyes daring me to say something.

"All right. Well, see you later," I said lamely. I watched her climb into Bakker's car and knew that if he hurt her, I would have no problem doing to him what I had done to Hunter. And in Bakker's case I wouldn't feel guilty.

"Whoa. I'm glad you're not looking at me like that," said Robbie, loping up to me. I shook my head.

"Yeah, just watch your step." I tried to sound light and teasing.

"Is Cal sick? I didn't see him all day," said Robbie. He smiled absentmindedly at a sophomore who was sending flirtatious looks his way.

"Morgan?" he prompted.

"Oh! Um, yes, Cal is sick," I said. I felt a sudden jangle of nerves. Robbie was a close friend, and I had told him about being adopted and a blood witch. He knew more about me than Bree did now. But I could never tell him about all that had happened on Saturday night. It was too horrible to share, even with him. "I'm going to call him right now—maybe go see him."

Robbie nodded. "I'm on my way to Bree's. Who knows, today might be the day I go for it." He wiggled his eyebrows suggestively, and I smiled. Robbie had recently admitted to me that he was totally in love with Bree and had been for years. I hoped she wouldn't break his heart the way she did with most of the guys she got involved with.

"Good luck," I said. He walked off, and I dumped my backpack in Das Boot and headed back to the pay phone in the school lunchroom.

Cal answered after four rings. His voice sounded better than it had the night before.

"Hi," I said, comforted just to talk to him.

"I knew it was you," he said, sounding glad.

"Of course you did," I said. "You're a witch."

"Where are you?"

"School. Can I come see you? I just really need to talk to you."

Groaning, he said, "I would love that. But some people just came in from Europe, and I've got to meet with them."

"Selene's been having people over a lot lately, it seems."

Cal paused, and when he spoke, his voice had a slightly different tone to it. "Yeah, she has. She's kind of been working on a big project, and it's starting to come together. I'll tell you about it later."

"Okay. How are your wrists?"

"They look pretty bad. But they'll be okay. I really wish I could see you," Cal said.

"Me too." I lowered my voice. "I *really* need to talk to you. About what happened."

"I know," he said quietly. "I know, Morgan."

In the background on Cal's end I heard voices, and Cal covered his mouthpiece and responded to them. When he came back on, I said, "I won't keep you. Call me later if you can, okay?"

"I will," he said. Then he hung up. I hung up, too, feeling sad and lonely without him.

I walked through the hall and out the door, got in Das Boot, and drove to Red Kill, to Practical Magick.

*　　　*　　　*

The brass bells over the door jingled as I pushed my way in. Practical Magick was a store that sold Wiccan books and supplies. Although I hadn't realized it until now, it was also becoming the place I went to when I didn't want to go anywhere else. I loved being there, and I always felt better when I left. It was like a Wiccan neighborhood bar.

At the end of the room the checkout desk was empty, and I figured Alyce and David must be busy restocking.

I began reading book titles, dreaming of the day I would have enough money to buy whatever books and supplies I wanted. I would buy this whole store out, I decided. That would be so much more fun than being a relatively poor high school junior who was about to wipe out her whole savings to pay for a crumpled headlight.

"Hi, there," came a soft voice, and I looked up to see the round, motherly figure of Alyce, my favorite clerk. As my eyes met hers, she stood still. Her brows drew together in a concerned look. "What's the matter?"

My heart thudded against my ribs. Does she know? I wondered frantically. Can she tell just by looking at me?

"What do you mean?" I asked. "I'm fine. Just a little stressed. You know, school, family stuff." I shut my mouth abruptly, feeling like I was babbling.

Alyce held my gaze for a moment, her eyes probing mine. "All right. If you want to talk about it, I'm here," she said at last.

She bustled over to the checkout counter and began to stack some papers. Her gray hair was piled untidily on top of her head, and she wore her usual loose, flowing clothes. She moved with precision and confidence: a woman at ease with herself, her witchhood, her power. I admired her, and it broke my heart to think how horrified she would be if she knew what I had done. How had this happened? How had this become my life?

I can't lose this, I thought. Practical Magick was my haven. I couldn't let the poison of Hunter's horrible death seep out and taint my relationships with this place, with Alyce. I couldn't bear it.

"I can't wait for spring," I said, trying to get my mind back on track. It wasn't even Thanksgiving yet. "I want to get started on my garden." I walked up the book aisle to the back of the store and leaned against a stool by the counter.

"So do I," Alyce agreed. "I'm already dying to be outside, digging in the dirt again. It's always a struggle for me to remember the positive aspects of winter."

I looked around at the other people in the store. A young man with multiple earrings in his left ear came up and bought incense and white candles. I tentatively sent out my senses to see if I could tell if he was a witch or not, but I couldn't pick up on anything unusual.

"Morgan, good to see you again."

I turned to see David stepping through the faded orange curtain that separated the small back room from the rest of the store. A faint scent of incense wafted in with him. Like Alyce, David was also a blood witch. Recently he'd told me that he was from the Burnhide clan. I felt honored to have gained his confidence—and terrified of losing it again if he ever found out what I'd done, that I'd killed someone.

"Hi," I said. "How are you?"

"I'm all right." He held a sheaf of invoices in his hand and looked distracted. "Alyce, did the latest batch of essential oils come? The bill is here."

She shook her head. "I have a feeling the shipment is lost somewhere," she said as another person checked out. This woman was buying a Wiccan periodical called *Crafting Our Lives*. I picked up on faint magickal vibrations as she passed me and was once again naively amazed that real witches existed.

I wandered around the store, fascinated as always by the candles, incense, small mirrors the shop contained. Slowly the place emptied, then new people came in. It was a busy afternoon.

Gradually the sunlight faded from the high windows, and I began to think about heading home. Alyce came up as I was running my fingers around the rim of a carved marble bowl. The stone was cool and smooth, like river stones. The stones Hunter had probably hit when he fell hadn't been smooth. They had been jagged, deadly.

"Marble is always thirteen degrees cooler than the air around it," Alyce said at my side, making me jump.

"Really? Why?"

"It's the property of the stone," she said, straightening some scarves that customers had rumpled. "Everything has its own properties."

I thought about the chunks of crystal and other stones I had found in the box containing my mother's tools. It seemed like ages ago—but it had actually been less than a week.

"I found Maeve's tools," I said, surprising myself. I hadn't planned to mention it. But I felt the need to confide *something* in Alyce, to make her feel I wasn't shutting her out.

Alyce's blue eyes widened, and she stopped what she was doing to look at me. She knew Maeve's story; it had been she who'd told me of my birth mother's awful death here in America.

"Belwicket's tools?" she asked unbelievingly. Belwicket had been the name of Maeve's coven in Ireland. When it was destroyed by a mysterious, dark force, Maeve and her lover, Angus, had fled to America. Where I'd been born—and they had died.

"I scryed," I told Alyce. "In fire. I had a vision that told me the tools were in Meshomah Falls."

"Where Maeve died," Alyce remembered.

"Yes."

"How wonderful for you," Alyce said. "Everyone thought those tools were lost forever. I'm sure Maeve would have been so happy for her daughter to have them."

I nodded. "I'm really glad about it. They're a link to her, to her clan, her family."

"Have you used them yet?" she asked.

"Um—I tried the athame," I admitted. Technically, since I was uninitiated, I wasn't supposed to do unsupervised magick or use magickal tools or even write in Cirrus's Book of Shadows. I waited for Alyce to chide me.

But she didn't. Instead she said briskly, "I think you should bind the tools to you."

I blinked. "What do you mean?"

"Wait a minute." Alyce hurried off and soon came back with a thick, ancient-looking book. Its cover was dark green and tattered, with stains mottling its fabric. She leaned the book on a shelf and flipped through pages soft and crumbling with age.

"Here we go." She pulled a quaint pair of half-moon glasses from her sweater pocket and perched them on her nose. "Let me copy this down for you." Then, just like the women at my church exchange recipes and knitting patterns, Alyce copied down an age-old Wiccan spell that would bind my mother's tools to me.

"It will be almost as if you're part of them and they are part of you," Alyce explained as I folded the paper and put it in my inside coat pocket. "It will make them more effective for you and also less effective for anyone else who tries to use them. I really think you should do this right away." Her gaze, usually so mild, seemed quite piercing as she examined me over the rims of her glasses.

"Um, okay, I will," I said. "But why?"

Alyce paused for a moment, as if considering what to say. "Intuition," she said finally, shrugging and giving me a smile. "I feel it's important."

"Well, all right," I said. "I'll try to do it tonight."

"The sooner the better," she advised. Then the bells over the door rang as a customer came in. I hastily said good-bye to Alyce and David and went out to Das Boot. I flipped on my one headlight, blasted the heater, and headed for home.

5

Bound

June 2000

Two covens in Scotland were wiped out: one in 1974 and one in 1985. The first was in the north, the second, toward the southeast. Now the trail is leading into northern England, so I am making plans to go. I have to _know_. This started out being about my parents. Now it's a much bigger picture.

I've heard that the council is seeking new members. I've put my name in. If I were a council member, I would have access to things that are usually not publicized. It seems the fastest way to have my questions answered. When I come back from the north, I'll learn of their decision.

I applied to become a Seeker. With a name like mine, it seems almost inevitable.

—Giomanach

Mary K. breezed in halfway through dinner. Her cheeks were pink. There was also something wrong with her shirt. I gazed in puzzlement at the two flaps of the hem. They didn't meet—the shirt was incorrectly buttoned. My eyes narrowed as I thought about what that meant.

"Where have you been?" Mom asked. "I was worried."

"I called and let Dad know I'd be late," my sister said, sitting down at the table. Seated, her telltale shirt wasn't so obvious. "What's that?" she asked, sniffing the serving platter.

"Corned beef. I made it in the Crock-Pot," Mom said.

Dad had glanced up at the sound of his name, pulled back to reality for a moment. He's a research-and-development guy for IBM, and sometimes he seems more comfortable in *virtual* reality.

"Hmmm," said Mary K. disapprovingly. She picked out some carrots, cabbage, and onions and conspicuously left the meat. Lately she'd been on a major vegetarian kick.

"It's delicious," I said brightly, just to needle her. Mary K. sent me a look.

"So I think Eileen and Paula have decided on the York Street house, in Jasper," my mom said.

"Cool," I said. "Jasper's only about twenty minutes away, right?" My aunt and her girlfriend had decided to move in together and had been house hunting with my mom, a real estate agent.

"Right," Mom said. "An easy drive from here."

"Good." I stood up and carried my plate to the kitchen, already anxious for my family to be asleep. I had work to do.

The spell for binding tools to oneself was complicated but not difficult, and it didn't involve any tools or ingredients that I didn't have. I knew I would need to work undisturbed, and I didn't want to do it outside. The attic seemed like a good place.

At last I heard my parents turn in and my sister brush her teeth noisily in the bathroom we shared. She poked her head into my room to say good night and found me hunched over a book discussing the differences between practicing Wicca on your own and within a coven. It was really interesting. There were benefits—and drawbacks—to both ways.

"Night," said Mary K., yawning.

I looked at her. "Next time you're late, you might want to make sure your shirt is buttoned right," I said mildly.

She looked down at herself, horrified. "Oh, man," she breathed.

"Just . . . be careful." I wanted to say more but forced myself to stop there.

"Yeah, yeah, I will." She went into her room.

Twenty minutes later, sensing that everyone was asleep, I tiptoed up the attic stairs with Maeve's tools, the spell Alyce had written out for me, and four white candles.

I swept one area clean of dust and set the four candles in a large square. Inside the square I drew a circle with white chalk. Then I entered the circle, closed it, and set Maeve's tools on one of my old sweatshirts. Theoretically, it would be full of my personal vibrations.

I meditated for a while, trying to release my anguish over Hunter, trying to sink into the magick, feeling it unfold before me, gradually revealing its secrets. Then I gathered Maeve's tools: her robe, her wand, her four element cups, her athame, and things I wasn't sure were tools but that I'd found in the same box: a feather, a silver chain with a claddagh charm on it, several chunks of crystal, and five stones, each one different.

I read the ritual chant.

"Goddess Mother, Protectress of Magick and Life, hear my song. As it was in my clan, so shall it be with me and in my family to come. These tools I offer in service to you and in worship of the glory of nature. With them I shall honor life, do no harm, and bless all that is good and right. Shine your light on these tools that I may use them in pure intent and in sure purpose."

I laid my hands on them, feeling their power and sending mine into them.

The same way it had happened in the past, a song in Gaelic came to my lips. I let it slip quietly into the darkness.

> *"An di allaigh an di aigh*
> *An di allaigh an di ne ullah*
> *An di ullah be nldi ruh*
> *Cair di na ulla nith rah*
> *Cair feal ti theo nith rah*
> *An di allaigh an di aigh."*

Quietly I sang the ancient words again and again, feeling a warm coil of energy circling me. When I had sung this before, it had drawn down an immense amount of power—I'd felt like a goddess myself. Tonight it was quieter, more focused, and the power flowed around and through me like water, going down my hands into the tools until I couldn't tell where the tools left off and I began. I couldn't feel my knees where I was kneeling, and giddily I wondered if I was levitating. Suddenly I realized that I was no longer singing and that the warm, rich power had leached away, leaving me breathing hard and flushed, sweat trickling down my back.

I looked down. Were the tools bound to me now? Had I done it correctly? I had followed the instructions. I had felt the power. There was nothing else on the paper Alyce had given me. Blinking, feeling suddenly incredibly tired, I gathered everything up, blew out the candles, and crept downstairs. Moving silently, I unscrewed the cover for the HVAC vent in the hallway outside my room and put my tools, except the athame, back into my never-fail hiding place.

Back in my room, I changed into my pajamas and brushed my teeth. I unbraided my hair and brushed it a few times, too tired to give it any real attention. Finally, with relief, I got into bed with Maeve's Book of Shadows and opened it to my bookmark. Out of habit I held my mother's athame, with its carved initials, in my hand.

I started to read, sometimes pointing the athame to the words on the page, as if it would help me decipher some of the Gaelic terms.

In this entry Maeve was describing a spell to strengthen her scrying. She mentioned that something seemed to be blocking her vision: "It's as if the power lines are clouded and dark. Ma and I have both scryed and scryed, and all we get is the same thing over and over: bad news coming. What that means, I don't know. A delegation is here from Liathach, in northern Scotland. They, like us, are Woodbanes who have renounced evil. Maybe with their help we can figure out what's going on."

I felt a chill. *Bad news coming.* Was it the mysterious dark force that had destroyed Belwicket, Maeve's coven? No, it couldn't be, I realized; that hadn't happened until 1982. This entry had been written in 1981, nearly a year earlier. I tapped the athame against the page and read on.

"I have met a witch."

The words floated across the page, written in light within the regular entry. I blinked and they were gone, and I stared at Maeve's angular handwriting, wondering what I had seen. I focused, staring hard at the page, willing the words, the writing to appear again. Nothing.

I took the athame, passing it slowly over the blue ink. Splashes, pinpricks of light, coalescing into words. "I have met a witch."

I drew in my breath, staring at the page. The words appeared beneath the athame. When I drew it away, they faded. I passed the knife over the book again. "Among the group from Liathach, there is a man. There is something about him. Goddess, he draws me to him."

Oh my God. I looked up, glanced around my room to make sure I was awake and not dreaming. My clock was ticking, Dagda was squirming next to my leg, the wind was blowing against my windows. This was all real. Another layer of my birth mother's history was being revealed: she had written secret entries in her Book of Shadows.

Quickly I flipped to the very beginning of the book, which Maeve had started when she was first initiated at fourteen. Holding the athame close to each page, I scanned the writing, seeing if other hidden messages were revealed. Page after page I ran the knife down each line of writing, each spell, each song or poem. Nothing. Nothing for many, many pages. Then, in 1980, when Maeve was eighteen, hidden words started appearing. I began reading, my earlier fatigue forgotten.

At first the entries were things Maeve had simply wanted to keep hidden from her mother: the fact that she and a girl-friend were smoking cigarettes; about how Angus kept pressuring her to go "all the way" and she was thinking about it; even sarcastic, teasing remarks or observations about people in the village, her relatives, other members of the coven.

But as time went on, Maeve also wrote down spells, spells that were different from the others. A lot of what Maeve and Mackenna and Belwicket had done was practical stuff: healing potions, lucky talismans, spells to make the crops perform. These new spells of Maeve's were things like how to communicate with and call wild birds. How to put your mind into an animal's. How to join your mind to another person's. Not practical, perhaps. But powerful and fascinating.

I went back to the passage I had found a few minutes ago. Slowly, word by word, I read the glowing letters. Each entry was surrounded by runes of concealment and symbols I didn't recognize. I memorized what they looked like so I could research them later.

Painstakingly, I picked out the message.

"Ciaran came to tea. He and Angus are circling each other like dogs. Ciaran is a friend, a good friend, and I won't have Angus put him down."

Angus Bramson had been my birth father. Ciaran must be the Scottish witch Maeve had just met. Previous entries had detailed Maeve and Angus's courtship—they'd known each other practically forever. When Belwicket had been destroyed, Maeve and Angus had fled together and settled in

America. Two years later I had been born, though I don't think they ever married. Maeve had once written about her sadness that Angus wasn't her *mùirn beatha dàn*—her preordained life partner, her soul mate, the person who was meant for her.

I believed Cal was mine. I'd never felt so close to anyone before—except Bree.

"Today I showed Ciaran the headlands by the Windy Cliffs. It's a beautiful spot, wild and untamed, and he seemed just as wild and untamed as the nature surrounding him. He's so different from the lads around here. He seems older than twenty-two, and he's traveled a bit and seen the world. It makes me ache with envy."

Oh, God, I thought. Maeve, what are you getting into?

I soon found out.

"I cannot help myself. Ciaran is everything a man should be. I love Angus, yes, but he's like a brother to me—I've known him all my life. Ciaran wants the things I want, finds the same things interesting and boring and funny. I could spend days just talking to him, doing nothing else. And then there's his magick—his power. It's breathtaking. He knows so much I don't know, no one around here knows. He's teaching me. And the way he makes me feel . . .

"Goddess! I've never wanted to touch anyone so much."

My throat had tightened and my back muscles had tensed. I rested the book on my knees, trying to analyze why this revelation shook me so much.

Is love ever simple? I wondered. I thought about Mary K. and Bakker, boy most likely to be a parolee by the time he was twenty; Bree, who went out with one loser after another; Matt, who had cheated on Jenna with Raven. . . . It was completely discouraging. Then I thought about Cal, and my spirits rose again. Whatever troubles we had, at least they were external to our love for each other.

I blinked and realized my eyelids were gritty and heavy. It was very late, and I had to go to school tomorrow. One more quick passage.

"I have kissed Ciaran, and it was like sunlight coming through a window. Goddess, thank you for bringing him to me. I think he is the one."

Wincing, I hid the book and the athame under my mattress. I didn't want to know. Angus was my birth father, the one who had stayed by her, who had died with her. And she had loved someone else! She'd betrayed Angus! How could she be so cruel, my mother?

I felt betrayed, too, somehow, and knowing that I was perhaps being unfair to Maeve didn't help. I turned off my light, plumped my pillow up properly, and went to sleep.

6

Knowledge

I'm going to have these scars forever. Every time I look at my wrists, I feel rage all over again. Mom has been putting salves on them, but they ache constantly, and the skin will never be the same.

Thank the Goddess Glomunach won't bother us anymore.

—Sgàth

"If you hum that song one more time, I may have to kick you out of the car," I informed my sister the next morning.

Mary K. opened the lid of her mug and took a swig of coffee. "My, we're grumpy today."

"It's natural to be grumpy in the morning." I polished off the last of my Diet Coke and tossed the empty can into a plastic bag I kept for recyclables.

"Tornadoes are natural, but they're not a *good* thing."

I snorted, but secretly I enjoyed the bickering. It felt so . . . normal.

Normal. Nothing would ever be normal again. Not after what Cal and I had done.

There'd been no mention of a body in the river in this morning's paper, either. Maybe he'd sunk to the bottom, I thought. Or snagged on a submerged rock or log. I pictured him in the icy water, his pale hair floating around his face like seaweed, his hands swaying limply in the current. . . . A sudden rush of nausea almost made me retch.

Mary K. didn't notice. She looked through the windshield at the thin layer of clouds blotting out the morning sun. "I'll be glad when vacation starts."

I forced a smile. "You and me both."

I turned onto our school's street and found that all my usual parking spaces were taken. "Why don't you get out here," I suggested, "and I'll go park across the street."

"Okay. Later." Mary K. clambered out of Das Boot and hurried to her group of friends, her breath coming out in wisps. Today it was cold again, with a biting wind.

Across the street was another small parking lot, in back of an abandoned real estate office. Large sycamores surrounded the lot, looking like peeling skeletons, and several shaggy cypresses made it feel sheltered and private—which was why the stoners usually hung out there when the weather was warmer. No one else was around as I maneuvered Das Boot into a space. Wednesday, after school let out at noon, I had an appointment to take it to Unser's Auto Repair to have the headlight repaired.

"Morgan." The melodious voice made me jump. I whirled to see Selene Belltower sitting in her car three spaces away, her window rolled down.

"Selene!" I walked over to her. "What are you doing here? Is Cal okay?"

"He's much better," Selene assured me. "In fact, he's on his way to school right now. But I wanted to talk to you. Can you get in the car for a moment, please?"

I opened the door, flattered by her attention. In so many ways, she was the witch I hoped someday to be: powerful, the leader of a coven, vastly knowledgeable.

I glanced at my watch as I sank into the passenger seat. It was covered with soft brown leather, heated, and amazingly comfortable. Even so, I hoped Selene could sum up what she had to say in four minutes or less since that was when the last bell would ring.

"Cal told me you found Belwicket's tools," she said, looking excited.

"Yes," I said.

She smiled and shook her head. "What an amazing discovery. How did you find them?"

"I saw Maeve in a vision," I said. "She told me where to find them."

Selene's eyebrows rose. "Goodness. You had a vision?"

"Yes. I mean, I was scrying," I admitted, flushing. I didn't know for sure, but I had a feeling scrying was another thing I wasn't supposed to do as an uninitiated witch. "And I saw Maeve and where the tools might be."

"What were you scrying with? Water?"

"Fire."

She sat back, surprised, as if I had just come up with an impossibly high prime number.

"Fire! You were scrying with fire?"

I nodded, self-conscious but pleased at her astonishment. "I like fire," I said. "It ... speaks to me."

There was a moment of silence, and I started to feel uneasy. I had been bending the rules and following my own path with Wicca practically from the beginning.

"Not many witches scry with fire," Selene told me.

"Why not? It works so well."

"It doesn't for most people," Selene replied. "It's very capricious. It takes a lot of power to scry with fire." I felt her gaze on me and didn't know what to say.

"Where are Maeve's tools now?" Selene asked. I was relieved that she didn't sound angry or disapproving. It felt very intimate in the car, very private, as though what we said here would always be secret.

"They're hidden," I said reassuringly.

"Good," said Selene. "I'm sure you know how very powerful those tools are. I'm glad you're being careful with them. And I just wanted to offer my services, my guidance, and my experience in helping you learn to use them."

I nodded. "Thank you."

"And I would hope, because of our close relationship and your relationship with Cal, that you might want me to see the tools, test them, share my power with them. I'm very strong, and the tools are very strong, and it could be a very exciting thing to put our strengths together."

Just then a familiar gold Explorer rolled into the parking lot. I saw Cal's profile through his smoked window, and my heart leaped. He glanced toward us, pausing for a moment before pulling into a spot and turning off the engine. Eagerly I rolled down my window, and as I did, I heard the morning bell ring.

"Hi!" I said.

He came closer and leaned on the door, looking through the open window. "Hi," he said. His injured wrists were covered by his coat sleeves. "Mom? What are you doing here?"

"I just couldn't wait to talk to Morgan about Belwicket's tools," Selene said with a laugh.

"Oh," said Cal. I was puzzled by the flat tone in his voice. He sounded almost annoyed.

"Um, I feel like I should tell you," I said hesitantly. "I, uh, I bound the tools to me. I don't think they'll work too well for anyone else."

Cal and Selene both stared at me as if I had suddenly announced I was really a man.

"What?" said Selene, her eyes wide.

"I bound the tools to me," I said, wondering if I had acted too hastily. But Alyce had seemed so certain.

"What do you mean, you bound the tools to you?" Cal asked carefully.

I swallowed. I felt suddenly like a kid called in front of the principal. "I did a spell and bound the tools to me, sending my vibrations through them. They're part of me now."

"Whoa. How come?" Cal said.

"Well," I said, "you know, to make it harder for others to use them. And to increase my power when I use them."

"Heavens," said Selene. "Who told you how to do that?"

I opened my mouth to say, "Alyce," but instead, to my surprise, what came out was, "I read about it."

"Hmmm," she said thoughtfully. "Well, there are ways to unbind tools."

"Oh," I said, feeling uncertain. Why would she want me to unbind them?

"I would love to show you some hands-on ways to use them." Selene smiled. "You can't get everything from books."

"No," I agreed. I still felt uncertain and indefinably uneasy. "Well, I'd better get going."

"All right," said Selene. "Congratulations again on finding the tools. I'm so proud of you."

Her words warmed me, and I got out of the car feeling better.

I looked at Cal. "You coming?"

"Yeah," he said. He hesitated as if he were about to say something else, then seemed to change his mind, calling merely, "Talk to you later, Mom."

"Right," she said, and the window rolled up.

Cal set off for school. His strides were so long that I practically had to run to keep up. When I glanced at his profile, I could see that his jaw was set. "What's wrong?" I asked breathlessly. "Are you upset about something?"

He glanced at me. "No," he said. "Just don't want to be late."

But I didn't need my witch senses to see that he was lying. Was he angry at me because I'd bound the tools to me and now no one else could use them?

Or was he angry with Selene? It had almost seemed like he was. But why?

My day went downhill from there. While I was changing classes at fourth period, I accidentally walked in on Matt Adler and Raven Meltzer making out in an empty chem lab. When our eyes met, Matt looked like he wanted to vaporize himself, and Raven looked even more smug than usual. Ugh, I thought. Then it occurred to me that I could never judge anyone again about anything because what I had done was so terrible, so unnatural. And as soon as I thought that, I went into the girls' bathroom and cried.

At lunchtime Cal and I sat with Cirrus at our usual table. The group was quiet today. Robbie was tight-faced, and I wondered how it had gone at Bree's house yesterday. Probably not well since Bree was across the lunchroom sitting on Chip Newton's lap and laughing. Great.

Jenna was even paler than usual. When Cal asked her where Matt was, she said, "I wouldn't know. We broke up last night." She shrugged, and that was that. I was surprised and impressed by how calm she seemed. She was stronger than she looked.

Ethan Sharp and Sharon Goodfine were sitting next to each other. After months of flirting, they were looking into each other's eyes as if they'd finally realized the other was a real person and not just a clever simulation. Sharon shared her bagel with him. It was the only cheerful thing that happened.

Somehow I slogged through the afternoon. I kept thinking about Selene teaching me to use Maeve's tools. One minute I would want to do it, and the next minute I would remember Alyce's warning and decide to keep them to myself. I couldn't make up my mind.

When the final bell rang, I gathered up my things with relief. Only half a day tomorrow, thank the Goddess, and then a four-day weekend. I walked outside, looking for Mary K.

"Hey," said my sister, coming up. "Cold enough for you?"

We glanced up at the striated clouds that scudded slowly across the sky.

"Yeah," I said, hitching up my backpack. "Come on. I'm parked over in the side lot."

Just as I turned, Cal came up. "Hey, Mary K.," he said. Then he ducked his head and spoke only to me. "Is it okay if I come over this afternoon?" There was an unspoken message—we had tons to talk about—and I nodded at once.

"I'll meet you there."

He touched my cheek briefly, smiled at Mary K., then walked beside us to his own car. My sister raised an eyebrow at me, and I shot her a glance.

Once we were in Das Boot and I was cranking the engine, Mary K. said, "So, have you done it yet?"

I almost punched the gas, which would have slammed us right into a tree.

"Good God, Mary K.!" I cried, staring at her.

She giggled, then tried to look defiant. "Well? You've been going out a month, and he's gorgeous, and you can tell *he's* not a virgin. You're my sister. If I don't ask you, who can I ask?"

"Ask about what?" I said irritably, backing out.

"About sex," she said.

I rested my head for a second against the steering wheel. "Mary K., this may surprise you, but you're only fourteen years old. You're a high school freshman. Don't you think you're too young to worry about this?"

As soon as the words were out of my mouth, I wished I could take them back. I sounded just like my mom. I wasn't surprised when my sister's face closed.

"I'm sorry," I said. "You just . . . took me by surprise. Give me a second." I tried to think quickly and drive at the same time. "Sex." I blew out my breath. "No, I haven't done it yet."

Mary K. looked surprised.

I sighed. "Yes, Cal wants to. And I want to. But it hasn't seemed exactly right yet. I mean, I love Cal. He makes me feel unbelievable. And he's totally sexy and all that." My cheeks heated. "But still, it's only been a month, and there's a lot of other stuff going on, and it just . . . hasn't seemed right." I frowned at her pointedly. "And I think it's really important to wait until it *is* exactly right, and you're totally comfortable and sure and crazy in love. Otherwise it's no good." Said the incredibly experienced Morgan Rowlands.

Mary K. looked at me. "What if the other person *is* sure and you just want to trust them?"

Note to self: Do a castration spell on Bakker Blackburn. I breathed in, turned onto our street, and saw Cal in back of us. I pulled into our driveway and turned off the engine but stayed in the car. Cal parked and walked up to the house, waiting for us on the porch.

"I think you know enough to be sure for yourself," I said quietly. "You're not an idiot. You know how you feel. Some people date for years before they're both ready to have sex." Where was I getting this stuff? Years of reading teen magazines?

"The important thing," I went on, "is that you make your own decisions and don't give in to pressure. I told Cal I wasn't ready, and he was majorly disappointed." I lowered my voice as if he could hear us from twenty feet away, outside the car. "I mean, *majorly*. But he accepted my decision and is waiting until I'm ready."

Mary K. looked at her lap.

"However, if for some reason you think it might happen,

for God's sake use nine kinds of birth control and check out his health and be careful and don't get hurt. Okay?"

My sister blushed and nodded. On the porch I saw Cal shifting his feet in the cold.

"Do you want me to send Cal home so we can talk some more?" Please say no.

"No, that's okay," said Mary K. "I think I get it."

"Okay. I'm always here. I mean, if you can't ask your sister, who can you ask?"

She grinned, and we hugged each other. Then we hurried inside. Twenty minutes later Mary K. was doing her homework upstairs and Cal and I were drinking hot tea in the kitchen. And I hoped my sister had taken my words to heart.

7
Self

July 2000

The council called me to London upon my return from the North. I spent three days answering questions about everything from the causes of the Clan wars to the medicinal properties of mugwort. I wrote essays analyzing past decisions of the elders. I performed spells and rituals.

And then they turned me down. Not because my power is weak or my knowledge scanty, nor yet because I am too young, but because they distrust my motives. They think I am after vengeance for Linden, for my parents.

But that's not it, not anymore. I spoke to Athar about it last night. She's the only one who truly understands, I think.

"You aren't after vengeance. You're after redemption," she told me, and her black eyes measured me. "But, Giomanach, I'm not sure which is the more dangerous quest."

She's a deep one, my cousin Athar. I don't know when she grew to be so wise.

I won't give up. I will write to the council again today. I'll make them understand.

—Giomanach

Our kitchen was about one-sixth the size of Cal's kitchen, and instead of granite counters and custom country French cabinets, we had worn Formica and cabinets from about 1983. But our kitchen felt homier.

I rested my legs over Cal's knees under the table and we leaned toward each other, talking. The idea that maybe someday we would have our very own house, just us two, made me shiver. I looked up at Cal's smooth tan skin, his perfect nose, his strong eyebrows, and sighed. We needed to talk about Hunter.

"I'm really shaken up," I said quietly.

"I know. I am, too. I never thought it would come to that." He gave a dry laugh. "Actually, I thought we would just beat each other up a bit, and the whole thing would blow over. But when Hunter pulled out the *braigh*—"

"The silver chain he was using?"

Cal shuddered. "Yes," he said, his voice rough. "It was spelled. Once it was on me, I was powerless."

"Cal, I just can't believe what happened," I said, my eyes filling with tears. I brushed them away with one hand. "I can't think about anything else. And why hasn't anyone found the body yet? What are we going to do when they do find it? I swear, every time the phone rings, I think it's going to be the police, asking me to come down to the station and answer some questions." A tear overflowed and ran down my cheek. "I just can't get over this."

"I'm so sorry." Cal pushed his chair closer to mine and put his arms around me. "I wish we were at my house," he said quietly. "I just want to hold you without worrying about your folks coming in."

I nodded, sniffling. "What are we going to do?"

"There's nothing we can do, Morgan," Cal said, kissing my temple. "It was horrible, and I've cursed myself a thousand times for involving you in it. But it happened, and we can't take it back. And never forget that we acted in self-defense. Hunter was trying to kill me. You were trying to protect me. What else could we have done?"

I shook my head.

"I've never been through anything like this before," Cal said softly against my hair. "It's the worst thing in my life. But you know what? I'm glad I'm going through it with you. I mean, I'm sorry you were involved. I wish to the Goddess that you weren't. But since we were in it together, I'm so glad I have you." He shook his head. "This isn't making sense. I'm just trying to say that in an awful way, this has made me feel closer to you."

I looked up into his eyes. "Yeah, I know what you mean."

We stayed like that, sitting at the table, our arms around each other, until my shoulder blades began to ache from the angle and I reluctantly pulled away. I had to change the subject.

"Your mom seemed really excited about my tools," I said, taking a sip of my tea.

Cal pushed his hands through his raggedy dark hair. "Yeah. She's like a little kid—she wants to get her hands on every new thing. Especially something like Belwicket's tools."

"Is there something special about Belwicket in particular?"

Cal shrugged, looking thoughtful. He sipped his tea and said, "I guess just the mystery of it—how it was destroyed, and how old the coven was and how powerful. It's a blessing the tools weren't lost. Oh, and they were Woodbane," he added as an afterthought.

"Does it matter that they were Woodbane since Belwicket had renounced evil?"

"I don't know," said Cal. "Probably not. I think it probably matters more what you *do* with your magick."

I breathed in the steam from my tea. "Maybe I bound the tools to me without thinking it through too well," I said. "What would happen if another witch tried to use them now?"

Cal shrugged. "It's not predictable. Another witch might subvert the tools' power in an unexpected way. Actually, it's pretty unusual for someone to bind a coven's tools only to themselves." He looked up and met my glance.

"I just felt they were mine," I said lamely. "Mine, my birth mother's, her mother's. I wanted them to be all mine."

Nodding, Cal patted my leg, across his knee. "I'd probably do the same thing if they were mine," he said, and I adored him for his support.

"And then Mom would kill me," he added, laughing. I laughed, too.

"Your mom said I was an unusually powerful witch, this morning in the car," I said. "So witches have different strengths of power? In one of my Wiccan history books it talks about some witches being more powerful than others. Does that mean that they just know more, or does it mean something about their innate power?"

"Both," Cal said. He put his feet on either side of mine under the table. "It's like regular education. How accomplished you are depends on how intelligent you are as well as how much education you have. Of course, blood witches are always going to be more powerful than humans. But even among blood witches there's definitely a range. If you're naturally a weak witch, then you can study and practice all you want and your powers will be only so-so. If you're a naturally powerful witch, yet don't know anything about Wicca, you can't do much, either. It's the combination that matters."

"Well, how strong is your mother, for example?" I asked. "On a scale of one to ten?"

Laughing, Cal leaned across and kissed my cheek. "Careful. Your math genes are showing."

I grinned.

"Let's see," he mused. He rubbed his chin, and I saw a flash of bandage on his wrist. My heart ached for the pain he had gone through. "My mother, on a scale of one to ten. Let's make it a scale of one to a hundred. And a weak witch without much training would be about a twelve."

I nodded, putting this mythical person on the scale.

"And then someone like, oh, Mereden the Wise or Denys Haraldson would be up in the nineties."

I nodded, recognizing the names Mereden and Denys from my Wiccan history books. They had been powerful witches, role models, educators, enlighteners. Mereden had been burned at the stake back in 1517. Denys had died in 1942 in a London bomb blitz.

"My mom is about an eighty or an eighty-five on that scale," Cal said.

My eyes widened. "Wow. That's way up there."

"Yep. She's no one to mess with," Cal said wryly.

"Where are you? Where am I?"

"It's harder to tell," Cal said. He glanced at his watch. "You know, it'll be dark soon, and I'd really like to put some spells on your house and car while Sky's still in town."

"Okay," I agreed, standing up. "But you really can't say where we are on the Cal scale of witch power? Which reminds me: is it Calvin or just Cal?"

He laughed and brought his mug over to the sink. From upstairs we heard Mary K. blasting her latest favorite CD. "It's Calhoun," he said as we walked into the living room.

"Calhoun," I said, trying it out. I liked it. "Answer my question, Calhoun."

"Let me think," said Cal, putting on his coat. "It's hard to be objective about myself—but I think I'm about a sixty-two. I mean, I'm young; my powers will likely increase as I get older. I'm from good lines, I'm a good student, but I'm not a shooting star. I'm not going to take the Wiccan world by storm. So I'd give myself about a sixty-two."

I laughed and hugged him through his coat. He put his arms around me and stroked my hair down my back. "But you," he said quietly, "you are something different."

"What, like a twenty?" I said.

"Goddess, no," he said.

"Thirty-five? Forty?" I made my eyes look big and hopeful. It made me happy to tease and joke with Cal. It was so easy to love him, to be myself, and to like who I was with him.

He smiled slowly, making me catch my breath at his

beauty. "No, sweetie," he said gently. "I think you're more like a ninety. Ninety-five."

Startled, I stared at him, then realized he was joking. "Oh, very funny," I said, laughing. I pulled away and put on my own coat. "We can't *all* be magickal wonders. We can't *all* be—"

"You're a shooting star," he said. His face was serious, even grave. "You *are* a magickal wonder. A prodigy. You could take the Wiccan world by storm."

I gaped, trying to make sense of his words. "What are you talking about?"

"It's why I've been trying to get you to go slowly, not rush things," he said. "You have a tornado inside you, but you have to learn to control it. Like with Maeve's tools. I wish you'd let my mother guide you. I'm worried that you might be getting into something over your head because you're not seeing the big picture."

"I don't know what you mean," I said uncertainly.

He smiled again, his mood lightening, and dropped a kiss on my lips. "Oh, it's no big deal," he said with teasing sarcasm. "It's just, you know, you have a power that comes along every couple of generations. Don't worry about it."

Despite my confusion, Cal really wouldn't talk about it anymore. Outside, he concentrated on spelling Das Boot and my house with runes and spells of protection, and once that was done, he went home. And I was left with too many questions.

That night after dinner my parents took Mary K. to her friend Jaycee's violin recital. Once they were gone, I locked all the doors, feeling melodramatic. Then I went upstairs, took out Maeve's tools, and went into my room.

Sitting on my floor, I examined the tools again. They felt natural in my hands, comfortable, an extension of myself. I wondered what Cal had meant about not seeing the big picture. To me, the big picture was: these had been my grandmother's tools, then my mother's; now they were mine. Any other big picture was secondary to that.

Still, I was sure Selene could teach me a lot about them. It was a compelling idea. I wondered again why Alyce had urged me to bind them to myself so quickly.

I was halfway through making a circle before I realized what I was doing. With surprise, I looked up to find a piece of chalk in my hand and my circle half drawn. My mother's green silk robe, embroidered with magickal symbols, stars, and runes, was draped over my clothes. A candle burned in the fire cup, incense was in the air cup, and the other two cups held earth and water. Cal's silver pentacle was warm at my throat. I hadn't taken it off since he'd given it to me.

The tools wanted me to use them. They wanted to come alive again after languishing, unused and hidden, for so long. I felt their promise of power. Working quickly, I finished casting my circle. Then, holding the athame, I blessed the Goddess and the God and invoked them.

Now what?

Scrying.

I looked into the candle flame, concentrating and relaxing at the same time. I felt my muscles ease, my breathing slow, my thoughts drift free. Words came to my mind, and I spoke them aloud.

"I sense magick growing and swelling.
I visit knowledge in its dwelling.
For me alone these tools endure,
To make my magick strong and sure."

Then I thought, I am ready to see, and then . . . things started happening.

I saw rows of ancient books and knew these were texts I needed to study. I knew I had years of circles ahead of me, years of observing and celebrating the cycles. I saw myself, bent and sobbing, and understood that the road would not be easy. Exhilarated, I said, "I'm ready to see more."

Abruptly my vision changed. I saw an older me leaning over a cauldron, and I looked like a children's cartoon of a witch, with long, stringy hair, bad skin, sunken cheeks, hands like claws. It was so horrible, I almost giggled nervously. That other me was conjuring, surrounded by sharp-edged, dripping wet stone, as if I stood in a cave by a sea. Outside, lightning flashed and cracked into the cave, shining on the walls, and my face was contorted with the effort of working magick. The cave was glowing with power, that other Morgan was giddy with power, and the whole scene felt awful, bizarre, frightening, yet somehow seductive.

I swallowed hard and blinked several times, trying to bring myself out of it. I couldn't get enough air and was dimly aware that I was gaping like a fish, trying to get more oxygen to my brain. When I blinked again, I saw sunlight and another, older Morgan walking through a field of wheat, like one of those corny shampoo commercials. I was pregnant. There was no dramatic power around me, no ecstatic conjuring or anything—just peace and quiet and calm.

Now I was breathing quickly, and every time my eyes closed, I alternated between the two images, the two Morgans. I became aware of a deep-seated pain in my chest and throat, and I started to feel panicky and out of control.

I want to get out of this, I thought. I want to get out. Let me *out*!

Somehow I managed to wrench my gaze away from the candle flame, and then I was leaning over, gasping on my carpet, feeling dizzy and sick. I was flooded with sensation, with memories and visions I couldn't interpret or even see clearly, and suddenly I knew that I was about to vomit. I staggered to my feet, breaking my circle, and lurched drunkenly to the bathroom. I yanked off my robe, slid across the tiled wall until I hovered over the toilet, and then I threw up, almost crying with misery.

I don't know how long I was in there, but it was a long while, and finally I started to cry, aching, deep sobs. I sat there till the sobs subsided, then shakily got to my feet, flushed the toilet, and crept to the sink. Splashing my face with cold water helped, and I brushed my teeth and washed my face again and changed into my pajamas. I felt weak and hollow, as if I had the flu.

Back in my room, Dagda sat in the middle of the broken circle, gazing meditatively at the candle. "Hi, boy," I whispered, then cupped my hand and blew out the candle. My hands trembling, I dismantled everything, storing the tools in their metal box, folding my mother's robe, which seemed alive, crackling with energy. The very air in my room felt charged and unhealthy. I flung open a window, welcoming the twenty-five-degree chill.

I vacuumed up my circle and hid the toolbox again, spelling the HVAC vent with runes of secrecy. Soon after that, the front door opened and I heard my parents' voices. The phone rang at the same moment. I sprang over to the hall extension and said breathlessly, "Hi. I'm glad you called."

"Are you okay?" Cal said. "I suddenly got a weird feeling about you."

He would not be thrilled to hear about my using my mother's tools in a circle. Lack of experience, lack of knowledge, lack of supervision. And so on.

"I'm okay," I said, trying to slow my breathing. I did feel much better, though still a bit shaky. "I just—missed you."

"I miss you, too," he said quietly. "I wish I could be there with you at night."

A cool breeze from my room gave me a quick shiver. "That would be wonderful," I said.

"Well, it's late," he said. "Sleep tight. Think of me when you're lying there."

I felt his voice in the pit of my stomach, and my hand tightened on the phone.

"I will," I whispered as Mary K. started coming upstairs loudly.

"Good night, my love."

"Good night."

8

Symbols

September 2000

I'm in Ireland. I went to the town of Ballynigel, where the Belwicket coven once was. It was wiped out around Imbolc in 1982, along with most of the town. So far it's the only Woodbane coven I've found that the dark wave has destroyed. But everyone knows Belwicket renounced evil back in the 1800s and had kept to the council's laws since the laws were first written. Did that have something to do with it? When I stood there and saw the bits of riven earth and charred stones that are all that's left, it made my heart ache.

Tonight I am meeting with Jeremy Mertwick, from the second ring of the council. I have written them a letter every week, appealing their decision. I still hope to make them see reason. I am strong and sure, and my pain has made me older than they know.

—Giomanach

"C'mon, last day before break," Mary K. coaxed, standing over my bed. She waved a warm Toaster Strudel under my nose. I sat up, patted Dagda, and then staggered unhappily to the shower.

"Five minutes," Mary K. called in warning. Then I heard her say, "Come on, little guy. Auntie Mary K. will feed you."

Her voice faded as the hot spray needled down my skin, making me feel semihuman.

Downstairs, my sister handed me a Diet Coke. "Robbie called. His car won't start. We need to pick him up on the way."

We headed out and detoured over to Robbie's house. He was waiting out front, leaning against his red Volkswagen.

"Battery dead again?" I greeted him as he climbed into Das Boot's backseat.

He nodded glumly. "Again." We drove on in companionable morning silence.

At school Mary K. was met as usual by Bakker.

"Young love," Robbie said dryly, watching them nuzzle.

"Ugh," I said, turning off the engine.

"Thanks for the ride," Robbie said. Something in his voice made me turn and look at him.

"So I kissed Bree on Monday," he said.

I sat back, taking my hand off the door handle. I had been so wrapped up in my own misery that I had forgotten to check in with Robbie about Bree. "Wow," I said, examining his face. "I wondered what had happened. I, um, I saw her yesterday with Chip."

Robbie nodded, scanning the school grounds through the car window. He said nothing, and I prompted him: "So?"

He shrugged, his broad shoulders moving inside his army surplus parka. He gave a short laugh. "She let me kiss her. It blew my mind. She just laughed and seemed into it, and I thought, All *right*. And then I came up for air and said that I loved her." He stopped.

"*And?*" I practically screeched.

"She wasn't into *that*. Dropped me like a stone. Practically pushed me out the door." He rubbed his forehead, as if he had a headache. Silently I offered him my soda, and he finished it off and wiped his mouth with the back of his hand.

"Hmmm," I said. I didn't trust Bree anymore. Before, she might have done the same thing to Robbie, but now I couldn't help wondering how her involvement in Kithic had affected her actions.

"Yeah. Hmmm."

"But the making out worked?" I asked.

"Worked fabulously. Hot, hot, hot." He couldn't help grinning at the memory.

"Okay, I don't need to know," I said quickly.

I took a minute to think. Was Bree capable of using Robbie for some dark purpose, or was she just toying with him in her usual way? I didn't know. I decided to take a chance.

"Well, my advice to you is," I said, "just make out with her. Don't talk to her about your feelings. Not yet, anyway."

He frowned. Outside the car, we saw Cal crunching toward us through the leftover snow, his breath puffing like a dragon's. As usual, my heart lurched when I saw him.

"Hey, I *love* her. I don't want to use her like that."

"No. My point is, let *her* use *you* like that."

"Like a boy toy?" He sounded outraged, but I saw a fleeting interest cross his face.

"Like someone who knocks her off her feet," I pointed out. "Someone who gives her something she can't get from Chip Newton or anyone else."

Robbie stared at me. "You are *ruthless*." I heard admiration in his voice.

"I want you to be happy," I said firmly.

"I think, deep down, you want *her* to be happy, too," Robbie said, unfolding his long frame from the backseat. "Hey, Cal," he said, before I could respond to his remark.

Cal leaned into the open door. "Getting out anytime soon?"

I looked at him. "How about you get in, we take off, and just keep driving until we run out of gas?" I checked my gauge. "Got a full tank." I was only half joking.

When I glanced up, I was startled by the look in his eyes. "Don't tempt me," he said, his voice rough. For a long moment I hung there, suspended in time, pinned by the fierce look of desire and longing. I remembered how it had felt, making out on his bed, touching each other, and I shuddered.

"Hey, Cal," said Ethan from the sidewalk, waving at us as he went into the building.

Cal sighed. "Guess we better go in."

I nodded, not trusting myself to speak.

Cal and I joined the other Cirrus members at the top of the basement stairs.

"Talk about brutal weather," said Jenna as we walked up. She hugged her Nordic sweater closely around her, looking ethereal. I wondered how her asthma was lately and if I could use my tools to help her breathing.

"It's not even officially winter yet. This is the third-coldest autumn on record," Sharon complained, and snuggled closer to Ethan, who looked pleased. Hiding a smile, I sank down on a step, and Cal sat next to me and twined his hand through mine.

"Oh, this is cozy," said Raven's voice. Her dark head appeared over the staircase, followed by another dark head: Matt's. He sat down on a step, the picture of guilt, and she stood there smiling down at us, the Wicked Witch of the Northeast.

"Hi, Raven," said Cal, and she looked him up and down with her shining black eyes.

"Hello, Cal," she drawled. "Having a coven meeting?" She didn't bother lowering her voice, and some students walking past glanced up, startled. And this was Bree's new best friend.

"How's *your* coven going?" I heard myself ask. "Everything okay with Sky?"

Raven's eyes focused on me. Her silver nose ring glinted, her full lips were painted a rich purple, and I was struck by her presence: she was bizarre and luxurious, silly and compelling at the same time.

"Don't talk about Sky," Raven said. "She's a better witch than you'll ever be. You have no idea what you're up against." She stroked two fingers along Matt's smooth cheek, making him flinch, and walked off.

"Well, that was fun," said Robbie when she was gone.

"Matt, why don't you just join Kithic?" Jenna said abruptly, her jaw tight.

Matt frowned, not raising his eyes. "I don't want to," he mumbled.

"Okay, we only have a minute," said Cal, getting down to business. "We have a circle coming up this Saturday, our first in two weeks, and I have an assignment for you."

"I'm sorry, Cal, I won't be here," said Sharon.

"That's okay," he said. "I know you have plans with your family. Do these exercises on your own, and tell us about it the next time we see you. Now, one of the basic platforms of Wicca is self-knowledge. One of my teachers once said, 'Know yourself, and you know the universe,' and that may have been overstating it a bit, but not entirely."

Jenna and Sharon nodded, and I saw Ethan gently massaging Sharon's shoulder.

"I want you to work on self-imaging," Cal went on. "You're going to find your personal correspondences, your own . . . what's the word? I guess *helpers* or *connectors* sort of comes close. They're the things that speak to you, that feel like you, that awaken something in you. Objects or symbols that strengthen your connection to your own magick."

"Not following you here," said Robbie.

"Sorry—let me give you some examples. Things like stones, the four elements, flowers, animals, herbs, seasons, foods," said Cal, ticking them off on his fingers. "My stone is a tigereye. I often use it in my rituals. My element is fire. My metal is gold. My personal rune is—a secret. My season is autumn. My sign is Gemini. My cloth is linen."

"And your car of choice is Ford," Robbie said, and Cal laughed.

"Right. No, seriously. Think especially about elements, stars, stones, seasons, and plants. Define yourselves, but don't limit yourselves. Don't force anything. If nothing speaks to you, don't worry about it. Just move on to something else. But explore your connection to earthly things and to unearthly things." Cal looked around at us. "Any questions?"

"This is so cool," said Sharon.

"I already know your correspondences," Ethan told her. "Your metal is gold, your stone is a diamond, your season is the post-Christmas sale season . . . ouch!" he said as Sharon clipped him smartly on the head. He laughed and raised his hands to defend himself.

"Very funny!" said Sharon, trying not to smile. "And your element is *dirt*, and your metal is *lead*, and your plant is *marijuana!*"

"I don't smoke anymore!" Ethan protested.

We were all laughing, and I felt almost lighthearted in a way that I hadn't since Hunter—

The first bell rang, and suddenly the halls were filled with students swarming to their homerooms. We gathered our various belongings and went our separate ways. And I wondered how much longer I could take this inner darkness.

After the school bell rang at noon, I waited for Cal and Mary K. by the east entrance. It was snowing again. Footsteps sounded behind me, and I turned to see Raven and Bree heading toward the double doors. Bree's face hardened when she saw me.

"So, what are you guys doing for Thanksgiving?" I blinked in surprise as the words left my mouth. Two pairs of dark eyes locked in on me as if I were glowing like a neon light.

"Um, well, gee," Raven said. "I guess I'm celebrating a day

of wonder and thankfulness in the arms of my loving family. How about you?"

Since I knew her loving family consisted of a mother who had too many boyfriends and an older brother who was away in the army, I guessed she didn't have plans.

I shrugged. "Family. Turkey. A pumpkin pie gone wrong. Keeping my cat off the dining room table."

"You have a cat?" Bree asked, unable to help herself. She had a major weakness for cats.

I nodded. "A gray kitten. He's incredibly adorable. Totally bad. Bad and adorable."

"This is delightful"—Raven sighed as Bree opened her mouth to speak—"but we really must be going. We have things to do, people to see."

"Sky?" I asked.

"None of your business," Raven said with a smirk.

Bree was silent as they thumped down the stairs in their matching heavy boots.

A second later Mary K. ran up to say she was going to Jaycee's and Mom had said it was okay, and then Cal came up and asked if I could come over and of course I wanted to. I called Unser's Auto Shop and canceled Das Boot's repair appointment. Then I followed Cal to his house, where we could be alone.

Cal's room was wonderful. It ran the whole length and breadth of the big house since it was the attic. Six dormer windows made cozy nooks, bookcases lined the walls, and he had his own fireplace and an outside staircase leading down to the back patio. His bed was wide and romantic-looking, with white bed linens and a gauzy mosquito net looped out of the way. The dark wooden desk where he did his home-work had rows of cream-colored candles lining its edge. I had never been in here without envying him this magickal space.

"Want some tea?" he asked, gesturing to the electric ket-tle. I nodded, and we didn't speak, enjoying the silence and safety of his room.

Two minutes later Cal put a cup of tea into my hand, and I adjusted its temperature and took a sip. "Mmm."

Cal turned away and stood looking out the window. "Morgan," he said. "Forgive me."

"For what?" I asked, raising my eyebrows.

"I lied to you," he said quietly, and my heart clutched in panic.

"Oh?" I marveled at how calm my voice sounded.

"About my clan." The words had almost no sound.

My heart skipped a beat, and I stared at him. He turned to me, his beautiful golden eyes holding promises of love, of passion, of a shared future. And yet his words . . .

He took a sip of tea. The pale light from the window outlined the planes of his cheekbones, the line of his jaw. I waited, and he came close to me, so that his shirt was almost brushing mine and I could see the fine texture of his skin.

Cal turned toward the window again and pushed his fingers through his hair, holding it back from his left temple. I caught a glimpse of a birthmark there, beneath the hair. I reached up and traced its outline with my fingers. It was a dark red athame, just like the one I had under my arm. The mark of the Woodbane clan.

"Hunter was right," Cal went on, his voice low. "I am Woodbane. And I've always known it."

I needed to sit down. I had been so upset when I first found out about my heritage, and Cal had said it wasn't so terrible. Now I saw why. I put down my tea and walked across the room to the futon couch. I sank onto it, and he came to kneel at my side.

"My father was Woodbane, and so is my mother," he said, looking more uncomfortable than I'd ever seen him. "They're not the Belwicket kind of Woodbanes, where everyone renounces evil and swears to do good." He shrugged, not looking at me. "There's another kind of Woodbane, who practices magick traditionally, I mean traditionally for their clan. For Woodbanes that means not being so picky about how you get your knowledge and why you use your power. Traditional Woodbanes don't subscribe to the council's edict that witches never interfere with humans. They figure, humans interfere with us, we all live in the same world, not two separate universes, so they're going to use their powers to take care of problems they might have with humans, or to protect themselves, or to get what they need. . . ."

I was unable to take my eyes off his face.

"After my dad married my mother, I think they started to go different ways, magickally," Cal continued. "Mom has always been very powerful and ambitious, and I think my father disagreed with some of the things she was doing."

"Like what?" I asked, a little shocked.

He waved an impatient hand. "You know, taking too many risks. Anyway, then my dad met Fiona, his second wife. Fiona was a Wyndenkell. I don't know if he wanted a Wyndenkell alliance or he just loved her more. But either way, he left my mother."

I was finally getting some answers. "But if Hunter was right and your father was also *his* father, then wasn't he half Woodbane himself?" This sounded like some awful soap opera. *The Young and the Wiccan.*

"That's the thing," said Cal. "Of course he was. So it made no sense for him to persecute Woodbanes. But he seemed to have a thing about them, like Mom said. An obsession. I wondered if he blamed my father—our father—for what happened to his parents and their coven, for some reason, and so decided to get all Woodbanes. Who knows? He was unhinged."

"So you're Woodbane," I said, still trying to take it all in.

"Yes," he admitted.

"Why didn't you tell me before? I was *hysterical* about being Woodbane."

"I know," he said, sighing. "I should have. But Belwicket was a different kind of Woodbane, a completely good Woodbane, above reproach. I wasn't sure you would understand my family's heritage. I mean, it isn't like they're all evil. They don't worship demons or anything like that. It's just—they do what they want to do. They don't always follow rules."

"Why are you telling me now?"

At last he looked at me, and I felt the pull of his gaze. "Because I love you. I trust you. I don't want any secrets to come between us. And—"

The door to his room suddenly flew open. I jumped about a foot in the air. Selene stood there, dressed beautifully in a dark gold sweater and tweed pants.

Cal stood with swift grace. "What the hell are you doing?"

I had never heard anyone speak to their mother this way, and I flinched.

"What are *you* doing?" she countered. "I felt—what are you talking about?"

"None of your business," he said, and Selene's eyes flashed with surprise.

"We discussed this," she said in a low voice.

"Mom, you need to leave," Cal said flatly. I was embarrassed and confused and also worried: no way did I want to get in between these two if they were fighting.

"How—how did you know he was telling me anything?" I ventured.

"I felt it," Selene said. "I felt him say Woodbane."

This was really interesting. Creepy, but interesting.

"Yes, you're Woodbane," I said, standing up. "I'm Woodbane, too. Is there a reason I shouldn't know your clan?"

"Mom, I trust Morgan, and you need to trust me," Cal said thinly. "Now, will you get back to your work and leave us alone, or do I have to spell the door?"

My lips curved into an involuntary smile, and a second later the tension on Selene's face broke. She breathed out. "Very nice. Threaten your mother," she said tartly.

"Hey, I'll make it so you'll *never* find your way up here again," Cal said, his hands on his hips. He was smiling now, but I felt he wasn't entirely joking. I thought of Selene walking in on us when we were rolling around on Cal's bed and secretly decided maybe spelling the door wouldn't be such a bad idea.

"Forgive me," Selene said at last. "I'm sorry. It's just—Woodbanes have a terrible reputation. We're used to guarding our privacy fiercely. For a moment I forgot who Cal was talking to—and how extraordinary and trustworthy you are. I'm sorry."

"It's okay," I said, and Selene turned around and left. Quickly Cal stepped to the door and snapped the lock behind her, then traced several sigils and runes around the frame of the door with his fingers, muttering something.

"Okay," he said. "That will keep her out." He sounded smug, and I smiled.

"Are you sure?"

The answering look he gave me took my breath away. When he held out his hand, I went to him immediately, and next we tumbled onto his wide bed, the white comforter billowing cozily beneath us. For a long time we kissed and held each other, and I knew that I felt even closer to him than before. Each time we were alone together, we went a little further, and today I needed to feel close to him, needed to be comforted by his touch. Restlessly I pushed my hands under his shirt, against his smooth skin.

I never wore a bra, having a distinct lack of need, and when his hands slipped under my shirt and unerringly found their way to my breasts, I almost cried out. One part of my mind hoped the spell on his door was really foolproof; the other part of my mind turned to tapioca.

I pulled him tightly to me, feeling his desire, hearing his breathing quicken in my ear, amazed at how much I loved him.

This time it was Cal who gradually slowed, who eased the fierceness of his kisses, who calmed his breathing and so made me calm mine. Apparently today would not be the day, either. I was both relieved and disappointed.

After our breathing had more or less returned to normal, he stroked my hair away from my face and said, "I have something to show you."

"Huh?" I said. But he was rolling off the bed, straightening his clothing.

Then he held out his hand to me. "Come," he said, and I followed him without question.

9

Secrets

It's odd to be the son of a famous witch. Everyone watches you, from the time you can walk and talk— watches you for signs of genius or of mediocrity. You're never offstage.

Mom raised me as she saw fit. She has plans for me, my future. I've never really discussed them with her, only listened to her tell me about them. Until recently, it never crossed my mind to disagree. It's flattering to have someone prepare you for greatness, sure of your ability to pull it off.

Yet since my love came into my life, I feel differently. She questions things, she stands up for herself. She's so naive but so strong, too. She makes me want things I've never wanted before.

I remember back in California—I was sixteen. Mom had started a coven. It was the usual smoke and mirrors—Mom using her circle's powers as sort of an energy boost so she wouldn't have to deplete her own—but then to our surprise she unearthed a very strong witch, a woman about twenty-five or so, who had no idea of her bloodlines. During circles she blew us away. So Mom asked me to get close to her. I did—it was surprisingly easy. Then Mom extinguished her during the Rite of Dubh Siol. It upset me, even though I'd known that it might happen.

It won't come to that this time. I'll make sure.

—Sgàth

As Cal led me down his outside steps to the back patio, the last flakes of falling snow brushed my face and landed on my hair. I held tightly to the iron rail; the metal stairs were slick with snow and ice.

Cal offered me his hand at the bottom of the stair. I crunched onto the snow, and he began to lead me across the stone patio. We were both cold; our coats had been in the downstairs foyer, and we hadn't gotten them.

I realized we were heading toward the pool. "Oh, God, you can't be thinking about going skinny-dipping!" I said, only half joking.

Cal laughed, throwing back his head as he led me past the big pool. "No. It's covered for the winter, underneath that snow. Of course, if you're willing . . ."

"I'm not," I said quickly. I had been the lone holdout from a group swim at our coven's second meeting.

He laughed again, and then we were at the little building that served as the pool house. Built to look like a miniature version of the big house, its stone walls were covered with clinging ivy, brown in winter.

Cal opened a door, and we stepped into one of the small

dressing rooms. It was decorated luxuriously, with gold hooks, spare terry-cloth robes, and full-length mirrors.

"What are we doing here?" I looked at my pale self in the mirror and made a face.

"Patience," Cal teased, and opened another door that led to a bathroom, complete with shower stall and a rack of fluffy white towels. Now I was really confused.

From his pocket Cal took a key ring, selected a key, and opened a small, locked closet. The door swung open to reveal shallow shelves with toiletries and cleaning supplies.

Cal stood back and gently swept his hands around the door frame, and I saw the faint glimmer of sigils tracing its perimeter. He muttered some words that I couldn't understand, and then the shelves swung backward to reveal an opening about five feet high and maybe two feet wide. There was another room behind it.

I raised my eyebrows at Cal. "You guys have a thing for hidden rooms," I said, thinking of his mother's concealed library in the main house.

Cal grinned. "Of course. We're witches," he said, and ducked through the door. I followed, stepping through, then straightening cautiously on the other side.

Cal stood there, expectant. "Help me light candles," he said, "so you can see better."

I glanced around, my magesight immediately adjusting to the darkness, and found myself in a very small room, perhaps seven feet by seven feet. There was one tiny, leaded-glass window set high up on the wall, beneath the unexpectedly high ceiling.

Cal started lighting candles. I was about to say it wasn't necessary, I could see fine, but then I realized he wanted to create an effect. I looked around, and my gaze landed on the burnt wick of a thick cream-colored pillar candle. I need fire, I thought, then blinked as the wick burst into flame.

It mesmerized me, and I leaned, timelost, into the wavering, triangular bloom of flame swaying seductively about the wick. I saw the wick shrivel and curl as the intense heat made the fibers contract and blacken, heard the roar of the victorious fire as it consumed the wick and surged upward in ecstasy. I felt the softening of the wax below as it sighed and acquiesced, melting and flowing into liquid.

My eyes shining, I glanced up to see Cal staring at me almost in alarm. I swallowed, wondering if I had made one of those Wiccan faux pas I was so good at.

"The fire," I murmured lamely in explanation. "It's pretty."

"Light another one," he said, and I turned to the next candle and thought about fire, and an unseen spark of life jumped from me to the wick, where it burst into a bloom of light. He didn't have to encourage me to do more. One by one, I lit the candles that lined the walls, covered the tiny bookcase, dripped out of wine bottles, and guttered on top of plates thick with old wax.

The room was now glowing, the hundreds of small flames lighting our skin, our hair, our eyes. In the middle of the floor was a single futon covered with a thin, soft, oriental rug. I sat on it, clasped my arms around my knees, and looked around me. Cal sat next to me.

"So this is your secret clubhouse?" I asked, and he chuckled and put his arm around me.

"Something like that," he agreed. "This is my sanctuary."

Now that I wasn't lighting candles, I had the time to be awestruck by my surroundings. Every square inch of wall and ceiling was painted with magickal symbols, only some of which I recognized. My brows came together as I tried to make out runes and marks of power.

My mathematician's brain started ticking: Cal and Selene had moved here right before school started—the beginning of September. It was almost the end of November now: that left not quite three months. I turned to look at him.

"How did you do all this in three months?"

He gave a short laugh. "Three months? I did this in three weeks, before school started. Lots of late nights."

"What do you do in here?"

He smiled down at me. "Make magick," he said.

"What about your room?"

"The main house is full of my mother's vibrations, not to mention those of her coven members. My room is fine for most things; it's no problem for us to have circles there. But for my stuff alone, sensitive spells, spells needing a lot of energy, I come here." He looked around, and I wondered if he was remembering all the warm late-summer nights he had been in here, painting, making magick, making the walls vibrate with his energy. Bowls of charred incense littered the floor and the bookshelves, and the books of magick lined up behind them were dark and faded, looking immeasurably old. In one corner was an altar, made of a polished chunk of marble as big as a suitcase. It was draped with a purple velvet cloth and held candles, bowls of incense, Cal's athame, a vase of spidery hothouse orchids, and a Celtic cross.

"This is what I wanted to show you," he said quietly, his arm warm across my back. "I've never shown this to anyone, although my mother knows it's here. I would never let any of the other Cirrus members see this room. It's too private."

My eyes swept across the dense writing, picking out a rune here and there. I had no idea how long we had been sitting there, but I became aware that I was sweating. The room was so small that just the heat of the candles was starting to make it too warm. It occurred to me that the candles were burning oxygen, and Practical Morgan looked for a vent. I couldn't see one, but that didn't mean anything. The room was so chaotic that it was hard to focus on any one thing.

I realized in surprise that I wouldn't be comfortable making magick in this room. To me it was starting to seem claustrophobic, jangling, as if all my nerves were being subtly irritated. I noticed that my breath was coming faster.

"You're my soul mate," Cal whispered. "Only you could handle being here. Someday we'll make magick here, together. We'll surprise everybody."

I didn't know what to think of that. I was starting to feel distinctly ill at ease.

"I think I'd better get home," I said, gathering my feet beneath me. "I don't want to be late."

I knew it sounded lame, and I could sense Cal's slight withdrawal. I felt guilty for not sharing his enthusiasm. But I really needed to get out of there.

"Of course," Cal said, standing and helping me to my feet. One by one he blew out the candles, and I could hear the minuscule droplets of searing wax splatting against the walls. One candle at a time, the room grew darker, and although I could see perfectly, when the room was dark, it felt unbearable, its weight pressing in on me.

Abruptly, not waiting for Cal, I stepped back through the small door, ducking so I wouldn't whack my head. I didn't stop till I was outside in the blessedly frigid air. I breathed in and out several times, feeling my head clear, seeing my breath puff out like smoke.

Cal followed me a moment later, pulling the pool-house door closed behind him.

"Thank you for showing it to me," I said, sounding stiff and polite.

He led me back to the house. My nerves felt raw as I collected my coat from the front foyer. Outside again, Cal walked me to my car.

"Thanks for coming over," he said, leaning in through the car window.

I was chilled in the frosted air, and my breath puffed out as I remembered the things we had done in his bedroom and the sharp contrast with how I had felt in the pool house.

"I'll talk to you later," I said, tilting my head up to kiss him. Then I was pulling out, my one headlight sweeping across a world seemingly made of ice.

10

Undercurrents

October 2000

I came home from Ireland this week for Alwyn's initiation. It's hard to believe she's fourteen: she seems both younger, with her knobby knees and tall, coltish prettiness, and somehow also older—the wisdom in her eyes, life's pain etched on her face.

I brought her a russet silk robe from Connemara. She plans to embroider stars and moons around its neck and hem. Uncle Beck has carved her a beautiful wand and pounded in bits of malachite and bloodstone along the handle. I think she'll be pleased when she sees it.

I know my parents would want to be here if they could, as they would have wanted to see my initiation and Linden's. I'm not sure if they're still alive. I can't sense them.

Last year I met Dad's first wife and his other son at one of the big coven meetings in Scotland. They seemed very Woodbane:

cold and hateful toward me. I had wondered if perhaps Dad still kept in touch with Selene—she's very beautiful, very magnetic. But his name seemed to set off a storm within them, which is not unreasonable, after all.

I must go—Alwyn needs help in figuring the positions of the stars on Saturday night.

—Giomanach

That night, after the house was quiet, I lay in bed, thinking. I had been disturbed by Cal's secret room. It had been so intense, so strange. I didn't really like to think about what Cal had done to make the room have those kinds of vibrations, vibrations I could only begin to identify.

And now I knew that Cal was Woodbane. So Hunter had been speaking the truth when he told me that. I understood why Cal and Selene would want to hide it—as Selene said, Woodbanes have a bad reputation in the Wiccan community. But it bothered me that Cal had lied to me. And I couldn't help remembering how he had said that he and Selene were "traditional" Woodbanes. What exactly did that mean?

Sighing, I made a conscious effort to set aside thoughts about my day and immerse myself in Maeve's BOS. Almost every entry in this section was overwritten with an encoded one, and painstakingly I made my way through several days' worth. I already knew that my birth mother had met a witch from Scotland named Ciaran and had fallen in love with him. It was horrible to read about, knowing the whole story of her and Angus. So far it didn't seem like she had slept with Ciaran—but still, the feelings she had for him must have broken Angus's heart. Yet Maeve and Angus had ended up together. And they'd had me.

At last I hid the book and the athame under my mattress. It was the night before Thanksgiving. Hunter's face rose once more before my eyes, and I shuddered. It would be hard, this year, to give thanks.

Downstairs the next morning the kitchen was a crazed flurry: a turkey on the counter, boiling cranberries spitting deep pink flecks of lavalike sauce, Dad—entrusted with only the simplest tasks—busily polishing silver at the kitchen table. Mary K. was wiping the good china, my mother was bustling about, flinging salad, hunting for the packages of rolls, and wondering out loud where she had put her mother's best tablecloth. It was like every other Thanksgiving, comforting and familiar, yet this year I felt something lacking.

I managed to slip outside without anyone noticing. The backyard was serene, a glittering world of icicles and snow, every surface blanketed, every color muted and bleached. What an odd, cold autumn it had been. Kneeling beneath the black oak, I made my own Thanksgiving offering, which I had planned almost a week ago, before the nightmarish events of the weekend. First I sprinkled birdseed on the snow, seeing how the smaller seeds pelted their way through the snow's crust but the large sunflower nuts rested on top. I hung a pinecone smeared with peanut butter from a branch. Then I put an acorn squash, a handful of oats, and a small group of pinecones at the base of the tree.

I closed my eyes and concentrated. Then I quietly recited the Wiccan Rede, which I had learned by heart. I was about to go inside to tell Mom that for some reason, she had left the bags of rolls in the hall closet, when my senses prickled. My eyes popped open, and I looked around.

Our yard is bordered on two sides with woods, a small parklike area that hadn't been developed yet. I saw nothing, but my senses told me someone was near, someone was watching. Using my magesight, I peered into the woods, trying to see beyond the trees.

I feel you. You are there, I thought with certainty, and then I blinked as a flash of darkness and pale, sun-colored hair whirled and disappeared from sight.

Hunter! Adrenaline flowed into my veins and I stood, taking a step toward the woods. Then I realized with a sick pang that it couldn't be him. He was dead, and Cal and I had killed him. It must have been Sky, with that hair. It was Sky, hiding in the woods outside my house, spying on me.

Walking backward, scanning the area around me intently, I moved toward the house and stumbled up the back steps. Sky thought I had killed her cousin. Sky thought Cal was evil and so was I. Sky was planning to hurt me. I slipped into the steamy, fragrant kitchen, soundlessly muttering a spell of protection.

"Morgan!" my mom exclaimed, making me jump. "There you are! I thought you were still in the shower. Have you seen the rolls?"

"Uh—they're in the hall closet," I mumbled, then I picked up a silver-polishing cloth, sat down next to my dad, and went to work.

Thanksgiving was the usual: dry turkey; excellent cranberry sauce; salty stuffing; a pumpkin pie that was an odd, pale shade but tasted great; soft, store-bought rolls; everyone talking over each other.

Aunt Eileen brought Paula. Aunt Margaret, Mom and Eileen's older sister, had finally broken down and started speaking to Aunt Eileen again, so she and her family joined us. She spent most of the evening silently but obviously stewing over the fact that her baby sister was going to roast in hell because she was gay. Uncle Michael, Margaret's husband, was jovial and good-natured with everyone; my four little cousins were bored and only wanted to watch TV; and Mary K. kept making faces at me behind our cousins' backs and giggling.

All par for the course, I guessed.

By nine o'clock people started trickling homeward. Sighing, Mary K. plunked down in front of the TV with a slice of pie. I went upstairs to my room, and I heard Mom and Dad turn in early and then the click of the TV turning on in their room.

I turned off my bedroom light, then crept to the window and looked out. Was Sky still out there, haunting me? I tried to cast out my senses, but all I got was my own family, their peaceful patterns in the house. Using my magesight, I looked deeply past the first line of trees and saw nothing unusual. Unless Sky had shape-shifted into that small owl on the third pine from the left, everything was normal.

Why had she been there? What was she planning? My heart felt heavy with dread, thinking about it. I turned my light back on, pulled down my shades, and twitched my curtains into place.

I hadn't talked to Cal all day, and I both wanted to and didn't want to. I longed for him, yet whenever I thought of his secret room, I felt unsettled.

I climbed into bed and took out one of my Wiccan books. I was working my way through about five Wiccan-related books at one time, reading a bit each day. This one was an English history of Wicca, and it was dry going sometimes. It was amazing that this writer had managed to suck the excitement out of the subject, but often he had, and only a determination to learn everything about everything Wiccan kept me going.

I made myself read the history for half an hour, then spent another hour memorizing the correspondences and values of crystals and stones. It was something I could spend years doing, but at least I was making a start.

Finally, my eyes heavy, I had earned the reward of reading Maeve's BOS.

The first section I read described a fight she'd had with her mother. It sounded awful, and it reminded me of the fights I'd had with my parents after I'd found out I was adopted.

Then I found another hidden passage. "September 1981. Oh, Goddess," I read. "Why have you done this? By meeting Ciaran, I have broken a heart that's true. And now my own heart is broken, too.

"Ciaran and I joined our hearts and souls the other night, on the headland under the moonlight. He told me about the depth of his love for me . . . and then I found out about the depth of his deception, too. Goddess, it's true he loves me more than anything, and I feel in my heart he's my soul mate, my one life love, my second half. We bound ourselves to each other.

"Then he told me another truth. He is already wed, to a girl back in Liathach, and has got two children with her."

Oh, no, I thought, reading it. Oh, Maeve, Maeve.

"Married! I couldn't believe it. He's twenty-two and has been married four years already. They have a four-year-old boy and a three-year-old girl. He told me he'd been forced to marry the girl to unite their two covens, which had been at war. He says he cares for her, but not the way he loves me, and should I give him the word, he would leave her tomorrow, break up his marriage, to be with me.

"But he will never be mine. I would never ask a man to desert his woman and children for me! Nor can I believe that he would even offer. Thank the Goddess, I kept a few of my wits and did not do anything that might see me with my own child by him!

"For this I broke Angus's heart, went against my ma and da, and almost changed the course of my life."

I rested the BOS on my comforter. Maeve's anguished words glowed beneath the blade of the athame, and I felt her pain almost as keenly as if it were my own. It was my own, in a way. It was part of my history; it had changed my future and my life.

I turned the page. "I have sent him away," I read. "He will go back to Liathach, to his wife, who is the daughter of their high priestess. Goddess, he was sickened with pain when I sent him away. If I willed it, he would stay. But after a night of talk we saw no clear path: this is the only way. And despite my fury at his betrayal, my heart tonight is weeping blood. I will never love another the way I love Ciaran. With him I could have drunk the world; without him I will be dosing runny-nosed children and curing sheep my whole life. If it were not a sin, I would wish that I were dead."

Oh, God, I thought. I pictured Cal and me being split apart and missed him with a sudden urgency. I looked at the clock. Too late to call. It would have to wait till morning.

I hid the athame and the Book of Shadows, which lately was seeming like a Book of Sorrows, turned out the light, and went to sleep.

My last thought before drifting off was something about Sky, but in the morning I couldn't remember what it was.

On Friday morning I was blessedly alone in the house. I showered and dressed, then ate leftover stuffing for breakfast. My parents had gone to see some old friends of my mom's who were in town for the weekend. Bakker had already picked up Mary K. He had looked less than enthusiastic about Mary K.'s plan to hit the mall for some early Christmas shopping.

After they left, I made an effort to sort through my troubled thoughts. Okay, number one: Hunter. Number two: Cal's secret room. Number three: The fact that Cal lied to me about his Woodbane heritage. Number four: Selene being upset that Cal had told me about their being Woodbane. Number five: Everything Maeve had gone through with Ciaran and my father. Number six: Sky spying on my house yesterday.

When the phone rang, I knew it was Cal.

"Hi," I said.

"Hi." His voice was like a balm, and I wondered why I hadn't wanted to talk to him earlier. "How was your Thanksgiving?"

"Pretty standard," I said. "Except I made an offering to the Goddess."

"We did, too," he said. "We had a circle with about fifteen people, and we did Thanksgiving-type stuff, witch style."

"That sounds nice. Was this your mom's coven?"

"No," said Cal, and I picked up an odd new tone in his voice. "These are some of the same people who have been coming and going for the last couple of weeks. People from all over. They're Woodbane, too."

"Wow, they're all over the place," I exclaimed, and he laughed. "You can't shake a stick around here without hitting a Woodbane," I added, enjoying his amusement.

"Not in my house, at least," Cal agreed. "Which is why I'm calling, actually. Besides just wanting to hear your voice. There are people here who really want to meet you."

"What?"

"These Woodbanes. Kidding aside, pure Woodbanes are few and far between," said Cal. "Often when they find out about others, they look them up, get together with them, exchange stories and spells and recipes and clan lore. Stuff like that."

I realized I was hesitating. "So they want to meet me because I'm Woodbane?"

"Yes. Because you're a very, very powerful pureblood Woodbane," Cal coaxed. "They're dying to meet the untrained, uninitiated Woodbane who can light candles with her eyes and help ease asthma and throw witch fire at people. And who has the Belwicket tools, besides."

Run, witch, run.

"What?" asked Cal. "Did you say something?"

"No," I murmured. My heart kicked up a beat, and I started breathing as if I had just run up a flight of stairs.

What was wrong? Glancing around the kitchen, everything looked fine, the same. But a huge, crashing wave of fear had slammed into me and was now engulfing me and making me shake.

"I feel odd," I said faintly, looking around the room.

"What?" said Cal.

"I feel odd," I said, more strongly. Actually, I felt like I was losing my mind.

"Morgan?" Cal sounded concerned. "Are you all right? Is someone there? Should I come over?"

Yes. No. I don't know. "I think I just need to, um, splash water on my face. Listen, can I call you back later?"

"Morgan, these people really want to meet you," he said urgently.

As he spoke, I was sucked under the swell of fear, so that I wanted to crawl under the kitchen table and curl into a ball. Ask him for help, a voice said. Ask Cal to come over. And another voice said, No, don't. That would be a mistake. Hang up the phone. And run.

Cal, I need you, I need you, don't listen to me.

Now I *was* under the kitchen table. "I have to go," I forced out. "I'll call you later." I was shaking, cold, flooded with so much adrenaline that I could hardly think.

"Morgan! Wait!" said Cal. "These people—"

"Love you," I whispered. "Bye." My trembling thumb clicked the off button, and the phone disconnected. I waited a second and hit talk, then put the phone on the floor. If anyone tried to call now, they'd get a busy signal.

"Oh my God," I muttered, huddled under the table. "What's wrong with me?" I crouched there for a moment, feeling like a freak. Trying to concentrate, I slowly took several deep breaths. For a minute I stayed there, just breathing.

Slowly I began to feel better. I crawled out from under the table, my knees covered with crumbs. Dagda gazed owlishly down at me from his perch on the counter.

"Please do not tell anyone about this," I said to him, standing up. By now I felt almost back to normal physically, though still panicky. Once more I glanced around, saw nothing different, wondered if Sky was putting a spell on me, if someone was *doing* something.

"Dagda," I said shakily, stroking his ears, "your mother is losing her mind." The next thing I knew, I was putting on my coat, grabbing my car keys, and heading outside. I ran.

11

Link

I've been studying formally since I was four. I was initiated at fourteen. I've taken part in some of the most powerful, dangerous, ancient rites there are. Yet it's very difficult for me to kindle fire with my mind. But Morgan . . .

Mom wants her desperately. (So do I, but for slightly different reasons.) We're ready for her. Our people have been gathering for weeks now. Edwitha of Cair Dal is staying nearby. Thomas from Belting. Alicia Woodwind from Tarth Benga. It's a Woodbane convention, and the house is so full of vibrations and rivulets of magick that it's hard to sleep at night. I've never felt anything like this before. It's incredible.

The war machine is starting to churn. And my Morgan will be the flamethrower.

—Sgàth

Outside of Practical Magick, I parked Das Boot and climbed out, not seeing the Closed sign until I was pushing on the door. Closed! Of course—it was the day after Thanksgiving. Lots of stores were closed. Hot tears sprang to my eyes, and I furiously blinked them back. In childish anger I kicked the front door. "Ow!" I gasped as pain shot through my toes.

Dammit. Where could I go? I felt weird; I needed to be around people. For a moment I considered going to Cal's, but another strange rush of fear and nausea swept over me, and gasping, I leaned my head against Practical Magick's door.

A muffled sound from within made me peer inside the store. It was dark, but I saw a dim light on in the back, and then the shadow moving toward me metamorphosed into David, jingling his keys. I almost cried with relief.

David opened the front door and let me in. He locked the door behind me, and we stood for a moment, looking at each other in the dimness.

"I feel odd," I whispered earnestly, as if this would explain my presence.

David regarded me intently, then began to lead me to the small room behind the orange curtain. "I'm glad to see you," he said. "Let me get you a cup of tea."

Tea sounded fabulous, and I was so, so glad I was there. I felt safe, secure.

David pushed aside the curtain and stepped into the back room. I followed him, saying, "Thanks for let—"

Hunter Niall was sitting there, at the small round table.

I screamed and clapped my hands over my mouth, feeling like my eyes were going to pop out of my head.

He looked startled to see me, too, and we both whirled to stare at David, who was watching us with a glint of amusement in his hooded eyes. "Morgan, you've met Hunter, haven't you? Hunter Niall, this is Morgan Rowlands. Maybe you two should shake hands."

"You're not dead," I gasped unnecessarily, and then my knees felt weak, just like in mystery novels, and I pulled out a battered metal chair and sank onto it. I couldn't take my eyes off Hunter. He wasn't dead! He was very much alive, though even paler than usual and still bearing scrapes and bruises on his hands and face. I couldn't help looking at his neck, and seeing me, he hooked a finger in his wool scarf and pulled it down enough for me to see the ugly, unhealed wound that I had made by throwing the athame at him.

David was pouring me a steaming mug of tea. "I don't understand," I moaned.

"You understand parts of it," David corrected me. He pulled up another chair and sat down, the three of us clustered around a small, rickety table with a round plywood top. "But you haven't quite got the big picture."

It was all I could do not to groan. I had been hearing about the big picture since I'd first discovered Wicca. I felt I would never be clued in.

I felt a prickle of fear. I disliked and distrusted Hunter. I'd grown to trust David, but now I thought of how he used to disturb me. Could I trust anyone? Was anyone on my side? I looked from one to the other: David, with his fine, short, silver hair and measuring brown eyes; Hunter, his golden hair so like Sky's but with green eyes where hers were black.

"You're wondering what's going on," said David. It was a massive understatement.

"I'm afraid," I said in a shaking voice. "I don't know what to believe."

As soon as I started speaking, it was as if a sand bagged levee had finally collapsed. My words poured out in a torrent. "I thought Hunter was dead. And . . . I thought I could trust *you*. Everything is upsetting me. I don't know who I am or what I'm doing." Do not cry, I told myself fiercely. Don't you *dare* cry.

"I'm sorry, Morgan," said David. "I know this is very hard for you. I wish it could be easier, but this is the path you're on, and you have to walk it. My path was much easier."

"Why aren't you dead?" I asked Hunter.

"Sorry to disappoint you," he said. His voice was raspier than before. "Luckily my cousin Sky is an athletic girl. She found me and pulled me out of the river."

So Sky had gotten my message. I swallowed. "I never meant to—hurt you that badly," I said. "I just wanted to stop what you were doing. You were killing Cal!"

"I was doing my *job*," Hunter said, his eyes flaring into heat. "I was fighting in self-defense. There was no way Cal would go to the council without my putting a *braigh* on him."

"You were killing him!" I said again.

"He was trying to kill me!" Hunter said. "And then *you* tried to kill me!"

"I did not! I was trying to stop you!"

David held up his hands. "Hold it. This is going nowhere. You two are both afraid, and being afraid makes you angry, and being angry makes you lash out."

"Thank you, Dr. Laura," I said snippily.

"I'm not afraid of *her*," Hunter said, like a six-year-old, and I wanted to kick him under the table. Now that I knew he was actually alive, I remembered just how unpleasant he was.

"Yes, you are," David said, looking at Hunter. "You're afraid of her potential, of her possible alliances, of her power and the lack of knowledge she has concerning that power. She threw an athame into your neck, and you don't know if she'd do it again."

David turned to me. "And you're afraid that Hunter knows something you don't, that he might hurt you or someone you love, that he might be telling the truth."

He was right. I gulped my tea, my face burning with anger and shame.

"Well, you're both right," said David, drinking from his mug. "You both have valid reasons to fear each other. But you need to get past it. I believe things are going to be very tough around here very soon, and you two need to be united to face them."

"What are you *talking* about?" I asked.

"What would it take for you to trust Hunter?" David asked. "To trust me?"

My mouth opened, then shut again. I thought about it. Then I said, "Everything I know—almost everything—seems to be secondhand knowledge. People *tell* me things. I ask questions, and people answer or don't answer. I've read different books that tell me different things about Wicca, about Woodbanes, about magick."

David looked thoughtful. "What do you trust?"

In a conversation I'd had once with Alyce, she'd said that in the end, I really had to trust myself. My inner knowledge. Things that just *were*.

"I trust *me*. Most of the time," I added, not wanting to sound arrogant.

"Okay." David sat back, putting his fingertips together. "So you need firsthand information. Well, how do you suggest getting it?"

On my birthday Cal and I had meditated together, joining our minds. Standing, I walked around the table, next to Hunter. I saw the tightening of his muscles, his wariness, his readiness for battle if that was what I offered.

Setting my jaw, focusing my thoughts, I slowly reached out my hand toward Hunter's face. He looked at it guardedly. When I was almost touching him, pale blue sparks leaped from my fingers to his cheek. We all jumped, but I didn't break the contact, and finally I felt his flesh beneath my curled fingertips.

In the street a couple of weeks ago I had brushed past him, and it had been overwhelming: a huge release of emotions so powerful that I had felt ill. It was something like that now, but not as gut-wrenching. I closed my eyes and focused my energy on connecting with Hunter. My senses reached out to touch his, and at first his mind recoiled from me. I waited, barely breathing, and gradually I felt his defenses weaken. His mind opened slightly to let me in.

If he chose to turn on me, I was cooked. Connected like this, I could sense how vulnerable we were to each other. But still I pressed on, feeling Hunter's suspicion, his resistance, and then very slowly his surprise, his acquiescence, his decision to let me in further.

Our thoughts were joined. He saw me and what I knew of my past, and I saw him.

Gìomanach. His name was Gìomanach. I heard it in Gaelic and English at the same time. His name meant Hunter. He really was a member of the High Council. He was a Seeker, and he'd been charged to investigate Cal and Selene for possible misuse of magick.

I almost pulled back in pain, but I stayed with Hunter, feeling him searching my mind, examining my motives, weighing my innocence, my connection to Cal. I felt him wonder if Cal and I had been lovers and was embarrassed when he was relieved that we hadn't.

Our breathing was slight and shallow, noiseless in the deep silence of the little room. This connection was deeper still than the one I had forged with Cal. This was bone deep, soul deep, and we seemed to sift through layer upon layer of connection, and suddenly I found myself in the middle of a sunny, grassy field, sitting cross-legged on the ground, with Hunter by my side.

This was nice, and I smiled, felt the sun heat warm my face and hair. Insects buzzed around us, and there was the fresh, sweet smell of clover.

I looked at Hunter, and he at me, and we needed no words. I saw his childhood, saw him with his cousin Athar, who I knew as Sky, felt the agony of his parents' leaving. The depth of his anguish over his brother's death was almost unbearable, though I saw that he had been tried and found not guilty. This was something about which Cal didn't know the truth.

Hunter saw my normal life, the shock of finding out I was a blood witch, the growing sweetness of my love for Cal, the disturbing feelings I'd had about his secret room. I couldn't hide my concern about Mary K. and Bakker, my love for my family, my sorrow over the sadness of my birth mother's life and her unsolved death.

Gradually I realized it was time to go, and I stood up in

the field, feeling the grass brush against my bare legs. Hunter and I didn't smile as we said good-bye. We had achieved a new level of trust. He knew I hadn't meant to kill him and that I wasn't part of any larger, darker plan. In Hunter, I had seen pain, anger, even vengefulness, all surrounded by a layer of caution and mistrust—but still, I hadn't seen what I had looked for. I hadn't seen evil.

When I came out of it, I felt light-headed, and David's hand guided me back to my chair. Shyly I glanced up to meet Hunter's eyes.

He looked back at me, seeming as shaken as I was.

"That was interesting," said David, breaking the silence. "Morgan, I didn't know you knew how to join with Hunter's mind, but I suppose I shouldn't be surprised. What did you learn?"

I cleared my throat. "I saw that Hunter wasn't—bad or anything."

Hunter was looking at David. "She ought not to be able to do that," he said in a low voice. "Only witches with years of training—she got right inside my mind—"

David patted his hand. "I know," he said ruefully.

I leaned across the table toward Hunter. "Well, if you're not evil," I said briskly, "why have you and Sky been stalking me? I saw you two in my yard a week ago. You left sigils all over the place. What were they for?"

Hunter twitched in surprise. "They're protection spells," he said.

Just then the back door, a door I had barely noticed, opened. Its short curtain swung in, and a blast of cold air swirled into the room.

"You!" Sky snapped, staring at me from the doorway. She

looked quickly at Hunter, as if to make sure I hadn't been trying to kill him in the last twenty minutes. "What is she doing here?" she demanded of David.

"Just visiting," David said with a smile.

Her black eyes narrowed. "You shouldn't be here," she snarled. "You almost killed him!"

"You made me think I *had* killed him!" I snapped back. "You knew what had happened, you knew he was alive, yet you let me think he was dead. I've been sick about it!"

She made a disbelieving face. "Not sick enough."

"What were you doing at my house yesterday? Why were you spying on me?"

"Spying? Don't flatter yourself," she said, flinging down her black backpack. "I've had more important things to do."

My eyes widened. "Liar! I saw you yesterday!"

"No, that was me," Hunter put in, and Sky and I both turned to stare at him.

He shrugged. "Keeping tabs."

His arrogance was infuriating. He might not be evil, but he was still a horrible person.

"How dare you—" I began, but Sky interrupted me.

"Of course he's keeping tabs on you!" she snapped. "He's on the council, and you tried to kill him! If another witch hadn't seen what you'd done and sent me a message to go get Hunter, he would have died!"

I exploded, leaping to my feet. "What other witch? *I* was the one who sent you the message that night! *I* was the one who told you to go get him! And I called 911, too!"

"Don't be ridiculous," Sky said. "You couldn't have sent that message. You're nowhere near strong enough."

"Oh, yes, she is," Hunter said mournfully, leaning his chin on his hand. "She just flushed out my brain. I have no secrets anymore."

Sky gaped at him as if he'd been speaking in tongues. He took careful sips of his tea, not looking at her. "What are you talking about?" Sky asked.

"She did *tàth meanma*," Hunter said, his accent thickening with the Gaelic words. A shiver went down my spine, and I knew instinctively he'd referred to what we had done, the thing I thought of as the "Wiccan mind meld."

Sky was taken aback. "But she can't do that." She stared at me, and I felt like an animal in a zoo. Abruptly I sat down again.

"You're Athar," I said, remembering. "Athar means Sky. Cousin Athar."

No one had much to say to that.

"She's not in league with Cal and Selene," Hunter offered finally. I got angry again.

"*Cal* and *Selene* aren't in league with Cal and Selene, either!" I said. "For your info, Cal and I have done . . . *tàth menama*—"

"*Meanma*," Hunter corrected.

"Whatever. And he wasn't evil, either!"

"Did he lead it or did you?" Hunter asked.

Nonplussed, I thought back. "He did."

"Did you go as deep as with me?" he pressed. "Did you see childhood and future, wake and sleep?"

"I'm not sure," I admitted, trying to think.

"You need to be sure," David told me, almost impatiently.

I looked at all three of them. They seemed to be waiting for my response, and I had nothing to give them. I loved Cal, and he loved me. It was ridiculous to think he might be evil.

A picture of the little room in the pool house suddenly rose in front of my mind's eye. I pushed it angrily away. My mind seized on something else.

"I heard Bree and Raven talking about how you were teaching them about the dark side," I accused Sky.

"Of course I was," she countered, black eyes flashing. "So they could recognize it and fight it! It seems someone should have been teaching you the same thing!"

I stood again, overwhelmed with anger. "Thanks for the tea," I told David. "I'm glad you're not dead," I growled at Hunter. Then I stalked out the back door.

As I stomped down the alley and back to my car, my brain pounded with possibilities. Hunter wasn't dead! It was a huge relief, and waves of thankfulness washed over me. And he wasn't evil! Just—misguided. Unfortunately, Sky was still a total bitch and leading Bree and Raven and the rest of Kithic into what seemed to me to be a gray area.

But first things first. Hunter was alive!

12

The Bigger Picture

October 2000

Alwyn's initiation went well. I was so proud of her, giving her answers in her clear, high voice. She will grow up Wyndenkell and, we hope, marry within Vinneag, Uncle Beck's coven.

For one moment, as Uncle Beck pressed his athame to her eye and commanded her to step forward, I wondered if her life would be better had she not been born a witch. She would be just a fourteen-year-old girl, giggling with her friends, getting a crush on a boy. As it is, she's spent the last six years memorizing the history of the clans, tables of correspondences, rituals, and rites; going to spell-making classes; studying astronomy, astrology, herbs, and a thousand other things along with her regular schoolwork. She's missed school functions and friends' birthdays. And she lost her parents when she was only four.

Is it better for her this way? Would Linden still be alive if he hadn't been a witch? I know our lives would have held less pain if we had been born just human.

But it's pointless to consider. One cannot escape one's destiny—if you hide from it, it will find you. If you deny it, it will kill you. A witch I was born, and my family, too, and witches we'll always be, and give thanks for it.

—Giomanach

When I got home, I found a note saying that Cal had stopped by while I was gone. I ran upstairs, brought the phone into my room, and called Cal's house. He answered right away.

"Morgan! Where have you been? Are you okay?"

"I'm fine," I said, the familiar feeling of warmth coming over me at the sound of his voice. "I don't know what was wrong with me this morning. I just felt so weird."

"I was worried about you. Where did you go?"

"To Practical Magick. And you'll never guess who I saw there."

There was silence on Cal's end, and I felt his sudden alertness. "Who?"

"Hunter Niall," I announced. I pictured Cal's eyes widening, his face showing astonishment. I smiled, wishing I could see him.

"What do you mean?" Cal asked.

"I mean he's alive," I said. "I saw him."

"Where has he been all this time?" Cal asked, sounding almost offended.

"Actually, I didn't ask," I said. "I guess he's been with Sky. She found him that night and brought him home."

"So he wasn't dead," Cal repeated. "He went over that cliff with an athame in his neck, and he wasn't dead."

"No. Aren't you thrilled?" I said. "The weight of this has been so awful. I couldn't believe I had done something so terrible."

"Even though he was killing me," Cal said flatly. "Putting a *braigh* on me. Trying to take me to the council so they could turn me inside out." I heard the bitterness in his voice.

"No, of course not," I said, taken aback. "I'm glad I stopped him from doing that. We *won* that battle. I don't regret that at all. But I thought I had killed someone, and it was going to be a shadow over my life forever. I'm really, really glad that it won't."

"It's like you've forgotten that he was trying to kill me," Cal said, his tone sharpening. "Do you remember what my wrists looked like afterward? Like hamburger. I'm going to have scars for the rest of my life."

"I know, I know," I said. "I'm sorry. He was—more than wrong. I'm glad I stopped him. But I'm also glad I didn't *kill* him."

"Did you talk to him?"

"Yes." I was getting so weirded out by how Cal sounded that I decided not to tell him about the *tàth menima—mamena*—whatever. "I also saw his charming cousin, Sky, and we got into an argument. As usual."

Cal laughed without humor, then was quiet. What was he thinking? I felt the need to meld with his mind again, to feel his inner self. But I wanted to lead it myself this time.

That was a disturbing thought. *Did* I have doubts about Cal?

"What are you thinking about?" he asked softly.

"That I want to see you soon," I said. I felt guilty at the partial truth.

"I wanted to see you today," he said. "I asked you, and you said no, and then you went to Practical Magick. You weren't even home when I came by to see if you were all right."

"I'm really sorry," I said. "I just—this morning I felt so strange. I think I was having a panic attack. I wasn't thinking clearly and just wanted to get out of here. But I'm sorry—I didn't mean to blow you off."

"There were people here who wanted to meet you," he said, sounding slightly mollified.

All the hairs on the back of my neck stood up. "I'm sorry," I said again. "I just wasn't up to it today."

He sighed, and I pictured him running a hand through his thick, dark hair. "I've got to do a bunch of stuff tonight, but we've got a circle tomorrow at Ethan's house. So I'll see you there, if not during the day."

"Okay," I said. "Give me a call if you can get away."

"All right. I missed you today. And I'm worried about Hunter. I think he's psycho, and I was relieved when I thought he couldn't hurt either of us anymore."

I felt a sudden twinge of alarm. I hadn't even considered that. I'd have to talk to Hunter and make sure he didn't try to go after Cal again. We'd have to find a way to straighten out all these—misunderstandings or whatever they were—without violence.

"I have to go. I'll see you soon." Cal made a kissing noise into the phone and hung up.

I sat on my bed, musing. When I talked to Cal, I hated the

whole idea of Hunter. But today, when Hunter and I were doing the *tàth* thing, he'd seemed okay.

I sighed. I felt like a weather vane, blowing this way and that, depending on the wind.

After dinner Mary K. and I were in the kitchen, cleaning up. Doing mundane things like working in the kitchen felt a little surreal after my conversation with Cal.

For the hundredth time I thought, Hunter is alive! I was so happy. Not that the world necessarily needed Hunter in it, but now I didn't have his death on my conscience. He was alive, and it felt like a thousand days of sunshine, which was bizarre, considering how I couldn't stand him.

"Any plans for tonight?" I asked Mary K.

"Bakker's picking me up," she answered. "We're going to Jaycee's." She made a face. "Can't you talk to Mom and Dad, Morgan? They still say that I can't go out on dates by myself, I mean, just me and Bakker. We always have to be with other people if it's at night."

"Hmmm," I said, thinking that it was probably a good idea.

"And my curfew! Ten o'clock! Bakker doesn't have to be home till midnight."

"Bakker's almost seventeen," I pointed out. "You're fourteen."

Her brows drew together, and she dropped a handful of silverware into the dishwasher with an angry crash.

"You hate Bakker," she grumbled. "You're not going to help."

Too right, I thought, but I said, "I just don't trust him after he tried to hurt you. I mean, he held my sister down and made her cry. I can't forget that."

"He's changed," Mary K. insisted.

I didn't say anything. After I'd scraped the last plate, I went up to my room. Twenty minutes later I picked up on Bakker's vibrations, and then the doorbell rang. I sighed, wishing I could protect Mary K. from afar.

Up in my room, I studied my book on the properties of different incenses, essential oils, and brews that one can make from them. After an hour I turned to Maeve's Book of Shadows once more, dreading what I would find out and yet compelled to keep reading. It was so full of sadness right now, of anguish over Ciaran. Even though he had concealed his marriage and proved ready to desert his wife and children, she still felt he was her *mùirn beatha dàn*. It was hard for me to understand how she could still love him after learning all that. It reminded me of Mary K. and Bakker. If someone had held me down and almost raped me, I knew there was no way I would ever forgive him or take him back.

Who's there? I looked up, my senses telling me that another person's energy was nearby. I scanned the house quickly. I did that so often and was so familiar with my family's patterns that it took only a second to know that my parents were in the living room, Mary K. was gone, and a stranger was in the yard. I flicked off my bedroom light and looked out my window.

I peered down into the darkest shadows behind the rhododendron bushes beneath my window, and my magesight picked out a glint of short, moonlight-colored hair. Hunter.

I ran downstairs and through the kitchen, grabbing my coat off the hook by the door. Boldly I crunched through the snow across the backyard, then down the side, where my bedroom window was. If I hadn't been looking for him, if I didn't have magesight, I never would have seen Hunter blending with the night's shadows, pressed against our house. Once again I got a strong physical sensation from his presence—an uncomfortable, heightened awareness, as if my system was being flooded with caffeine over and over.

Hands on hips, I said, "What the hell are you doing here?"

"Can you see in the dark?" he asked conversationally.

"Yes, of course. Can't every witch?"

"No," he said, stepping away from the house, dusting off his gloves. "Not every witch has magesight. No uninitiated witch does, except you, I suppose. And not even every full-blood witch has it. It does seem to run strongly in Woodbanes."

"Then you must have it," I said. "Since you're half Woodbane."

"Yes, I do," he said, ignoring the challenge in my voice. "In me it developed when I was about fifteen. I thought it had to do with puberty, like getting a beard."

"What are you doing here?"

"Redrawing the protection sigils on your house," he said, as if he was saying, Just neatening up these bushes. "I see Cal laid his own on top of them."

"He was protecting me from you," I said pointedly. "Who are you protecting me from?"

His grin was a flash of light in the darkness. "Him."

"You're not planning to try to bind him again, are you?" I asked. "To put the *braigh* on him? Because you know I won't let you hurt him."

"No fear, I'm not trying that again," Hunter said. He touched his neck gingerly. "I'm just watching—for now, anyway. Until I get proof of what he's up to. Which I will."

"This is great," I said, disgusted. "I'm tired of both of you. Why don't you two leave me out of whatever big picture you're playing out?"

"I wish I could, Morgan," said Hunter, sounding sober. "But I'm afraid you're part of the picture, whether you want to be or not."

"But why?" I cried, fed up.

"Because of who you are," he said. "Maeve was from Belwicket."

"So?" I rubbed my arms up and down my shoulders, feeling chilled.

"Belwicket was destroyed by a dark wave, people said, right?"

"Yes," I said. "In Maeve's Book of Shadows, she said a dark wave came and wiped out her coven. It killed people and destroyed buildings. My dad went to look at the town. He said there's hardly anything left."

"There isn't," said Hunter. "I've been there. The thing is, Belwicket wasn't the only coven destroyed by this so-called dark wave. I've found evidence of at least eight others, in Scotland, England, Ireland, and Wales. And those are only the ones where it was obvious. This—force, whatever it is—could be responsible for much more damage, on a smaller scale."

"But what is it?" I whispered.

"I don't know," Hunter said, snapping a small branch in frustration. "I've been studying it for two years now, and I still don't know what the hell I'm dealing with. An evil force of some kind. It destroyed my parents' coven and made my parents go into hiding. I haven't seen them in almost eleven years."

"Are they still alive?"

"I don't know." He shrugged. "No one knows. My uncle said they went into hiding to protect me, my brother, my sister. No one's seen them since."

The parallels were clear. "My birth parents went into hiding, here in America," I said. "But they were killed two years later."

Hunter nodded. "I know. I'm sorry. But they're not the only ones who have died. I've counted over a hundred and forty-five deaths in the eight covens I know about."

"And no one knows what it is," I stated.

"Not yet." His frustration was palpable. "But I'll find out. I'll chase it till I know."

For a long minute we stood there, not speaking, each lost in our thoughts.

"What happened with Linden?" I asked.

Hunter flinched as if I'd struck him. "He was also trying to solve the mystery of our parents' disappearance," he said in a low voice. "But he called up a force from the other side, and it killed him."

"I don't understand," I said. A chill breeze riffled my hair, and I shivered. Should I ask Hunter in? Maybe we could hang in the kitchen or family room. It would be warm there.

"You know, a dark spirit," Hunter said. "An evil force. I'm guessing the dark wave is either an incredibly powerful force like that or a group of many of them, banded together."

This was too much for me to take in. "You mean, like a dead person?" My voice squeaked. "A ghost?"

"No. Something that's never been alive."

I shivered again and wrapped my arms around myself. Before I knew it, Hunter was rubbing my back and arms, trying to warm me up. I glanced up at his face in the moonlight, at his carved cheekbones, the green glitter of his eyes. He was beautiful, as beautiful as Cal in his own way.

This is who hurt Cal, I reminded myself. He put a *braigh* on Cal and hurt him.

I stepped away, no longer wanting to ask him inside. "What will you do with this dark force when you find it?" I asked.

"I won't be able to do anything to it," he said. "What I hope to do is to stop the people who keep calling it into existence."

I stared at him. He held my gaze; I saw him glance at my mouth.

"And then," he said quietly, "maybe then people who have been hurt by this, like you, like me . . . will be able to get on with their lives."

His words fell like quiet leaves onto the snow as I stood, trapped by his eyes. My chest hurt, as if I had too much emotion inside, and to let it all out was unthinkable: I wouldn't know where to begin.

Frozen, I watched Hunter lean closer to me, and then his hand was on my chin, and it was cold, like ice, and he tilted up my face. Oh, Goddess, I thought. He's going to kiss me. Our eyes were locked on each other, and again I felt that connection with him, with his mind, his soul. A small spot of heat at my throat reminded me that I wore Cal's silver pentacle on a cord around my neck. I blinked and heard a car drive up and realized what we were doing, and I stepped back and pushed against him with my hands.

"Stop that!" I said, and he looked at me with an unfathomable expression.

"I didn't mean to," he said.

A car door opened, then slammed shut, then opened, and Mary K.'s voice said, "Bakker!" Her tone was shrill, alarmed.

Before the door slammed shut again, I was running across the yard to find Mary K., with Hunter right behind me.

Bakker had parked in front of our house. Inside the dark car I caught glimpses of arms and legs and the auburn flash of my sister's hair. I yanked the car door open, spilling Mary K. on her back into the snow, her legs up on the car seat.

Hunter reached down to help Mary K. up. Tear tracks were already frosting on my sister's face, and one of her jacket's buttons had been ripped. She was starting to cry and hiccup at the same time. "M-m-morgan," she stammered.

I leaned into the car to glare at Bakker.

"You stupid bastard," I said in a low, mean voice. I felt cold with rage. If I'd had an athame right then, I would have stabbed him.

"Stay out of it," he said, sounding upset. He had scratch marks on one cheek. "Mary K.!" he called, shifting in his seat as if he would get out. "Come back—we need to talk. "

"If you ever look at, touch, talk to, or stand next to my sister again," I said very softly, "I'll make you sorry you were ever born." I didn't feel at all afraid or panicky: I wanted him to get out of the car and come after me so I could rip him apart.

His face turned red with anger. "You don't scare me with all that witch crap," he spat.

An evil smile snaked across my face. "Oh, but I should," I whispered, and watched the color drain from his cheeks. I narrowed my eyes at him for a second, then drew out of the car and slammed the door shut.

Hunter was watching us from a few feet away. Mary K. was holding his arm, and now she blinked up at him, saying, "I know you."

"I'm Hunter," he said as Bakker peeled away, burning rubber.

"Come on, Mary K.," I said, taking her arm and leading her toward the house. I didn't want to look at Hunter—I was still trying to process that almost kiss.

"Are you okay?" I asked, hugging Mary K. to my side as we went up the steps.

"Yes," she said shakily. "Just get me upstairs."

"Will do."

"I'll see you later, Morgan," said Hunter. I didn't reply.

13

The Circle

Giomanach is alive. Back from the dead. Dammit! Having the council's dog breathing down our necks could ruin everything. I need to take care of him. It's my responsibility.

I'll put the braigh on him, around his neck, and he can see how it feels.

—Sgàth

The next day Mary K. came into the family room as I was researching correspondences on the computer. There were dozens of Wiccan sites online, and I loved cruising from one to another.

"Morgan?"

"Yeah? Hey." I turned to look at her. Head hanging down, she looked uncharacteristically drawn and defenseless. I stopped what I was doing and pulled her into a tight hug.

"Why did he do it?" she whispered, her tears making my cheeks wet. "He says he loves me. Why does he try to hurt me?"

A rage began to boil in me. Was there some kind of spell I could do to Bakker that would teach him a lesson?

"I don't know," I told her. "He can't take no for an answer. Somehow he doesn't mind hurting you."

"He *does* mind," Mary K. cried. "He doesn't want to hurt me. But he always does."

"If he can't control himself, he needs help," I said slowly and carefully. "He needs to be in therapy. He's going to end up killing someone someday, a girlfriend or a wife." I pulled away and looked my sister in the eyes. "And Mary K.? That person will not be you. Understand?"

She looked at me helplessly, her eyes awash with tears. I shook her shoulders gently, once, twice, until she nodded.

"It won't be me," she said.

"It's over this time," I said. "Right?"

"Right," she said, but her eyes slid away, and I swore to myself.

"Do you want to tell Mom and Dad about him, or should I?" I said briskly.

"Oh, uh . . ."

"I'll tell them," I said, setting off to find them. In my opinion, keeping this a secret only made it more likely it would happen again. If my folks knew, Mary K. would have a harder time forgiving Bakker and going back to him again.

My parents did not take it well. They were angry with me for not telling them sooner, furious with Mary K. for continuing to see Bakker after the first time, and almost murderous in their rage toward Bakker, which cheered me up. In the end there was a big group hug, complete with tears and sobbing.

Half an hour later I paced off a small plot in the backyard, where my parents had agreed I could have a garden. The ground was too hard to dig, but I hammered in stakes and string to show where next spring's herbs would be. Then I sat on the snowy ground and tried to meditate for a while, clearing my mind and sending good thoughts into the earth below me, thanking it for being receptive to my garden. Feeling refreshed, I went back inside to look for a spell to put on Bakker.

Technically, of course, I wasn't supposed to do spells. I wasn't initiated, and I'd been a student for barely a couple of months. So I wasn't *committed* to spelling Bakker. But if the necessity arose . . .

Once more we had turkey sandwiches for dinner. I was approaching my saturation point with turkey and was glad to see the carcass was almost bare.

"Any plans for tonight?" my mom asked me.

"Cal's going to pick me up," I said. "Then we're going to Ethan's." Mom nodded, and I could almost see her weighing my boyfriend against Mary K.'s. On the one hand, Cal was Wiccan. On the other hand, he had never hurt me.

By the time Cal rang our doorbell, I had dressed in faded gray cords and the purple batik blouse he had given me for my birthday. I'd French braided my hair to the nape of my neck, then let the rest hang down. In the mirror I looked excited, pink-cheeked, almost pretty: a vastly different crea-ture than the Morgan I had been two months ago and a different Morgan than just two days ago. Now I knew I wasn't a murderer. I knew I wasn't guilty. I could breathe again, and enjoy life, without Hunter's death hanging over me.

"Hi!" I greeted Cal, shuffling into my coat. I said good-bye to my parents, and we walked down the salt-strewn pathway to the Explorer. In the dark car he leaned over and kissed me, and I welcomed his familiar touch, the faint scent of incense that clung to his jacket, the warmth of his skin.

"How's Mary K.?"

"So-so." I rocked my hand back and forth. I'd told him the gist of what had happened last night, omitting the Hunter part. "I've decided to fix it so that every time Bakker speaks, a toad or snake will slither from his mouth."

Cal laughed and turned onto the main street that would take us to Ethan's. "You are one bloodthirsty woman," he said. Then he flicked me a serious glance. "No spells, okay? Or at least, please talk to me about them first."

"I'll try," I said with exaggerated virtue, and he laughed again.

He parked in back of Robbie's red Beetle outside Ethan's house and turned to me again. "I haven't seen you in days, it feels like." He looped his hand around my neck and pulled me closer for a breathless kiss.

"Just one day," I answered, kissing him back.

"I wanted to ask you—what did you think about my seòmar?"

"What's a shomar?"

"Seòmar," Cal corrected my pronunciation. "It's a private place, usually used by one witch alone, to work magick. Different from a place where you meet with others."

"Does every witch have one?" I asked.

"No. Quit evading the question. What did you think of *mine?*"

"Well, I found it sort of disturbing," I said. I didn't want to hurt his feelings, but I couldn't lie, either. "After a while I wanted to get out of there."

He nodded, then opened the car door and got out. We walked up the pavement to Ethan's small, split-level brick rambler. "That's natural," he said, not sounding offended. "I'm the only one who's worked there, and I've done some intense stuff. I'm not surprised it seemed a little uncomfortable." He sounded relieved. "You'll get used to it pretty fast."

He rang the doorbell while I wondered if I even wanted to get used to it.

"Hey, man," said Ethan. "Come on in."

This was the first time I'd been to Ethan's house: before we were coven mates, we'd never socialized in or out of school. Now I saw that his house was modest but tidy, the furniture worn but cared for. Suddenly two small apricot bundles skittered around the corner from the hall, barking wildly, and I backed up a little.

Jenna laughed from the couch. "Here, pup dogs," she called. The two doglets ran toward her, panting happily, and Jenna gave them each a tortilla chip. She'd obviously been here before and knew Ethan's dogs. Another surprise.

"I never figured you for Pomeranians," Cal told Ethan with a straight face.

"They're my mom's," Ethan said, scooping one under each arm and carrying them back down the hall.

Robbie came out of the kitchen, munching a chip. Matt arrived last, and we went downstairs to the basement, which had been finished to be a large family room.

"Is Sharon still out of town?" I asked, helping Ethan push back furniture.

"Yeah. In Philly," he said. He pushed one of his straggly ringlets out of his eyes.

Once the furniture was out of the way, Cal started unpacking his leather satchel, taking out his Wiccan tools.

"Hey, Jenna," Matt said, since she had ignored him upstairs. His usual pressed appearance had taken a downslide in the last few days: his hair was no longer brushed smooth, his clothes looked less carefully chosen.

Jenna met his gaze squarely, then turned away from him with no expression on her face. Matt flinched. I'd always thought of Jenna as being kind of needy and dependent on Matt, but now I was beginning to suspect that she'd always been the stronger one.

"Last Wednesday, I asked you to choose your correspondences," Cal said as we settled on the floor around him. "Did anyone have any success?"

Jenna nodded. "I think I did," she said, her voice firm.

"Let us have it," said Cal.

"My metal is silver," she said, showing us a silver bracelet on her wrist. "My stone is rose quartz. My season is spring. My sign is Pisces. My rune is Neid." She lifted her hand and drew Neid in the air. "That's all I have."

"That's plenty," said Cal. "Good work. Your rune, standing for delay and the need for patience, is very apt."

He fished in his satchel and took out a squarish chunk of rose quartz the size of an egg. It was pale pink, mostly clear, not milky, and inside were cracks and flaws that looked like broken windowpanes, trapped inside. I thought it looked like pink champagne, frozen in time. Cal handed it to Jenna. "This is for you. You'll use it in your spells."

"Thanks," Jenna said, looking deeply into it, pleased.

"Your rune, Neid, will also become important. For one thing, you can use it as a signature, either on your spells or even in notes and letters."

Jenna nodded.

I sat forward, excited. This was cool stuff—this was what I really loved about Wicca. In my Wicca books the use of quartz in various spells had come up again and again. It had been used religiously for thousands of years. In particular, pink or rose quartz was used to promote love, peace, and healing. Jenna could use all three.

"Robbie?" Cal asked.

"Yeah," he said. "Well, I'm a Taurus, my rune is Eoh, the horse, which also symbolizes travel or change of some kind. My metal is copper. My herb is mugwort. My stone is emerald."

"Interesting." Cal grinned at us. "This is really interesting. You guys are doing a great job of feeling your way to your essences. Robbie, I didn't even associate emerald with you, but as soon as you said it, I thought, yeah, of course." He reached into his bag, rejecting several stones, then brought one out.

"This is a rough emerald," he said, holding it toward Robbie. It was about the size of a pat of butter, a dark, greenish lump in his hand. Robbie took it. "Don't get excited—it's not gem quality. No jeweler would buy it from you. Use it in good health," said Cal, and I was oddly reminded of taking communion at church. Cal went on,

"Emerald is good for attracting love and prosperity, to strengthen the memory, to protect its user, and also to improve the eyesight."

Robbie turned and wiggled his eyebrows at me. Until about a month ago, he'd worn thick glasses. My healing potion had had the unexpected side benefit of perfecting his vision.

"So do you just have every stone possible in that bag?" Ethan asked.

Cal grinned. "Not every one. But I have one or two of the most typical."

I had been wondering the same thing myself.

"Okay, Matt?" Cal prompted

Matt swallowed. "I'm a Gemini," he said. "My rune is Jera. My stone is tourmaline."

"Jera, for karma, a cyclical nature, the seasons," said Cal. "Tourmaline."

"The kind with two colors," Matt said.

"They call that watermelon tourmaline," said Cal, and took one out. It looked like a hexagonal piece of quartz, about an inch and a half long and as thick as a pencil. It was green on one end, clear in the middle, and pink on the other end. Cal handed it to Matt, saying, "Wearing this balances the user. Use it in good health."

Matt nodded and turned the stone over in his hand.

"I can go next," said Ethan. "I know what Sharon's are— should I tell them to you?"

Cal shook his head. "She can tell us at the next circle or at school."

"Okay, then, mine," said Ethan. "I'm a Virgo. My season is summer. My stone is brown jasper. I don't have a plant or anything. My favorite jellybean flavor is sour apple."

"Okay," said Cal, smiling. "Good. I think I have a piece of brown jasper . . . hang on." He looked at the stones in his bag and pulled out one that looked like solidified root beer. "Here you go. Brown jasper is especially good for helping you keep your feet on the ground."

Ethan nodded, looking at his stone.

"I think for your rune, you should use . . ." Cal considered Ethan thoughtfully while we all waited. "Beorc. For new beginnings, a rebirth. Sound okay?"

"Yeah," Ethan said. "Beorc. Cool."

Cal turned to me with a special look. "Last but not least?"

"I'm on the Scorpio-Sagittarius cusp," I said. "Mostly Sagittarius. My herb is thyme. My rune is Othel, which stands for an ancestral home, a birthright. My stone is bloodstone."

I might have been the only one to see Cal's pupils dilate and then contract in an instant. Was my choice wrong? Maybe I should have run my ideas by him first, I thought uncertainly. But I had been so sure.

Cal let a stone drop unseen into his bag; I heard it click faintly. "Bloodstone," he said, trying it out. I met his gaze as he looked at me. "Bloodstone," he repeated.

"What are its properties?" Jenna asked.

"It's very old," said Cal. "It's been used in magick for thousands of years to give strength to warriors in battle, to help women through childbirth. They say it can be used to break ties, open doors, even knock down barriers." He paused, then reached into his bag again, rummaged around, and pulled out a large, dark green stone, smooth and polished. When he tilted it this way and that, I could see the dark, blood-colored flecks of red within its darkness.

"Bloodstone," repeated Cal, examining it. "Its ruling

planet is Mars, which lends it qualities of strength, healing, protection, sexual energy, and magick involving men."

Jenna grinned at me, and I felt my cheeks flush.

"It's a fire stone," Cal went on, "and its associated color is red. In spells you could use it to increase courage, magickal power, wealth, and strength." His eyes caught mine. "Very interesting." He tossed me the stone, and I caught it. It felt smooth and warm in my hand. I had come across another bloodstone among the things in Maeve's toolbox. Now I had two.

"Okay, now let's make a circle," said Cal, standing. He quickly drew a circle, and we all helped cast it: purifying it, invoking the four elements and the Goddess and God, linking hands within it. Without Sharon there were only six of us. I looked around and realized that I was starting to feel like these people were my second family.

Each of us held our stones in our right palm, sandwiched with the left palm of the person next to us. We moved in our circle, chanting. Looking forward to the rush of ecstatic energy I always got in a circle, I moved around and around, watching everyone's faces. They were intent, focused, perhaps more so than during other circles: their stones must be at work. Jenna looked lovely, ethereal as delight crossed her features. Wonderingly she glanced at me, and I smiled at her, waiting for my own magick to take me away.

It didn't. It was a while before I realized I was deliberately holding it down, not letting it go, not letting myself give in to the magick. It occurred to me: I didn't feel safe. There was no reason I could think of not to, but I simply didn't. My own magick stayed dampened, not the enormous outpouring of power that it usually was. I let out a deep breath and put my trust in the Goddess. If there was danger here that I couldn't see, I hoped she would take care of me.

Gradually Cal took us down, and as we slowed, my coven members looked at me expectantly. They were used to me having to ground myself after a circle, and this time, when I shook my head, they seemed surprised. Cal gave me a questioning look, but I just shrugged.

Then Jenna said, "I feel kind of sick."

"Sit down," Cal said, moving to her side. "Ground yourself. All of you may feel some increased sensations because of your stones and the inner work you did over the week."

Cal helped Jenna sit cross-legged on the carpeted floor, her forehead touching the floor, both hands out flat. He took her chunk of pink quartz and placed it on the back of her slender neck, exposed because her ash blond hair had slipped down on both sides.

"Just breathe," he said gently, keeping one hand on her back. "It's okay. You're just getting in touch with your magick."

Robbie sat down, too, and assumed the same position. This was amazing. The others were finally picking up on the kind of magickal energy I'd been overwhelmed by since the beginning. Forgetting about my own weird feelings, I met Cal's eyes and smiled. Our coven was coming together.

An hour later Cal ended the circle. I stood and got my coat from the hall.

"It was a great circle tonight, guys," Cal said, and everyone nodded enthusiastically. "School starts again Monday, and we'll all be distracted again, so let's try to keep focused. I think you'll find it's easier to do now that you have your working stones. And just remember, we have a rival coven,

Kithic. Kithic is working with witches who are untrustwor-thy, who have an agenda. For your own sake, I want you all to stay away from anyone associated with them."

I looked at Cal in surprise. He hadn't mentioned his inten-tion of telling us this, but I supposed it was only natural, given the connection between Hunter and Sky, Sky and Kithic.

"We can't just be friends with them?" asked Jenna.

Cal shook his head. "It might not be safe. Everyone, be careful, and if anything feels strange or you feel things you can't figure out, please tell me right away."

"You mean like spells?" Ethan asked with a frown. "Like if they put spells on us?"

"I don't think they will," Cal said quickly, raising his hands. "I'm just saying be alert and talk to me about everything and anything, no matter how small."

Robbie looked impassively at Cal. I doubted he planned to quit seeing Bree. Matt looked completely depressed—he didn't seem to have a choice about seeing Raven or not: she wanted to see him, and so far he hadn't been able to say no.

Cal and I went out to the car, and I was silent with thought.

14
Finding

December 2000

My petition to become a Seeker has gone to the top. Yesterday I met with the seven elders of the council. They once again turned me down. What to do now?

I must curb my anger. Anger cannot help me here. I will ask Uncle Beck to intercede on my behalf. In the meantime I am taking classes with Nera Bluenight, of Calstythe. With her guidance I can school my emotions more and petition the council once again.

—Giomanach

On Sunday morning I realized that one week ago today I had turned seventeen. Looking back, it had been an intensely unhappy day: trying to appear normal while reliving the horror of watching Hunter go over the ledge, the dismay over Cal's wounds, the temporary loss of my magick. This week was going better. Thank the Goddess and God, Hunter was alive. I felt reassured by knowing that he wasn't inherently evil—and neither was I. Yet there were still huge, unresolved issues in my life. Questions about Cal and the things he might or might not be hiding from me, questions about myself and the depth of my commitment to Cal, to Wicca itself . . .

I went to church with my family because I knew my mother would make a fuss if I tried to duck out for the second week in a row, and I just wasn't ready to fight that battle. I sleepwalked through the service, my mind churning ideas incessantly. I felt I was two people: Catholic and not Catholic. Part of my family and not part of my family. In love with Cal, yet holding back. Loathing Hunter and yet full of joy that he was alive. My whole life was a mishmash, and I was being divided in two.

When the time for communion approached, I slipped out of our pew as if I was heading for the bathroom. I stood in the drafty hall behind the organist's cubby for a couple of minutes, then came back and fell in line with the people who had just taken communion. I took my seat, dabbing my lips as if I'd just sipped from the chalice. My mother gave me a questioning look but didn't say anything. Leaning back, I let my thoughts drift away once again.

Suddenly Father Hotchkiss's booming voice startled me. From the pulpit he thundered, "Does the answer lie within or without?"

It was like a bolt of lightning. I stared at him.

"For us," Father Hotchkiss went on, gripping the pulpit, "the answer is both. The answers lie within yourselves, as your faith guides you through life, and the answer lies without, in the truth and solace the church offers. Prayer is the key to both. It is through prayer we connect with our Maker, through prayer we reaffirm our belief in God and in ourselves." He paused, and the candles glowing behind him seemed to light the whole nave. "Go home," he went on, "pray thoughtfully to God, and ask him for guidance. In prayer will be your answer."

"Okay," I breathed, and the organ started playing, and we stood to sing a hymn.

After church my family had lunch at the Widow's Diner as usual, then headed home. Up in my room I sat on my bed. It was time to take stock of my life, decide where I was going. I wanted to follow the path of Wicca, but I knew that it wouldn't be easy. It would need more commitment from me than the things I was doing. It had to be woven into the everyday cycles of my life. I needed to start living mindfully in every moment.

Serious Wiccans maintain small altars at home, places to meditate, light candles, or make offerings to the Goddess and God, like the one in Cal's *seòmar*. I wanted to set one up for myself as soon as possible. Also, I had been meditating a bit, but I needed to set aside time to do it every day.

Making these simple decisions felt good—they would be outward manifestations of my inner connection to Wicca and my witch heritage. Now for another outward manifestation. Quickly I changed into jeans and a sweatshirt. When the coast was clear, I retrieved Maeve's tools from behind the vent and threw my coat over the box.

"I'm going for a drive," I told Mom downstairs.

"Okay, honey," she replied. "Drive carefully."

"Okay." Out in Das Boot, I put my coat on the seat

beside me and cranked the engine. A few minutes later I was approaching the edge of town.

Surrounding Widow's Vale are farmlands and woods. As soon as we had gotten our driver's licenses the year before, Bree and Robbie and I had gone on many day trips, exploring the area, looking for swimming holes and places to hang out. I remembered one place not too far out of town, a large, undeveloped tract that had been cleared for lumber back in the 1800s and was now covered with second-growth trees. I headed there, trying to remember the turns and forks, looking for familiar landmarks.

Soon I saw a field I remembered, and I pulled Das Boot over and put on my coat. I left the car on the shoulder of the road, took Maeve's box, and set off across the field and into the woods. When I found the stream I remembered, a sense of elation came over me, and I blessed the Goddess for leading me there.

After following the stream for ten minutes, I came upon a small clearing. Last summer, when we'd found it, it had seemed a magickal place, full of wildflowers and damselflies and birds. Robbie and Bree and I had lain on our backs in the sun, chewing on grass. It had been a golden day, free of worries. Today I had come back to partake of the clearing's magick again.

The snow here was deep—it had never been plowed, of course, and only faint animal tracks disturbed it. With each step I sank in over my ankles. A boulder at the edge of the clearing made a convenient table. I set Maeve's box there and opened it. Cal had said that witches wore robes instead of their everyday clothes during magickal rites because their clothes carried all the jangled, hectic vibrations of their lives. When I had worn Maeve's robe and used her tools a few days ago, I had felt nauseated, confused. It had occurred to me today that perhaps it was because of the clashing vibrations of my life and my magick.

Father Hotchkiss had advised us to pray, to look within for answers before we tackled outside problems. I was going to take his advice. Witch style.

Luckily for me, it was another one of those weird, warm days. The air was full of tiny dripping sounds as snow melted around me. I shucked my coat, sweatshirt, and undershirt.

It might have been warm for late autumn, but still, it wasn't summer. I began to shiver, and quickly pulled Maeve's robe over my head. It fell in folds to midcalf. I untied my boots, took off my jeans, and even my socks.

Miserably I peered down at my bare ankles, my feet buried in the snow. I wondered how long I would have the guts to stick this out.

Then I realized I no longer felt even the tiniest bit cold.

I felt fine.

Cautiously I lifted one foot, it looked pink and happy, as if I had just gotten out of the bath. I touched it. Warm. As I was marveling about this, I felt a focused spot of irritation at my throat. I touched it and found the silver pentacle Cal had given me weeks ago. I was so used to wearing it that I hardly noticed it anymore, but now it felt prickly, irritating, and regretfully I took it off and put it on the boulder with my other things. Ah. Now I was completely comfortable, wearing nothing but my mother's robe.

I wanted suddenly to sing with joy. I was completely alone

in the woods, enveloped in the warm, loving embrace of the Goddess. I knew I was on the right path, and the realization was exhilarating.

I set up the four cups of the compass. In one I put snow, then took out a candle. Fire, I thought, *flame,* and the charred wick burst into life. I used that candle to melt the snow into water. It was harder to find earth, but I dug a hole in the snow and then scraped at the frozen ground with my athame. I'd brought incense for air, and of course I used the candle for fire.

I made a circle in the snow with a stick, then invoked the Goddess. Sitting on the snow, as comfortable as an arctic hare, I closed my eyes and let myself sink through layer upon layer of reality. I was safe here; I could feel it. This was a direct communion between me and nature and the life force that exists within everything.

Slowly, gradually, I felt myself joined by other life forces, other spirits. The large oak lent me its strength, the pine, its flexibility. I took purity from snow and curiosity from the wind. The frail sun gave me what warmth it could. I felt a hibernating squirrel's small, slow heartbeat and learned reserve. A fox mother and her kits rested in their den, and from them I took an eager appetite for survival. Birds gave me swiftness and judgment, and the deep, steady thrumming of the earth's own life force filled me with a calm joy and an odd sense of expectation.

I rose to my feet and stretched my bare arms outward. Once again the ancient song rose in me, and I let my voice fill the clearing as I whirled in a circle of celebration.

Both times before, the Gaelic words had seemed like a call to power, a calling down of power to me. Now I saw that it was also a direct thread that connected me to Maeve, Maeve to Mackenna, Mackenna to her mother, whose name, it came to me, had been Morwen. For who knows how long I whirled in a kaleidoscope of circles, my robe swirling, my hair flying out in back of me, my body filled with the power of a thousand years of witches. I sang, I laughed, and it seemed that I could do it all at once, could dance and sing and think and see so startlingly clearly. Unlike the last time, I felt no unease, no illness, only an exhilarating storm of power and connection.

I am of Belwicket, I thought. I am a Riordan witch. The woods and the snow faded around me, to be replaced by green hills worn smooth by time and weather. A woman strode forward, a woman with a plain, work-lined face. Mackenna. She held out tools, witch's tools, and a young woman wearing a clover crown took them. Maeve. Then Maeve turned and handed them to me, and I saw my hand reaching out to take them. Holding them, I turned again and held them out to a tall, fair girl, whose hazel eyes held excitement, fear, and eagerness. My daughter, the one I would have one day. Her name echoed in my mind: Moira.

My chest swelled with awe. I knew it was time to let the power go. But what to do with it, where to direct this power that could uproot trees and make stones bleed? Should I turn it inward, keep it within myself for a time when I might need it? My very hands could be instruments of magick; my eyes could be lightning.

No. I knew what to do. Planting my feet in the churned snow beneath me, I flung my arms outward again and came to a stop. "I send this power to you, Goddess!" I cried, my throat hoarse from chanting. "I send it to you in thanks and blessing! May you always send the power for good, like my mother, her mother, her mother before her, and on through the generations. Take this power: it is my gift to you, in thanks for all you have given me."

Suddenly I was in the vortex of a tornado. My breath was pulled from my lungs, so that I gasped and sank to my knees. The wind embraced me, so that I felt crushed within strong arms. And a huge clap of thunder rang in my ears, leaving me shaken and trembling in the silence that followed, my head bowed to the snow, my hair wet with perspiration.

I don't know how long I crouched there, humbled by the power I myself had raised. I had left this morning's Morgan behind, to be replaced by a new, stronger Morgan: a Morgan with a newfound faith and a truly awesome power, gifted by the Goddess herself.

Slowly my breathing steadied, slowly I felt the normal silence of the woods fill my ears. Both drained and at peace, I raised my head to see if the very balance of nature had shifted.

Before me sat Sky Eventide.

15

Visions

February 2001

They have accepted me at last. I am the council's newest member—and its youngest, the most junior member of the third ring. I'm one of more than a thousand workers for Wiccan law. But my assigned role is that of Seeker, as I requested. I've been given my tools, the braigh and the books, and Kennet Muir has been assigned as my mentor. He and I have spent the past week going over my new duties.

Now I have been given my first task. There is a man in Cornwall who is accused of causing his neighbor's milk cows to sicken and die. I'm going down there today to investigate.

Athar has offered to come with me. I didn't tell her how glad I was of her offer, but I could see that she understood it nonetheless. She is a good friend to me.

—Giomanach.

Sky was perched on a snow-covered log about fifteen feet away from me. Her eyes were almond-shaped pools of black. She looked pale with cold and very still, as if she had been waiting a long time. Kicking in after the fact, my senses picked up on her presence.

She casually brushed off one knee, then clasped her gloved hands together.

"Who are you?" she said conversationally, her English accent as crisp and cool as the snow around us.

"Morgan," I was startled into replying.

"No. Who *are* you?" she repeated. "You're the most powerful witch I've ever seen. You're not some uninitiated student. You're a true power conduit. So who are you, and why are you here? And can you help me and my cousin?"

Suddenly I was chilled. Steam was coming off me in visible waves. My skin was damp and now turning clammy with sweat, and I felt vulnerable, *naked* beneath my robe.

Keeping one eye on Sky, I dismantled my circle swiftly and packed away my tools. Then I sat on the boulder and dressed, trying to act casual, as if getting dressed in front of a relative stranger in the woods was an everyday thing. Sky waited, her gaze focused on me. I folded Maeve's robe and put it back in my box, and then I turned to face Sky again.

"What do you want?" I demanded. "How long have you been spying on me?"

"Long enough to wonder who the hell you are," she said. "Are you really the daughter of Maeve of Belwicket?"

I met her eyes without responding.

"How old are you?"

A harmless question. "I just turned seventeen."

"Who have you been studying with?"

"You know who. Cal."

Her eyes narrowed. "Who else? Who before Cal?"

"No one," I said in surprise. "I only started learning about Wicca three months ago."

"This is impossible," she muttered. "How can you call on the power? How can you use those tools without being destroyed?"

Suddenly I wanted to answer her, wanted to share with her what I had just experienced. "I just—the power just comes to me. It *wants* to come to me. And the tools . . . are mine. They're for me to use. They *want* me to use them. They beckon me."

Sky sighed.

"Who are *you?*" I asked, thinking it was time she answered some questions herself. "I know you're Sky Eventide, you're from England, you're Hunter's cousin, and he calls you Athar." I thought back to what I had learned during the *tàth* thing with Hunter. "You grew up together."

"Yes."

"What are you doing with Bree and Raven?" I demanded.

After a pause she said, "I don't trust you. I don't want to tell you things only to have you tell Cal and his mother."

I crossed my arms over my chest. "Why are you even here? How did you know where to find me? Why do you and Hunter keep spying on me?"

Conflicting emotions crossed Sky's face.

"I felt a big power draw," she said. "I came to see what it was. I was in my car, heading north, and suddenly I felt it."

"I don't trust you, either," I said flatly.

We looked at each other for long minutes, there in the woods. Sometimes I heard clumps of snow falling off branches or heard the quick flap of a bird's wings. But we were in our own private world, Sky and I, and I knew that whatever happened here would have far-reaching consequences.

"I'm teaching Bree, Raven, Thalia, and the others basic Wiccan tenets," Sky said stiffly. "If I've told them about the dark side, it was only for their protection."

"Why are you in America?"

She sighed again. "Hunter had to come here on council business. He told you he's been doing research about the dark wave, right? He's combining his research with his duties as a Seeker. I get worried about him—all our family does. He's treading on dangerous ground, and we didn't want something bad to happen to him. So I offered to keep him company."

Remembering what Hunter's council duties were, I felt my fists clench. "Why is he investigating Cal and Selene?"

Sky regarded me evenly. "The council suspects they've been misusing their powers."

"In what way?" I cried.

Her dark eyes gazed deeply into mine. "I can't tell you," she whispered. "Hunter believes you're not knowingly involved with their plan. He saw that when you two were in tàth meanma. But I'm not so sure. Maybe you're so powerful that you can hide your mind from others."

"You can't believe that," I said.

"I don't know what to believe. I do know that I don't trust Cal and Selene, and I fear they're capable of more evil than you can imagine."

"Okay, you're pissing me off," I said.

"You need to face the facts. So we need to figure out the facts first. Hunter thinks Selene has a big plan that you're a key element of. What do you think they'll do to you if you don't want to be part of it?"

"Nothing. Cal loves me."

"Maybe he does," Sky said. "But he loves living more. And Selene would stop at nothing to have you—not even her own son."

I shook my head. "You're crazy."

"What does your heart tell you?" she asked softly. "What does your mind tell you?"

"That Cal loves me and accepts me and has made me happy," I said. "That I love him and would never help you hurt him."

She nodded thoughtfully. "I wish you could scry," she said. "If you could see them . . ."

"Scry?" I repeated.

"Yes. It's a somewhat precarious method of divination," Sky explained.

I nodded impatiently. "I know what it is. I scry with fire."

Her eyes opened so wide, I could see the whites around her black irises.

"You don't."

I just looked at her.

Disbelieving, she said, "Not with fire."

Not answering, I shrugged.

"Have you scryed to see what's happening in the present?"

I shook my head. "I just let the images come. It seems to be mostly the past, and sometimes I see possible futures."

"You can guide scrying, you know. You focus your energy on what you want to see. With water you'll see whatever your mind wants to see. A stone is the best, most accurate, but it offers less information. Do you think you could control scrying with fire?"

"I don't know," I said slowly, my mind already leaping with possibilities.

Ten minutes later I found myself in a situation I never could have dreamed up. Sky and I sat cross-legged, our knees touching, our hands on each other's shoulders. A small fire burned on a flat stone I had unearthed in the snow. It crackled and spat as the snow in the cracks of the burning branches boiled. I'd lit it with my mind, and had felt a stealthy surge of pride at the way Sky's eyes widened in shock.

Our foreheads touched; our faces were turned to the fire. I took a deep breath, closed my eyes, and let myself drift into meditation. I tuned out the fact that my jeans were getting wet and my butt would probably never thaw again. I had never scryed while doing the Wiccan mind meld, but I was into trying it.

Gradually my breathing deepened and slowed, and sometime later I sensed that Sky and I were breathing in unison. Without opening my eyes I reached out to touch her mind, finding the same suspicious brick wall that I had with Hunter. I pushed against it, and I felt her reluctance and then her slow acceptance. Cautiously she let me into her mind, and I went slowly, ready to pull out if this was a trap, if she tried to attack. She was feeling the same fear, and we paused instinctively until we both decided to let down our guards.

It wasn't easy. She had always rubbed me the wrong way, and she just about hated me. Surprisingly, it hurt to see the depth of her dislike for me, the rage she felt over what I had done to Hunter, her suspicion of my powers and their possible sources. I didn't realize witches could transfer their powers to another until I saw her worry that Selene had done this to me.

We breathed together, locked in a mental embrace, looking deeply into each other. She loved Hunter dearly and was very afraid for his safety. She missed England and her mother and father terribly. In her mind I saw Alwyn, Hunter's younger sister, who looked nothing like him. I saw her memory of Linden, how beautiful he had been, how tragic his death was.

Sky was in love with Raven.

What? I followed that elusive thought, and then it was there, in the forefront, clear and complete. Sky was in love with Raven. Through Sky's eyes I saw Raven's humor, her strength, her gutsiness, her determination to study Wicca. I felt Sky's frustration and jealousy as Raven chased Matt and flirted with others and had no reaction to Sky's tentative overtures. To Sky, slender, blond, restrained English Sky, Raven was almost unbearably lush and sexy. The bold way she spoke, her vivid appearance, her brash attitude all fascinated Sky, and Sky wanted her with a frank desire that took me aback and almost embarrassed me.

Then Sky was leading me, asking questions about Cal. Together we saw my love for him, my humiliating relief that someone finally wanted me, my awe at his beauty and respect for his power. She saw my uncertainty about and fascination with Selene and my discomfort about Cal's *seòmar*. As Hunter had, she saw that Cal and I hadn't made love yet. She saw that Hunter had almost kissed me, and she nearly broke off contact in surprise. I felt like she was paging through my private diary and began to wish I'd never agreed to this. My mind told Sky I had been shocked to find out I was Woodbane and extra shocked just four days ago to learn Cal was Woodbane also.

Now, together, she thought, and I opened my eyes. After looking at each other for a moment, weighing what we had learned, we turned, staying connected, and looked into the fire.

Fire, element of life, Sky thought, and I heard her. Help us see Cal Blaire and Selene Belltower as they are, not as they show themselves to us.

Are you ready to see? I heard the fire whisper back to us seductively. Are you ready, little ones?

We are ready, I thought, swallowing hard.

We are ready, Sky echoed.

Then, as it had for me in the past, the fire created images that drew us in. I felt Sky's awe and joy: she had never scryed with fire before. She strengthened her mind and concentrated on seeing the here and now, seeing Cal and Selene. I followed her example and focused on that also.

Cal, I thought. Selene. Where are you?

An image of Cal's huge stone house formed within the flames. I remembered how I could never project my senses through its walls and wondered if that applied to scrying. It didn't. The next time I blinked, I found myself in Selene's circle room, the huge parlor where she regularly held her coven's circles. It had once been a ballroom and now seemed like a grand hall of magick. Selene was there, in her yellow witch's robe, and I recognized Cal's dark head standing out from a group of people I didn't recognize.

"Do we really need her?" a tall, gray-haired woman with almost colorless eyes asked.

"She's too powerful to let go," said Selene.

An icy trickle down my back told me they were speaking of me.

"She's from Belwicket," a slender man pointed out.

"Belwicket is gone," Selene said. "She'll be from anywhere we want her to be."

Oh, God, I thought.

"Why haven't you brought her to us?" asked the gray-haired woman.

Selene and Cal met eyes, and to me it felt like they fought a silent battle.

"She'll come," said Cal in a strong voice, and inside me I felt a piercing pain, as if my heart were being rent. "But you don't understand—"

"We understand that it's past time for action," another woman said. "We need this girl on our side now, and we need to move on Harnach before Yule. You had an assignment, Sgàth. Are you saying you can't bring her to us?"

"It will be done," said Selene in a voice like marble. Again her gaze seared Cal, and his jaw set. He gave an abrupt nod and left the room, graceful in his heavy white linen robe.

I can't see any more, I thought, and then I said the words aloud. "I can't see any more."

I felt Sky pulling back as I did, and I shut my eyes and deliberately came back to the snowy woods and this moment. Opening my eyes, I looked up to see that the sky was darkening with late afternoon, that my jeans were soaked through and miserably uncomfortable, that the trees that had made a circle of protection around me now seemed black and threatening.

Sky's hands slid off my shoulders. "I've never done that,"

she said in a voice just above a whisper. "I've never been good at scrying. It's—awful."

"Yes," I said. I looked into her black eyes, reliving what I had just seen, hearing Selene's words again. Shakily I uncoiled and stood, my leg muscles cramped, my butt beyond feeling, and an unsettling feeling of nausea in my stomach. As Sky stood, stretching and groaning under her breath, I knelt and scooped up some clean snow, putting it in my mouth. I let it melt and swallowed the cold trickle of water. I did this again, then rubbed snow on my forehead and on the back of my neck under my hair. My breath was shallow, and I felt shaky, flooded with fear.

"Feel ill?" Sky asked, and I nodded, eating more snow.

I stayed on all fours, melting small mouthfuls of snow while my brain worked furiously, trying to process what we had seen. When Bree and I had fought over Cal and I had realized that we were no longer friends after eleven years, it had been shockingly painful. The sense of betrayal, of loss, of vulnerability had been almost unbearable. Compared to what I was feeling now, it had been a walk in the park. Inside, my mind screamed, No, no, no!

"Were those images true?" I choked out.

"I think so," Sky said, sounding troubled. "You heard them mention Harnach? That's the name of a Scottish coven. The council sent Hunter here to investigate evidence that Selene is part of a Woodbane conspiracy that's trying, basically, to destroy non-Woodbane covens."

"She's not the dark wave?" I cried. "Did she destroy Belwicket?"

Sky shrugged. "They don't see how she could have. But she's been linked to other disasters, other deaths," she said, hammering my soul with each word. "She's been moving around all her life, finding new Woodbanes wherever she goes. She makes new covens and ferrets out blood witches. When the coven is solid, she breaks it up, destroying the non-Woodbane witches and taking the Woodbanes with her."

"Oh my God," I breathed. "She's killed people?"

"They believe so," Sky said.

"Cal?" I said brokenly.

"He's been helping her since he was initiated."

This was all too much for me to take in. I felt frantic. "I have to go," I said, looking around for my tools. It was now almost dark. I grabbed Maeve's box and shook some of the snow off my boots.

"Morgan—" Sky began.

"I have to go," I said, more strongly.

"Morgan?" she called as I took the first step into the woods. I turned back to look at her, standing alone in the clearing. "Be careful," she said. "Call me or Hunter if you need help."

Nodding, I turned again and made my way back to my car. Inside, my heart began screaming again: No, no, no . . .

16

Truth

I've always wondered if my mother killed my father. After all, he left her, not the other way around. And then he had two more kids right away with Fiona. That really freaked Mom out.

Dad "disappeared" when I was almost nine. Not that I'd seen anything of him before that. I was the forgotten son, the one who didn't matter.

When Mom got the phone call, she just told me that Dad and Fiona had vanished. She didn't say anything about them being dead. But as the years have worn on and no one's heard from him—that I know about, anyway—it seems safe to assume he's dead. Which is convenient, in a way. It means Giomanach doesn't have Dad's power behind him. But still, I wish I knew what really happened. . . .

—Sgàth

The sun had faded away. My wheels crunched ice on the road as I drove past old farms, fields of winter wheat, silos.

Cal and Selene. Selene was evil. It sounded melodramatic, but what else do you call a witch who works on the dark side? Evil. Woodbane.

No! I told myself. I'm Woodbane. I'm not evil. Belwicket wasn't evil; my mother wasn't. My grandmother wasn't. But somewhere along the line, my ancestors had been. Was that why Selene wanted me? Did she see the potential for evil in me? I remembered the vision I'd had of myself as a gnarled crone, hungry for power. Was that my true future?

I choked back a sob. Oh, Cal, I screamed silently. You betrayed me. I loved you, and you were just playing a *part*.

I couldn't get over this. It was a physical pain inside me, an anguish so devastating that I couldn't think straight. Tears rolled down my cheeks, leaving hot tracks and tasting of salt when they touched the edges of my lips. A thousand images of Cal bombarded my brain: Cal leaning down to kiss me, Cal with his shirt open, Cal laughing, teasing me, offering to help me with Bakker, making me tea, holding me tight, kissing me hard, harder.

I was flying apart inside. I began to pray desperately that the scrying had been a lie, that Sky had tricked me, made me see things that weren't there, she had lied, had lied. . . .

I needed to see him. I needed to find out the truth. I'd had my questions answered by Hunter and by Sky, and now only Cal remained to fill me in on the big picture, the dangers I was blundering into, the reasons I needed to be careful, to watch myself, to rein in my power.

But first—I had to hide my mother's tools. With all my

heart, I hoped that Cal would convince me of his innocence, convince me that Sky was wrong, convince me that our love was true. But the mathematician in me insisted that nothing is one hundred percent certain. I had bound my mother's tools to me, they were mine, and now I had to make sure no one would take them away or make me use them for evil.

But where to stash them? I couldn't go home. I was already almost late for dinner, and if I went home, I wouldn't be able to turn around and leave. Where?

Of course. Quickly I made a right turn, heading to Bree's house. Bree and I were enemies: no one would suspect I would hide something precious in her yard.

Bree's house looked large, immaculately kept, and dark. Good—no one was home. I popped the trunk on my car and took out the box. Whispering, "I am invisible, you see me not, I am but a shadow," I slunk up the side yard, then quickly ducked beneath the huge lilac bush that grew outside the dining room window. It was mostly bare this time of year, but it still hid the opening to the crawl space beneath Bree's house. I tucked the toolbox out of sight behind a piling, traced some fast runes of secrecy, and stood up.

I was opening my car door when Bree and Robbie drove up in Bree's BMW. They pulled up beside me and stopped.

Ignoring them, I started to swing into the driver's seat of my car. The passenger window scrolled down smoothly. Crap, I thought.

"Morgan?" said Robbie. "We've been looking for you. We were talking to Sky. You've got to—"

"Gotta go," I said, climbing in and slamming the door shut before he could say anything else. I had already talked to Sky, and I knew what she'd said.

Robbie opened his door and started toward me. I peeled off, watching him get smaller in the rearview mirror. I'm sorry, Robbie, I thought. I'll talk to you later.

On the way toward the river, thoughts of exactly what I would say to Cal raced through my mind. I was in the middle of my ninth hysterical scenario when—

Morgan.

My head whipped around. Cal's voice was there, right beside me, and I almost screamed.

Morgan?

Where are you? my mind answered frantically.

I need to see you. Please, right away. I'm at the old cemetery, where we had our circle on Samhain. Please come.

What to do? What to think? Had everything he'd told me been a lie? Or could he explain it all?

Morgan? Please. I need you. I need your help.

Just like that night with Hunter, I thought. Was he in trouble? Hurt? Blinking, I wiped away some stray tears with the back of my sleeve and peered through the windshield. At the next intersection I turned right instead of left, and then I was on the road leading north, out of town. Oh, Cal, I thought, a new wave of anguish sweeping over me. Cal, we have to have it out.

Five minutes later I turned down a side road and parked in front of the small Methodist church that had once shepherded the people who now lay in its graveyard.

Shuddering with leftover sobs, I sat in my car. Then I felt Cal, coming closer. He tapped gently on my window. I opened the door and got out.

"You got my message?" he said. I nodded. He examined my face more closely. Then he caught my chin in his hands and said, "What's wrong? Why were you crying? Where were you? I tried going by your house."

What should I say?

"Cal, is Selene trying to hurt me?" I asked, my words like shards of ice in the night air.

Everything in him became still, centered, and focused. "Why would you say that?"

I felt his senses reaching out to me, and quickly I shut myself down, refusing him entrance.

"Is Selene part of an all-Woodbane coven that wants to erase non-Woodbanes?" I asked, pushing my hair out of my face. Please tell me it's a lie. Please convince me. Tell me anything.

Cal gripped my hair in his hand, making me look at him. "Who have you been talking to?" he demanded. "Dammit, has that bastard Hunter been—"

"I scryed," I said. "I saw you with Selene and other people. I heard them talking about your 'assignment.' Was I your assignment?"

He was silent for a long time. "Morgan, I can't believe this," he said at last. "You know you can't believe stuff you see in scrying—it's all nebulous, uncertain. Scrying shows you only possibilities. See, this is why I always want you to wait until I guide you. Things can be misunderstood—"

"Scrying showed me the possibility of where my mother's tools were," I said, my voice stronger. "It's not always lies— otherwise no one would use it."

"Morgan, what's this all about?" he asked in a loving voice. He gently pulled me to him so that my cheek rested against his chest, and it felt wonderful and I wanted to sink into him. He kissed my forehead. "Why are you having doubts? You know we're *mùirn beatha dàns*. We belong together; we're one. Tell me what's wrong," he said soothingly.

With those words the pain in my chest intensified, and I took deep breaths so I wouldn't cry again. "We're not," I whispered, as the truth broke over me like a terrible dawn. "We're not."

"Not what?"

I tilted back my head to look into his gold eyes, his eyes full of love and longing and fear. I couldn't bring myself to say it outright.

"I know you slept with Bree," I lied instead. "I *know* it."

Cal looked at me. Before Bree and I had broken our friendship, she had been chasing Cal hard, and I knew from past experience that she always got whatever guy she wanted. One day she had been happy, saying she and Cal had finally gone to bed, so now they were going out. But they hadn't started going out, and he had come after me. I'd asked him about it before, and he had denied sleeping with her, with my best friend. Now I needed to know the truth of it, once and for all, even as I was being hit with other painful truths from every direction.

"Just once," Cal said after a pause, and inside, I felt my heart cease its pumping and slowly clog shut with ice.

"You know what Bree's like," he went on. "She won't take no for an answer. One night, before I really knew you, she jumped on me, and I let her. To me it was no big deal, but I guess she was hurt that I didn't want more."

I was silent, my eyes locked on his, seeing in their reflection all my dreams exploding, all my hopes for our future, all shattering like glass.

"The only powers she had were reflections coming from

you," he said, the barest trace of disdain in his voice. "Once I realized you were the one, Bree was just ... unimportant."

"Realized I was the one what?" My voice sounded tight, raspy, and I coughed and spoke again. "The one Woodbane around? The Woodbane princess of Belwicket?" I pushed him away. "Why do you keep lying to me?" I cried in anguish. "Why can't you just tell me who you are and what you want?" I was practically screaming, and Cal winced and held up his hands.

"You don't love me," I accused him, still pathetically hoping he would prove me wrong. "I could be *anyone,* young or old, pretty or ugly, smart or stupid, as long as I was *Woodbane.*"

Cal flinched and shook his head. "That isn't true, Morgan," he said, a note of desperation in his voice. "That isn't true at all."

"Then what *is* true?" I asked. "Is anything you've told me true?"

"Yes!" he said strongly, raising his head. "It's true that I love you!"

I managed a credible snort.

"Morgan," he began, then stopped, looking at the ground. His hands on his hips, he went on. "This is the truth. You're right. I was supposed to find a Woodbane, and I did."

I almost gasped with pain.

"I was supposed to get close to her, and I did."

How could I still be standing, I wondered in a daze.

"I was supposed to make her love me," he said quietly. "And I did."

Oh, Goddess, oh, Goddess, oh, Goddess.

He raised his head and looked at me, my eyes huge and horrified.

"And you were the Woodbane, and you didn't even know

it. And then you turned out to be from the Belwicket line, and it was like we'd hit gold. You were the one."

Oh, Goddess, help me. Help me, please, I beg you.

"So I got close to you and made you love me, right?"

I had no answer. My throat was closed.

Cal gave a laugh laced with bitterness. "The thing is," he said, "no one said I had to love you back. No one expected me to, including me. But I do, Morgan. No one said I had to fall for you, but I did. No one said I had to desire you, enjoy your company, admire you, take pride in your strength, but I do, dammit! I do." His voice had been rising, and he stepped closer to me. "Morgan, however it started, it isn't like that now. I feel like I've always loved you, always known you, always wanted a future with you." He put his hand on my shoulder, gently kneading and squeezing, and I tried to back up. "You're my *mùirn beatha dàn*," he said softly. "I love you. I want you. I want us to be together."

"What about Selene?" My voice sounded like a croak.

"Selene has her own plans, but they don't have to include us," he said, stepping closer still. "You have to understand how hard it is to be her son, her only son. She depends on me—I'm the heir to the throne. But I can have my own life, too, with you, and it doesn't have to include her. It's just— first I have to help her finish some things she's been working on. If you help us, too, it will all go so much faster. And then we can be free of her."

I looked at him, feeling a cold, deadly calm replacing the panic and wretchedness inside me. I knew what I had seen in my vision, and I knew Cal was either lying or kidding himself about Selene's plans. They didn't include letting him—or me—be free.

"I'm free of her now," I said. "I know that Selene needs me for something. She's counting on you to sign me up. But I'm not going to, Cal. I'm not going to be part of it."

His expression looked like he had just watched me get hit by a car.

"Morgan," he choked out, "you don't understand. Remember our future, our plans, our little apartment. Remember? Please just help us with this one thing, and then we can work out all the details later. Trust me on this. Please."

My heart was bleeding. I said, "No. Selene can't have me. I won't do what she wants. I won't go with you. It's all over, Cal. I'm leaving the coven. And I'm leaving you."

His head snapped up as if I had hit him, and he stared at me. "You don't know what you're saying."

"I do," I said, trying to make my voice strong, though I really wanted only to crumple in misery on the ground. "It's over. I won't be with you anymore." Each word scarred my throat, etching its pain in acid.

"But you love me!"

I looked at him, unable to deny it even after all this.

"I love *you*," he said. "Please, Morgan. Don't—don't force my hand. Just come with me, let Selene explain everything herself. She can make you understand better than I can."

"No."

"Morgan! I'm asking you, if you love me, come with me now. You don't have to do anything you don't want to. Just come and tell Selene herself that you won't be part of her coven. That's all you need to do. Just tell her to her face. I'll back you up."

"You tell her."

His eyes narrowed with anger, then it was gone. "Don't

be unreasonable. Please don't make me do anything I don't want to do."

Fear shot through me. "What are you talking about?"

His face had a strange look, a look of desperation. I was suddenly terrified. The next second I whirled, broke into a run, and was digging my car keys out of my pocket. I ripped open the car door, hearing Cal right behind me, then he yanked the door open, hard, and shoved me in.

"Ow!" I cried as my head hit the door frame.

"Get in!" he roared, pushing against me. "Get in!"

Goddess, help me, I prayed as I scrambled to let myself out the other side. But when I grabbed the door handle, Cal put his hand on my neck and squeezed, muttering words that I didn't understand, words that sounded ancient and dark and ugly.

I tried to counter with my Gaelic chant, but my tongue froze in my mouth and a paralyzing numbness swept over me. I couldn't move, couldn't look away from him, couldn't scream. He had put a binding spell on me. Again.

I'm so stupid, I thought ridiculously as he started Das Boot with my keys.

17

The Seòmar

February 2001

I did it. I put a witch under the braigh.

The fellow in Cornwall was mad, there is no question of that. When I came to question him he first tried to evade me, then when he saw that I would not give up, he flew into a frenzy. He gibbered about how he would curse me and my whole family, that he was one of the Cwn Annwyn, the hounds of Hell. He began to shout out a spell and I had to wrestle him to the ground and put the braigh on him. Then he began to weep and plead. He told me how it burned him, and begged me to let him go. At last his eyes rolled back in his head and he lost consciousness.

I put him in the car, and Athar drove us to London. I left him with Kennet Muir. Kennet told me I'd done well; the man might be mad but he also had true power and was therefore dangerous. He said my task was done, and now it was the seven elders' job to determine the man's future.

I left, and then Athar and I went to a pub and got very drunk. Later, she held me while I wept.

—Giomanach

"You just don't get it, do you?" Cal said angrily, taking a corner too fast. I slumped against the car door helplessly. Inside, my mind was whirring like a tornado, a thousand thoughts spinning out of control, but the binding spell he had put on me weighted my limbs as thoroughly as if I were encased in cement.

"Slow down," I managed to whisper.

"Shut up!" he shouted. "I can't believe you're making me do this! I love you! Why can't you listen to me? All I need is for you to come talk to Selene. But no. You can't even do that for me. The one thing I ask you to do, you won't. And now I have to do this. I don't want to do this."

I slanted my eyes sideways and looked at Cal, at his strong profile, his hands gripping Das Boot's steering wheel. This was a nightmare, like other magickal nightmares I'd had before, and soon I would wake up, panting, in my own bed at home. I just needed to wake up. Wake up, I told myself. Wake up. You'll be late for school.

"Morgan," Cal said, his voice calmer. "Just think this through. We've been working with witchcraft for years. You've only been doing it a couple of months. At some point you'll just have to trust us with what we're doing. You're only resisting because you don't understand. If you would calm down and listen to me, it would all make sense."

Since I was in essence deadweight right now, his telling me to calm down seemed particularly ironic. Cal kept on talking, but my brain drifted away from his monologue. Focus, I thought. Focus. Get it together. Make a plan.

"I thought you would be loyal to me always," Cal said. My eyes were just above the window ledge, and I saw that we were just entering Widow's Vale. Were we going to Cal's house? It was so secluded—once he got me there, I'd never get out. I thought about my parents wondering where I was and wanted to cry. Focus, dammit! Think your way out of this. You're the most powerful witch they've ever seen; surely there must be something you can do. Think!

Cal flew through a red light at the edge of town, and involuntarily I flinched as I heard the squeal of brakes and an angry horn. I realized he hadn't even put my seat belt on me, and in my present helpless state I couldn't do it myself. Fresh, cold fear trickled down my spine when I pictured what would happen to me in an accident.

Think. Focus. Concentrate.

"You should have just trusted me," Cal was saying. "I know so much more than you do. My mother is so much more powerful than you. You're a student—why didn't you just trust me?"

My door was locked. If I could open it, I could maybe tumble out somehow. And get crushed beneath the wheels since I probably couldn't leap out of the way. Could I unroll my window and shout for help? Would anyone in town recognize my car and wonder why I wasn't driving it?

I tried to clench my right hand and saw with dismay that I could barely curl up my first knuckle.

The night of my birthday, when Cal had put the binding spells on me, I had somehow managed to break free. I had—pushed, with my mind, like tearing through plastic, and then I had been able to move. Could I do that now?

We raced through downtown Widow's Vale, the three stoplights, the lit storefronts, the cars on their way home. I peered up over my window, hoping someone, anyone, would see me. Would Cal get stopped for speeding? I almost cried as a moment later we passed through downtown and were on the less-traveled road that led toward Cal's house. Panic threatened to overtake me again, and I stamped it down.

Bree's face floated suddenly into my mind. I seized on it. Bree, Bree, I thought, closing my eyes and concentrating. Bree, I need your help. Cal has me. He's taking me to Selene. Please come help me. Get Hunter, get Sky. I'm in my car. Cal is desperate. He's going to take me to Selene. Bree? Robbie? Hunter, please help, Hunter, Sky, anyone, can you hear me?

Working this hard mentally was exhausting, and my breath was coming in shallow pants.

"You don't understand," Cal went on. "Do you have any idea what they'd do to me if I showed up without you?" He gave a short, barking laugh. "Goddess, what Hunter did to me that night was child's play compared to what they would do." He looked at me then, his eyes glittering eerily. He looked belovedly familiar and yet horribly different. "You don't want them to hurt me, do you? You don't know what they could do to me...."

I closed my eyes again, trying to shut him out. Cal had always been so in control. To see him this way was sickening, and a cold sweat broke out on my forehead. I swallowed and tried to go deep inside myself, deep to where the power was. Bree, please, I'm sorry, I thought. Help. Help me. Save me. Selene is going to kill me.

"Stop that!" Cal suddenly shouted, leaning over and shaking my shoulder hard.

I gasped, opening my eyes. He glared at me in fury.

"Stop that! You don't contact anyone! Anyone! Do you hear me?" His angry voice swelled in the car's interior, filling my ears and making my head hurt. One hand shook me until my teeth rattled, and I clenched my jaws together. I felt the car making big swerves on the road and prayed to the Goddess to protect me.

"Don't you wreck this car," I said, unclenching my lips enough to speak.

Abruptly he let go of me, and I saw the glare of headlights coming at us and then the long, low blare of a truck horn blowing. It swept past us as I drew in a frightened breath.

"Shit!" Cal said, jerking the steering wheel to the right. Another horn blared as a black car screeched to a halt just before ramming my side. I started to shake, slumped against my door, so afraid, I could hardly think.

You, afraid? part of me scoffed. You're the Woodbane princess of Belwicket. You could crush Cal with the power in your little finger. You have the Riordan strength, the Belwicket history. Now, save yourself. Do it!

Okay, I could do this, I told myself. I was a kick-ass power conduit. Letting my eyes float closed again, trying not to think about the chaos raging around me, I let the music come to me, the timeless music that magick sent. *An di allaigh an di aigh,* I thought, hearing the tune come to me as if borne on a breeze across clover-covered hills.

An di allaigh an di ne ullah. Was that my voice, singing in a pure ribbon of glorious sound that only I could hear? My fingers tingled, as if coming awake. *An di ullah be nith rah.* I drew in a deep, shuddering breath, feeling my muscles twitch, my toes curl. I am breaking this binding spell, I thought. I am smashing it. I am tearing it like wet tissue. *Cair di na ulla nith rah, Cair feal ti theo nith rah, An di allaigh an di aigh.*

I was myself. I had done it. I stayed exactly where I was, opening my eyes and gazing around. With a flare of alarm I recognized the tall hedges that surrounded Cal's property. He swung Das Boot into a side road, skidding a bit, and we began to crunch on icy gravel.

Bree, Sky, Hunter, Robbie, anyone, I thought, feeling my radiating power. Alyce, David, any witch, can you hear me?

The side road to Cal's driveway was long, with tall, overhanging trees. It was pitch-black except where moonlight glistened off snow. The dashboard clock said six-thirty. My family was sitting down to eat. At the thought I felt a surge of anger so strong it was hard for me to hide it. I couldn't accept the possibility that I might never see them again, Mom, Dad, Mary K., Dagda. I would escape. I would get out of this. I was very powerful.

"Cal, you're right," I said, making my voice sound weak. I couldn't even feel the effects of the binding spell anymore, and a surge of hope flamed in my chest. "I'm sorry," I said. "I didn't realize how important this was to you. Of course I'll go talk to your mom."

He turned the wheel and paused, reaching out his left hand and pointing it ahead of him. I heard the metallic rumbling of heavy gates, heard them swing on hinges and clunk open with a bang.

Then, as if he had finally heard me, Cal looked over. "What?" He stepped on the gas, and we rolled through the gate. Ahead of me was a dark roofline, and I realized we were in the backyard, and the building in front of me was the little pool house. Where Cal had his *seòmar*.

"I said, I'm sorry," I repeated. "You're right. You're my *mùirn beatha dàn*, and I should trust you. I do trust you. I just—felt unsure. Everyone keeps telling me something different, and I got confused. I'm sorry."

Das Boot rolled slowly to a halt, ten feet from the pool house. It was dark, with the car's one headlight shining sadly on the dead brown ivy covering the building.

Cal turned off the engine, leaving the keys in the ignition. He kept his eyes on me, where I leaned awkwardly against the door. It was all I could do to keep my hand from grasping the door handle, popping the door, and running with all my might. What spell could I put on Cal to slow him down? I didn't know any. Suddenly I remembered how his pentacle had burned at my throat when I used Maeve's tools. I'd felt better without it on. Was it spelled? Had I been wearing a spell charm all this time? I wouldn't doubt it at this point.

With agonizingly slow movement, I slipped my right hand down into my pocket and pulled out Cal's pentacle. He hadn't noticed I wasn't wearing it yet, and I let it slip from my fingers to the floor of the car. As soon as it left my hand, my head felt clearer, sharper, and I had more energy. Oh, Goddess, I was right. The pentacle had been spelled all this time.

"What are you saying?" Cal said, and I blinked.

"I'm sorry," I repeated, making my voice a little stronger. "This is all new to me. It's all confusing. But I've been thinking about what you said, and you're right. I should trust you."

His eyes narrowed, and he took hold of my hand. "Come on," he said, opening his door. His grip on my hand was crushing, and I dismissed the possibility that I could slip out suddenly and run. Instead he pulled me out the driver's-side door and helped me stand. I pretended to be weaker than I was and leaned against him.

"Oh, Cal," I breathed. "How did we get into such a fight? I don't want to fight with you." I made my voice soft and sweet, the way Bree did when she talked to guys, and I leaned against Cal's chest. Seeing the mixture of hope and suspicion cross his face was painful. Suddenly I pushed hard against him, shoving with every bit of strength in my arms, and he staggered backward. I raised my right hand and shot a spitting, crackling bolt of blue witch fire at him, and this time I didn't hold anything back. It blasted Cal right in the chest, and he cried out and sank to his knees. I was already running, my boots pounding heavily toward the metal gates that were swinging closed.

The next thing I knew my knees had crumpled and I was falling in slow motion to land heavily, face-first, on the icy gravel. The breath left my lungs in a painful whoosh, and then Cal stood over me, cradling one arm against his chest, his face a mask of rage.

I tried to roll quickly to shoot witch fire again, the only defensive weapon I knew, but he put his boot on my side and pressed down, pinning me to the cold ground. Then he grabbed one of my arms, hauled me to my feet, and squeezed the back of my neck, muttering another spell. I screamed, "Help! Help! Someone help me!" but of course no one came. Then I sagged, a deadweight.

"*An di allaigh*," I began in a choking voice as Cal hauled me toward the pool house. I knew where we were going, and I absolutely did not want to go there.

"Shut up!" Cal said, shaking me, and he pushed open the changing room door. Bizarrely, he added, "I know you're upset, but it will all be okay. Everything will be all right soon."

Reaching out, I grasped the door frame, but my limp fingers brushed it harmlessly. I tried to drag my feet, to be an awkward burden, but Cal was furious and afraid, and this fed his strength. Inside we lurched through the powder room, and Cal let me slump to the floor while he unlocked the closet door. I was trying to crawl away when he opened the door to his *seòmar*, and I felt the darkness come out of it toward me, like a shadow eager to embrace.

Goddess, I thought desperately. Goddess, help me.

Then Cal was dragging me by my feet into his room. With my magesight I saw that it had been cleared of everything, everything I could have used for a weapon, everything I could have used to make magick. It was bare, no furniture, no candles, only thousands and thousands of dark spells written on the walls, the ceiling, the floor. He'd prepared my prison in advance. He'd known this would happen. I wanted to gag.

Panting, Cal dropped my feet. He hovered over me, then narrowed his eyes and grabbed at the neck of my shirt. I tried to pull away, but it was too late.

"You took off my charm," he said, sounding amazed. "You don't love me at all."

"You don't know what love is," I croaked, feeling ill. I raised my hands over my eyes and clumsily brushed my hair out of the way.

For a moment I thought he was going to kick me, but he didn't, just looked down at me with the devastating face that I had adored.

"You should have trusted me," he said, sweat running down his face, his breathing harsh.

"You shouldn't have lied to me," I countered angrily, trying to sit up.

"Tell me where the tools are," he demanded. "The Belwicket tools."

"Screw you!"

"You tell me! You should never have bound them to you! How arrogant! Now we'll have to rip them away from you, and that will hurt. But first you tell me where they are—I didn't feel them in the car."

I stared at him stonily, trying to rise to my feet.

"Tell me!" he shouted, looming over me.

"Bite me," I offered.

Cal's golden eyes gleamed with hurt and fury, and he shot out his hand at me. A cloudy ball of darkness shot right at me, hitting my head, and I crashed headlong to the floor, sinking into a nightmarish unconsciousness, remembering only his eyes.

18

Trapped

June 2001

Litha again. It's now fully ten years since my parents disappeared. When they left, I was a boy, concerned only with building a working catapult and playing Behind Enemy Lines with Linden and my friends.

At the time we were living in the Lake District, across Solway Firth from the Isle of Man. For weeks before they left, they were in bad moods, barking at us children and then apologizing, not having the time to help us with our schoolwork. Even Alwyn started coming to me or Linden to help her dress or do her hair. I remember Mum complaining that she felt tired and ill all the time, and none of her usual potions seemed to help. And Dad said his scrying stone had stopped working.

Yes, something was definitely oppressing them. But I'm sure they didn't know what was really coming. If they had, maybe things would have turned out differently.

Or maybe not. Maybe there is no way to fight an evil like that.
—Giomanach

When I awoke, I had no idea how much time had passed. My head ached, my face burned and felt scraped from the gravel, and my knees ached from when I had fallen on them. But at least I could move my limbs. Whatever spell Cal had used on me, it wasn't a binding one.

Cautiously, silently, I rolled over, scanning the *seòmar*. I was alone. I cast out my senses and felt no one else near. What time was it? The tiny window set high on one wall showed no stars, no moon. I crawled up on my hands and knees, then unfolded myself and stood slowly, feeling a wave of nausea and pain roll over me.

Crap. As soon as I stood, I felt the weight of the spelled walls and ceilings pressing in on me. Every square inch of this tiny room had runes and ancient symbols on it, and without understanding them, I knew that Cal had worked dark magick here, had called on dark powers, and had been lying to me ever since the day I met him. I felt incredibly naive.

I had to get out. What if Cal had left only a minute ago? What if even now he was bringing Selene and the others back to me? Goddess. This room was full of negative energy, negative emotions, dark magick. I saw stains on the floor that had been hidden by the futon the first time I was here. I knelt and touched them, wondering if they were blood. What had Cal done here? I felt sick.

Cal had gone to get Selene, and they were going to put spells on me or hurt me or even kill me to get me to tell them where Maeve's tools were. To get me to join their side, their all-Woodbane clan.

No one knew where I was. I had told Mom I was going for a drive more than six hours ago. No one had seen me meet Cal at the cemetery. I could die here.

The thought galvanized me into action. I got to my feet again, looking up at the window, gauging its height. My best jump was still two feet short of the window ledge. I pulled off my jacket, balled it up, and flung it hard at the window. It bounced off and clumped to the floor.

"Goddess, Goddess," I muttered, crossing to the door. Its edge was almost invisible, a barely seen crack that was impossible to dig my nails into. In the car I had my Swiss Army knife—patting my pockets quickly yielded me nothing. Still I tried, wedging my short nails into its slit and pulling until my nails split and my fingers bled.

Where was Cal? What was taking so long? How long had it been?

Panting, I backed up across the room, then launched myself shoulder first at the small door. The impact made me cry out, and then I slid down to the floor, clutching my shoulder. The door hadn't even shuddered under the blow.

I thought of how my parents had been so devastated when I took up Wicca, how afraid they had been for me after what happened to my birth mother. I saw now that they'd had good cause to worry.

An unwanted sob choked my throat, and I sank to my knees on the wooden floor. The back of my head ached sickeningly. How could I have been so stupid, so blind? Tears edged from my eyes and coursed down my bruised and dirty cheeks. Sobs struggled to break free from my chest.

I sat cross-legged on the floor. Slowly, knowing it was pointless, I drew a small circle around myself, using my index finger, wetting the floor with my tears and my blood. Shakily I traced symbols of protection around me: pentacles, the intersected circles of protection, squares within squares for orderliness, the angular runic þ for comfort. I drew the two-horned circle symbol of the Goddess and the circle/half circle of the God. I did all these things with only the barest amount of thought, did them by rote, over and over, all around me on the floor, all around me in the air.

Within moments my breathing calmed, my tears ceased, my pain eased. I could see more clearly, I could think more clearly, I was more in control.

Evil pressed in around me. But I was not evil. I needed to save myself.

I was the Woodbane princess of Belwicket. I had power beyond imagining.

Closing my eyes, I forced my breathing to calm further, my heartbeat to slow. Words came to my lips.

> "Magick, I am your daughter,
> I am following your path in truth and righteousness.
> Protect me from evil. Help me be strong.
> Maeve, my mother before me, help me be strong.
> Mackenna, my grandmother, help me be strong.
> Morwen, who came before her, help me be strong.
> Let me open the door. Open the door. Open the door."

I opened my eyes then and gazed before me at the spelled and locked door. I looked at it calmly, imagining it opening before me, seeing myself pass through it to the outside, seeing myself safe and gone from there.

Creak. I blinked at the sound but didn't break my concentration. I was unsure whether I had imagined it, but I kept thinking, Open, open, open, and in the darkness I saw the minuscule crack widen, just a hair.

Elation, as strong as my earlier despair had been, lifted my heart. It was working! I could do this! I could open the door!

Open, open, open, I thought steadily, my focus pure, my intent solid.

I smelled smoke. That fact registered only slightly in my brain as I kept concentrating on opening the door. But I realized that my nose was getting irritated, and I kept blinking. I came out of my trance and saw that the *seòmar* was becoming hazy, and the scent of fire was strong.

I stood up within my circle, my heart kicking up a beat. Now I could hear the joyful crackling of flames outside, smell the acrid odor of burning ivy, and see the faint, amber light of fire reflected in the high window.

They were burning me alive. Just like my mother.

As my concentration broke, the door clicked shut again.

Panic threatened to drown me. "Help!" I screamed as loud as I could, aiming my voice at the window. "Help! Help! Someone help me!"

From outside, I heard Selene's voice. "Cal! What are you doing?"

"Solving the problem," was his grim response.

"Don't be stupid," Selene snapped. "Get away from there. Where are the tools?"

I thought fast. "Let me out and I'll tell you, I promise!" I shouted.

"She's lying," said another voice. "We don't need her, anyway. This isn't safe—we have to get out of here."

"Cal!" I screamed. "Cal! Help me!"

There was no answer, but I heard muffled voices arguing outside. I strained to hear.

"You promised she would join us," someone said.

"She's just an uneducated girl. What we really need is the tools," said someone else.

"I'll tell you!" I shouted. "They're in the woods! Let me out and I'll take you there!"

"I'm telling you, we have to leave," someone said urgently.

"Cal, stop it!" said Selene, and suddenly the sound of flames was louder, closer.

"Let me out!" I screamed.

"Goddess, what is he doing? Selene!"

"Get back or I'll torch the whole place with all of us in it," said Cal, sounding steely. "I won't let you have her."

"The Seeker will be here any minute," said a man. "There's no way he won't come for this. Selene, your son—"

I heard more arguing, but I was choking now, the smoke stinging my eyes, and then I heard the popping of the wooden rafters up above. I pressed my ear to the wall and listened, but there were no more voices. Had they all just gone away? If I died in the fire, they would never find Maeve's tools. That wasn't true, I realized. They could scry to find them; they could do spells to find them. The simple concealment runes I had traced around the box wouldn't deceive any of them. They wanted me to tell them only to save time. They didn't really need me at all.

I tried once again to open the door with my mind, but I couldn't focus. I kept coughing and my mind was starting to feel foggy. I slumped against the wall in despair.

It had all been for *nothing*: Maeve hiding her tools to keep them safe, coming to me in a vision to tell me where they were, my finding them with Robbie, my learning how to use them. For nothing. Now they would be in Selene's hands, under her control. And maybe the tools were so old that they had been used by the original members of Belwicket—before the clan promised to forsake evil. Maybe the tools would work just as well for evil as they could for good.

Maybe this was all my fault. This was the big picture everyone kept talking about. This was the danger I was blundering into. This was why I needed guidance, a teacher.

"Goddess, forgive me," I muttered, lying belly down on the smooth wooden floor. I pulled my jacket over my head. I was going to die.

I was very tired. It was hard to breathe. I was no longer panicking, no longer full of fear or hysteria. I wondered how Maeve had faced her death by fire, sixteen years before. With each moment that passed, I had more in common with her.

19

Burn

June 2001

Here's an interesting thing: I went today to Much Bencham, which is the little town in Ireland next to where Ballynigel used to be. No one there wanted to talk to me, and I got the feeling the whole village was anti-witch. Having seen their closest neighbors turn to dust all those years ago, I'm not surprised. But as I was leaving the town square, an old woman caught my eye. She was probably on the dole—making ends almost meet by selling homemade pasties. I bought one, and as I bit into it she said, very quietly, "You're the lad's been asking questions about the town next door." She didn't name Ballynigel, but of course that was what she meant.

"Aye," I said, taking another bite. I waited.

"Odd things," she murmured. "Odd doings in that town, sometimes. Whole town wiped off the face of the earth. It's not natural."

"No," I agreed. "Not natural at all. Did no one survive, then?"

She shook her head, then frowned as if remembering something. "Though that woman last year said as how some did survive. Some escaped, she said."

"Oh?" I said, though inside my heart was pounding. "What woman was this?"

"She were a beauty," said the old woman, thinking back. "Dark and exotic. She had gold eyes, like a tiger. She came here asking about them next door, and someone—I think it was old Collins, at the pub—he told her they were dead, all of them, and she said no, she said that two made it away to America."

"Two people from Ballynigel went to America?" I said, to make certain. "After the disaster, or before?"

"Don't know, do I," said the woman, starting to lose interest. "She just said that two from there had gone to New York years ago, and that's in America, isn't it."

I thanked her and walked away, thinking. Damn me if that tiger woman didn't sound like Dad's first wife, Selene.

So now I am on my way to New York. Is it really possible two witches from Belwicket escaped the disaster? Could they be in New York? I won't rest until I know.

—Giomanach

Dying from smoke inhalation is not the worst way to go, I thought sleepily. It's uncomfortable and gives you a drowning sort of feeling, but it must be better than being shot or actually burned to death or falling off a cliff.

It wouldn't be long now. My head ached; smoke filled my

lungs and made me cough. Even lying on the floor, with my head covered by my jacket, I wouldn't last much longer. Was this how it had been for Maeve and Angus?

When I heard the voices calling my name from outside, I figured I was hallucinating. But the voices came again, stronger, and I recognized them.

"Morgan! Morgan! Are you in there? Morgan!"

Oh my God, it sounded like Bree! Bree and Robbie!

Sitting up was a mistake because even a foot above me, the air was heavier. I choked and coughed and sucked in air, and then I screamed, "I'm in here! In the pool house! Help!" A spasm of coughing crushed my chest, and I fell to the floor, gasping.

"Stand back!" Bree shouted from outside. "Get away from the wall!"

Quickly I rolled to the wall farthest away from her voice and lay there, huddled and coughing. My mind dimly registered the familiar, powerful roar of Das Boot's engine, and the next thing I knew, the wall across from me was hit with a huge, earthshaking crash that made the plaster pop, the window shatter and rain glass on me, and the wall bulge in. I peeped out from under my coat and saw a crack where smoke was rising, pouring out into the sky, grateful for release. I heard the roar of the engine, the squeal of wheels, and the whole building shook as my car rammed the wall violently once more. This time the stone and plaster broke, studs snapped, and then the crumpled, ash-strewn nose of my car was perched in the wall, opening like the mouth of a great white shark.

The driver's door opened, and then Bree was scrambling over rubble, coughing, and I reached out to her, and she grabbed my arms and hauled me out over the wreckage. Robbie was there outside, waiting for us, and as my knees buckled he ran over and caught me. I bent over, coughing and retching, while he and Bree held me.

Then we heard the nearing sounds of wailing fire sirens, and in the next few minutes three fire trucks appeared, Sky and Hunter arrived, and Cal's beautifully manicured lawn was ruined.

And I was alive.

Book Five

SWEEP
Awakening

All quoted materials in this work were created by the author.
Any resemblance to existing works is accidental.

Awakening

SPEAK
Published by the Penguin Group
Penguin Group (USA) Inc., 345 Hudson Street, New York, New York 10014, U.S.A.
Penguin Group (Canada), 90 Eglinton Avenue East, Suite 700, Toronto, Ontario, Canada M4P 2Y3
(a division of Pearson Penguin Canada Inc.)
Penguin Books Ltd, 80 Strand, London WC2R 0RL, England
Penguin Ireland, 25 St Stephen's Green, Dublin 2, Ireland (a division of Penguin Books Ltd)
Penguin Group (Australia), 250 Camberwell Road, Camberwell, Victoria 3124, Australia
(a division of Pearson Australia Group Pty Ltd)
Penguin Books India Pvt Ltd, 11 Community Centre, Panchsheel Park, New Delhi - 110 017, India
Penguin Group (NZ), 67 Apollo Drive, Rosedale, North Shore 0632, New Zealand
(a division of Pearson New Zealand Ltd)
Penguin Books (South Africa) (Pty) Ltd, 24 Sturdee Avenue, Rosebank, Johannesburg 2196, South Africa

Registered Offices: Penguin Books Ltd, 80 Strand, London WC2R 0RL, England

Published by Puffin Books, a division of Penguin Young Readers Group, 2001
Published by Speak, an imprint of Penguin Group (USA) Inc, 2007
This omnibus edition published by Speak, an imprint of Penguin Group (USA) Inc., 2010

1 3 5 7 9 10 8 6 4 2

Copyright © 2001 17th Street Productions, an Alloy company
All rights reserved

Produced by 17th Street Productions,
an Alloy company
151 West 26th Street
New York, NY 10001

17th Street Productions and associated logos
are trademarks and/or registered trademarks of Alloy, Inc.

Speak ISBN 978-0-14-241020-2
This omnibus ISBN 978-0-14-241897-0

Printed in the United States of America

Except in the United States of America, this book is sold subject to the condition that
it shall not, by way of trade or otherwise, be lent, re-sold, hired out, or otherwise
circulated without the publisher's prior consent in any form of binding or cover
other than that in which it is published and without a similar condition
including this condition being imposed on the subsequent purchaser.

The publisher does not have any control over and does not assume any
responsibility for author or third-party Web sites or their content.

To GC and EF, with many thanks

1

Embers

They fled tonight, the lot of them. Selene Belltower, Cal Blaire, Alicia Woodwind, Edwitha of Cair Dal, and more—all slipped through my fingers. They knew I was closing in on them. It's my fault. I was too cautious, too worried about proving the case against them beyond all doubt, and so I left it too long. I've failed, and badly. And worse, Morgan nearly died because I didn't stop them.

I've got to break the warding spells and get into Selene's house. She can't have had time to pack up all her things. Maybe I can find some clue, something to tell me where she went or what her group is planning.

Damn, damn, damn!

—Giomanach

I stood with Bree Warren and Robbie Gurevitch, my two oldest friends, on the lawn in back of Cal Blaire's house. Together we stared at the flames that leaped hungrily up from the pool house and cast a smoky pall over the stark November moon. Somewhere in the inferno there was a crash as a section of the roof caved in. A fountain of white-hot sparks flew skyward.

"My God," Bree said.

Robbie shook his head. "You got out of there just in time."

Sirens wailed in the distance. Though it was the last night of November and snow lay inches deep on the ground, the night air felt hot and dry as I gulped in a deep breath. "You guys saved my life," I managed to choke out. Then I doubled over, coughing. It hurt just to breathe. My throat was raw and my chest ached and every cell in my body craved oxygen.

"Barely," Robbie murmured. He tucked an arm under my elbow, supporting me.

I shuddered. I didn't need Robbie to tell me how close I had come to dying, trapped in the tiny, spell-wrapped room that had been hidden in the pool house. Trapped by Cal Blaire, my boyfriend. My eyes, already stinging from the smoke, blurred again with tears.

Charismatic, confident, inhumanly beautiful, Cal had woken something that had been sleeping inside me for six-teen years. It was Cal who had first loved me, as no boy ever had. It was Cal who had helped me to the realization that I was a blood witch, with powers I'd never even known could exist in the real world. It was Cal who had shown me how love and magick could twine together until it seemed that all the energy in the universe was enfolding me, stream-ing through me, there for the taking.

And it was Cal who had lied to me, used me. Cal who,

less than an hour ago, had tried to kill me by setting the pool house on fire.

The wailing sirens of the fire trucks sounded closer now, and I could see the reflection of their whirling lights faintly in the dense clouds of smoke. The red made a hellish glow against the roiling gray. I turned to see where the trucks were, then gasped as two dark, faceless silhouettes loomed up in front of me.

They resolved into Hunter Niall and his cousin, Sky Eventide, two English witches who'd arrived in our little town a few weeks ago. Oh, right, I realized foggily. I'd sent them a witch message, too, begging them to help me. I'd forgotten.

"Morgan, are you all right?" Hunter asked in his crisp, accented voice. "Do you need a doctor?"

I shook my head. "I think I'm okay." Now that I could breathe, my body was starting to thrum with adrenaline, and I was getting a weird, disconnected feeling.

"There'll be an ambulance coming with the fire trucks," Bree pointed out. "You should let them check you out, Morgan. You inhaled a lot of smoke."

"Actually, if Morgan's up to it, it would be better if we left now." Hunter cast a glance over his shoulder. The first of the fire trucks was turning into the curved gravel driveway in front of the big house where Cal and his mother, Selene Belltower, lived. "I don't think we want to talk to anyone official. Too many awkward questions. Sky, if you wouldn't mind delaying them for a moment so we can make our getaway . . ."

Sky nodded and set off across the lawn at a smooth lope. Stopping a few yards from the house, she held up her hands. I watched, puzzled, as she moved her fingers in a complicated dance in the air.

"What's she doing?" Robbie asked.

"Casting a glamor," Hunter explained. "She's making the firemen believe the fire has spread to the house. The illusion won't last more than a few moments, but it'll keep them from noticing our cars while we're driving away." He nodded his approval to Sky as she hurried back toward us. "Let's get going. No time to waste. Robbie, if you'll drive Morgan's car, we can all meet down at the end of the block."

I was dimly amazed by the swift way he took charge of the situation. No exclaiming over what had happened. No expressions of shock or horror. Just business. Normally that would have irritated me. But at that moment I felt reassured; safe, almost.

Robbie hurried toward my car. I started to follow him, but Bree took my arm. "Come on, you can ride with me," she said.

My gaze met hers. Even at the scene of a fire, her glossy, shoulder-length hair looked perfect. But the shock of what had happened showed in her dark eyes.

Once we'd been so close that we'd finished each other's sentences. That was before she'd fallen for Cal, before he'd chosen me. This morning Bree and I had been enemies. But tonight I had called her, sent her a witch message with my mind, when I was facing my darkest hour. I had called out to *her*. And she had heard me and had come to my aid. Maybe there was hope for us yet.

"Come on," Bree repeated, and led me toward her BMW. She helped me into the passenger seat, then went around to the driver's side. As we drove down the narrow, winding back driveway, she glanced anxiously in her rearview mirror.

"They're still running around the main house. No one's

even gone into the backyard yet," she said. A smile tugged at her lips. "Sky's spell really worked, I guess. All this witchcraft stuff really blows my mind."

She gave me a sideways look. "It was wild hearing your voice so clearly in my mind," she added after a moment. "I thought I was going nuts. But then I figured, enough bizarre things have happened lately that I probably should take this seriously."

"I'm glad you did. You saved me," I replied. My voice was hoarse, and the act of speaking triggered another coughing fit.

"Are you sure you're okay?" Bree asked when I straightened up. "No burns or anything?"

Not on the outside, I thought bleakly. I shook my head. "I'm alive," I said. "Thanks to you." It wasn't exactly a reconciliation, but it was all I could manage at the moment.

At the end of the dark, quiet block we pulled up to the curb behind Sky's green Ford. Robbie was already there, leaning against the door of my car, Das Boot. I winced as I looked at the battered '71 Valiant. It was already dented and missing a headlight from a minor accident I'd had a week ago. Then, moments ago, Robbie had used Das Boot to ram through the wall of the pool house where I was trapped. Now the hood was badly dented, too.

"Right, then," Hunter said. He spoke briskly, but I felt like I was hearing him through a layer of heavy cloth. Somehow I just couldn't focus. "People are going to be asking a lot of questions about what happened here tonight; how the fire started, and so forth. We need to get our stories straight. Robbie, Bree, I think it's best if you simply pretend you weren't here. That way no one will question you."

Robbie folded his arms. "I'm going to tell our friends

in Cirrus the truth," he said. "They have a right to know." Cirrus was the coven Cal had started. Robbie and I were members, along with four other people.

"Cirrus," Hunter said. He rubbed his chin thoughtfully. "You're right, they should know. But please, ask them to keep it to themselves." He turned to me. "Morgan, if you can bear it, I need to talk to you. I'll drive you home in your car afterward."

I cringed. Talk? Now?

"Can't it wait until tomorrow?" Bree asked sharply.

"Yeah," Robbie agreed. "Morgan's a mess. No offense, Morgan."

"I'm afraid it can't," Hunter said. His voice was quiet, but there was a final tone in it.

Robbie looked like he was about to argue, but then he simply handed Hunter my car keys.

Sky turned to Hunter. "I'll try to find out where they've gone, as we discussed," she said.

"Right," Hunter agreed. "I'll see you at home later."

"Where who's gone?" I asked. This was all moving too fast for me.

"Cal and Selene," Sky told me. She pushed a hand through her short, silver-blond hair. "Their house is sealed with warding spells, and both their cars are gone."

I swallowed hard. The thought that they were out there, who knew where, was terrifying. I had a sudden, irrational conviction that they were hiding behind a tree or something equally melodramatic, spying on me at this very moment.

"They're not in Widow's Vale anymore," Hunter said, as if he'd read my mind. "I'm sure of it. I'd be able to tell if they were."

Though the logical part of my brain told me that nothing is ever certain, something in the way Hunter spoke made me believe him. I felt a burst of relief, followed by a wash of intense pain. Cal was gone. I'd never see him again.

Hunter put one hand under my elbow and steered me over to my car. He opened the passenger door, and I slid in. The inside of the car was frigid and that, combined with the adrenaline still pumping through my body, made me shake so hard, my muscles started to ache. Hunter cranked the engine, flipped on the one remaining headlight, then pulled out onto the quiet, tree-lined street.

He didn't say anything, and I was grateful. Usually Hunter and I were like sparks and gunpowder. He was a Seeker, sent by the International Council of Witches to investigate Cal and Selene for misuse of magick. He'd told me they were evil. Before I'd learned, to my horror and shock, that he was right, Cal and I had almost killed him. That was just one of the things that made me intensely uneasy around him.

In one of those weird connections that seemed common among blood witches, Hunter was Cal's half brother. But where Cal was dark, Hunter was fair, with sunlight-colored hair, clear green eyes, and sculpted cheekbones. He was beautiful, but in an entirely different way than Cal. Hunter was cool, like air or water. Cal smoldered. He was earth and fire.

Cal. Every thought led back to him. I stared out my window, trying to blink back tears and not succeeding. I wiped them away with the back of my hand.

Gradually it dawned on me that I didn't recognize the road we were on. "Where are we going?" I asked. "This isn't the way to my house."

"It's the way to *my* house. I thought it would be better if you washed up first, got the smell of smoke out of your hair and so forth, before you faced your parents."

I nodded, relieved that once again he'd thought it out. My parents—my adoptive parents, really—weren't comfortable with my powers or with me practicing witchcraft. Besides the fact that they're Catholic, they were frightened by what had happened to my birth mother, Maeve Riordan. Sixteen years ago Maeve and my biological father, Angus Bramson, had burned to death. No one knew exactly how it had happened, but it seemed pretty clear that the fact that they were witches had had everything to do with it.

I pressed my hand against my mouth, trying desperately to make sense of the last few weeks. Just a month ago I'd discovered that I was adopted and that by birth I was a descendant of one of the Seven Great Clans of Wicca—a blood witch. My birth parents had died when I was only a baby. Tonight I had almost shared their fate.

And it had been at Cal's hands. At the hands of the guy with whom I'd hoped to share the rest of my life.

Ahead of us, a fat brown rabbit sat frozen in the middle of the icy road, paralyzed by my car's headlight. Hunter brought the car to a stop, and we waited.

"Can you tell me what happened tonight?" he asked, surprisingly gently.

"No." My hand was still pressed against my mouth, and I had to take it away to explain. "Not right now." My voice cracked with a sob. "It hurts too much."

The rabbit came out of its paralysis and scampered to safety on the other side of the road. Hunter pressed the gas pedal, and Das Boot surged forward again. "Right, then," he said. "Later."

Hunter and Sky's house was on a quiet street somewhere near the edge of Widow's Vale. I didn't really pay attention to the route. Now that the adrenaline of escaping the fire was leaking away, I felt exhausted, groggy.

The car pulled to a stop. We were in a driveway beneath a canopy of trees. We got out to the night's chill and walked up a narrow path. I followed Hunter into a living room where a fire burned in a small fireplace. A worn sofa covered in dark blue velvet stood against one wall. One of its legs had broken off, and it listed at a drunken angle. There were two mismatched armchairs across from it, and a wide plank balanced on two wooden crates served as a coffee table.

"You'll need a shower and clean clothes," Hunter told me.

I glanced at a small clock on the mantel. It was nearly nine. I was more than late for dinner. "I've got to call my folks first," I said. "They've probably called the police by now."

Hunter handed me a cordless phone. "Should I tell them about the fire?" I asked him, feeling lost.

He hesitated. "The choice is yours, of course," he said at last. "But if you do, you'll have a lot of explaining to do."

I nodded. He was right. One more thing I couldn't share with my family.

Nervously I dialed my home number.

My dad answered, and I heard the relief in his voice as I greeted him. "Morgan, where on earth are you?" he asked. "We were about to call the state troopers!"

"I'm at a friend's house," I said, trying to be as honest as I could.

"Are you all right? You sound hoarse."

"I'm okay. But Cal and I . . . we had a fight." I fought to keep my voice steady. "I'm—I'm kind of upset. That's why I didn't call earlier. I'm sorry," I added lamely.

"Well, we were very worried," my dad said. "But I'm glad you're all right. Are you coming home now?"

The front door opened, and Sky walked in. She glanced at me, then looked at Hunter and shook her head. "Not a trace," she said in a low voice.

Ice trickled down my spine. "In a little while, Dad," I said into the phone. "I'll be home in a little while."

Dad sighed. "Don't forget that tomorrow is a school day."

I said good-bye and hung up. "You didn't find them?" I asked Sky anxiously.

"They're gone. They hid their tracks with so many concealing spells that I can't even tell which direction they went," Sky said. "But they're definitely nowhere nearby."

I stood there, feeling my heart beat, not knowing how to process that information. After a moment, Sky took my arm and gently led me upstairs. I was too out of it to notice much more than that there were two doors up there that were closed. The third, in between them, opened into a narrow bathroom.

Sky disappeared through one of the doorways, then reappeared a moment later holding a bathrobe. "You can wear this when you come out," she said. "Leave your clothes outside the door, and I'll throw them in the washer."

I took the robe and closed the door, feeling suddenly self-conscious. I turned and dared a look in the mirror. My nose was red and swollen, my eyes puffy, and my long dark hair matted and flecked with ash. Soot streaked my face and clothes.

I'm hideous, I thought, as Cal's face rose in my mind again. He'd been so incredibly beautiful. How could I ever have believed he could really love someone like me? How could I have been so blind? I was such an idiot.

Clenching my jaw, I stripped down. I opened the door a crack and dropped my clothes in a heap on the hall floor. Then I got into the shower and scrubbed my body and my hair hard, as if the water could wash away more than dirt and smoke, as if it could take my sorrow and terror and rage and sluice them down the drain.

Afterward I dried off and put on the robe. Sky was taller than I was, and the robe bunched at my feet, looking shapeless and drab. I pulled a comb through my wet hair and went back downstairs.

Sky was sitting in one of the armchairs, but as I came down, she rose gracefully to her feet and went up to her room. As she passed me, she let her hand rest briefly on my shoulder.

Hunter stood at the fireplace, feeding a log to the fire. A small ceramic teapot and two mugs sat on the coffee table. He turned to face me, and I was keenly aware of how good-looking he was.

I settled myself on the sofa, and Hunter sat in a worn armchair. "Better?" he asked.

"A little." My chest and throat weren't quite as sore, and my eyes had stopped stinging.

Hunter's green eyes were locked on me. "I need you to tell me what happened."

I took a deep breath; then I told him how Sky and I had scryed together. How she'd helped me to spy on Cal and his mother in their spell-guarded house as they talked to their coconspirators about killing me if I refused to join them. How I saw that Cal had been assigned to seduce me, to get me onto their side so that my power could be joined with theirs. How I'd learned that they were also after my birth mother's coven tools, objects of enormous power that they wanted to add to their arsenal of magickal weapons. How I'd gone to talk to Cal, how he'd overpowered me with magick and taken me back to his house.

"He put me in a *seòmar* in the back of the pool house," I said, a vivid picture of the horrible little secret room rising in my mind. "The walls were covered with dark runes. He must have knocked me unconscious. When I came to, I heard Selene arguing with him outside. She was telling him not to do it, not to set it on fire. But Cal said"—my voice broke again—"he said he was solving the problem. He meant me. I was the p-p-problem."

"Shhh," Hunter said softly. Reaching out, he laid his palm flat against my forehead. I felt a tingling warmth spread outward from the spot, like a thousand little bubbles. His eyes held mine as the sensation washed over me, dulling the edge of my pain to the point where I could just bear it.

"Thanks," I said, awed.

He smiled briefly, his face transforming for a moment. Then he said, "Morgan, I'm sorry to press you, but this is important. Did they get your birth mother's tools?"

Maeve had fled her native Ireland after her coven, Belwicket, had been decimated. I had recently found her tools, the ancient tools of her coven. Selene had wanted them badly. "No," I told Hunter. "They're safe. I'd know if they weren't—they're bound to me. Anyway, I hid them."

Hunter poured us each a cup of tea. "Where?"

"Um—under Bree's house. I put them there right before I went to see Cal," I said. It sounded so lame as I said it that I cringed, waiting for Hunter to yell at me.

But he just nodded. "All right. I suppose they'll be safe enough for now, since Cal and Selene have fled. But get them back as soon as you can."

"What can they do with them?" I asked. "Why are they so dangerous?"

"I'm not sure exactly what they could do," Hunter said. "But Selene is very powerful and very skilled in magick, as you know. And some of the tools, the athame and the wand in particular, were made long ago, back before Belwicket renounced the blackness. They've since been purified, of course, but they were made to channel and focus dark energies. I'm sure Selene could find a way to return them to their original state. I imagine, for example, that Maeve's wand in Selene's hands could be used to magnify the power of the dark wave."

The dark wave. I felt a coldness in the pit of my stomach. The dark wave was the thing that had wiped out Maeve's coven. It had also destroyed Hunter's parents' coven and had forced his mother and father into hiding ten years ago. They were still missing.

No one seemed to know exactly what the dark wave was—whether it was an entity with a will of its own or a force of mindless destruction, like a tornado. All we did know was that where it passed, it left death and horror behind it, entire towns turned to ash. Hunter believed that Selene was somehow connected to the dark wave. But he didn't know how.

I put my head in my hands. "Is all of this happening because Cal and Selene are Woodbane?" I asked in a small voice. Woodbane was the family name of one of the Seven Great Clans of Wicca. To be Woodbane meant, traditionally, to be without a moral compass. Woodbanes throughout history had used any means at their disposal, including calling on dark spirits or dark energy, to become more powerful. Supposedly this had all changed when the International Council of Witches had come into being and made laws to govern the use of magick. But as I was learning, the world of Wicca was as fractured and divided as the everyday world I'd known for the first sixteen years of my life. And there were many Woodbanes who didn't live by the council's laws.

I happened to be Woodbane, too. I hadn't wanted to believe it when I first found out, but the small, red, dagger-shaped birthmark on the inside of my arm was proof of it. Many, if not most, Woodbanes had one somewhere. It was known as the Woodbane athame, because it looked like the ceremonial dagger that was part of any witch's set of tools.

Hunter sighed, and I was reminded that he was half Woodbane himself. "That's the question, isn't it? I don't honestly know what it means to be Woodbane. I don't know what's nature and what's nurture."

He set down his mug and rose. "I'll see if your clothes are dry. Then I'll run you home."

Sky followed us to my house in her car so that she could drive Hunter home. He and I didn't talk on the way.

Whatever calming effect his touch had had on me was entirely gone now, and my mind kept replaying Cal lying to me, shouting at me, using his magick to nearly kill me. How could something that had been so sweet, that felt so good, have turned into this? How could I have been so blind? And why, even now, was some shameful part of me wanting to call to him? Cal, don't leave me. Cal, come back. Oh, God. I swallowed as bile rushed up into my throat.

"Morgan," Hunter said as he pulled up in front of my house. "You do understand, don't you, that you can't let your guard down? Cal may be gone, but it's likely he'll come back."

Come back? Hope, fear, rage, confusion swept over me. "Oh, God." I doubled over in my seat, hugging myself. "Oh, God. I loved him. I feel so *stupid*."

"Don't," Hunter said quietly. I looked up. His face was turned away from me. I saw the plane of his cheek, pale and smooth in the milky starlight that filtered in through Das Boot's windshield.

"I know how much you loved Cal," Hunter said. "And I understand why. There's a lot in him that's truly beautiful. And—and I believe that he loved you, too, in his own way. You didn't imagine that. Even though I was one of the ones telling you otherwise."

He turned to face me then, and we stared at each other. "Look. I know you feel like you'll never get past this. But you will. It won't ever go away, but it *will* stop hurting quite so much. Trust me. I know what I'm talking about."

I was reminded of the time he and I had joined our minds, and I'd seen that he had lost not only his parents but also his brother to dark magick. He'd suffered so much that I felt I could believe him.

He made a movement as if he were going to touch my face with his hand. But he seemed to stop himself and pulled his hand back. "You'd better go in before your parents come out here," he said.

I bit the inside of my cheek so I wouldn't start crying all over again. "Okay," I whispered. I sniffed and looked at my house. The lights were on in the living room.

I felt suddenly awkward. After that moment of connection, should I shake Hunter's hand? Kiss his cheek? In the end I just said, "Thanks for everything."

We both got out of the car. Hunter gave me my keys and headed down the dark street to where Sky waited in her car. I walked up the drive, my body on autopilot. I hesitated at the door. How was I going to act normal around my parents when I felt like I'd been ripped apart?

I opened the front door. The living room was empty, and the house smelled of chocolate chip cookies and wood smoke. There were still embers in the fireplace, and I could smell a faint tinge of the lemon oil that my mom used on the furniture. I heard my parents' voices in the kitchen and the sound of the dishwasher being unloaded.

"Mom? Dad?" I called nervously.

My parents, Sean and Mary Grace Rowlands, came into the living room. "Morgan, you look like you've been crying," my mom said when she caught sight of me. "Was the fight with Cal very bad?"

"I—I broke up with Cal." It wasn't exactly true, but it wasn't the falsehood that shocked me as much as the truth of my situation. Cal and I were no longer together. We were not a couple. We were not going to love each other forever. We were not going to be together again. Ever.

"Oh, honey," said my mom. The sympathy in her voice made me want to cry for the hundredth time that awful night.

"That's too bad," my dad chimed in.

"Um, I also had a little accident in Das Boot," I said. The lie slipped out before I'd even fully formulated it. I just knew I had to explain the crumpled hood of my car somehow.

"An accident?" my dad exclaimed. "What happened? Are you all right? Was anyone else hurt?"

"No one got hurt. I was pulling out of Cal's driveway and I hit a light pole. I kind of messed up the hood of my car." I swallowed. "I guess I was pretty upset."

"Oh my God," Mom said. "That sounds serious! Are you sure you're all right? Maybe we should run you over to the ER and have them take a look at you."

"Mom, I didn't hit my head or anything." I smothered a cough.

"But—" my dad began.

"I'm fine." I cut him off. I had to get to my room before I had a nervous breakdown right in front of them. "I'm just beat, that's all. I really just want to go to bed."

Then, before they could ask any more questions, I fled up the stairs. I was relieved to see that the door to my sister's room was closed. I couldn't handle another explanation. Or even another syllable.

In my room I paused briefly to pet Dagda, my little gray kitten, who was curled up on my desk chair. He mewed a sleepy hello. I went over to my dresser to get out my softest flannel pajamas. But I paused, staring at a tiny gift box on top of my dresser. It was one of the birthday gifts Cal had given me last week: a pair of earrings, golden tigereyes set in silver. I couldn't stop myself from opening the box to look at them again. They were as beautiful as I remembered: the silver swirling in delicate Celtic knots and the stones that were the same color as Cal's eyes. I could still see him, his dark, raggedly shorn hair, his sensual mouth, the golden eyes that seemed to see right into me. The way he used to laugh. The way he had felt like a soul mate from the start.

I laid the earrings on my palm. They gave off a little pool of heat. They're spelled, I realized with a rush of nausea. Goddess, they're just another tool to control me, to spy on me. I remembered thinking, when he gave them to me, that these gifts were wrapped in his love. But the fact was, they were wrapped in his magick.

I couldn't keep them anywhere near me, I realized. I would have to find a safe way to dispose of everything Cal had given me. But not tonight. I stashed the earrings in the back of my closet, together with his other gifts. Then I put on my pajamas.

As I was pulling back my covers, there was a soft knock at my door. A moment later my mom stepped in. "Are you going to be all right?" she asked. Her voice was quiet.

And then the tears were flooding down my cheeks, my defenses completely overwhelmed. I sobbed so hard, my whole body shook.

I felt my mom beside me, her arms encircling me, and I clung to her as I hadn't in years. "My darling," she said into my hair. "My daughter. I'm so sorry. I know how much you must be hurting. Do you want to talk about it?"

I raised my head and met her eyes. "I can't . . . ," I whispered, gasping. "I can't. . . ."

She nodded. "All right," she said. "When you're ready."

When I'd crawled into bed, she pulled the comforter up to my chin and kissed my forehead as if I were six. Reaching over, she turned off my light. "I'm here," she murmured, taking my hand in hers. "It'll be all right."

And so, clutching her hand tightly, I fell asleep.

2

Changes

I went back to Selene's house tonight after I drove Morgan home. I waited until the police and firefighters were all gone, and then I spent an hour trying to get in, but I couldn't break through the thicket of spells she put round the place. It's bloody frustrating. I felt like chucking a rock through one of those big plate glass windows.

I wonder if Morgan could do it? I know she got into Selene's hidden library without even trying. She is incredibly strong, though incredibly untutored, too.

No. I can't ask her. Not after what she went through at that place. Goddess, the pain in her face tonight—and all over that bastard Cal. It made me sick to see it.

—Giomanach

I drifted awake on Monday, aware that the house was awfully quiet. Was I actually up before my parents or my sister? It didn't seem possible. They were all morning people, insanely perky long before noon, a trait I could not fathom. It should have been the great tip-off that I was adopted.

I squinted at my clock. Nine forty-eight?

I bolted upright. "Mary K.!" I yelled.

No answer from my sister's room. I cast my senses out and realized I was alone in the house. What is going on? I wondered, sitting up.

A cough tore at my throat. Within the next instant everything that had happened last night came back to me. The enormity of it overwhelmed me. I dropped back against my pillows again and took a deep breath.

Nine forty-eight. Calculus would be starting soon. It suddenly hit me that I would never share my calculus and physics classes with Cal again, and anguish clawed at me. How stupid are you? I asked myself in disgust.

I staggered to my feet and padded downstairs. A note from my mom lay on the kitchen counter.

> Sweetie,
>   I think you need to rest today. Dad gave Mary K. a ride to school, and she'll go to Jaycee's later. There's left-over chili in the fridge for lunch. Give me a call and let me know how you're feeling.
>   Love, Mom
> P.S. I know you won't believe me yet, but I promise you will get over this.

I blinked, feeling both grateful and guilty. There was so much they didn't know; so much I could never tell them.

I stuck a Pop-Tart in the toaster and got a Diet Coke

from the fridge. The first sip, though, convinced me it was a mistake. The bubbles of carbonation stung like little pin-pricks as they went down my throat. I made some tea instead and skimmed through the newspapers. The local paper came out only twice a month, and of course there was nothing in *The New York Times* or the *Albany Times Union* about a minor fire in Widow's Vale, two hours away from either city. I could watch the local news later on TV. I wondered if my school would have some kind of explanation for Cal's disappearance.

By the time I'd finished breakfast, it was after ten. For a moment I debated crawling back under the covers with Dagda. But I needed to deal with Cal's gifts right away, so a trip to Practical Magick was in order. I figured the people who ran the shop, Alyce and David, would know what to do.

Then a horrible thought occurred to me: David and Alyce were part of Starlocket, Selene's coven. Could they have had anything to do with what happened to me?

I sank back into the chair, resting my elbows on the kitchen table, my forehead in my hands. My stomach roiled. Had everyone I'd trusted betrayed me? Practical Magick was almost a sanctuary to me; Alyce, in particular, a kind of guide. Even David, who had initially made me feel uncomfortable, was turning out to be someone whose friendship I valued.

Think, I told myself. I'd felt awkward with David but never threatened. I hadn't heard their voices while I was trapped in the pool house. And Hunter had explained to me that Selene created covens wherever she went—and then destroyed the non-Woodbane members. Neither David nor Alyce was Woodbane. They would have been in danger from Selene as well—wouldn't they?

It's okay, I told myself. David and Alyce are my friends.

I called my mom at her office and thanked her for letting me stay home.

"Well, I know that you share some classes with Cal," Mom said. "I thought it might be hard to see him today."

Her words reminded me: she didn't even know he was gone. My stomach knotted up again. My mom thought all I was suffering from was my very first broken heart. That was certainly true, but it was also so much more than that, Cal's betrayal so much deeper.

"I'm sorry, sweetie, but I've got to run," she said. "I've got an appointment to show a house in Taunton. Will you be all right? Want me to come home at lunch?"

"No, I'm okay," I said. "I think I'll go out and run some errands."

"Staying busy is a good idea," she said. "And if you feel like calling later, just to talk, I'll be here most of the afternoon."

"Thanks." I hung up and went upstairs. I changed into jeans and a heavy ski sweater that my aunt Margaret had given me last Christmas. I don't ski, and the sweater was kind of snowflaky for my taste, but I was cold, and it was the warmest thing I owned.

I went into my closet, where I had shoved Cal's gifts. My hands shook as I put them in my backpack. I set my jaw and willed myself not to grieve over them, over him. Then I grabbed my parka and hurried out of the house.

I drove north in my battered, rattly car, beneath bleak, wintry skies that seemed leached of all color. Despite the salt on the roads, a thin sheet of ice covered the ground. All the cars were moving slowly. I switched on the radio, hoping for the local news, but instead got a weather report stating that the temperature was currently eighteen degrees and would drop to ten by evening. With the wind chill, it was even more brutal.

I pulled into a parking spot right in front of Practical Magick; for a change, parking was easy, as the block was practically empty. Only after I had climbed out of my car did I remember that there was one more gift from Cal, the one I'd loved best of all: the pentacle that he had worn around his neck. It was somewhere on the floor of my car, where I'd let it fall the day before when it had hit me that Cal was using it to enhance his control over me. I leaned down, searched the damp floor mats, and found the little silver circle with its five-pointed star. Without looking at it, I slipped it into the outer pocket of my pack.

I pushed through the heavy glass doors into Practical Magick. The shop was dark and cozy; half of it given to books on every aspect of Wicca, the occult, and New Age spiritual practices; the other half filled with a huge variety of supplies: candles, herbs, powders, crystals, ritual tools like athames, pentacles, robes, even cauldrons. The warm air was scented with herbs and incense. It all felt familiar, reassuring, safe—all feelings I had in very short supply at the moment.

I was surprised to see a customer in the shop, since there weren't any cars out front. Alyce was talking to a young woman who wore a sling with a baby in it and was holding the hand of a boy who looked to be about four years old.

As the woman spoke to her, Alyce nodded, dislodging several strands of gray hair from her long braid. She tucked them back in without ever taking her blue eyes from the young woman's face. It looked like a serious conversation. I wandered along the rows of books, waiting until they were done. I wanted to be able to talk to Alyce and David privately.

Then I heard more voices and saw an elderly couple emerge from behind the curtain that blocked off the tiny back room that David used as an office. They looked upset, as the woman talking with Alyce did. I wondered what was going on. Were there all kinds of magickal emergencies requiring Alyce and David's help today?

The elderly couple spoke with Alyce and the young woman. From the way they were behaving, they all seemed to know one another. They must be the people who lived upstairs, I realized. Practical Magick was on the ground floor of a three-story building. There were apartments above it, but I had never seen any of the tenants before. That would explain why there were no cars outside and why the elderly couple wore only sweaters.

They all left together. Alyce watched them for a moment, shook her head sadly, and then went back behind the counter.

I studied her quietly. Could she have had any part in what had happened to me?

Sensing my gaze, Alyce glanced up. "Morgan," she said, and I could see nothing but concern in her face. She came out from around the counter and took both my hands. "Hunter came by this morning and told us what happened. Are you all right?"

I nodded, looking at her. I let my senses seek for danger from her. I sensed nothing.

"Let's go in the back and talk," Alyce said. "I'll put the teakettle on."

I followed her behind the counter to the small back room, where David, the other clerk, sat at the square, battered table he used as a desk. An open ledger, its columns filled with numbers, lay in front of him. David, who was in his early thirties, was prematurely gray, a trait that he said was typical of his clan, the Burnhides. Today his face looked drawn and weary, as if he were aging to match his hair.

"Morgan," he said, "I was horrified to hear what happened to you. Please, sit down."

He closed the ledger as Alyce put a mixture of dried herbs into a metal tea ball. Then she turned to face me. "We owe you an apology," she said. David nodded his agreement.

I waited nervously. An apology for what?

"We were too slow to see what Selene was really after," David said. "Too slow to stop her."

I could feel truth, and sorrow, in his statement. My nerves began to unwind.

"It wasn't your fault," I said. It felt strange to have these adult witches apologizing to me. "I should have seen through Selene and . . . and the rest of them." I couldn't bring myself to say Cal's name.

The kettle on the hot plate began to steam, and Alyce poured the boiling water into a teapot. She set it on a trivet to let the tea steep.

"Selene is a very seductive woman," David said. "All of Starlocket was taken in by her, even those of us who should have been wary. Cal might have been the only one who truly knew her nature."

"She's pure evil," I said angrily. The force of my words surprised me.

David raised one silver eyebrow. "It's more complex than that, I think. Very few things are purely black or white."

"Plotting to kidnap or kill me?" I demanded. "To steal my

mother's coven's tools? Doesn't that count as evil?"

"Yes, of course," David said. He wasn't flustered by my outburst. In fact, it occurred to me that I'd never seen him flustered about anything. "Her actions *were* evil. But her intentions may have been more complicated than that."

"Her intentions aren't at issue," Alyce said, and I heard a note of steel in her voice.

David looked thoughtful but didn't say anything.

Alyce poured the tea. "Mint, motherwort, lemongrass, and a pinch of catnip. It's a very soothing brew," she announced, as if she wanted to change the subject. She sat down and took my hand. "This must be so awful for you," she said.

All I could do was nod. I took a deep breath. "Did you know they were both Woodbane?" I blurted. I hadn't realized how much that troubled me until this moment.

Alyce and David exchanged glances. "Yes," said David. "But that name doesn't mean what it used to."

"Morgan," Alyce said, closing her hand over mine, "you know that being Woodbane doesn't make you evil. A person chooses his or her own way."

"I guess," I mumbled. In a way I wanted to believe that Cal had had no choice but to be evil because of his Woodbane blood. But that would mean that I didn't either. I sighed. Wicca had seemed such a beautiful thing at first. How had it all become so complicated and frightening?

"If you need anything," David said, "if you have a question, need someone to talk to . . ."

"A shoulder to cry on," Alyce added. "Please, come to us. We are so sorry we weren't able to protect you from Selene. You are so new to this world, so vulnerable."

"Maybe you can help me now," I said, pulling my pack up

into my lap. I removed the things I'd packed. "I got some birthday gifts from . . . from Cal." There, I'd said it. "Plus his pentacle. They're all spelled. What should I do with them?"

"Burn them," David advised. "Cast a purification spell so that even the ashes will be free of his magick."

"I agree," said Alyce. "You have to break their powers. They could still be acting on you, influencing you, as long as they exist."

"Okay." As I gazed at the pile of gifts, the enormity of Cal's betrayal rose up and threatened to drown me again. I swallowed, fighting back a sob as I put them back into my pack.

"It will be hard, but it's something only you can do for yourself," Alyce said. "If you'd like, you can come back here after the ritual."

"Maybe I will," I said. I took another sip of tea.

The bells over the front door jangled, indicating that someone had come into the store. "I'd better go and see who that is," Alyce said, standing up.

The phone rang, and David looked at it, frowning. "Here we go again. Would you two excuse me, please?"

A shadow seemed to pass over Alyce's face. "Come on, Morgan," she said. "Let me take care of this customer. Then I'll help you find a purification spell. A really strong one."

In the main room I skimmed the bookcases, looking for purification spells, while I waited for Alyce.

Suddenly I heard David's voice raised from the back room. It was so unusual to hear him excited that I glanced up, startled. "Look, it's not just me. Two families will lose their homes!" he shouted. "I need more time." Then he said something else, but his voice had dropped to its normal, quiet pitch, which put an end to my eavesdropping.

I glanced at Alyce. Her face wore its usual air of calm, but I saw that her shoulders had tightened. They relaxed only once David's voice returned to normal.

After her customer paid for his purchase, she joined me. She scanned the shelves, then took down a slender book titled *Rituals for Purification and Protection.* "Try page forty-three. I think you'll find what you need for dealing with Cal's gifts."

As I read through the spell, David's voice rose again, and of course I listened. I couldn't help it. "I can't afford that, and you know it!" he shouted.

Alyce gave me a quick glance. She knew I had heard David, so I figured, why not just ask? "Alyce, what's going on?" I asked bluntly. "Who is David talking to?"

Alyce took a deep breath. "It sounds like he's talking to Stuart Afton or, more likely, Afton's lawyers."

"But why?" I asked. "Is something wrong? And who's Stuart Afton?"

"It's a long story," Alyce said. "David's aunt Rosaline, who owned the store—this entire building, actually—died last week."

"I'm sorry to hear that." So much for my witch senses. I hadn't even detected David's grief. My own problems had overwhelmed me. "Is he okay?"

Alyce bit her lip as if she was trying to decide how much to say. "Well, Rosaline's death wasn't unexpected. She'd been ill for a while. But that's only the beginning, I'm afraid. David had always assumed that, as her only living relative, he'd inherit the shop. But Rosaline died without a will and, unbeknownst to David, heavily in debt to a local real estate developer named Stuart Afton."

Now I realized why the name had sounded familiar. "Afton as in Afton Enterprises?" I'd seen the sign on a gravel pit just down the road from Unser's Auto Repair, where I always took Das Boot for service.

Alyce nodded. "Rosaline had been borrowing for years to keep the store afloat, using the building itself as collateral. The store barely makes any money, and Rosaline couldn't bear to raise the rent on the Winstons and the Romerios."

"Who are the Winstons and the Romerios?" I asked.

"They were all here when you arrived, actually," Alyce replied. "Lisa Winston is the woman I was talking to; she lives with her two boys on the top floor. The Romerios were that sweet old couple that came out of David's office. They were living on the second floor when Rosaline bought the building, years ago—that's how far back they go. They never had any children; they live on social security." She shook her head. "It would be impossible for them to move. And it would be a struggle for Lisa Winston. Her husband left her with those two little boys and nothing else."

I shook my head, confused. "But what's the problem? Why would they have to move?"

"Well, Rosaline didn't borrow from a bank; she borrowed from Afton. I'm not sure why—maybe the bank wouldn't give her a loan. Anyway, Afton essentially took over her mortgage. He doesn't have to follow the same rules as a bank. And now he wants the loan repaid in full at once, or the building is his." Alyce sighed. "Unless David can raise the money to repay him or Afton forgives the debt, this building will go to Afton. That was obviously his plan all along. He owns the buildings on either side already. Apparently he's been soliciting buyers, and rumor has it one of the big bookstore chains is interested in buying the whole block of properties and converting it into one big superstore."

"So Afton's just going to throw the tenants out?" I asked.

"More or less," Alyce agreed. "He can't flat out evict them, but he can raise their rents to market value, which comes to the same thing. If they lose those apartments, they'll never find anything else they can afford in this area."

"And Afton doesn't care?"

Alyce shrugged. "He's a businessman. He doesn't like losing money. Believe me, David and I have spent this entire week on the phone, trying everything we could think of to raise the money, but without much success."

My stomach dropped as the implication hit me. "What will happen to the store?"

Alyce looked at me with a steady gaze. "We'll sell off the stock and close. We can't afford rent in this area, either."

I looked at her in dismay. "Oh, no. You can't close. We all need you here, as a resource." Panic made my breath come faster. Having lost the anchor of Cal in my life, the idea of losing Practical Magick, my haven, threatened to push me over the edge.

"I know, my dear. It's a shame. But some things are out of our hands," Alyce said.

"No," I said. "We can't just accept this." I was stunned that she seemed so calm.

"Everything in life has its own cycle," Alyce said gently. "And the cycle always includes a death of sorts. It's the only way you get to a new cycle, to regeneration. If it's time for Practical Magick to come to an end, it will end."

"It's awful," I said in dismay. "I can't believe Afton can do this. Why can't someone get through to him, show him what he's doing?"

"Because he doesn't want to see," Alyce replied. Her

brow furrowed. "I'm worried more about David than myself. I can always go back to teaching. But I'm not sure what he'll do. This store has been more or less his home since he got out of college. It will be much harder for him than for me."

I clenched my teeth in frustration, wondering if there was anything at all I could do. Organize a protest? A petition? A sit-in? Surely there must be some spell that could be done? But I wasn't supposed to do spells. That was the one thing all the more experienced witches agreed upon—that I didn't have enough knowledge yet. Besides, I told myself, if there were spells, well, David and Alyce would surely have already done them.

"All right, enough gloom," said Alyce briskly. "Tell me, do you have Maeve's cauldron?" Alyce knew I'd found my birth mother's tools.

"No."

"Well, pick out a nice cauldron, then," she said.

"Do I need one?" I asked.

"It's something every witch should have as part of her tools," she explained. "And you need it to make the fire to burn Cal's gifts. You want the fire contained in something round that you can circle with protection spells."

I went and chose a small cauldron from the ones on display and brought it back to the counter. Alyce nodded her approval. "Do you have all the herbs you need?" she asked.

I checked my spell, and Alyce filled a small paper bag with the ingredients I needed. "Make sure that before you start, you purify the cauldron with salt water," she said. "And then purify it again when you're done to ensure that none of Cal's magick lingers."

"I will," I promised. "Thanks, Alyce. And please tell David

how sorry I am about his aunt and the store. If there's anything I can do to help . . ."

"Don't worry about us," she replied. "This is a time to heal yourself, Morgan."

After I'd paid and left Practical Magick, depression settled on me again. Cal had been not only my first love, but my first teacher as well. I hadn't realized this before, but right up until the moment Alyce told me the store might close, some part of me had already assumed that even without Cal, I'd have a place to learn about Wicca. Now it looked like I was going to lose that, too.

3

Purified

December 1982

A year ago I had no children. Now I have two—and I can't be a father to either of them.

Cal, the elder, was born in June. I love him; how could I help it? He's so beautiful, so sweet and trusting. But I can't bear it when he looks at me with his mother's golden eyes. I can't bear the growing fear that he is Selene's creation, that she'll mold him to follow her in her madness and that nothing I do can stop it.

Yet still, I feel bound to stay. Bound to try to save him.

Giomanach, my younger son, was born just three nights ago. I felt, across an ocean and a continent, Fiona's pain and joy as he came out of her body. I ache to be with her, with my dearest love, my soul mate—and I ache to see my newborn son. But I don't dare go to them for fear that Selene will take some terrible vengeance on them.

Goddess. I'm being ripped in two. How much longer can I bear this?
—Maghach

I made one quick detour on the way home, pulling into Bree's driveway. I climbed out and glanced around to see if anyone was watching me. Even though it was noon on Monday in a residential neighborhood and not many people were around, I whispered, "You see me not: I am but a shadow," as I hurried around to the side of Bree's house.

I knelt next to a big, winter-bare lilac that grew outside the dining room window and reached deep into the crawl space hidden by the cluster of woody stems. Tucked behind a piling was a rusted metal box. I'd hidden it there less than twenty-four hours earlier, on my way to see Cal.

I pulled the box out carefully. It contained my most precious possessions—the tools that Cal, Selene, and the people with them had almost killed me for. Tucking the box and its contents under my coat, I hurried back to my car.

When I got home, I glanced at the kitchen clock. I had a few hours before anyone got home. It was time to get rid of Cal's gifts.

I read over the spell Alyce had recommended. As she'd advised, I purified the cauldron first with boiling, salted water, then with plain salt rubbed over the interior and exterior. In my room I opened the metal box and looked through Maeve's tools. I took out the athame. Since I was planning to perform the ritual in our yard, I decided against using Maeve's green silk robe. You never know when a meter reader will show up or a neighbor will traipse into the yard, chasing after a dog. It wasn't a good idea to risk being seen in full witch regalia.

I was about to close the box when my fingertips brushed

against my mother's wand. It was made of black wood, inlaid with thin lines of silver and gold. Four small rubies studded its tip. I'd never used it before, but now I closed one hand around it and instinctively knew it would focus my energy, concentrate and store my power.

The ground was covered with a thick, crunchy sheet of snow. The temperature must have been close to the promised ten degrees; it was bitterly cold. The wind was battering sky, trees, and ground as if determined to whip the warmth from the earth.

Carrying the cauldron and the rest of my supplies, I crossed the yard to a big oak in the back. In a book of Celtic lore, I'd read that the oak was considered a guardian. I stared up into its bare branches, realizing that I actually did feel safer beneath it. I knew that the tree would lend its energy and protection to my ritual.

I set down the cauldron and began to collect fallen branches, shaking off the snow. Giving thanks to the oak for its kindling, I broke the branches and arranged them in the cauldron. Then, using Maeve's athame, I traced a circle in the snow. I sprinkled salt over the line traced by the athame, and I started to feel the earth's power moving through me. I drew the symbols for the four directions and for fire, water, earth, and sky, invoking the Goddess with each one.

I brushed the snow off a boulder and sat down, trying to ignore the cold wind. Closing my eyes, I began to follow my breath, aware of the rise and fall of my chest, the rhythm of my heartbeat, the blood coursing through my veins. Gradually my awareness deepened. I felt the roots of the oak tree stretching through the frozen ground beneath the circle, reaching toward me. I felt the earth itself echoing with all the years that our family had lived in this house. It was as if all the love in my adoptive family had penetrated the earth, become part of it, and was now surging up to steady me.

I was ready. Opening my eyes, I put the herbs that Alyce had given me into the cauldron. Most of them I recognized: a lump of myrrh, its scent unmistakable, dried patchouli leaves, and wood betony. Two of them I didn't recognize, but as I added them, their names came to me: olibanum tears and small pieces of a root called ague. Finally I added a few drops of pine and rue oil and mixed the ingredients until I felt their essences swirl together.

I concentrated on the cauldron. Fire, I thought. A moment later a spark flickered, and I heard the sound of flames crackling. A thin line of smoke rose from the cauldron.

"Goddess, I ask your help," I began. I glanced at the spell book. "These gifts were given to bind me. Take them into your fire, cleanse them of their dark magick, and render them harmless."

Then, swallowing hard, I took Cal's gifts and one by one dropped them into the cauldron. The beautiful batik blouse whose colors reminded me of a storm at sunset, the book of herbal magick, the earrings, the pentacle, even the bloodstone he'd given me at our last circle. The flames crackled, licked at the rim of the cauldron. I watched the pages of the book curl into glowing whorls of ash. The burning ink gave off a faint, acrid smell. Wisps of glowing thread drifted upward as the batik blouse was consumed by the fire.

It burned hotter, hotter, until it gave off an incandescence that was almost too much for my eyes. The flames leaped to meet the wind high above the cauldron. I gasped, my heart aching with sadness. There, in the center of the white-hot flames, I saw Cal exactly as he had been when he gave me my gifts, a look of pure tenderness on his face. I felt myself falling deeper then, my heart opening to him the way a flower opens to the sun. Tears blurred my vision.

"No," I said, suddenly furious that here, in *my circle,* Cal's magick was still rising up to control me. I reached for Maeve's wand and aimed it at the cauldron. I felt my power pour into it and intensify. Beyond that I felt the power of Maeve and her mother, Mackenna, high priestesses both. I began to move deasil, chanting the words from the book aloud:

"Earth and air, flame and ice,
Take darkness from me.
Cleanse these things of ill intent.
Let this spell cause no harm nor return any on me."

On the last words of the spell the flames crackled, as if in answer to me, then died out completely. A white, nearly transparent smoke rose. The wand in my hand felt weightless. I gently laid it on the ground.

After a moment I gathered my courage and peered into the cauldron. The blouse was gone entirely, as was the book. There were a few darkened lumps of metal, which I took to be the earrings and the pentagram. The tigereyes seemed to be gone. I could still see the shape of the bloodstone, though, covered in a fine ash. I touched the edge of the cauldron. It was already cool, despite the white-hot flames that had blazed there just moments earlier.

I reached in for the bloodstone. White ash fell from it; it was cool to the touch. I gingerly extended my senses, examining it for any trace of Cal's magick. I couldn't find any.

My fist tightened around it, and something deep inside me snapped. It was a crackling, heartrending release, as if the ritual had broken not only Cal's magickal bonds on me, but my own bonds on my reined-in pain and anger. I flung the bloodstone away as hard as I could. "You bastard, Cal!" I screamed into the bitter wind. "You bastard!"

Then I dropped to my knees, sobbing. How could he have done this to me? How could he have taken something as precious as love and corrupted it so horribly? I crouched, praying to the Goddess to heal my heart.

It was a long time before I straightened up again. When I did, I felt that magick had left the circle. Things were back to normal—whatever normal was.

I opened the circle, grabbed my tools, and took them back into the house. I returned the tools to their old hiding place in the HVAC vent in the upstairs hallway. I made a mental note to find a new hiding place soon. I repurified the cauldron with salt water before stuffing it in the back of my closet. Then I took a hot shower and finally did what I'd wanted to do since that morning.

I got Dagda, crawled into bed, and went back to sleep.

4

Celebration

August 1984

    I've made my choice, if you can call it a choice. I'm with Fiona now, back home in England. Our second son will be born in a week, and I simply could not stay away any longer. She is my mùirn beatha dàn, my soul's true mate.

    I think—I hope—that Selene has at last accepted this. When I left this time, she didn't plead. She said only, "Remember the threefold law. All that you do comes back to you." She turned away, and I watched Cal carefully copy her. I've lost him. He is wholly Selene's now.

    Giomanach is so changed from the last time I saw him. He's nearly two years old now, no longer a baby but a wiry little boy with hair like bleached corn silk and Fiona's dancing green eyes. He's a happy child but still shy and a little fearful around me. I try not to let him see how it hurts me.

I try, too, not to think too often of Cal, and of the battle that I lost.

—*Maghach*

"Morgan." My sister was sitting on the edge of the bed, shaking my shoulder. "Mom asked me to wake you up."

I opened my eyes and realized it was dark outside. I felt like I'd been asleep for days. "What time is it?" I asked groggily.

"Five-thirty." Mary K. turned on the light on my night table, and I saw the concern in her warm brown eyes. "Aunt Eileen and Paula are on their way over for dinner. They should be here any minute. Hey, Mom told me about you and Cal. And I saw Das Boot. Are you okay?"

I drew in a shaky breath, then nodded. Something had shifted during the purification ceremony. Though I still felt deeply wounded, I didn't have quite the same sense of hope-lessness I'd had this morning. "I've been better, but I'll live."

"Cal wasn't in school today," Mary K. said. She hesitated. "There's a rumor going around that he and his mom left town over the weekend. That there was some kind of suspi-cious fire on their property and now they've disappeared."

"They did leave, it's true," I said. I sighed. "Look, I can't talk about this right now. I'll tell you the whole story soon. But you have to promise to keep it to yourself."

"Okay." She looked solemnly at me, then went through the connecting door to her room.

I pulled on a pair of sweats and a red thermal top and brushed my long hair into a ponytail. Then I went down-stairs. In the front hall I heard the doorbell, then a babble of excited voices. "What's going on?" I asked as I went out to greet them. They all sounded cheerful and happy.

"We made an offer on a house today, and it was accepted!" Aunt Eileen told me. When my aunt Eileen and her girlfriend, Paula Steen, decided to move in together, my mom had made it her personal mission to find them the house of their dreams.

Moments later we were all gathered around the dining room table. Mary K. set out silverware and plates, my dad set out wineglasses, and Mom, Aunt Eileen, and Paula opened container after container of takeout food.

I sniffed the air, not recognizing the smells of either Chinese or Indian food, the two usual choices. "Wow. Smells great. What'd you bring?"

"We splurged at Fortunato's," Paula told me. Fortunato's was a trendy gourmet place that had opened a couple of years ago in Widow's Vale. Our family didn't shop there much, due to their insane prices.

"What's your pleasure?" Aunt Eileen asked. "We've got filet mignon with wild mushrooms, herb potatoes, cold salmon, asparagus vinaigrette, spinach salad, clam fritters, and chicken dijonnaise."

"And save room for chocolate-hazelnut cake," Paula added.

"Oh my God, I'm never going to be able to move again," Mary K. moaned.

Paula popped the cork on a champagne bottle and poured it into glasses as we all took our seats. She even gave Mary K. and me about a swallow each, though I noticed my mom raise her eyebrows as Aunt Eileen handed the glasses to us. "A toast!" Paula said, and lifted her own glass high. "To our new, absolutely perfect home and the absolutely brilliant real estate agent who found it for us!"

My mom laughed. "May you always be happy there!"

We began passing around the food. It felt good to see everyone so cheerful, even Mary K., who had been looking pretty down since she and her boyfriend, Bakker, had broken up. I was glad to be able to focus on someone's good news. I felt myself start to relax, felt my anxiety recede a bit.

"So tell me all about this perfect house," I said to Eileen.

"It's in Taunton," Eileen began, naming a town about ten miles north of us. "It's a little house with bay windows, set back from the street, with a beautiful garden out back. Wood-burning stove downstairs and a fireplace in the master bedroom. The only bad part is, it's covered with ugly green vinyl siding."

"Which is old and needs to be replaced, anyway," Mom stuck in. "Apart from that, it oozes charm."

"Yeah." Paula grinned. "Just ask the Realtor."

"When do you think you'll move in?" Mary K. asked Aunt Eileen.

Aunt Eileen had just taken a huge bite of spinach salad, so Mom answered for her. "The closing is scheduled for next week, after the inspection," she said.

"That's fantastic!" Mary K. said. "You could actually be in by next weekend."

Aunt Eileen took Paula's hand and with her other hand crossed her fingers. "That's what we're hoping," she said.

The rest of dinner went by quickly, with talk of moving plans, house plans, and a heated discussion about how many pets they would adopt once they were settled. Paula was a veterinarian, so Aunt Eileen thought they should have a good menagerie, including several cats and dogs and a rabbit or two. By the time we got to dessert, everyone was laughing.

All at once my smile froze into place as I felt Hunter on our front walk outside. His presence always had a weird effect on me. The doorbell rang a moment later, and I stood quickly. "I'll get it," I said.

I went to the front hall and opened the door. Hunter stood there in a thick green sweater that perfectly matched his eyes. His hands were shoved into the pockets of a worn brown leather jacket that emphasized his broad shoulders.

"You weren't in school today," he stated.

"Hello to you, too," I said dryly.

He ducked his head and kicked snow off his boot. "Uh, right. Hello. How are you feeling?"

"Better, thanks."

He brought his gaze back up to mine, his eyes glinting in the reflection from the little light over the door. "As I was saying—you weren't in school."

My forehead crinkled. Had he gone to my school to check up on me? Was Hunter actually concerned about me?

I must have been staring at him because I noticed the tips of his ears begin to turn pink. Was he blushing? Surely not. Not Hunter. He must really be cold.

"Morgan, who is it?" my mom called.

"Um—it's my friend Hunter," I called back. "I'll just be a second."

"Well, invite him in and shut the door. You're letting in cold air."

Silently I held the door, and Hunter stepped inside. "We need to talk," he said.

I knew he was right, but I wasn't ready yet. "It's not a good time."

"I don't mean about Cal," he said. "I mean about Cirrus."

Cirrus was the coven that Cal had started. I was a member, along with Robbie, Jenna Ruiz, Sharon Goodfine, Ethan Sharp, and Matt Adler. Bree had originally been part of Cirrus, too, but when she and I split up over Cal, she and Raven Meltzer had formed Kithic, a coven that was now led by Hunter's cousin Sky.

"Cirrus?" I repeated, confused. "What about it?"

"With Cal gone, you need someone else to lead it. An initiated witch."

I hadn't even thought about that. With Cirrus, Cal had opened up the world of Wicca to me, permanently altering my world. His betrayal had left a deep black hole in my life, and my few new support systems were now being sucked away into it.

I didn't want to lose the coven. "I could ask Alyce or David if they'll take over."

"Alyce and David are already part of Starlocket. I hear Alyce has been asked to lead it now that Selene is gone," Hunter said.

I was silent, thinking, and then Hunter broke in.

"I want to lead Cirrus," he said.

Now I was seriously at sea. "Why?" I asked. "You don't know any of us. You don't even live here. Not permanently, anyway."

"I'll probably be here for a while. I've asked the council to give me time to come up with new leads on Cal and Selene. I want to see if I can track them down."

"But you don't know how long that will take," I argued. "Anyway, there are five other people in our coven. They might have something to say about who leads us."

"I already discussed it with them," Hunter said. "I went to

your school today. That's how I know you weren't there."

So he hadn't gone there out of concern for me. To my surprise, I felt a stab of disappointment. Then my anger rose. How could he be so presumptuous? "So you talked to them and they said yes? You're it?"

"We're going to see how it goes," he said cautiously. "There's a circle tomorrow night at my house at seven. I hope you'll be there. I think it would be good for . . . everyone."

"A circle on a Tuesday night?"

"We can't wait until Saturday," Hunter said. "It's important that Cirrus re-form quickly. When a circle is broken in this way, it can be devastating to the members. Besides, we don't know what magick Cal might have used on the members. I've asked everyone to bring the stones Cal gave them so we can purify them. You should bring yours, too, along with anything else he gave you."

"I already purified everything," I said, and felt a childish triumph when I saw the surprise in his eyes. Now maybe he'd stop being so superior, so remote, making me feel like he was ten years older than me rather than two.

Even as the thoughts formed, I knew I wasn't being fair to him. He really was trying to help. But his very competence irked me, made me feel clumsy, naive.

He must have sensed a change in my attitude and figured the circle issue was a done deal, because he moved on. "Now, the second thing," he said, "is you. You've come into quite a birthright—far more power than most blood witches ever experience, and Belwicket's tools besides. But you know only the most rudimentary things about how to focus and control your power. And you know even less about how to protect yourself."

I took it as an accusation and felt anger flare again. "I've only known I was a blood witch for a month. I know I have a long way to go."

Hunter sighed. "All I'm saying is that you've got a hell of a lot of catching up to do. Most blood witches are initiated at age fourteen, after studying for years. Witches need to know the history of Wicca and the Seven Great Clans; the rituals of the Goddess and the God and the eight great sabbats; herbalism; the basics of numerology; the proper use of talismans and runes; the properties of minerals, metals, and stones and how they interact with the cycles of the celestial bodies. The full correspondences; reading auras; spells of protection, healing, binding, and banishment. And though it's more advanced, you really ought to learn about the Guardians of the Watchtowers—"

A sudden burst of laughter came from the kitchen, where Aunt Eileen and Paula and my family were lingering over coffee. It sounded so safe and comforting in there, a world I was not fully part of anymore, a world I had taken for granted. An awful thought occurred to me. "Is my family in danger?" I blurted out.

Hunter ran a hand through his pale blond hair. Tiny crystals of ice had beaded up in it, so now bits of it stuck up in spiky tufts, making him look about eight years old.

"I don't think so," he said. "At least, not now. With Selene's plan exposed, I suspect she and her cronies will lie low for a while. You have a window of safety here, which is why it's vital that you don't waste it. You need to begin studying."

I gnawed my thumbnail. He was right.

"I have some books that I bought at Practical Magick," I

told him. "I haven't read them cover to cover, but I've skimmed them." I told him the titles. "And of course I've read most of Maeve's Book of Shadows."

He nodded approvingly. "Those are all good. Keep working with them and we'll talk in a few days. Write down any questions you have. I'll give you a reading list after I have a better sense of what you know."

"Hey." Mary K. came out into the hall. "Hunter, right? How are you?"

"Fine, thanks," he said, flashing her a surprisingly warm smile. "You?"

"Good." Mary K. twisted a strand of auburn hair around her finger.

Was she *flirting* with him? "Hunter's got to go now," I said.

He looked at me, then nodded. "Good night," he called to my sister. To me he said, "You look tired. Get some sleep."

"What a hottie," Mary K. said as the door clicked shut behind him.

"Oh, please," I groaned, then went back to the kitchen to join the group.

5

Darkness

With Athar's help, I broke the warding spells today. It took the two of us the better part of the day—Athar was annoyed because I made her take a day off from her job.

But I found nothing useful inside. If Selene did leave anything, it's locked in that library of hers, and I can't get at it. The council is sending a fellow down from Boston next week to help me bind the house in spells. Perhaps he'll be able to help me get in. I will not ask Morgan for her help. It's clear that she dislikes me enough already.

I wish she didn't. There's something in her eyes, in the way she holds her head, that somehow draws me to her.

—Giomanach

Something was after me, I could feel it. Deep darkness was surrounding me, trying to find me, to envelop me. I tried to make the rune signs for protection, but I couldn't lift my hands: my fingers weren't working. I'd been bound, just as Cal had bound me to entrap me.

Smoke and flames burned in the back of my throat, and I heard a voice screaming, "Not again!" Somehow I knew the voice belonged to my birth mother, Maeve.

Then faces rose up out of the smothering darkness: Selene and Cal. I begged them to leave me alone. I pushed my lips together tightly, knowing, somehow, that they wanted me to breathe in the darkness, wanted it to become a part of me.

Just as I felt myself about to suffocate, I saw a tiny sliver of light. The faces of Cal and Selene dissolved as the light approached. And then I began to see a new face in its midst.

Hunter.

I woke up, sweaty and gasping for breath. My heart raced, pounding hard in my chest. I pushed my hair away from my damp forehead and looked around the room. I was in my own bedroom. I was alone. Dagda was sleeping on a pillow that had fallen to the floor. It was still pitch-dark outside my window.

I shuddered. The dream had been so intense, it felt like it was still with me. I pulled at the sheets. They were completely wrapped around my body. I let out a shaky laugh. No wonder I'd thought I was being smothered. Those sheets were wound as tightly as a straitjacket. I struggled free, then reached over to my bedside table and flicked on the lamp. Not so good. The lamp cast spooky shadows all around my room. I got up and turned on my overhead light. Dagda stretched and blinked sleepily. I picked him up and brought him back into bed with me.

"It was just a nightmare," I told my purring kitten. "It's

just my brain trying to process all that I've been through."

I pulled the comforter up around my shoulders. I'd gone from sweaty to freezing. Was my window open? I glanced over, but no, it was shut. I still felt anxious, unsettled. My heart started its syncopated beat again. Was it just the aftermath of the dream, or was I picking up something with my witch senses?

Cradling Dagda close to my body, I got up and went to the window. I took in deep breaths, trying to calm my mind. Dagda squirmed, so I put him down. I didn't want to be distracted.

Willing myself to breathe evenly, I opened myself to the night. I could feel the sting of frosty air on my face as my senses moved out of my cozy bedroom and into the back-yard. The world was quiet under its blanket of snow, and the trees themselves seemed to be asleep. The houses were filled with sleeping bodies; a car drove slowly along the road. Beyond that, I didn't get much sensation, just vague cold.

Then a wave of nausea hit me. My veins felt like they were filled with cold sludge. The only other time I'd felt any-thing like this horrible sensation was when Cal had used magick to bind me.

There was dark magick in Widow's Vale tonight. I knew that with certainty.

Stay clear, stay calm, a voice said in my head. Was it my own? Don't fight the sensation, the voice told me. Examine it.

As I stopped fighting the nausea, it seemed to dissipate. I realized that I wasn't being acted upon. This wasn't an attack—it felt oddly impersonal. The energy, whatever it was, wasn't directed at me. It was as if I'd gotten a whiff of something really foul but hadn't actually come into contact with it.

But what was it? And where was it coming from?

Suddenly I could see the field where Cal had brought us for our very first circle. I couldn't make out what was happening there, but I was certain that I was seeing the place where the magick was being worked.

I gasped. It could only mean one thing. Cal and Selene were back. Who else would go to that particular field? They were there, working their dark spells. Whatever they were doing right now wasn't aimed at me. But it was only a matter of time before they came for me.

6

A New Circle

Kennet Muir, my council mentor, rang from London to say he'd got a new assignment for me. There was a cat found in a suburb of Montreal with its throat cut, and the council fears a rogue coven may have resurrected the blood rituals that were banned in the nineteenth century.

On the strength of one dead cat! It's ridiculous: it's a fool's errand, and I told Kennet so. I told him I needed to stay here, that I had many things to finish. He finally agreed, but only after warning me not to allow myself to become too emotionally wrapped up in my work.

Athar laughed when I told her that. "Too late," she said.

I had the feeling she was not referring only to finding Cal and Selene.

—Giomanach

I didn't sleep at all during the rest of the night. Whenever I shut my eyes, images of Selene and Cal rose up, unbidden. By dawn I gave up and used my nervous energy to do the next week's math problems. The only thing that kept me from jumping out of my skin was the knowledge that the dark magick hadn't been focused on me.

I knew I had to tell Hunter about what I had experienced, and I didn't want to wait until the circle that night. I went out to the hall phone.

Mary K. walked by on her way to the bathroom. Her eyes widened when she saw me. "You're up early," she said. "You even have time to eat breakfast sitting down."

"I may be up, but I'm not awake," I warned her. I dialed Hunter's number, hoping he and Sky were early risers.

No answer. And no voice mail. I banged the phone down in frustration. Where the hell were they at this ridiculous hour?

Luckily Mary K. misinterpreted my mood as my usual morning crabbiness, so she didn't ask any questions. Stay calm, I ordered myself. Selene and Cal may be back, but you'll find some way to be ready for them.

Since I was already up, Mary K. and I set out for school early. She was stunned since she usually had to nag me into my car. I figured I'd use the opportunity to find out what the other members of Cirrus really thought about Hunter taking over.

I could feel Mary K.'s eyes on me while I drove. Did she sense my tension?

"Do you want to talk about it now?" she asked hesitantly.

I sighed. I felt bad for not telling her the full story. But I just wasn't up to it yet. I squeezed Das Boot into a snug parking space. "Soon, I promise. It's really . . . really hard.

Cal—he wasn't who I thought he was." Understatement of the year.

She sighed. "Is it the Rowlands's curse to have bad judgment when it comes to guys?" Mary K.'s ex-boyfriend, Bakker, had tried to force himself on her. I had been so furious that I'd shot witch fire at him without even realizing what I was doing. Still, that didn't stop her from taking him back. Or him from trying it again. Luckily she'd been stronger the second time. He was out of her life for good. I hoped.

"Mom did okay," I said.

"She wasn't a Rowlands," Mary K. pointed out darkly.

"True!" I said, and unbelievably, I giggled. Then we were hugging in the front seat of my demolition-derby car. "I'm glad you're my sister," I whispered.

"Back atcha," Mary K. said, and then her friend Jaycee ran up to the car, bundled in a Day-Glo–pink ski jacket.

"Mary K.," she cried excitedly, tapping the window. "You are *not* going to believe who Diane D'Alessio is going out with!"

"Just a sec," Mary K. told her. She turned back to me. "I'll talk to you later, okay?"

"Yep," I told her.

Mary K. and Jaycee hurried across the icy parking lot toward school. I grabbed my backpack and followed them.

Inside the redbrick building, I headed to the basement stairs, where our coven usually hung out on cold mornings. Jenna and Sharon were already there, along with Ethan. Matt, Jenna's ex, was nowhere to be seen, and neither was Robbie.

"Hey," I said.

Sharon looked up at me, relief evident in her expression. "Morgan! Are you all right? Robbie told us about Sunday night."

I sat down on the step beside Jenna. "Yeah, I'm okay. I guess."

Ethan shook his head. "That totally blew me away. I can't believe I missed all the signs that Cal was lethal."

"We all missed them," Sharon said, shuddering. Ethan put his arm around her shoulders.

Jenna tucked a strand of her pale blond hair behind her ear. "I feel so stupid. Like we were all taken in by a con artist or something. That the whole thing was just part of a plot to get at you."

"It's strange, but I can't help feeling that a lot of what he was doing was sincere," I said thoughtfully. Then I caught myself, wondering if I had a total victim personality or what. "Of course, he seemed pretty sincere about trying to kill me, too," I added briskly. "So now we know. Wicca definitely has a dark side, and Cal and Selene were practicing it."

Ethan stood up and shoved his hands into the pockets of his jeans. "You know, I like the part of Wicca that's about connecting with nature, understanding yourself. But this dark stuff scares me."

"I don't think any of us realized what we might be getting into when Cal started Cirrus," I said. "Now I guess we have to decide whether we want to go on with it."

"Did you hear that Hunter wants to lead the coven?" Jenna asked.

I nodded. "He told me last night. How do you all feel about it?"

"Weird," Jenna said. "I mean, we started with Cal. Being in the coven is so much connected with him for me. I don't know what it will be like. Plus it seems weird that Hunter would even want to lead us. He doesn't know us."

"He's worried about us being exposed to dark magick, and he wants to make sure no one gets hurt. That's what he said, anyway," Sharon said. She smiled. "In his sexy English accent."

"Hey!" Ethan protested. "What about *my* sexy accent?"

"He does seem to know what he's talking about," Matt said. "He's been doing this a lot longer than we have. I know he's not much older than we are, but he seems . . . I don't know . . . more grown-up or something."

"It's just the accent," Ethan said, poking Sharon in the ribs. "It makes him seem older."

"Cut it out." Sharon wiggled away, laughing.

"You're right," I admitted. Hunter did seem older than his years. It probably had to do with all he'd been through. He'd had to grow up fast.

"I loved Cal's circles," Sharon said wistfully. "He was totally laid-back but at the same time encouraging."

"That last circle with him, I felt real magick," Jenna agreed. "Still, it might be interesting to see how Hunter handles things. For variety." The first bell rang, and she got to her feet. "All I know is, I'm not joining Sky's coven," she said. We all knew what she meant. Along with Bree, Raven Meltzer also belonged to Sky's coven. Raven had tried to seduce Matt, and Matt had pretty much gone for it. Hence the end of the four-year romance between Matt and Jenna.

Sharon said, "I think we ought to give him a chance."

"Yeah," Ethan said. "If we hate it, we can just quit."

For a moment, I envied them. If they didn't enjoy Wicca, they could drop it, the way you drop a boring after-school activity. I didn't have that option. Wicca had chosen me as much as I'd chosen it.

I'd hoped to get to Hunter and Sky's place early so that I could talk to Hunter about what I'd sensed the night before, but in the dark I missed the turn to his street and was out of Widow's Vale completely before I figured it out. By the time I pulled up in front of the house, it was already after seven, and everybody else's cars were parked against the curb. I wedged Das Boot in between Robbie's Beetle and Jenna's Corolla and started up the narrow path.

Hunter must have sensed me coming before I reached the porch. The front door opened, framing him in warm golden light. I caught my breath—it was so similar to the image of him in my dream, bathed in light, pushing back the darkness. I blinked to shake off the image. He watched me from the doorway, looking like one of those ads for an après-ski drink, and I suddenly felt self-conscious, as if I were about to slip and fall facedown on the walk.

"Welcome," he said.

"Morganita." Robbie came up behind him. "You've got to check this place out. It's very cool."

"I've been here before," I mumbled, oddly flustered.

Hunter stood aside to let me pass, and I walked into the living room. Sharon and Ethan were sharing an ottoman, leaning companionably against each other's backs. Jenna and Matt were in the armchairs, not looking at each other. Robbie sat down at one end of the blue velvet sofa and waved a hand at the seat next to him. I could sense that everyone was unsure about Hunter leading us, and I knew that Hunter sensed it, too.

"You know what's strange about this living room?" Robbie said. "There's no TV."

Hunter arched one blond eyebrow. "We don't have time for it," he said. The implication was that neither should we. Not a great way to start.

"Is Sky here?" Jenna asked.

"No. She's out this evening," Hunter replied. He was wearing a deep-blue denim shirt, and worn black jeans hung loosely on his hips. I suddenly had a vivid flashback to the moment he'd almost kissed me, standing in the dark outside my house. That had been only three nights ago, but until this minute I'd forgotten about it.

I felt my cheeks burn. Where had that stray thought come from?

Hunter moved to stand in front of the hearth. "Welcome, everyone. I appreciate your showing up on a weeknight. I know this change is difficult. And I understand that despite the way things turned out with Cal, you liked the way he led Cirrus.

"My approach will inevitably be different," he went on. "But I'll try to see that Cirrus remains a coven where you feel comfortable, where you can be open with one another, where you can learn to safely draw on the power that lies within you, and where you will enter into a true connection with your magick."

Sharon smiled at that. But all I could think about was how with Cal the circles had seemed natural and comfortable. With Hunter it felt like we were getting the Wicca version of a Rotary Club speech.

"So," Hunter said, "let's begin. If you'll follow me, please . . ."

We followed him from the living room through a short hallway that I hadn't noticed when I'd been there before. It was lined with bookshelves that held a small collection of clothbound volumes. Through an arched doorway I could see into a small kitchen, where dried herbs and flowers hung from the ceiling.

At the end of the hall was a set of double wooden doors. Hunter opened them into a long, narrow room that was lit by candles and the glow of a wood-burning stove. The room ran the length of the house. Its back wall was covered with windows. A door led out to what seemed to be a deck. The windows rattled slightly, and I could hear the wind sighing through the trees.

An altar sat at one end of the room, holding more candles, a stick of burning incense, a shell, a dish of water in which purple blossoms floated, a pale blue crystal, and a stone sculpture of a woman. The sculpture was rough, the face barely defined, yet it was completely sensuous, a vision of the Goddess. You had only to look at it to know that it was made with love. I looked at Hunter. Had he sculpted it?

"Will you form a circle, please?" Hunter began. He sounded terribly proper and polite, very British. Once again I missed Cal with a pang and once again felt stupid and angry at myself for missing someone who had hurt me so badly.

I joined the others as Hunter drew a circle with white chalk around us. It was reassuring to feel Robbie on one side of me and Sharon on the other. I felt uneasy, though. I wondered if it was the threat of Selene and Cal or if it was Hunter. His presence always unsettled me, and being in a circle was so intimate. I wondered what it would be like to share this experience with him.

With the chalk Hunter traced four runes on each of the directional points. "I've chosen these runes specifically for our first circle together," he said. "Thorn is for new beginnings and opening gateways," he said, pointing to the rune at the east. "Beorc is a rune of growth. Ur is to create change and healing and strengthen all magick. Eolh is for protection."

I tried to quell the flutters in my stomach. What was my problem? Hunter hadn't done anything unusual so far.

"Did everyone bring the stones Cal gave out?" Hunter asked. When people nodded, he added, "Toss them into the middle of the circle, please."

Everyone but me pulled their stones out of their pockets. When they were all in a heap in the center of the chalk ring, Hunter drew a pentagram around them. At each of the five points he drew a symbol I didn't recognize.

"These sigils are from an older runic alphabet than the one we usually work with," he explained. "They're for protection and purification and will help strengthen our spell. We're going to use the circle itself to purify these stones. Now, have you all done the basic breathing exercises?"

Matt spoke up. "Cal taught us that."

"Then let's begin there," Hunter said. "May the circle of Cirrus always be strong."

We all joined hands, and I heard the familiar sound of Sharon's bracelets jingling against each other. I began to concentrate on my breathing, on pulling each inhalation deep into my stomach and then releasing it. Gradually I felt myself relax and become aware of the pattern of breathing within the circle. Hunter had the deepest, slowest breaths. Jenna, who was asthmatic, had the shallowest.

Hunter began to sing in a low voice. It was a simple chant in English, praising moon and sun, Goddess and God, asking them to be with us in our circle, to protect us from all evil intent, and to guide us through the cycle of the seasons, the cycle of life. His voice was lilting, smooth and soft, yet with a core of strength. It resonated beautifully in the space. I never would have imagined that he could sing with such passion and simplicity. But for some reason, I couldn't hold on to the words. The others did, though, and as they sang together and we all moved widdershins, I saw their faces change. They were feeling something that I wasn't. A connection. Their voices gained power as some kind of energy surged through them. And I, the blood witch, the prodigy of Cirrus coven, felt nothing.

I became aware of Hunter's gaze on me. I closed my eyes, trying futilely to deepen my concentration, to snatch at the ethereal thread of magick that seemed to dance just out of reach. But I couldn't touch it, and finally, when I was almost weeping with frustration, Hunter slowed the circle and brought the song to an end. "Don't break the circle," he told us. "But everyone sit down."

We sat in place, our legs crossed.

"That was really good, everyone," Hunter said. His face glowed, his features relaxed in a way that I rarely saw, as if the circle was the place he felt most comfortable. It upset me that he could feel so at ease here in my coven while I, for the first time, felt like an outsider. He looked at each one of us in turn and then asked, "Do you want to share your thoughts?"

Ethan said, "That was . . . intense. The Wicca books talk about the Wheel of the Year. This time I felt like I could sort of . . . feel all of us traveling on it, our whole lives."

"Yeah," Matt said. "It was like I was both in this room and out there in the ravine."

"Me too." Robbie looked awestruck. "I felt like I was the wind in the trees."

Hunter looked at Sharon. "I didn't get anything cosmic," she admitted, sounding embarrassed. "I just felt how much my family cares about me. It was like I got this blast of mother-father love that I haven't been paying attention to lately."

Hunter smiled. "What makes you think that isn't cosmic?"

Robbie said, "What about you, Jenna?"

Jenna laughed softly. "I had a vision of myself being really *strong.*"

It was my turn next, and I was dreading it. What had gone wrong? I wondered. Maybe Hunter was just the wrong person for me to be working with. Now I was going to have to say I hadn't felt anything, and everyone was going to wonder what was wrong with me, if I could only reach my power with Cal. I took a deep breath, trying to calm down.

"All right, then." Hunter got to his feet. "That was good work, everyone. Let's call it a night and meet again on Saturday."

I looked up, startled. He had skipped me!

When he walked over to blow out the altar candles, I followed him. "Do I not count?" I asked in a low voice. "Doesn't it matter what I felt?"

He glanced at me in surprise. "I could tell you didn't connect," he replied softly. "I thought you'd rather not talk about it. I'm sorry if I made the wrong assumption."

I couldn't think of a reply to that. It was the right assumption, in fact. It just bothered me, the way he could read me. I found it incredibly disconcerting.

He turned back to the others. "On Saturday we'll work with the pentagram," he said. "Read up on it and spend some time visualizing it. See what it tells you."

I thought of Cal's pentacle necklace, and a shudder went through me.

"We can meet at my house," Jenna volunteered.

"Perfect," Hunter said. "Thank you all."

I knew I should seize the moment and tell him I needed

to speak to him privately, but I just couldn't do it. I felt too off balance, too out of sorts. Before I'd made up my mind to do anything, Robbie came up and handed me my coat.

"So do you have a good book about pentagrams?" he asked as we walked out toward the cars.

"No," I said tiredly. "I don't seem to have anything right now."

7

Intruder

April 1986

Today I found Glomanach, all of three and a half years old,
hunched over a bowl of water, staring into it so intently that his eyes
were almost crossing. When I asked him what he was doing, he told
me he was scrying for his sister. Goddess, I was startled. We'd not told
him that Fiona is carrying another child, yet he knew. He's amazingly
quick.

I asked him if he'd seen anything, expecting him to say he hadn't.
He's too young to scry. But he said he'd seen a little girl with dark
hair and eyes. I smiled and told him we'd have to wait and see. But
my lueg told me our Alwyn will have red hair and green eyes like
Fiona's, so I'm afraid the water lied to my boy. Unless it showed him
its own riddling truth.

Then Glomanach smacked his hand down so the water spilled out *of the bowl. I opened my mouth to scold him, but he looked up at me with that little mischievous smile, and I hadn't the heart. He's like sunshine to me. After looking over my shoulder for two years, I'm finally beginning to accept that nothing is going to happen, that life can actually be this good.*

—Maghach

I sat in Das Boot on Wednesday morning, thinking again about last night's circle. The truth was, part of me loved being the star pupil, the one who had off-the-charts power. In our coven, right from the start, I'd been the gifted one. It had made me feel special for the first time in my life. Was that over, too?

"Morgan?" a muffled voice called. "Morgan!"

I blinked and glanced up. My friend Tamara Pritchett was tapping on the window, her breath coming out in white puffs. "You're going to be late," she said as I rolled down the window. "Didn't you hear the bell?"

"Um . . . ," I mumbled. "Sorry. I was just thinking."

We walked to class together, and all the way there I was aware of the curious looks Tamara kept giving me. By now everyone knew that Cal was gone, that there had been a fire at his house. I'd told everyone who asked the standard story: that we'd broken up and I didn't know anything about the fire or where he was. But the people I'd been good friends with before Wicca came into my life, people like Tamara and Janice Yutoh, could tell there was a lot I wasn't saying.

I got through my morning classes, and then at lunch period I left school. I had an appointment for Das Boot at the body shop to get an estimate for the repairs. Unser's Auto Repair was off the highway on the outskirts of Widow's Vale. It was a big fenced lot, filled with cars, with a garage in the middle of it. With the exception of the Afton Enterprises gravel pit, which I passed about a quarter of a mile before Unser's, the road stretched out bleak and empty. I gave the gravel pit a glare as I drove past it, thinking of Practical Magick.

I pulled into the garage. Bob Unser, a gruff, gray-haired man in coveralls, wiped his hands on a rag and came over to the car as I got out. His big German shepherd, Max, bounded over, shoved his wet nose into my palm and licked it, then bounded away again. Max was technically a guard dog, but he was a total sweetheart. He and Bob both knew me pretty well. Being a genuine antique, Das Boot had had its share of problems, though nothing as major as this before.

Bob squinted at Das Boot's crumpled, scorched nose and smashed headlight. "What happened?"

"It kind of . . . collided with a building that was on fire."

He grunted "That's original."

I huddled in my coat while he looked over Das Boot and made notes on a clipboard. "Let me call and get an estimate on the parts," he said. "Then I'll give you a total."

"Great." I had a feeling this repair was going to cost a fortune, and I wasn't sure how I was going to pay for it. I didn't want to put it on my parents' insurance and risk raising their rates.

Bob went into the little office, and I stayed in the garage. Max trotted back to my side, and I ran my hand through his thick coat. Then I felt the fur near his neck start to rise, and a low, rumbling growl filled the garage. I let go of him at once, wondering what was wrong.

Max swung his head toward the entrance of the garage.

His growl deepened, and he loped outside. Then my own senses prickled. Something was out there. Something magickal.

My pulse rate picked up. I stood still, trying to get a better sense of the presence. It didn't feel human. Cautiously I stepped outside. Max stood on an icy patch of gravel a short distance from the garage, fur bristling and teeth bared. Then he began to race around the perimeter of the lot, barking furiously.

I cast out my senses and got feelings of stealth, concealment, malevolent power. Cold fear coursed through me, and my breath came fast as I traced the shape of Peorth in the air, the rune for revealing what is hidden. I visualized the rune, tracing it in my mind in bright red light until I felt its shape become a three-dimensional entity. Instinctively I began saying my power chant. *"An di allaigh . . ."*

There was a weird, whooshing noise, as if a whole flock of birds had started up from the ground at once. Something that felt like an ill wind brushed past me, making the tiny hairs on my arms stand up. I gasped. Max raced over to me, barking frantically. I saw nothing, but the air felt lighter, and I knew that the intruder was gone.

Bob walked out of the shop. "What's going on out here?" He frowned at Max, then at me. "What was all that noise about?"

I leaned against the car so he wouldn't see how I was shaking. "I guess Max heard something."

Max sat down in front of Bob and elaborated with short, eloquent barks.

"Okay, boy, okay." Bob was petting him now, comforting him. "We'll lock up good tonight."

We went back inside, and he handed me a written esti-mate for $750. That made me gasp again. "I'll have to special-order you a bumper and hood," he explained. "They don't make parts for this model anymore. I'll have to get them from a used-parts dealer in Pennsylvania. You call me and let me know when you're ready to go ahead."

I thanked him, barely even listening. Before I left I traced the rune Eolh on Max's forehead for protection. What had that mysterious presence been? Was it after me? Was it connected to the dark force I had felt the other night? Was it Cal or Selene?

Though the sun was shining brightly, I felt like a black veil had been pulled across the sky. Shivering, I got into my car and drove back to school.

Mary K. went to Jaycee's house after school, as she often did, so I drove straight home. I was still shaken up from the incident at the garage. I had no idea what it had been, but I didn't want to take any chances. I had felt something evil. If it was after me, I'd better start protecting myself fast.

In the empty house I went upstairs and took my birth mother's athame from its hiding place in the HVAC vent. Then I walked around the outside of my house, running the athame lightly over the clapboard siding. Hunter and Sky had placed runes of protection all around the house about two weeks ago. The athame revealed the magick signs to me, and I breathed a sigh of relief. They were still there and still glowing with potency.

Next I went up to my room and closed the door. I'd been planning to make an altar for some time, but now it seemed doubly urgent. If there really was someone or something after me, I needed to be as strong and sure in my magick as possible.

The problem was, the altar had to be somewhere my family wouldn't notice. Although my parents now seemed to realize that they couldn't prevent me from being a witch, there was no point in setting up an altar where they would see it and get upset.

I looked around my room. It wasn't big. There was no obvious place to set up an altar—certainly none that wouldn't be totally noticeable. I thought a moment and opened the door to my closet. It was a deep walk-in, with a long hanging rod running the length of it. I began taking clothes off the rod, laying shirts, dresses, jackets, and skirts on my bed. "Yuck," I said as a sundress with an enormous tropical flower print surfaced. It was time to give some things away.

When the closet was empty, I stared at the back of it. A small footlocker from when I went to summer camp sat on the floor. It had potential.

I rummaged in my dresser drawer for the length of plum-colored Irish linen that Aunt Eileen had brought back from her trip to Ireland. It covered the trunk perfectly, as if that's exactly what it had been woven for. Voilà. One altar.

Next I opened the junk drawer of my desk. I sorted through the crap until I found a small, perfect, pink-and-white scallop shell. I set it on one corner of the altar to represent water. On another I put a chunk of amethyst that had been among the crystals in Maeve's box of tools. That was for earth. On the remaining corners I set a candle for fire and a stick of incense for air. Of course, I wouldn't actually be able to light the candle or incense inside the closet. For that the altar would have to come out into my room. But I liked having all four elements in place.

I sat before my altar. It was pretty simple, as basic as you can get. Yet it felt right.

Something soft nudged me. Dagda. I ran my hand down his silky little back. "This is where we're going to invoke the Goddess," I explained. He purred as if in approval.

May I work strong, pure magick here, I said silently, spells of healing and wholeness.

And may they keep me safe, I couldn't help adding.

8

Potential

Litha, 1991

Goddess, help us. How can we go on from here? We've lost everything—our home, our coven, our children. Our children.

It all came so suddenly. We'd both been feeling ill and out of sorts for weeks, but I didn't think much of it. Then, late yesterday evening, I was working in my study when I heard Fiona scream. I raced to her workroom and found her lying on the floor, her leug clutched in her hand. She had been scrying to find the source of her illness and had seen something hideous in the stone. She described it as a wave of darkness, like a swarm of black insects or a pall of smoke, sweeping over the land. "It was evil," she whispered. "It wants us. It's . . . searching for us. We've got to warn the others, and then we've got to go. Now. Tonight."

"Tonight? But—the children. Giomanach's got an herbology lesson tomorrow," I objected stupidly.

The look she gave me broke my heart. "We can't take them," she said. "It wouldn't be safe. Not for them or for us. We've got to leave them."

I argued, but in the end she convinced me that she was right. The only hope for any of us was for Fiona and me to disappear, to try somehow to draw the evil away from our children.

Fiona left a frantic message for her brother Beck, who lives in Somerset. Then we laid the strongest protections we could on our house. I kissed my children as they slept, smoothing Alwyn's tangled red curls, pulling the covers back up over Linden. Last of all I stood by Giomanach, watching the rise and fall of his chest. I tucked my lueg under his pillow, where he'd find it in the morning.

And then, once again, I abandoned my children.

—Maghach

I left a note for my mom saying that I'd be back for dinner, then drove over to Hunter's house. As much as being around him upset me, I realized Hunter needed to know about the dark presence I'd sensed at Unser's and the dark magick I had felt on Monday night. He might be able to tell me what it was, where it had come from, how I could protect myself from it effectively.

I started up the narrow path. Even in daylight it was hard to be sure that there was a house tucked away behind all the trees. The porch was even ricketier than it had seemed at night. A post was missing from the railing, and the stairs had a split tread.

I reached the door and hesitated. Should I knock? I suddenly felt reluctant to bring my troubles to this particular door.

I chickened out. I'd turned and started off the porch when I heard the door open behind me. "Morgan," Hunter's voice said.

Caught. I turned to face him and felt myself blush. "I should have called first. Maybe this isn't a good time."

"It's fine," he said. "Come in."

Inside there was no sign of Sky. I settled myself in one of the living room armchairs. The house was as cold as it had been last night, the fire in the little fireplace giving off hardly any warmth at all. I was shivering, growing more uncomfortable by the second. This had been a bad idea.

"So," Hunter said as he sat across from me. "Why are you here?"

To my surprise, I blurted, "I didn't feel anything at our circle last night. I'm the one who always gets swept away, but . . . Everyone else was transported, but I didn't get anything. I don't know if Cirrus is right for me anymore."

"Wicca isn't about getting things," Hunter said.

"I know that," I said defensively. "It's just—it's just that it doesn't usually happen to me." I studied his face, wondering how much to confide in him. "It scared me," I admitted. "Like my powers would be gone forever." A thought occurred to me. "Did you do something to damp down my power during the circle in any way?"

He raised his eyebrows. "If I were trying to control your power, you'd have known it. And it's not something I would do unless it were an extreme emergency."

"Oh." I sank back into the chair.

He crossed a booted foot over his knee. He tapped it a few times. "Perhaps . . . my style doesn't bring out your potential."

He sounded disappointed. In me, I wondered, or in himself? "Everyone else, it worked for them," I said grudgingly. "They really liked how you did things."

His face brightened, making him look more like an ordinary teenager. Extraordinarily handsome, maybe, but less intense. "They did? I'm glad. I haven't been that nervous since . . . well, never mind." He pressed his lips together as if he wanted to make sure he didn't say anything else. He looked almost startled—as if he hadn't meant to say those words aloud.

"You were nervous?" I couldn't help enjoying that. "The mighty Hunter?"

Hunter leaned forward, gazing into the hearth. "Don't you think I know how highly you all thought of Cal? Especially you. I knew no one really wanted me taking over. And a part of me thought: Well, maybe they're right. Maybe I can't lead a circle as well as he did. God knows he's more at ease with people than I'll ever be."

I stared at him, stunned to hear him admit to so much vulnerability. I thought back to times when I'd watched Cal move from one clique at school to another, fitting in wherever he went. It was part of what had made him so good at manipulating people—he could present them with what they wanted to see. And what made it so powerful was that at some level, it was real. Hunter, on the other hand, could only be himself.

He and I had that in common.

A sadness clouded his clear green eyes. "I always thought my father would be there when I took over as a coven leader. It feels strange to take the step without him."

I nodded, aware of another connection we had. "Like my

trying to learn about my birthright without my birth parents. I feel like something is missing."

"Yes," Hunter agreed. "Without Dad, being coven leader is all that more daunting."

"What made you decide to do it, then?" I asked.

He gave me a sudden, lopsided grin, gazing up at me from under a shock of pale hair. "The thought that *you* might try to lead them. I couldn't risk that."

If that was a joke, I didn't find it particularly funny. "Hey, I didn't come here to be insulted."

"Oh, stop." He laughed. "I didn't mean it as an insult. I only meant that you're a bit of a loose cannon because you've got all this power and no training. It's not an incurable condition."

"Glad to know it's not terminal," I muttered.

He looked at me more seriously now. "Morgan, listen to me. You have so much potential—it's very exciting, I know. But you've got to learn how to rein in and focus your power. For your own good as much as anything else. All that power makes you like a beacon. You're a walking target."

Abruptly I remembered the real reason I'd come here. I sat forward in my chair.

"There's something I need to tell you about," I said. I described the dark force I'd felt after my dream and then again at the garage. "I tried to get it to reveal itself by drawing Peorth, but it just sort of evaporated," I said. "Do you have any idea what it was?"

He was frowning. "This is not good. It could have been another witch, cloaking him, or herself. It sounds more like some sort of a *taibhs*, a dark spirit, though."

"The first time, when I sensed it in the middle of the

night, I had the impression that whatever it was, it wasn't aimed at me," I said. "But after what happened at the garage, I'm not so sure. Do you think it's been following me?"

"You would have sensed that, I think." Hunter got to his feet, went to the window, and peered out into the trees that surrounded the house. "But we've got to assume that it wasn't coincidence, either. It was looking for you. And it found you."

"Did Selene send it? Or . . . Cal?" I asked in a low voice, not really wanting to know the answer.

"More likely Selene," Hunter said. "To her your power is an irresistible lure, almost as much as Belwicket's tools are. If she can't coerce you to join her group, she wants to absorb your power. It would increase her own to the point where she'd be practically invincible."

My skin crawled. I thought of David, saying that we had to take Selene's intentions into account as well as her actions. Maybe he was right, but her intentions sounded pretty awful in themselves. "They're really evil, aren't they?" I asked. "Selene and . . . and Cal?"

He took some branches from the box of kindling, snapped them in half, and added them to the fire. "Cal . . . is his mother's creation. I don't know if I'd call him evil." Glancing up, he gave me that quick grin again. "Besides, that's not a nice thing to say about one's own kin, is it?"

I grinned back. Hunter did have a sense of humor, I realized. It was just an offbeat one.

"As for Selene," Hunter went on, getting serious again. "She's ambitious and ruthless. She studied with Clyda Rockpel."

I shook my head, indicating that I didn't know the name.

"Clyda Rockpel was a Welsh Woodbane who was legendarily vicious. She's said to have murdered her own daughter to enhance her power. And it's certainly true that wherever Selene goes, witches tend to disappear or die. Destruction seems to follow in her wake. Yes, I would agree that she is truly evil."

I felt a wave of pity for Cal. With a mother like that, he'd never really had a choice. Or a chance.

As if he'd read my mind, Hunter said in a quiet voice, "Poor Cal." His eyes met mine, and I was startled by the depth of compassion in them.

We stared at each other, and then we were both suspended in a strange, timeless moment. I felt like I was falling into Hunter's gaze, and again I remembered the night when he'd almost kissed me. Of the profound connection I'd felt with him, the lightness I'd experienced when he and I had done *tàth meànma*, the intense sharing of minds I thought of as the Wiccan mind meld.

I wanted to feel Hunter's mouth on mine, his arms around me. I wanted to kiss away that sadness, all that had happened to him before we'd met. To tell him that his father would be proud of him if only he could be here. I could feel him wanting to do the same for me; I could sense his aching to stroke my face until he had wiped away all the tears I'd shed over Cal.

Then I blinked. What was I *thinking*? Here I was, talking to my ex-boyfriend's half brother and fantasizing about making out with him. Was I insane?

"I—I've got to go home," I said.

A faint flush had risen under Hunter's clear, pale skin. "Right," he said, standing up. He cleared his throat. "Wait just a moment. I've got some books for you."

He strode into the hallway and began pulling books off the shelves. "Here," he said, his voice back to its usually proper tone. "An advanced compendium of runic alphabets, Hope Whitelaw's critique of Erland Erlandsson's numerological system, and a guide to the properties of stones, minerals, and metals. Start with these, and when you've finished them, we'll talk about them. Then I'll give you more."

I nodded, not trusting myself to speak. When I took Hunter's books, I was careful to not allow our hands to touch.

Outside, the late afternoon sky was a harsh, glaring white. I drove home in a daze, my mind whirling, barely noticing the cold at all.

9

Almost Normal

It happened again this afternoon. Just the way it did that other night. We were talking—talking about how to protect her, actually—and then, suddenly, I looked at her and it was as if I'd found an entire universe within her eyes. And I wanted so badly just to touch her, to kiss her mouth . . . I can't stop thinking about her. She moves me so strongly, so strangely. I've never felt like this before.

I'm an idiot. She can barely stand me.

—Giomanach

Thursday and Friday, I worked really hard on keeping things normal. I went to school. I talked to my friends. I worked at my mom's office—I'd made a deal with my parents in which they'd front me the money for my car repairs in exchange for my getting all my mom's real estate listings entered into the computer. I cheered when the news came that Aunt Eileen and Paula had closed on their house and that they would start moving in over the weekend. I tried not to think about Cal. Or Hunter. Or the bad news about Practical Magick. Or dark forces that might be out to get me. I made it through the days like other teenage girls.

On Saturday, Robbie picked me up in his red Beetle. By now everyone in the coven had heard about Practical Magick closing, and Robbie had suggested a trip over there to see if there was anything we could do to help. I didn't think there was, but I was glad to go, anyway.

"So, how'd it go last night?" I asked as I buckled my seat belt. I knew that Robbie had gone out with Bree. It was a new direction for their age-old friendship.

Robbie shook his head, gazing through the windshield. "Same as before. We hung out, watched a video. Then we made out, and it was great. Fantastic. But the second I tried to talk about how I felt, she got all squirrelly." He grinned. "But this time I had the sense to shut up and kiss her again before she kicked me out of her house."

I laughed. "Quick thinking."

The fact was, Robbie had been in love with Bree for years. But Bree was gorgeous, while Robbie . . . well, he'd been a pizza face. It had made him afraid to approach her. Then, in trying out my newfound power, I'd made a potion to clear up the acne that for years had obliterated his looks. The potion had worked and kept on working in an almost frightening way. The scars had disappeared completely, and then his poor vision had improved, to the point where he no longer wore the thick glasses that he'd had ever since I'd known him. Without the acne or the glasses, he turned out to be amazingly good-looking and was now considered a major hottie at school.

With his new looks, Robbie had found the courage to go after Bree. But the results so far were uneven. They weren't exactly seeing each other but were definitely more than friends. On Robbie's side, it was love. For Bree . . . it was impossible to tell. Even back when we told each other everything, she'd always been hard to figure out when it came to relationships.

Thinking about Bree, I felt another pang of loss. With all that had happened to me in such a short amount of time, it was painful not to be able to confide in her. But the wounds were still too fresh. Maybe, just maybe, with Cal gone, we could begin to be friends again. I hoped so.

Robbie and I talked about Practical Magick's problems for the rest of the drive. Robbie's brow creased as he hunted for a parking space in front of the store. "There's something I don't get," he said. "I mean, we've got you, David, Alyce, Hunter, and Sky—that's five blood witches. And I assume you'd all like Practical Magick to stay open. Why can't you just all do a spell together so David hits the lottery or something?"

"I'm sure that kind of thing isn't allowed under Wiccan law," I said gloomily. "Otherwise David and Alyce would have done it already."

"That's a drag," Robbie said. He squeezed into a space behind a minivan, and we started for the store.

I nodded, but I couldn't help thinking—there must be some kind of spell to increase wealth. After all, going by the listings I'd seen in my mom's office, Selene Belltower's property must be worth at least a million dollars. And although Cal had told me that Selene's employers had transferred her to Widow's Vale, I never had found out what she supposedly did for a living. I had a feeling her money didn't come through any of the usual channels.

Robbie pushed open the door, and I followed him into the store. I was stunned by Alyce's reception.

"Morgan!" she called. Her eyes were sparkling, her cheeks were pink, and she sounded almost giddy. "Robbie! I'm so glad to see you. I have excellent news!"

"What happened?" I asked.

"It's almost unbelievable. Stuart Afton has forgiven Rosaline's debt!" Alyce said.

"What?" I practically shrieked. "How did that happen?"

"Do rich people really do that?" Robbie asked.

"Apparently this one does," Alyce said, laughing. "Afton called David late last night to say he'd made a sudden windfall on the stock market and he'd decided to pass on some of his good fortune. I suppose it's the Yule spirit."

David stepped out from the little back room. "Have you heard?"

"Alyce was just telling us," I answered. "It's too good to be true."

David gave a faint smile. "It is rather surprising," he said.

"So the deal with the bookstore chain is off?" Robbie asked.

"That's right," David said. "And the upstairs tenants can stay, with their same rent."

"Best of all, Practical Magick stays," Alyce added. "We're throwing a party here tonight to celebrate. I was just going to start making calls to invite all of you, in fact. We want everyone to come—Wiccans, Catholics, Buddhists, atheists, you name it."

This was such great news. Even the idea of dark forces around couldn't keep me from a celebratory mood. "We'll be here," I promised.

"Uh, Morgan." Robbie elbowed me. "Hunter scheduled a circle tonight, remember?"

I'd forgotten, in fact. My stomach did a flip-flop at the thought of seeing Hunter again.

"I already spoke to Hunter. He's going to reschedule," Alyce said. She was practically giggling. "You don't get a gift like this every day, and we must give it a proper welcome. I've already arranged for The Fianna to play. It was the first thing I did when I heard the news." The Fianna was a hot Celtic pop band. Mary K. and I had tried to get tickets to one of their concerts last spring, and they had been totally sold out.

I glanced at David, who was methodically counting Tarot decks. Compared to Alyce's high-energy happiness, he seemed subdued. Then I remembered that this positive out-come came from a loss—the death of David's aunt. Perhaps now that the immediate crisis about the building was over, he had more time actually to feel his grief. Well, as Wicca teaches, everything is cyclical. Life leads to death leads to rebirth.

I wondered what kind of cycle I was in with Hunter. Annoyance leads to dreaming of kissing him to . . . irritation again?

"So what non-Wiccans are going to be at this party?" Mary K. asked as we waited for Das Boot's windshield to defrost. I'd come home that afternoon to find her so down about her breakup with Bakker that I'd talked her into com-ing with me to the Practical Magick party. Mary K. felt pretty much the same way that my parents did about Wicca, so she'd been reluctant—until I mentioned that The Fianna was going to play.

"The Fianna?" she'd gasped. "For real?"

After that she couldn't say no.

I wasn't just being nice by inviting her; I needed her support. I've never been the most comfortable person at a party. And knowing that Hunter would be there made me even more nervous.

I blew on my fingers to warm them up. "I'm not sure who'll be there," I said. "Probably the people who live above the shop. Plus you'll know Robbie and Bree and the other kids from school. They're Wiccans, but they're still people you've known forever."

I glanced at Mary K. She was wearing a short brown wool skirt and a russet-colored sweater. Citrine earrings sparkled against her auburn hair. As usual she looked perfect—neither too casual nor too dressy, just undeniably pretty.

"Well, you look great," she said, sounding uncharacteristically nervous.

On her advice, I had worn a lavender sweater, a long forest green skirt, an amethyst necklace, and brown lace-up boots. Did I really look good? Except when I was making magick, I usually felt depressingly plain. I'm five-foot-six, completely flat chested, with boring, medium-brown hair and what my mother calls "a strong nose." I mean, I'm not revolting or anything, but I'm not pretty.

At least, I was never pretty until Cal. Cal himself was so beautiful, he could have had any girl he wanted—and he chose me. Of course, he had chosen me for awful reasons, but in spite of that I didn't believe he'd totally faked the way he looked at me, touched me, kissed me. It seemed like I'd become beautiful. Now, without him, I felt plain again.

Mary K. fiddled with her seat belt and turned to me. "So . . . what happened with you and Cal? I mean, the real story."

My fingers tightened on the steering wheel. I took a deep breath. Then I finally told her everything that had happened the day of the fire. Everything I hadn't told my parents.

"Oh my God," was all she could say when I was done. "Oh my God, Morgan."

"You know, I owe you an apology for being so judgmental about you and Bakker," I told her. "I guess I expected you to handle the whole situation according to a simple, rational formula: Bakker hurts Mary K.; Mary K. dumps Bakker."

"That's how it should have been." Mary K.'s voice was so quiet, I could barely hear her. "I can't believe I gave him another chance."

"Two weeks ago I couldn't understand that," I said slowly, my thoughts forming my words. "But feelings don't work rationally. I did the same thing. All last week I knew things were wrong with Cal. But I didn't want to believe he could hurt me, even after he used his magick against me."

"He'd done it before?"

"The night before my birthday." The night we almost killed Hunter, I thought. Mary K. didn't need to know that part. I swallowed hard. "Cal—put a binding spell on me. I couldn't move. It was like I was drugged."

"Oh, great. All these things you're telling me really make me want to walk into a room full of witches." Mary K. peered out through her window as I pulled into a parking spot down the block from Practical Magick. "Is it too late to turn around and go home?"

"Yes. It's too late." I smiled and shut off the engine, but Mary K. just sat there, tugging her glove off and then on again. When she spoke, she sounded young and vulnerable.

"I appreciate what you said about me and Bakker. And I know that Wicca and your—your birth mother mean a lot to you. But all this witch stuff—it scares me. Especially when you tell me what's happened to you because of it."

I sighed. Maybe I'd told her too much.

"That's why it's so important to me that you come to this party," I tried to explain. "I want you to meet these people, to see that they're not all weird or scary or evil. I don't want to have to hide what I am. Please, Mary K. If you're really uncomfortable, we won't stay. I promise."

She looked down at her lap. After a moment she nodded.

"Okay," I said, trying to sound cheery. "Let's party."

10

The Party

July 1991

    We are in Bordeaux, staying with Leandre, a Wyndenkell cousin of Fiona's. Fiona is not well. She says it's only a chill she caught during the channel crossing, but I'm afraid it's something more serious. For a week now she's had a fever every night, and none of the usual remedies seem to help it. I'm almost ready to suggest that she go to a doctor of Western medicine.

    I went out today and hunted through the fields until I found a chunk of quartz the size of my fist. It's not as good as obsidian, but I think it will serve. I'm going to scry for our children, our town, our coven. I feel heavy with dread at the thought of what I might see.

    —Maghach

Mary K. wasn't the only one who was nervous. I felt flutters in my stomach as we walked up the block toward the store. It had occurred to me that I was going to have to walk into a room full of people who all probably knew exactly what had happened with me and Cal. I pictured the talk stopping and all eyes turning toward me and Mary K. the minute we opened the door. My pace slowed to a halt.

Mary K. looked at my face. "Want to go home?" she asked shrewdly.

I swallowed. "No. Come on."

As it turned out, our entrance hardly attracted any notice at all. I stood by the glass doors, peeling off my gloves and gathering my courage. The party was already in full swing. Practical Magick was lit with candles and tiny white Christmas lights, and fragrant pine boughs decked the molding. Shelves had been moved into the nonbook half of the store so a platform stage could be set up. A cloth printed with Celtic knots was draped over the counter and covered with platters of food.

Alyce, wearing a long blue velvet dress, was the first to greet us. "Morgan," she said, folding me into a hug. "You look wonderful. I'm so glad you made it. And this is . . . ?"

"My sister, Mary K."

"Welcome," she said, clasping both of Mary K.'s hands in hers. "What a pleasure to meet you." Mary K. smiled; it was impossible not to respond to Alyce's warmth.

Alyce waved us in. "It's crowded already," she warned. "There's a coatrack set up against the back wall, cold drinks by the stockroom door, and hot apple cider on the little table by the Books of Shadows."

"Are The Fianna really playing?" asked Mary K.

"They are. They're in the back room, going over their set list."

"How did you ever get them?" Mary K. was clearly awestruck.

"Connections," Alyce told her. "The lead guitarist is my nephew. Would you like to meet them?"

My sister's eyes widened. "Are you serious?"

"Now's your chance." Alyce slipped an arm through Mary K.'s and led her behind the counter and into the back room.

I surveyed the other guests. It *was* crowded. I spotted the elderly couple from upstairs holding hands and beaming happily. Even from across the room, I could sense their relief. I felt a rush of pleasure, knowing that some problems had quick and happy solutions.

Sharon and Ethan were standing near an aluminum tub filled with ice and canned drinks, their heads bent toward each other. Jenna, wearing a silky slip dress with a cropped cardigan, was chatting animatedly to a guy who'd been in the shop the other day. He was laughing at something she said, and I noticed her ex, Matt, watching them. From the way Jenna cast a subtle glance in Matt's direction, I could tell she enjoyed knowing that Matt was watching her flirt.

Things are getting more and more complicated, I thought. I glanced around, looking for Hunter. I almost missed him because he was kneeling down in deep conversation with a little boy I recognized as the four-year-old son of the other tenant, Lisa Winston. The little boy seemed to be explaining something very important to Hunter, and Hunter was nodding seriously. Then Hunter said something, and the boy laughed with delight. Hunter must have felt my eyes on him because he suddenly glanced my way. I felt my heart catch; was it nerves?

Hunter went back to talking to the boy, and I was wondering if I should go join them when I heard someone say my name behind me.

"Morgan, isn't it?" I turned to see a middle-aged woman with salt-and-pepper hair in a thick French braid. She looked familiar, yet I couldn't place her.

"I'm Riva. I met you once at Selene's. I'm part of Starlocket," she explained. "I heard about what Selene and Cal tried to do to you," she added, staring at me.

"Oh," I said. This was just what I'd been afraid of. I felt like a zoo exhibit and wished desperately that she'd just go away and leave me alone.

"I couldn't believe it," she went on. "I had no idea Selene was mixed up with dark magick. I promise you, if any of us had known, we wouldn't have let her lead us."

"Thanks," I said awkwardly "That's good to know."

She nodded and moved on to talk with another woman I recognized from Starlocket.

The mention of dark magick made me think again of the presence I'd felt at home and at the garage. I had checked to be sure that the protective sigils that Sky and Hunter had left at the house were still there, and it was reassuring that they were. Knowing that I had my altar set up also gave me something approaching peace of mind. Maybe I should find a book on altar magick, I thought. At least it would give me something to do besides standing here like a dork.

As I moved to the book section of the store, I felt a cold draft and turned to see the front door open.

"We're here!" Raven Meltzer announced from the open

doorway. "The party can start now!" She strode into the store, Bree and Sky following her.

Raven took the prize for most outrageous outfit—no surprise there. She hadn't even bothered to wear a coat; she probably didn't want anything to spoil her dramatic entrance. Her black leather bustier showed off both the circle of flames tattooed around her belly button and a generous amount of cleavage. She wore tight black leather hip huggers, heavy-soled biker boots, hematite bracelets on her wrists, silver chains around her throat, and glittery eye shadow that went clear out to her temples. She'd put blue highlights in her dyed black hair. Catching sight of Matt, she gave him a smile and then ran her tongue over her lips in a slow, deliberate way. He flushed heavily.

As Bree shrugged off her heavy coat, Robbie stepped up to take it from her. But he was too late; a guy I knew from English class had already grabbed it, and Bree was thanking him sweetly, touching his arm. She was looking even more glamorous than usual in a slim coppery sheath of a dress.

Sky was as beautiful as Bree and Raven but in a completely different way. She was more subdued, more contained, in a pair of black jeans and a midnight blue camisole that set off her pale complexion and dark eyes. Those eyes never left Raven. She watched her in fascination, with yearning. I had been shocked to discover that Sky had a serious thing for Raven; they were so different. Maybe for Sky that was part of the attraction.

I sighed. Matt wanted Raven but sort of still wanted Jenna, too. Raven wanted to tease Matt and maybe Sky as well. Sky wanted Raven. Robbie wanted Bree, who only wanted boys she didn't have to take seriously. And I still wanted Cal, who had tried to kill me. Except when I wanted Hunter, whom I couldn't stand . . . Suddenly the idea of joining a convent sounded very appealing.

I snorted a laugh. Could witches even join convents? Well, this was one mess that I couldn't blame on Wicca, I realized. Wicca might have brought us together and intensified our feelings, but this little soap opera had high school hormones written all over it. In a weird way, the normalcy of these huge problems felt comforting.

And here I was, back to feeling my normal wallflower self.

Bree caught my eye and gave me a cautious little grin. She knew how uncomfortable I was in social situations. I had always counted on her to get me through them. I smiled back.

To my surprise, she walked over to me. "Hey, Morgan. That skirt looks great on you."

"Mary K. put this outfit together for me," I confessed.

Bree laughed, not meanly. "I figured." We stood side by side for a moment, looking out at the crowd. Then she asked quietly, "Is it hard for you, being here without Cal?"

I glanced at her, startled. I hadn't expected anything that direct. But as I met her gaze, I wanted so badly to reconnect with her.

"Everything feels hard with him gone," I said. My words tumbled out. "I miss him all the time. I feel like such a moron. It's like something out of a tabloid: High School Witch Grieves for Would-be Murderer."

"You're not a moron," she said. "You really cared about him. And—and maybe in some twisted way, he really cared about you, too."

I nodded numbly. I knew that it had been hard for her to say that. She had wanted Cal for herself. And it made me feel less like an idiot to think that he did care for me, even just a little.

Bree hesitated. "You know, I've been thinking about the way he played us."

I froze. Bree was treading on dangerous ground here.

"What I'm saying is . . ." She looked massively uncomfortable, then plunged ahead. "I think Cal deliberately slept with me, knowing it would set us against each other."

I gaped at her. "What?"

"He wanted to isolate you," she explained. "Come on, Morgan. You and I were best friends. We talked about everything. We trusted each other." Bree's voice started to quaver, and I could see her fighting to steady it. "Cal was trying to take you over, to control you completely. It would make sense for him to make sure he was the only one you talked to, the only one you really trusted. If he split us up, you'd be more dependent on him."

In a flash of sickening clarity, I realized she was right. I felt like I'd just been punched in the stomach. Every time I thought I'd faced the worst about Cal, I found more—new and deeper layers of deception on his part, blindness on mine.

"He pitted us against each other. He used us both," Bree said.

I nodded, unable to speak, seeing more layers falling away.

But as I stood there, trying to process it all, it occurred to me that even if Bree was right about Cal, no one had forced her to do the cruel things she'd done to me. Maybe things were mending between us, but they could never go back to what they had once been. We'd never trust each other the way we used to. I felt incredibly sad.

"What happened to David?" Bree said, pulling my attention back to the room.

"What?" I asked.

She nodded toward the counter. David was dipping a carrot stick into some hummus. His left hand was wrapped in a white gauze bandage.

"I don't know," I said. "Let's go find out."

Before I could move, Mary K. emerged from the back room and, to my astonishment, walked up onto the platform and took the mike. "Excuse me. Could I have everyone's attention, please?" she said. When the room was quiet, she announced with a huge grin, "I'm pleased to introduce The Fianna!"

Practical Magick erupted into applause as The Fianna made their way onto the stage. They were four skinny young guys and a wisp of a girl with short red hair. She launched into an a cappella verse in a voice that was positively haunting. It reminded me of Hunter's voice when he sang the chant in our circle, a voice drawn out of the world of our ancestors, a pure, shimmering thread that connected us to the past.

I jumped when I heard Hunter's voice behind me. "I need to talk to you," he said quietly.

Bree gave me a questioning look and then moved to rejoin Sky across the room.

"Not here," Hunter said. Taking my elbow, he led me through the crowded room and out the door.

"It's freezing out here," I complained, crossing my arms over my nonexistent chest. "And I want to hear The Fianna."

"Morbid Irish ballads later," he said. "Believe me, there are plenty more where those came from." He opened the door to Sky's green car. "Get in."

I ducked into the passenger seat, muttering, "Do you always have to order me around?"

He grinned. "It's the cold," he said. "Don't have time for the niceties. Don't want you freezing in that pretty outfit." He shut my door, then climbed into the driver's seat.

Flustered at hearing the word *pretty* come out of his mouth in reference to me, I sat there in silence.

He turned on the heat, then rubbed his hands to warm them up. "I went to that field. Where you thought the first dark presence might have been."

"Wh-what did you find out?" I wasn't sure if I wanted to hear his answer.

He shook his head. "I don't think it was Selene."

"Really?" My heart returned to its normal rhythm. But then it sped up again as I asked, "But then who? What?" Hunter let out a sigh. "That's just it. I'm not entirely sure. There was a dark ritual performed there—you were right about that." He gave me a quick glance. I knew my abilities as a beginning witch still surprised him. "But the traces I found of the ritual suggested to me that whoever performed it was someone who had to work quite hard to conjure power."

"What kind of traces?" I was fascinated in spite of myself.

"Blood, among other things," Hunter said, and I gasped. "One of the ways to summon a dark spirit is with a blood offering. But that isn't something Selene would need to do."

I shut my eyes. "Do you think it was Cal?" I asked in a low voice.

"It could be. But why he'd do work like that without Selene . . . well, it just doesn't add up."

I felt a tiny flicker of hope. Maybe Cal had left Selene.

Maybe he was on his own because he'd come back to be with me. I doused that flame by reminding myself that it had been dark magick that I had felt, which would mean that Cal would still be incredibly dangerous.

I shivered, and it wasn't with cold. "If it's not Cal and Selene, who could it be? Who would perform a dark magick ritual?" I asked. I glanced at the door to Practical Magick, wondering if the wayward witch was inside. Among us. And what he or she would do next.

Hunter didn't respond. He looked straight ahead.

"What?" I demanded, a prickle of foreboding making the hairs on my arms stand up. "What aren't you telling me?" I was so sick of secrets and lies that my voice was louder than I had planned.

Hunter's jaw tightened, then he turned to face me. "You won't like this. I don't, either. But hasn't it occurred to you that Practical Magick was saved just in the nick of time? Don't you find it convenient that Stuart Afton has forgiven this huge debt, out of the blue?"

I stared at him. "Alyce said the guy had a windfall," I explained. "If I suddenly came into lots of money, I'd be generous, too."

Hunter smirked at me. "You, clearly, are not a business-man."

"It's not possible," I snapped. "Are you really suggesting that David and Alyce used some kind of dark magick to get Stuart Afton to cancel the debt?"

"Not necessarily Alyce," Hunter said. "But David, yes—I think it's possible. Did you notice the bandage on his hand?"

"What about it?" I asked, nonplussed.

"Remember the blood I found in the field?"

"Huh?" At first I didn't understand what he was trying to say. But then I got it, and it was so absurd, I let out a sharp laugh. "Oh, please. Are you saying David hurt his hand making a blood offering to a dark spirit? Come on! There are a dozen other ways he could have hurt himself. Did you even ask him about it?"

"Not yet," Hunter admitted.

"I can't believe you're thinking this way," I said. "I mean, we *know* Cal and Selene use dark magick, and we know the magick was done in a place Cal used to go to. Why are you even bringing David into it? Why do you have to be suspicious about *everything*?" I was starting to get worked up again. "Why can't good news just be good news?"

Hunter was silent. The door to Practical Magick opened as a couple entered, and the singer's voice drifted into the night. She was singing a joyful song of coming spring, and I was suddenly impatient to share in that pleasure, not sit out here listening to Hunter's ridiculous theories. I flung open the car door and hurried back inside.

The Fianna played for almost an hour, and practically everyone in the room danced. Mary K. even tugged me out onto the floor for a song. I ignored Hunter as best I could and noticed he left early.

After another hour or so, people began to filter out. Mary K. and I got our coats. As she went to say good night to the band, David joined me at the cider table.

"Did you enjoy yourself?" he asked.

I nodded and gave him a smile. "What happened to your hand?" I asked.

David shrugged. "My knife slipped as I was trimming pine boughs."

Ha, I thought. Wait until I tell Hunter. So much for his suspicions.

Mary K. returned, proudly displaying her autographed Fianna CD. "I can't wait until Jaycee gets a load of this," she declared as we headed for the car.

"So now do you believe that all Wiccans aren't evil and weird?" I asked Mary K.

"I'll say one thing for them," she answered. "They know how to throw a party. I still can't believe I met The Fianna!" She clutched the CD to her chest.

As I kicked Das Boot into gear, she went on. "It's just that . . . well, Wicca isn't my way. And the fact that the Church is against it doesn't help," she added more quietly. Mary K. wasn't as religious as Mom or our aunt Margaret, but she did basically believe in what Catholicism taught. "I have to say I was never totally comfortable in there."

I nodded. I'd already pretty much known that my sister felt like this. But to hear it confirmed so baldly was painful. So that was it, I thought. The essence of my identity, the core of who I was, was the very thing that created an unbridgeable gap between me and my family.

We drove the rest of the way home in silence.

11

Hunted

July 1991

In Milan now. A close escape. It was my scrying, I think, that alerted the evil to our presence in Bordeaux.

First I sought our children and found them, as I had prayed they would be, safe with Beck. Then I asked my quartz to help me see our coven, and I saw. Oh, Goddess.

I saw the utter devastation of our town, the swathe of burnt houses, charred cars, blackened tree trunks whose branches seemed to claw at the sky in their agony. . . . Nothing, it seemed, was spared. Nothing except our house. It stood there, the mellow brick darkened by a pall of ash but otherwise untouched.

Then, from our bedroom, I heard Fiona screaming. I ran in and found her sitting upright in bed, her eyes wild. "It's coming," she cried. "It's found us. We have to go!"

She's calling me. More later.

—Maghach

My dad was in the kitchen when I came down the next morning, wearing his usual winter outfit of khakis, button-down shirt, and knit vest. He was peeling potatoes for dinner, then dropping them into a bowl of ice water. My dad has a thing about preparing far in advance.

"Your cat would like you to feed him," my dad greeted me.

Sure enough, Dagda was sitting on the floor next to his bowl, looking up with a hopeful expression. He wound himself around my ankles, arching his little back against my hand. I bent and picked up the dish.

"How was the party?" my dad asked as I spooned canned food into Dagda's bowl.

"Okay," I replied. Disturbing, I added silently. I went to the fridge and scanned for food.

"Morgan, don't just stand there with the door open," he admonished me.

"Sorry," I said. I grabbed a box of waffles and shut the fridge. As I crossed to the toaster, I noticed the local newspaper on one of the kitchen chairs. It was open to the business section, which my father reads religiously.

"Dad," I said, "have you ever heard of a guy named Stuart Afton?"

"You mean the cement-and-gravel tycoon?" Dad asked.

"He's a tycoon?"

Dad paused. "Maybe not exactly. But he is a big player in the local building supplies industry. I've heard he's kind of ruthless, like a strong-arm guy."

"Hmmm." I had to admit that Afton didn't sound like the kind of person to forgive a debt. No, I told myself, rummaging for syrup, people can surprise you. Maybe Afton is tough on the outside but a softie on the inside. I pushed aside the thought that came after that: that David could also surprise me and that Hunter could be right.

Get your mind off it, I ordered myself. "Where are Mom and Mary K.?" I asked Dad.

"They went to church early to help with the Christmas clothing drive." He wiped his hand on a dish towel. "We're meeting them there for mass."

I brought my waffle over to the table and fiddled with my fork. "Um, I have a lot of studying to do," I said at last. "Is it all right if I skip church?"

Behind his tortoiseshell glasses, Dad's eyes were troubled. "I suppose so," he said after a moment.

"Thanks." I put a big bite of waffle into my mouth so I didn't have to say anything else. Since discovering Wicca, my relationship to Catholicism was changing, like everything else in my life. Though I still found the services beautiful, they didn't speak to me in the way they once had. I was pleased, though, that my parents were at a point where they accepted my ambivalence, despite the worry it caused them.

I spent most of the rest of the day tucked away in my room, studying the books Hunter had lent me. I copied spells and lessons into my Book of Shadows and even, feeling a little silly, made myself a set of rune flash cards. I wasn't going to leave Hunter any room to reprimand me for being lax in my studies.

As if he'd heard me thinking, Hunter called to suggest that I come over Tuesday afternoon for some more lessons. I couldn't think of a legitimate excuse, so I agreed.

That night I had trouble sleeping again. I was troubled by Hunter's suggestion that dark magick had anything to do with Stuart Afton's change of heart regarding Practical Magick. I couldn't believe that David would be involved in anything like that. How would I know for sure? It wasn't as if I could just go up to him and ask him.

I could scry, I realized. Maybe I'd find the proof I needed for Hunter to back off on this crazy idea. I hated that he could make me suspicious of my friends.

I peered out into the hallway. The light in my parents' room was out and so was Mary K.'s. Quietly I took the candle from the altar in my closet, set it on my desk, and lit it.

I stared into the flame, burning bright yellow with streaks of orange and blue. It seemed so insignificant. One breath could annihilate it. When I'd scryed before, I'd done it with a full, blazing fire, but in theory there was no reason why a candle shouldn't work just as well. Fire was fire, wasn't it? And right now the thought of any fire greater than this one made me shudder.

I closed my eyes and began to clear my mind. Breathe in, breathe out. In, out. I was aware of my pulse slowing, my muscles relaxing, the tiny fibers smoothing themselves into shining ribbons.

Fire, help me to see the truth. I am ready to see what you know, I thought, and opened my eyes.

The small flame of the candle had blazed up into a molten, white-hot teardrop. From its brilliant center, a face gazed back at me: a familiar nose and mouth, smooth skin, dark, thick hair, and golden eyes. That isn't David, I thought stupidly.

I stared, frozen, as Cal's image floated before me. His lips moved, and then I heard his voice.

"Morgan, I'm sorry. I love you. I'll love you forever. We're soul mates."

"No," I breathed, feeling my heart implode. It wasn't true. We weren't destined to be together. I knew that now.

"Morgan, forgive me. I love you. Please, Morgan . . ."

The last word was a whisper, and I struck out blindly with my hand and brought it down on the candle flame. There was a hiss and a faint, charring smell. And I was alone in the darkness.

12

Ugly

July 1991

I thought Fiona was delirious from the fever, but her terror was so intense that I ended up bundling her up and putting her into Leandre's car. I chose a direction at random: east. We had driven for less than an hour when Fiona let out a cry. "Leandre!" She grasped my arm. "I can _feel_ him. He's dying."

I pulled up at the first little village bistro I could find and rushed in to phone Leandre, but I couldn't get through. Not until late that night did we find out that his farm had been consumed by a mysterious wildfire. He and all his family had been trapped in their house.

"It was the dark wave," Fiona whispered, shuddering. "It's hunting for us."

Without discussing it, we got back into the car and continued east, fleeing across France. As I drove through the clear *summer night. I kept remembering something Selene had said shortly before I left her the first time. She'd come back from a meeting with her Woodbane friends, the ones I feared, and once again she'd been in an oddly frenetic state, as if she had so much energy within her that she must keep moving or catch fire. I asked her what they'd done. "Watched the wave," she said with a strange, sharp laugh. Of course, I thought she meant <u>waves</u>: we lived on the Pacific Coast. But now, as I drove, I wondered if she'd meant something else altogether.*

Did Selene have something to do with sending the dark wave? Is she taking her revenge at last?

—Maghach

I don't know how long I sat there, shaking, too shocked even to cry. Goddess, help me, I thought desperately.

Cal. Oh, Cal. Tears began to rain down my cheeks, scalding and salty. I wrapped my arms around myself and rocked back and forth, keening quietly, trying to smother the sound. My palm throbbed where I'd crushed the candle flame, and as I sat there, the pain seemed to spread until my whole body was one pulsing, raw wound.

After a while Dagda mewed and tapped me tentatively with one paw. I looked at him numbly.

At some point my brain began to work again. How had that happened? How had Cal gotten into my vision? Was it his dark magick? Or had I summoned him somehow—had my own subconscious betrayed me?

He'd said he still loved me. He'd said he'd love me forever. Wasn't that truth I'd heard in his voice?

I gasped and squeezed my head between my hands. "Stop it. Stop it!" I muttered.

I sat there for another few minutes. Then I forced myself to climb into bed. Dagda sprang up and curled himself into a ball on my stomach. I lay there, staring blindly at the ceiling as tears ran down the sides of my face to soak my pillow.

I went through school the next day like an automaton. The burn on my palm had swelled into a shiny blister that burst halfway through the day. It hurt to write, so I just sat in class, not bothering to take notes. Not that my notes would have been much good, anyway. For all I got, my teachers might as well have been speaking Swahili. All I could think was: Cal. He had spoken to me.

What did it mean? Did he still hope to convince me to join him and Selene? Or was this some cruel plan to make me go crazy? If that was it, it was working. I'd never experienced such a horrible mixture of longing and revulsion. I felt like I was going to split apart.

When I got home from school, I had a message from Bob Unser, saying that Das Boot's parts had come in and asking me to drop off the car tomorrow morning. I could pick it up again on Wednesday morning, he said. Perfect, I thought. I couldn't possibly go to Hunter's on Tuesday since I wouldn't have transportation. I knew I was being incredibly stupid, not telling him about seeing Cal, but I just couldn't do it. I couldn't share it, especially with him. Not yet, anyway.

I shot off an e-mail to Hunter, saying I had to cancel tomorrow because I would be vehicularly challenged. I also told him what David had told me about how he hurt his hand.

Then I sat at the kitchen table, drumming my fingers on the Formica surface. I had to do something to distract myself. I knew Aunt Eileen and Paula were moving in all week; some manual labor would be just what the doctor ordered. So I set off for Taunton.

Taunton was a smaller town than either Widow's Vale or Red Kill. Both Widow's Vale and Red Kill had had their town centers "revitalized," but Taunton was more mainstream America. There were the usual strip malls with the predictable fast-food joints, auto supply places, megastores, and video and drugstore chains.

Eileen and Paula's neighborhood was older. Although each house was different, they fit together harmoniously. Huge old trees shaded the lawns and arched out over the center of the street. The neighborhood had a nice, settled feel to it.

Paula and Eileen's house was at the very end of the street. I wanted to surprise them, so I parked at the other end of the block. I started walking.

As I got closer to the end of the block, I saw three teenage boys standing in front of one of the houses. Two of them wore parkas with shiny reflective tape on the seams. The third wore a loose camouflage jacket over camouflage pants. At first I thought they were having a snowball fight with some other kids I couldn't see; then I realized that they were throwing *rocks* at Paula and Eileen's house. My mouth dropped open, and I froze in my tracks.

"Queer!" one of them shouted.

"We don't need dykes in this neighborhood!" called another.

In one instant I got it, and then I was running hard toward

the house, anger coursing through my veins like alcohol.

"Come on out, bitch!" one of the boys yelled. "Meet your neighbors! We're the welcome wagon!"

I heard the sound of glass shattering as at least one of the rocks connected. The boy closest to me looked up, his alarm quickly replaced by naked aggression.

"What the hell are you doing?" I demanded, breathing hard. "Get out of here, and don't come back!"

The boy couldn't be older than me, I saw. He had a shaved head, a nose that was nearly flat, and pale blue eyes. "Who are you?" He sounded amused. "One of their dyke friends? You don't know what you're missing, baby."

"Get. Out. Of. Here," I said, my voice vibrating with only marginally controlled fury. I felt on fire with rage.

The guy with the shaved head advanced on me, and his two friends closed in behind him. "Or what?" he said nastily. "You'll hit me with your purse?" He turned around to his friends, and the three of them laughed. My hands were trembling, clenched into fists, and I felt almost ill.

"Leave," I said, eerily calm. My voice didn't sound like my own. "Don't make me hurt you."

He burst into laughter. "Baby, maybe what you need is a man. Like those other dykes." He opened his arms wide. "Let me show you how it's supposed to be."

One of his friends laughed.

"You don't know what you're doing," I almost whispered.

Grinning, Flat Nose reached out to grab my arm, but before he touched me, I shot out my hand and sent a burning, crackling ball of blue witch fire at his throat. I didn't even think about it—I just unleashed my fury. The fire hit him so quickly, he had no time to react. His hands went to his throat, and he dropped to his knees. He doubled over, making little whimpering sounds of pain.

I felt encased in ice, completely calm, ready to annihilate them all. I began to call on my power. *"An di allaigh, re nith la,"* I murmured.

The two friends were staring at Flat Nose and then back at me as they tried to figure out what happened. Flat Nose was gagging and retching on the cold sidewalk. He glared up at me and tried to climb to his feet. I pushed the air and he sank, crumpled, to the cement. I used my power to pin him like a bug without even touching him. Adrenaline coursed through my veins, and I felt unbelievably powerful.

"Shit," said the second guy. He and the third guy stared fearfully at each other. Then they turned and pounded down the street, looking back over their shoulders.

I leaned over the worm who lay writhing and frightened on the sidewalk. He was getting just what he deserved, I gloated with satisfaction. I felt filled with power, and I liked it.

I took a deep breath and stepped back, smelling the acrid scent of his fear. "Go," I whispered, and released him with my mind.

Clumsily he scrambled to his feet and backed away from me. Then he spun around and ran off. It was over, and I had won.

I felt dizzy, a little nauseous, the way I sometimes felt in circles when power rushed through me. I took a few moments to ground myself, then I looked up at the house.

The bay window was smashed, as well as another one on the first floor. Where were Eileen and Paula? I wondered. Were they hurt? Or had they seen what I'd done?

Wondering how I would explain it, I walked up to the door and rang the bell. Winter-bare rosebushes in front of the house were sparkling with shards of glass.

No one answered. I cast my senses and felt both Eileen's and Paula's familiar energy inside the house. They were okay. They were just afraid to answer the door, and I felt angry all over again. Prisoners in their own house. It was disgusting!

"Aunt Eileen, it's me, Morgan!" I called through the broken window.

"Morgan?" A minute later the door opened, and my aunt swept me into her arms. "Are you okay? There were these idiot boys outside—"

She hadn't seen me. Relief.

"I saw them," I told her.

Paula gave me a hug, too. "Welcome to the neighborhood," she said shakily.

We all stepped in, and Aunt Eileen shut the front door, locking the dead bolt. She crossed her arms over her chest, rubbing her own shoulders as if for comfort. "I'm glad they left before you got here," she said. "But I'm sorry they didn't stick around long enough for the police to show up. I just called them."

"We probably shouldn't clean up the glass until the police have seen it." Paula ran a hand through her sandy blond hair. "I guess we're an official crime scene now."

I felt so sorry for them—and so furious at those small-minded idiots.

"It's just glass," Aunt Eileen said, putting an arm around her. "We can have new glass put in." She looked at me. "I'm sorry, Morgan. This isn't a good welcome for you. Come in, take off your coat, and we'll give you the grand tour of broken glass and packed boxes."

We walked through the empty rooms, and Paula and Aunt Eileen explained their plans for decorating and renovating to me. They were both doing their best to sound excited, but I could sense their tension. The thugs had shaken them badly.

When the doorbell rang, we all jumped. My senses told me it was safe, though, and when Aunt Eileen opened the door, we saw two cops. Officer Jordan was a tall man and black. His partner was a younger woman with short, curly blond hair, whose badge said Officer Klein. I stood by as Aunt Eileen and Paula gave their report and showed them the damage.

"Did you get a good look at these boys?" Officer Jordan asked.

"We know there were three of them," Aunt Eileen told him. "But we stayed in the house."

"I saw them as I came up," I said. "They were about my age, juniors or seniors in high school. One of them was wearing camouflage. Another was bald with a flat, broken nose and blue eyes."

Paula looked at me in surprise. "How did you get such a good look at them?"

"They, um, they ran right past me," I explained. "Another guy was little, maybe five-five, with a brown crew cut. The third guy had blond hair, slicked back, and thick lips."

Officer Jordan took notes on all of that, then looked at my aunt. "It looks like you people just moved in. Any idea of why these kids went after you?"

"Because we're gay," Aunt Eileen said matter-of-factly. "They called us dykes."

I noticed Officer Klein's lips tighten. "Some people are just ignorant," she muttered.

"I hope you catch them," Paula said. "Before they actually hurt someone."

The police left, and I helped Aunt Eileen and Paula clean up the shattered glass and seal off the broken windows with cardboard and tape.

"God, that's ugly," Paula said, looking at our handiwork.

"It's temporary," Aunt Eileen assured her. "I'll call a glass company tomorrow."

I glanced at my watch. "Oh, wow, I'd better get home. It's after six."

Aunt Eileen and Paula both hugged me and told me to come back anytime.

As I walked down the front steps, I turned back to wave and saw the two of them hugging each other tightly. Paula's face was buried in Aunt Eileen's shoulder. I could feel their tension from where I stood. And I knew what they were worried about. I'd had the same thought.

This wasn't over. Those kids would talk themselves out of their fear at what I'd done. And then they'd be back.

13

Protection

Litha, 1993

We're in Prague now, but Fiona feels we'll have to leave again soon. A dubious legacy of the dark wave—ever since she saw it in her lueg, she can sense it coming.

It's been two years now since we left our lives behind us. Two years of running, hiding, locking our magick away to keep it from betraying us. Two years of longing for news of our children, yet not daring to reach out to them. Two years of Fiona gradually withering, racked by ailment after ailment. We've come to believe it's the effect of the dark wave itself—that it crippled her somehow when she saw it in her lueg. So far we've found no cure.

—Maghach

That night I blew off my homework. I went through every magick book I had, looking for something that would help me protect Aunt Eileen and Paula. I could put runes of protection around their house, I reasoned. That would be a start, at least.

Too bad I couldn't get them to wear talismans for personal safety. Somehow I couldn't picture either of them wearing Wicca paraphernalia, no matter how open-minded they might be.

"Ew," I said as I found the instructions for making an old protection called a Witch's Bottle. The Witch's Bottle was not only supposed to shield you from evil but also to send the evil back to its source. It called for filling a small glass bottle halfway to the top with sharp objects: old nails, pins, razor blades, needles, and so on. Then you filled the bottle the rest of the way with urine and, ideally, some blood, too. Then you sealed the jar and buried it twelve inches deep. The bottle and its protection was supposed to last until the bottle was dug up and smashed.

I put down the book, completely grossed out. Did I have the stomach to be a witch? This was disgusting. But if it would really protect Eileen and Paula . . . I read it through again. No, it wouldn't work. The Witch's Bottle was to protect against negative *magick*. The guys who'd attacked Aunt Eileen and Paula's house were negative, all right, but they weren't using magick.

I finally settled on a protection charm that I could place in their house without their noticing. It called for ingredients that I didn't have, and I decided to make a trip to Practical Magick as soon as I had my car back.

Robbie followed me and Mary K. out to Unser's on

Tuesday morning, then drove us to school. My plan was to go to my mom's office after school and spend some time inputting listings, then get a ride home with her. Mary K. was going to Jaycee's house. Jaycee's mom would drop her at our house in time for dinner.

After school I set out alone on the long walk to Mom's office, shivering and hoping someone I knew would drive by and offer me a ride.

Be careful what you wish for. A familiar pale green Ford pulled up at the curb, and the passenger window rolled down. Sky Eventide leaned over from the driver's seat, her white-blond hair luminous. "Hop in," she said.

"Were you out looking for me?" I asked, perplexed. "Or is this just a coincidence?"

Sky raised an eyebrow. "Haven't you yet learned that there are no coincidences?"

I stood on the sidewalk, staring stupidly at her. Was she joking or not? I wasn't sure. Just like Hunter, Sky wasn't easy to read.

Seeing my confusion, she said, "Hunter asked me to come pick you up. I even left work early. You're supposed to come to our house for lessons."

I had heard that Sky worked at a used-record store. She was so ethereal, it was hard to picture her doing mundane things like working a cash register. "But I already told Hunter I couldn't come," I protested. "And my mom's expecting me."

Sky tapped a gloved finger on the steering wheel impatiently. "Call her from our place. This is important, Morgan."

She was right, I realized, though not for the reasons she thought. I couldn't keep putting off talking to Hunter. Biting my lip, I opened the passenger door and climbed in.

My stomach felt fluttery. I still didn't feel ready to talk about seeing Cal, but I knew I had to face it sooner or later. And sooner was probably safer.

Sky pulled out into traffic and accelerated. She drove fast and tended to stomp on the brakes harder than she needed to at red lights. "Sorry," she said as I jerked forward against my seat belt. "I'm not used to all this power-assisted driving."

I glanced at her as she made a right turn. Her profile was pure, almost childlike, with its perfect nose and arched brows, the smooth curve of cheek covered with the finest, faintest golden down. She and Hunter looked very much alike, but while Sky seemed deceptively fragile, Hunter's face had a masculine angularity that projected strength.

"Why is Hunter doing this?" I found myself asking. "Why is he so concerned about making sure that I become a proper witch?"

Sky smiled slightly. "Wicca isn't something you can learn in a correspondence course or figure out on your own. It's experiential. You need someone who's gone through it before you as a guide. Otherwise bad things can happen. Especially with the kind of power that you've inherited."

"That's not what I was asking," I said. "Why Hunter? Doesn't he have more important things to do than worry about me?"

"He's a Seeker," Sky replied. "It's his job to make sure witches don't misuse their magick. And—" She broke off. Then, after a moment's hesitation, she added, "And you're Woodbane."

I bristled. "So he's waiting for me to turn bad?"

"You might," Sky said bluntly. "He can't ignore the possibility."

I folded my arms and pressed my back against the cushioned seat. So Hunter was acting as my watchdog, making sure I stayed on the path of righteousness. I was his assignment, just as I had been Cal's assignment.

I remembered how much I had hated both Sky and Hunter when I'd first met them. With Sky it was mostly from jealousy—her beauty and poise were intimidating to me. But, I realized now, it was also that I'd sensed their suspicion. I could feel that Sky still didn't truly trust me; even though we'd scryed together, she continued to scrutinize me. Apparently Hunter was doing the same thing. The thought sent a sharp pain through me.

Hunter looked up when I walked in with Sky. "Thanks," he said to her.

"Ta," Sky said. She tossed her leather jacket on the sofa, then pointed to the phone. "Feel free," she said, then disappeared up the stairs.

"How long can you stay?" Hunter asked me. "We've got a lot to talk about."

"I'm not staying," I said. "Sorry Sky went to all that trouble, but I have work to do." I crossed to his phone. "If you won't drive me, I'll call a taxi."

Hunter rubbed a hand across his chin. "What is the matter with you?" he asked mildly.

"I don't appreciate you sending your cousin to practically kidnap me off the street," I snapped. "I told you I didn't have a ride, so I couldn't make it."

"I'm sorry." To my astonishment, he actually sounded abashed. "I—well, I thought I was doing you a favor."

"No, you didn't," I retorted. "You just wanted me to stick to your plan. What gives you the right to just waltz in out of nowhere and take charge? You think just because the International Council of Witches told you to keep an eye on me that gives you the right to run my life?"

"They—" Hunter began, but I cut him off.

"You know what? I'm really sick of being somebody's assignment." Tears filled my eyes. I blinked furiously, trying to keep them from falling. "No one seems to care about who I really am, or what I want! What about *me* in all of this?"

"Morgan—" Hunter began, but I cut him off again.

"No!" I cried. "Don't! It's my turn." My fingers curled into fists, and I felt pressure build in my chest. "You're so self-righteous about your mission and the council and all that crap, but really you want exactly the same thing as Cal and Selene did—to control me. To use me for your own purposes." To my humiliation, my voice broke. I turned my back on Hunter and stood there, biting down hard on my lower lip as I struggled to hold myself together.

He didn't say anything at first, and silence stretched between us. At last he spoke in a curiously subdued voice.

"You're not my assignment. The council didn't tell me to keep an eye on you, actually," he said.

I fought to regain my normal pattern of breathing so that I would be able to understand what he was telling me. I wanted so much to understand, to be wrong.

I heard Hunter take a deep breath, too. "I'm here of my own choice, Morgan. I did contact them about you, that's true. I told them you were a witch of exceptional power and that I wanted to see if I could help guide you. They said I could do that as long as it didn't interfere with my primary work as a Seeker—which is to track down Cal and Selene and others like them."

He paused, and I heard him take a step toward me. Then I felt a featherlight touch on my shoulder. "I don't want to control you, Morgan," he said. "That's the last thing I want."

His hand left my shoulder, his fingers lightly stroking my long hair. He was just inches behind me; I could feel the warmth of his body, and I held my breath.

"What I'm trying to do," he went on softly, "in my own clumsy way, is to give you the tools you need to understand the forces that you will inevitably come up against."

I turned to face him, searching his eyes, wondering what it was that he wanted, what I wanted. His eyes are so green, I found myself thinking, so gentle. I could feel his breath on my cheek, warm everywhere except on the wet trail of tears.

"I just want . . . ," he whispered, and trailed off.

We stood there, our gazes locked, and it seemed to me that once again the universe suspended its motion around us and the only warm, living things in it were the two of us.

Then Sky's voice called down from upstairs, "Hunter, did you remember to get cheese and biscuits?" and suddenly everything started moving again, and I stepped backward until the backs of my knees hit the worn ottoman and I sat down. I was trembling, and I found I couldn't look at Hunter.

"Um—yes, I got them," Hunter replied, his voice raspy and a little breathless.

"Right, then. I'm going to make a cheese-and-tomato omelette. I'm starved." I heard Sky's boots clattering down the stairs. "Want some?"

"Sounds great," Hunter said. "Morgan, how about you?"

"Um—no thanks, my family will be expecting me for dinner at six-thirty," I said shakily. "In fact, I'd better give my mom a call right now and let her know where I am."

"Tell her I'll run you home by six," he said. Then he added, "If that's all right with you, I mean. If you want to stay."

"It's all right," I told him. I didn't feel ready to leave.

By the time I hung up, I felt more normal. Hunter led me to the back of the house, where the wood-burning stove filled the long room with warmth. The windows were fogged with condensation, but I rubbed one with my sweater and looked outside. Another rickety porch lined the back of the house, and beyond it I could see trees growing from the sides of the ravine: oak, maple, birch, hemlock, and pine. The woods around Widow's Vale tended to have a well-trod, gentle feel to them. But the land behind Hunter and Sky's house felt raw, wild, as though floodwaters had just swept through and carved out something new and highly charged.

"It feels different here," I said.

"It is. It's a place of power." Hunter lit the candle and incense stick on the altar. He gestured to the floor where we'd held the circle. A worn Oriental carpet now covered the center of the floor. "Have a seat."

I settled myself on the carpet.

He didn't sit. "There's something we need to discuss," he said.

"What?" I asked, feeling wary again.

"I did some checking on David's story, yesterday and today. That's why I couldn't come pick you up myself." Hunter paced toward the woodstove, then swung around to face me. "First of all, he lied about how he hurt his hand. I asked Alyce, and she told me he'd come in with it bandaged up two days *before* the party. He didn't do it trimming boughs for the party."

My heart lurched. David had lied to me?

Wait. I thought back. Not so fast. He never said he cut his hand trimming boughs *for the party*. He could have been trimming some other boughs. Couldn't he?

"Second, Stuart Afton didn't make any money on stocks last week," Hunter said.

I frowned. "I'm not following you."

Hunter made an impatient gesture with his hand. "David said Afton forgave his debt because he'd made a killing on the stock market last week," he reminded me. "But I checked, and it never happened."

"You checked? How?"

"If you must know," Hunter said, looking uncharacteristically self-conscious, "I chatted up his secretary. No man has secrets from his secretary. She knew nothing about any sudden windfall."

"And why is this your business?"

"Because I'm a Seeker," Hunter said. "It's my job to investigate misuses of magick."

"This doesn't have anything to do with magick," I said, standing up. "Maybe there was a stock split and Afton's secretary was at lunch when the call came in. Maybe he got the news by e-mail. Maybe there was no stock split but Afton forgave the debt anyway, out of the simple goodness of his heart. This isn't council business, Hunter."

"Open your eyes, " Hunter said flatly. "There's magick involved here. Dark magick. We both know that."

I realized I had no choice. I had to tell him about seeing Cal.

I took a deep breath. "There's something I have to tell you."

I explained how I'd scryed for the truth two nights ago

and how instead of seeing David, Cal had appeared. I didn't speak about the feelings seeing Cal's face had induced, nor did Hunter ask. But two white creases appeared on the outsides of his nostrils.

"The way I see it, this is the strongest proof we've had yet that Cal is behind the dark magick we've detected," I said. "It isn't David at all."

I could see Hunter weighing this new information. "You say you asked to see the truth?" he asked after a moment. "Were those the words you used? Did you mention David's name?"

"No," I answered, puzzled. "Why?"

"You weren't very specific. And fire can be a capricious scrying tool," Hunter replied.

"Are you trying to tell me the fire lied to me?" I asked. I was starting to get angry again.

"No," Hunter said. "Fire doesn't lie. But it reveals the truths *it* wants to reveal, especially if you're not specific with your questions."

I put my head in my hands, feeling suddenly weary. "I don't get it, Hunter," I said. "I keep giving you clues that point clearly to Cal and Selene, the witches you came here to investigate—the witches you're still trying to track down. I don't want it to be them—I don't want to even think about them. But it makes total sense that they're the ones whose presence I felt. Why do you keep trying to make this about David and Practical Magick?"

Hunter was silent for a moment. At last he said, "It's a feeling I have. I've got an instinct for darkness. It's what makes me so good at my job." The words weren't a boast. His voice was quiet. For the first time I began to really wonder. Was it possible that he was right?

"Enough of this," he said with a sigh. "We're not getting anywhere, and it's nearly six. I'd better run you home."

We walked out to his car without talking. I noticed with a shock that it was the same gray rental sedan he'd had the week before. Selene had hidden it in an abandoned barn when she thought Cal and I had killed Hunter.

"I tracked it down," Hunter remarked, eerily echoing what was on my mind. We climbed into the car, and he drove me home in silence, each lost in our own thoughts. He pulled into my driveway. Then, as I reached for the door handle, he put his hand on mine. "Morgan."

A jolt of sensation ran up my arm, and I turned to face him.

"Please think about what we discussed, about David. I'm almost certain Stuart Afton didn't forgive that debt out of kindness."

"I just don't believe David would mess with dark magick," I said. As he began to reply, I cut him off. "I know, I know, you have a special sense for evil. But you're wrong this time. You have to be."

I climbed out and hurried up the walk to my house, hoping I was right.

14

Old Wounds

Beltane, 1996

We are in Vienna, where I have found work tutoring college students in English. Evenings, Fiona and I walk along the Danube or in the Stefansplatz. She has gained some much needed weight and is looking better. The other night we even went on the Ferris wheel in the Volksprater. But the amusement park made us think of the children. Have Beck and Shelagh ever taken them to such a place?

Giomanach is now thirteen, Linden almost twelve, and Alwyn, nine. I wonder what they look like.

—Maghach

At dinner Mom reported that so far there had been no new incidents at Aunt Eileen and Paula's house. "They're hoping that those creeps saw the police show up at the house and have backed off."

"I hope so," I said. I reminded myself to get to Practical Magick for those ingredients soon.

Mom dished out some goulash and handed me the plate. "Will you be able to finish inputting our real estate listings this week?" she asked.

"I'm getting Das Boot back tomorrow afternoon," I said. "So I can stop by your office around three-thirty, after I drop Mary K. at home."

"I forgot to tell you. I'm not coming straight home tomorrow after school," said Mary K. "I'm going shopping with Olivia and Darcy."

Shopping. I wasn't ordinarily a big fan of shopping, but suddenly I felt a sharp pang of envy. How long had it been since I'd gone shopping with my friends or just hung out after school, doing nothing in particular?

Since you and Bree stopped being friends, I answered myself.

After dinner I went upstairs and tried to do my math homework, but my brain was too overloaded with thoughts of Hunter, Cal, David. I sighed. With its connection to the harmony of nature, Wicca was about balance, something I sorely needed. I had to bring balance back into my life, and the only way I could think of doing that was with a healthy dose of non-Wicca normalcy.

Surprising myself, I opened my door and padded out into the hall, where I picked up the phone. I took it back into my room and perched cross-legged on my bed.

My heart pounded as I dialed Bree's number. It had been so long since I'd done this. Would she want to talk to me?

Bree picked up on the third ring. "Hi, it's Morgan," I said quickly, before my nerve failed me.

"Hi." She sounded uneasy. "What's up?"

"Um—" I hadn't thought this through. "Not a whole lot. I just . . . you know, wanted to say hi. Catch up."

"Oh. Well, hi," she said.

Then we had one of those long, awkward silences, and I wondered if maybe it was crazy of me to have called her. Maybe she didn't want to be friends with me anymore. Maybe there was just too much water under the bridge.

I was about to mumble that I had to go when she spoke. "Morgan." She hesitated. "Some of things I did to you—I know they really hurt. I can't undo them. But I'm really sorry. I was a complete bitch."

"I—I was, too," I admitted.

Another silence. Clearly neither one of us wanted to go into the details. It was still too raw to bring all that up again.

"So," she said, "what's been happening in your life? Robbie told me—well, he told me about your being adopted. About being a blood witch."

"He did?" I tried to decide how I felt about Bree and Robbie discussing my personal life.

"Yeah. I've been wanting to talk to you about it. If you want to," she said.

"I've been wanting to talk to you about it, too," I confessed. "But when we're face-to-face. Not on the phone."

"Okay," she said. "I'd like that."

"Meanwhile Hunter's got me in a Wicca study intensive," I told her. "You know, he's taken over the leadership of Cirrus now that . . ." I trailed off. Now that Cal's gone, I thought. Quickly changing the subject, I asked, "How's Kithic? How is it having Sky lead a coven?"

"Challenging," Bree said in a thoughtful tone. "We've been doing visualization exercises. At our last circle we were outside under the moon, and Sky told us to visualize a pentagram. At first everyone was distracted by the cold and the noise of cars going by. Finally, though, we got it together. We all closed our eyes, visualizing away, and there was this moment of absolute silence, then Sky told us to open our eyes, and there was this perfect pentagram, etched in the snow. It was amazing."

"Cool," I said enviously. It sounded like her coven was really growing. I leaned back against my pillows.

Bree's voice went conspiratorial. "Sky and Raven are flirting, I think. Isn't that wild?"

"Very wild." It was so easy to fall back into gossiping with Bree again. "I never figured Raven would turn out to be gay."

"I don't think she really is. I think she just really likes Sky. It's an attraction of opposites," Bree said with a laugh. There was another pause, but this time it didn't feel awkward. It was just—natural.

"Speaking of attractions," I ventured, "how's your love life?"

"Robbie." I heard a guarded note in her voice.

"Yeah," I said, hoping I hadn't shattered our new, fragile bond.

But Bree just sighed. "Well, it's—it's kind of weird," she said slowly. "I don't know . . . we've been buddies forever, and now all of a sudden we're making out. I guess I'm just sort of taking it as it comes and seeing what happens." She gave a little laugh. "I have to say, though, we really click physically. It's very hot."

"Wow." I felt voyeuristic but also fascinated. It was strange to hear these two people I'd known since childhood talk about each other in these new, romantic terms.

"Listen, I've got to go," Bree said. "I've got a history paper due tomorrow, and I'm still on page one."

"You'll crank it out," I told her. "You always do."

"Yeah, I do, don't I," she replied. "I'll talk to you later, okay? And—Morgan?"

"What?"

"Thanks for calling," she said softly. "I know it couldn't have been easy to do."

"You're welcome," I said.

We hung up, and I replaced the phone on the hall table. I was smiling as I went back into my room, feeling happier than I had for days.

15

Threads

Imbolc, 1997

Imbolc is a day for light. Fiona reminds me that Imbolc means "in the belly," in the womb of the Goddess, and celebrates the seeds hidden in the earth that are just beginning to stir. Even though it's dark and cold here in Helsinki, it's a day of hope, and we must light the sacred fire.

In England, among the covens, there are great bonfires. Here we lit candles throughout our small rented house. Then the two of us did a quiet ceremony as we fed kindling into our woodstove.

The cold is hard on Fiona. She is always shivering and in pain. We can't live this far north for long. Where next, I wonder?

—Maghach

After my conversation with Bree the night before, I felt so much better able to face the next day. I knew she and I still had many, many fences to mend, but for the first time it actually seemed possible.

"You're in a good mood," Mary K. commented as we were getting ready for school. "Is that because you were talking to Hunter on the phone last night?" she added, wiggling her eyebrows at me.

She shrieked as I threw a damp dish towel at her.

"It wasn't Hunter. If you must know," I said, grabbing my backpack, "I was talking to Bree."

Mary K. beamed at me. "That's great!" She knew how much my friendship with Bree meant to me. "Maybe now things will get back to normal around here."

Robbie honked outside. He was giving us another lift to school. I'd pick up Das Boot later, and then things really *would* get back to normal!

Just as I was slipping into my coat, the phone rang. My witch senses tingled. What could Hunter want so early in the day? I picked up the phone. "Hi, Hunter."

"Good morning."

"I can't really talk," I told him. "I'm on my way to school, and Robbie and Mary K. are waiting for me."

"I'll make this quick," he said. "I just—I feel I need to prepare you. I know you're being loyal to David, and that's good. But I don't want you to be blind to dark forces just because you like him."

"I'm not," I said, stung. "Don't you think, after what Cal did to me, that I've learned my lesson? It just doesn't make sense to me, that's all. David's not like Selene or

Cal. He's not power hungry. He's not even Woodbane."

He drew a long breath. "Listen, I told you how my brother, Linden, died. How he called up a dark spirit and it overpowered him."

That wasn't the whole story, I knew. When we'd joined our minds, I had learned that Hunter had been accused of causing Linden's death and had stood trial before the International Council of Witches. He'd been found innocent, but he still carried the pain of his loss and the conviction of his own guilt.

"I remember," I said.

"What I didn't tell you is that Linden had called up dark spirits many times before," Hunter went on. "After that first time, when he did it with me—it was as if the door had been opened for him. He liked working dark magick. It spoke to him. But the first time, Morgan—the first time we did it for the purest of reasons."

"And you think David did the same thing," I said. "You think he opened the door."

"I think it's possible, yes."

Robbie honked again outside. "I have to go," I told Hunter. "They're waiting for me."

"We'll talk more later," Hunter said.

"Fine. Whatever." I hung up and stared at the phone for a minute. I remembered my own pleasure when I fought off those horrible guys at Aunt Eileen and Paula's. I had enjoyed it. Did that count as dark magick? No. Even if I had felt a rush from it, I was defending people I loved against an attack. That couldn't be bad.

As I walked out to the car, I made a decision. I was going to prove that David was innocent. That Cal was the source of the evil energy Hunter was feeling. I'd go talk to Stuart Afton myself and get this all straightened out.

After school I called Stuart Afton's office to make an appointment. His secretary told me that he wasn't in the office.

"Is he sick?" I asked.

She hesitated. "He's . . . indisposed. He's been out since the middle of last week."

Something in her voice made me extend my witch senses. I picked up on strong confusion and unease. She didn't know what was wrong with her boss, I sensed, and that was very unusual.

It also occurred to me that I'd first sensed the dark presence in the middle of last week. Around the same time Afton had stopped coming into his office.

Coincidence, I told myself.

There are no coincidences, my inner witch voice said.

"Did Mr. Afton come into any large sums of money recently?" I asked on impulse.

"Not that I have any intention of answering a question like that—but you're the second person to ask it in the last few days," the secretary said, sounding amazed. "What is going on?"

"I'm not sure," I said. "Thanks for your help."

I hung up and looked up Afton's home address. He lived in a fancy section of town, but one I could get to by bus. I didn't want Robbie to know what I was doing. Somehow I felt I needed to do this alone. I'd just take the bus back to pick up Das Boot.

The bus let me off a few blocks from Afton's house. The houses were enormous, with wide lawns. Even the snow looked more elegant in this neighborhood. I walked fast, trying to stay warm, my breath forming a little fog in front of me.

I rang the bell and stamped my booted feet on the welcome mat. Was I nuts coming here? Would Afton even see me? I heard footsteps on the other side of the door, and then it swung open. A thick woman in a maid's uniform looked at me. A wave of worry radiated from her.

"Yes?" she asked. "May I help you?"

"Uh," I said brilliantly. "I was wondering if I could talk to Mr. Afton?"

She pursed her lips, and I realized she looked pale. "Oh, dear, I'm sorry. Mr. Afton . . . Mr. Afton . . . was taken to the hospital earlier this morning."

"What?" I gasped.

She nodded. "The paramedics thought he'd had a stroke."

"I—I'm so sorry," I stammered. My heart thudded hard. It's just a coincidence. It has nothing to do with magick, I told myself.

A crumpled shopping bag sitting in the hallway behind her caught my eye. It seemed so out of place, just lying there, as if perhaps Mr. Afton had been holding it when he'd suffered from his stroke. The forest green color and silver handles looked familiar. I was about to ask the maid about it when my witch senses tingled. Hunter was coming up the walk.

What was he doing here? I whirled and stared at him.

"Is everything all right?" he asked as he reached the door.

"Stuart Afton is in the hospital," I blurted. "He had a stroke this morning."

Hunter's green eyes widened slightly. He glanced at the maid. "I'm sorry to hear that. Can you tell me what hospital he's in? I'd like to send over some flowers."

"Yes—Memorial. That's the closest." She shook her

head. "He runs six miles a day, more on weekends. You've never met anyone who takes better care of their health than Mr. Afton. A stroke just doesn't make sense."

I didn't need to do a mind meld to know what Hunter was thinking. A stroke made sense if dark magick was involved.

"Thank you. We're sorry to have bothered you," I said to the maid. Then I grabbed Hunter's arm and pulled him down the porch steps. "What are you doing here?" I demanded.

"The same thing you are, I suppose," he replied. "Trying to get some answers."

I didn't want to think about the conclusions I knew he was jumping to.

"Where's your car?" he asked as we reached the curb.

"I have to go pick it up from the shop," I said.

"Hop in. I'll give you a lift."

I stood on the sidewalk. I wasn't sure if I wanted to get into the car with him, knowing the conversation we were about to have. My stomach felt knotted.

"Morgan, make up your mind. I'm freezing." Hunter walked around the car and slid in behind the steering wheel.

I was freezing, too. I climbed into the car and told him how to get to Unser's.

I didn't know what to think and was lost in my own thoughts while Hunter drove. True, sometimes people did have inexplicable strokes. Maybe he had some congenital defect.

"Someone like Stuart Afton is a very unusual candidate for a stroke," Hunter pointed out, and though it was exactly what I'd been thinking, I felt a flash of irritation. Hunter always had to be right.

"It happens," I said. "All kinds of freak things happen. Look at my life."

Hunter nodded. "Exactly. Your life was straight-on normal until magick kicked in. I could say the same for Afton, except magick has dealt with him far more harshly than it has with you."

"You don't know that this has anything to do with magick," I reminded him tightly. "You're jumping to conclusions."

"Am I?" he asked.

I took a deliberate breath and tried to keep my tone reasonable. "Okay, for the sake of argument, let's say David did have something to do with Afton erasing the debt. Well, Afton did it. David has the shop. So why would David hurt him now? He's grateful to Afton. Hurting him now doesn't make sense."

"Unless David made mistakes, got involved with forces he can't control, lost his power over what was supposed to happen," Hunter said. "The darkness is not predictable. It often has effects beyond the immediate, planned ones."

He sounded so self-righteous that I lost my temper and words shot out of my mouth. "You know what? I think being a Seeker makes you suspicious of everyone. I think you're furious because Cal and Selene escaped, so now you're determined to get someone else. David just happens to be a convenient target."

The brakes squealed as Hunter suddenly swerved and pulled off the road. I barely had time to brace myself before he cut off the engine and turned to face me, his eyes blazing with anger. "You have no idea what you're talking about! Do you think this a *game* for me, where I cut notches in my belt for every renegade witch I run in? Do you think I get off on going after other witches?"

My own temper caught fire. "You do it, though, don't you? You *chose* it."

The muscle in his jaw twitched, and one hand clenched the steering wheel, his knuckles white. Then Hunter relaxed suddenly, releasing the tension from his body on a deep breath. He rubbed his hand over his chin, the way he did when he was thinking. The car was filled with the vanishing traces of our anger, our quiet breathing. The air seemed alive and crackling, and it occurred to me that when I was with Hunter, I literally felt more alive. Probably because I was so often angry at him. But when I was with him, I didn't have time to be crushed with sorrow over Cal.

"Morgan, it's important to me that you understand that what you accused me of—is not true," Hunter said, his voice low. "That's not what being a Seeker is. If the council even suspected me of acting that way, they'd strip me of my powers in a heartbeat. I don't understand how you could think that of me."

His gentle answer made me ashamed. "Okay," I said. "Maybe I was wrong." I've always been a rotten apologizer. It was one of the things I wanted to work on.

"Maybe?" He shook his head and started the car again. Neither one of us spoke after that until we were almost at Unser's. We drove past the entrance to the Afton Enterprises gravel pit, and I saw him turn his head to read the sign. When he faced front again, he was frowning.

We pulled into Unser's yard. "Is this where you felt that dark energy?" Hunter asked me, his frown deepening. "Right here?"

"Yes," I said, puzzled.

"What day was it?" Hunter asked.

"Last Wednesday," I said, but then I saw Das Boot parked over to the side, and I forgot everything else. My beloved white car had a new hood and new bumper, but the hood was *blue*.

"Oh my God," I gasped. "My car!"

Bob Unser heard Hunter's car and came out of the garage, wiping his hands on a rag. Max, the German shepherd, loped out at his side, grinning amiably. Hunter and I climbed out of his car, and I walked slowly to my Valiant, feeling like I was about to cry.

Bob looked over Das Boot with pride. "Good fit, huh?" he asked. "That hood is perfect. We got lucky."

I was speechless. The two front sides of my car had been hammered out and covered with Bondo body filler to fix the crumpling. The Bondo was sanded and looked like steel-gray dusty spackle all over the front of my car. And the hood was *blue*. The bumper looked all right, but was unusually shiny and looked out of place. My beautiful, lifesaving car looked like crap.

"Uh . . . uh . . ." I began, wondering if I was going to hyperventilate. After losing my boyfriend, almost being killed, having my magick disappear on me in a circle, worrying about David Redstone; now, ridiculously, what was finally sending me over the edge was owing my parents almost a thousand dollars so my car could look like *crap*.

Hunter patted my shoulder. "It's just a car," he offered hesitantly.

I couldn't even respond. My mouth just hung open.

Bob gave me a look. "Course, it needs to be painted," he said.

"Painted?" I was amazed at how calm my voice was.

"I didn't want to do that without talking to you," he explained, scratching his head. "We can paint it white, to match the rest of the car, but to tell you the truth, the whole car needs a paint job. See those bits of rust under the door? We should really sand those out, give it a coat of rust protector, then paint the whole body. If we Bondo the other dings, this car could look brand-new." The idea seemed to fill him with enthusiasm.

"How much?" I whispered.

"Another four hundred, five hundred, max," he said.

I gulped and nodded. "Um, does it run okay?"

"Sure. I had to tighten the engine block a bit, knock a few hoses tighter. But this baby's a tank. It was mostly bodywork."

Max panted his agreement.

Silently I handed Bob Unser the check my mother had made out, and he dropped the keys into my hand. "Let me think about the paint job," I said.

"Sure thing. Take care of this car, now." He headed back into the warmth of the garage, and I turned to face Hunter. It was dark now, but I could still see Das Boot's tricolored nose, and it made me incredibly upset.

"I'm sorry about your car," Hunter said. "I'm sure it will be fine."

I closed my eyes and nodded. It was obvious he didn't understand at all.

16

Uncertain

The witch from Boston came today. We spent the morning purifying Selene Belltower's house. But we had no luck getting into her library. In fact, this time I couldn't even find the door.

Then, in the afternoon, I fought with Morgan. I pushed her too hard about David. She's resisting me all the way. And why not, when it seems I'm doing nothing but persecute the people she cares for? Am I trying to make her hate me?

No, it's not that simple. I need her to be able to face the truth, even when it's ugly or painful. I need her to believe in her own strength, the strength that I see every time I look at her.

I've never met anyone who affects me the way she does. We argued today, and the things she said were so wrong and hurtful that I wanted to shake her. But then, later, when she saw what the mechanic had done to that old wreck of a car she drives, she *looked so shattered, so utterly forlorn, that it was all I could do not to take her in my arms and kiss away the tears.*

—Giomanach

In my hideous, piebald car, I drove to a fabric shop to get gold cloth and crimson embroidery thread. I needed them for the protection charm I was going to make for Aunt Eileen and Paula. It would be a little pouch embroidered with the rune Eolh, containing herbs and a crystal.

After that I drove to my mom's realty office. Das Boot no longer made a grinding metallic noise; in fact, the engine sounded perfect. But I was ashamed of how my beloved car looked. I parked at an angle and tried not to look at the nose as I walked to Mom's office.

Widow's Vale Realty was in a small, white-shingled building. Inside, the look was deliberately cozy, with polished hardwood floors, lots of plants, and arts-and-crafts-style rugs and furniture.

"Oh, Morgan, honey. Hi. Did you get your car?" My mom peered out from a desk piled high with three-ring binders, file folders, and loose computer printouts. She looked overworked and overwhelmed. I sighed. I was glad I'd be able to help.

"Yes," I said. "It's fixed. But please don't make me talk about how it looks."

My mom tried unsuccessfully to bite back a smile. A non–car lover, like Hunter. What strange creatures they were.

Thursday and Friday were uneventful days at Widow's Vale High. I met with Cirrus on Friday morning before classes. Everyone was excited about having a circle the following night with Hunter.

"I've been reading this guy, Eliade, who's an expert in the history of religions, and Eliade talks about sacred space," Ethan said. "I'm thinking that's where Hunter took us. And that's exactly what ritual is supposed to do."

I tried not to gape. If anyone had told me two months ago that Ethan Sharp would be discoursing on ritual and sacred space, I'd have told them they were nuts.

"That never happened with Cal," Jenna pointed out. "We did feel magick that one time, but with Hunter it was different. It was just this incredible . . . connection."

"That first circle with Hunter changed me," Sharon stated. "I can never go back to thinking about anything the way I did before."

Suddenly I realized they were all feeling something similar to what I'd felt during our very first circle with Cal, when he'd opened me up to magick. It *had* changed everything. And I ought to be feeling glad instead of resenting the coven and Hunter because my own experience in the circle had been so frustrating.

Matt, whom I'd considered totally self-absorbed, caught me off guard. "But Morgan didn't like it," he said. "It's funny that Hunter has all this power and the one blood witch among us doesn't think he's so great."

Blood witch? I looked up.

"Robbie told us. It sort of came out when he was explaining about Cal," Jenna said gently. "It's okay. We pretty much knew, anyway."

"Uh," I started, flustered. "It's not that I don't like Hunter."

"What is it, then?" Sharon asked.

It was complicated. It was Cal, losing Cal. Hunter being a Seeker and the one who'd made me see the truth about Cal. Hunter suspecting David of dark magick. I shook my head. I couldn't even begin to explain it. So I just shrugged and said, "I don't know, exactly."

Fortunately the first bell rang then. I hurried away, mumbling about how I had to get to my locker. How could I explain my feelings about Hunter to them when I couldn't even explain them to myself?

Saturday dawned cold and bleak. I woke up just after sunrise—unusual for me—shaken by a dream I couldn't remember. Dagda was curled up against my chest. I kissed the top of his silky head and tried to fall back asleep, but it was useless. My thoughts were already roiling. Hunter's face kept rising in front of my eyes. I wondered how Stuart Afton was doing. I needed to get a start on my physics homework and also get back to the realty office to input listings.

That night I had a circle, and Hunter wanted to get together on Sunday for a lesson. I'd told Aunt Eileen and Paula that I'd help them unpack sometime during the weekend, but what I really needed to do was get the last ingredients for my protection charm so I could place it in their house. That meant I had to go to Practical Magick and face David. Would he be able to sense my uncertainty about him?

Already totally stressed, I gave up on sleep, got out of bed, and got dressed. Then I settled at my desk and opened my physics book. *Plot the trajectory of a baseball that's been struck by a batter at a 45-degree angle and is traveling at 100 mph (assuming no air resistance),* read the first problem. "Why?" I muttered. It was hard to imagine anything more irrelevant to my life, but I started crunching numbers and kept at it until nine, which seemed a respectable hour for me to show up for breakfast on a Saturday morning.

My mom was already gone when I got downstairs, the weekends being prime workdays for Realtors. My dad sat at the table, reading the paper. "Morning, sweetie," he said.

Mary K. was standing at the stove, stirring something in a pot. "Want some oatmeal?" she asked.

"No thanks." I started to prepare my own nutritious breakfast regimen of Pop-Tarts and Diet Coke.

She scraped her oatmeal into a bowl. "I talked to Aunt Eileen last night, and I'm going over there after church tomorrow to help them unpack. Want to come?"

"Yes, I told them I would. But can we talk about it later?" I said. "I've got a million things to do this weekend, and I'm not sure how the timing's going to work out."

My father lowered the paper. "What do you have to do?"

I blew out a stream of breath as I carefully edited my answer. "Um . . . working at Mom's office, errands, schoolwork, and getting together with friends tonight." My parents knew that on Saturday nights I attended Wiccan circles, but I tried not to mention it directly too often.

My father studied me with concern. "I trust schoolwork isn't coming last on your list?"

"No," I assured him. "I already did my physics. I've still got a history paper to work on, though."

He smiled at me. "I know you've got a lot going on. I'm proud of you for keeping your grades up, too."

Just barely, I thought.

Twenty minutes later I was out the door.

The light scent of jasmine was in the air when I entered Practical Magick, and Alyce was dressed in an ivory knit dress with a pale pink tunic over it. A strand of rose quartz beads hung from her neck.

"You look ready for spring." I said. "Three months early."

"There's nothing wrong with wishful thinking," she told me with a smile. "How are you, Morgan?"

"Overwhelmed but okay." I couldn't help asking, "Did you hear about what happened to Stuart Afton?"

"Yes, poor man. It's awful." She shook her head, her blue eyes troubled. "I thought maybe we would try to send him healing energy at our next circle."

"So . . . how is your coven going?" I knew that Alyce had been asked to lead Starlocket now that Selene was gone.

Alyce tucked a strand of gray hair back into its twist. "Selene is a hard act to follow. I don't have nearly the power she had. Then again, I've never abused my power the way she did. Our coven has a great deal of healing to do, and since I've always loved healing work, that will be my focus, at least for the present."

"Morgan, good morning," David said, emerging from behind a bookshelf. I noticed his hand was still bandaged and that some blood had seeped through it, staining the gauze. "Nice to see you."

I hoped my voice sounded natural as I said, "You too. Um, I need some ingredients." I took my list out of my pocket.

If he noticed anything in my manner, he didn't mention it. He simply took the list and scanned it. "Oils of cajeput, pennyroyal, lavender, and rose geranium," he murmured, nodding. "We've just gotten in a fresh stock of pennyroyal, haven't we, Alyce?"

"Yes. I'll get the oils," Alyce said. To me she explained, "We keep the big bottles in the back, by the sink. They're rather messy to handle. I'll be back in a few minutes."

She bustled off, leaving me alone with David. He looked up from my list. "Burdock, frankincense, and a sprig of ash," he said in a neutral voice.

"Do you have them?" I asked. I couldn't read him at all, and it was making me nervous.

"We've got them," he replied. He added in a conversational tone, "These are the ingredients for a protection charm. So what are you protecting yourself against?"

"It's not for me," I told him. "It's for my aunt and her girlfriend. They just moved into a house in Taunton, and they're being harassed because they're gay."

"That's a shame. It's never easy to be different," David said thoughtfully. "But I guess you know that, being a witch."

"Yes," I agreed. "Do you think this charm will really help?"

"It's worth trying."

"I used my power to stop the guys who were scaring them," I admitted. "With witch fire." I wanted to see how he would react to this turn in the conversation.

David raised one silver eyebrow but said nothing.

"Even now I want to see them suffer. It makes me worry about myself," I added.

David pursed his lips. "You're being very hard on yourself. You're a witch, but you're human, too, with human weaknesses. Anyway, dark energy is not in and of itself necessarily evil." He slid his hand into the display case beneath the counter and took out a necklace with the yin-yang circle worked in white and black onyx. "To me, the most interesting part of this symbol is that the white half contains a tiny spot of black and the black a tiny spot of white," he said. "You need both halves—bright and dark—to complete the circle. They're part of a whole, and each contains the seed of the other. So there's no such thing as dark magick without a bit of light in it or bright magick without a bit of dark."

Alyce, who'd returned with some vials of oil while he was speaking, shook her head. "That's fine as philosophy, David, but on a purely practical level, I think we'd all do well to shun the dark."

David smiled at me. "There you have it, the combined wisdom of Practical Magick. Make of it what you will."

A customer came in, and Alyce went over to help her.

David rang up my items. Then he reached down and pulled up a paper shopping bag and put it on the counter. He set the vials inside it. "Like it?" he asked, seeing my eyes on the bag. "We had them made as part of our celebration of Practical Magick's new lease on life, as it were."

"It's nice," I managed. Grabbing the bag, I mumbled a good-bye and hurried out of the store.

Outside, I held up the bag and stared at it. It was forest green, with silver handles. Just like the bag I had seen lying crumpled in Stuart Afton's hallway the day he'd had a stroke.

17

Breaking In

August 1999

Beck contacted us today. I knew as soon as I saw his face in my lueg that the news was bad. But I didn't imagine it would be this bad.

Linden was killed, Beck told us, trying to summon the dark spirits. "He called on the dark side to ask how to reach you and Fiona," was what Beck said in his blunt way.

Goddess, what have I wrought? I've abandoned four children, and now one is dead because of me. I didn't know this kind of pain was possible.

—Maghach

I sat in Das Boot, trying to take meditative breaths to calm down. It doesn't mean anything, I told myself. It's just a shopping bag.

Right. Afton was just the type to shop at Practical Magick.

Twenty minutes later I pulled up in front of Afton's sprawling home. What was I doing here? How was I going to prove anything?

I gazed gloomily out my car window. It must be garbage day, I realized, spotting the cans lining the curbs.

Could my proof be in those cans? I wondered. I scrambled out of the car and raced to the cans in front of Afton's house. I opened one, and the stink hit me. Ew. Was I really going to paw through someone else's trash?

I held a hand over the can, trying to get a sense of what I was looking for. I seek witch power, I thought. If there is an object that has been handled by a witch, lead me to it, please. The tips of my fingers tingled, and I ripped open one of the black plastic bags.

A green shopping bag with silver handles lay on top. The logo for Practical Magick was stamped on its side in silver. A gift card was tied to one of the handles. With shaking hands, I pulled it out of the garbage. I flipped open the card and gasped. *These are for you,* the card read. *You know why.*

The card was signed, *Blessed be, Alyce.*

I dropped the bag as if it had bitten me. Home-baked muffins tumbled out into the snow.

A car drove up and stopped behind me. Once again, I realized, Hunter had tracked me down.

"Morgan, what is it?" he asked.

I lifted my stricken face to him. "It can't be," I whispered.

If Alyce had used dark magick to cause Stuart Afton's stroke, then everything that I thought I knew or understood was wrong. And no one was to be trusted.

"Get in the car," Hunter ordered.

I simply obeyed. My mind whirled. Alyce? Then she was an amazing liar because she had seemed to be very certain that no one should mess with dark forces.

Hunter got out of the car and picked up the bag I had dropped. He gathered up the muffins, sniffed them, gazed at them. Then he dumped everything back into the garbage can. He climbed back into the car.

"They're not spelled," he said.

"Wh-what?" I asked.

"The muffins, the bag, the note," he explained. "None of it is spelled. Alyce had nothing to do with Afton's stroke."

I leaned back and let out a sigh of relief.

I felt Hunter's eyes on me. "You suspected David, though, didn't you? That's why you came back out here?"

"I—I don't know what I thought," I said.

"I went to Red Kill, to Memorial Hospital. I saw Stuart Afton," Hunter said.

I didn't bother to ask how he had been able to see Afton since he wasn't a relative or even a friend.

"I had heard he'd been acting strangely for days, which they believe may have been signaling the stroke, despite the fact that there was no medical reason for it to have happened. And he was sort of babbling while I was there."

"What did he say?" I asked apprehensively.

"He said, 'I did what they wanted. Why isn't it over?'"

"That doesn't mean anything," I felt compelled to say. "He could have been talking about work or something."

"There's more," Hunter said. "Remember the dark presence you felt at your garage? I hadn't realized until I drove you there that the garage is right down the road from the Afton gravel pit. But when I saw that, I realized that the dark presence might not have been looking for you at all."

I gaped at him. "You mean . . . ?".

Hunter nodded. "Maybe it was looking for Stuart Afton."

I put a hand to my forehead. I didn't know whether to be relieved or upset. If the dark presence had been after Afton instead of me, that meant I wasn't being stalked. But it also meant that Hunter was right and David had called on the dark side.

"Anyway, I was heading over to his office to do some more checking, then I got this sense that you needed me," Hunter said.

I bristled. "I was fine," I said. "It was just upsetting to think that Alyce might have been involved somehow."

"Well . . . good," Hunter said. "So I'll see you later."

I turned in my seat to face him. "I'm going with you."

"What?"

"I am part of this now," I said firmly. "If you're going to check out Afton's office, then I'm going, too."

For a moment it seemed like he was going to argue with me, but then he sighed. "Fine. You'd just follow me, anyway."

I managed a grin. "Gee, I guess you do know me after all."

I scrambled out of his car and into mine. Then I followed him to Stuart Afton Enterprises. Hunter took my arm, and we crossed the street to Afton's building. "I want to get into his office and search for signs of magick."

"You mean like breaking and entering?" My voice sounded strangled. I'd never even so much as shoplifted.

"Well, yes," Hunter said. "Not to put too fine a point on it."

"Don't tell me: You're a Seeker and have some sort of magickal permission that lets you break all kinds of human laws." I crossed my arms over my chest.

Hunter smiled, and I caught my breath at how boyish he suddenly looked. "That's right," he said. "You can back out anytime. I didn't invite you, remember?"

I rolled my eyes. "I'm in."

"Fine. Just so long as you remember who's in charge here."

I gritted my teeth in irritation as he murmured under his breath, quickly tracing runes and other sigils in the air. "This is a spell of illusion," he told me. "Anyone looking at us here will see something else—a cat, a banner, a tall plant—anything but us."

I was impressed and also envious of Hunter's ability. I realized again how much I had to learn.

"All right, now. Here's something for you to do," Hunter instructed. "There's an alarm wired into this door. It runs on electricity, which is just energy. Focus your own energy, then probe inside for the energy of the security system and do something with it."

I didn't want this responsibility. "What if I short-circuit the microwave by mistake?"

"You won't," he assured me.

I sent my energy inside the building. It was the first time I'd ever tried to focus on energy that wasn't attached to a person or somehow linked to the land. This was searching for electric currents that had no character or easily recognizable pattern; they were simply circuits, designed to register a response when they were opened or closed.

At first all I felt was a general emptiness within the rooms of the building. I probed again and this time felt a lower-level energy around the perimeter of the building, steady and unobtrusive, designed to be noticed only if it were broken. It ran across all the doors and through the glass of the windows. I went deeper into the building and picked up other kinds of energy—ultrasonic sound waves and, upstairs, a laser, both motion detectors. And something else on the ground floor: a passive infrared light, designed to pick up on the infrared energy given off by an intruder's body heat.

"Well?" Hunter asked.

"This is so cool," I murmured.

"Find the security system," he reminded me.

"Right." I cast my energy again, found the security control box in the basement, and let my mind examine it. I concentrated harder, sensing a pattern that had been punched in time and time again.

"Six-two-seven-three-zero," I said. "That's the code."

"Excellent." Hunter tapped the numbers into the keypad by the door, and we heard a quiet click. "Let's go."

Inside, Hunter headed for a big, windowed room at the back of the first floor: Stuart Afton's office. Inside the room he looked around, closed his eyes for a moment, and controlled his breathing. Then he reached into his jacket pocket and pulled out an athame. The hilt had a simple design, set with a single dark blue sapphire.

Hunter unsheathed the blade and pointed it at Afton's desk. A sigil flickered, lit with sapphire blue light. Magick had been done here.

Hunter pointed the blade at Afton's chair and I saw the rune Hagell, for disruption. The rune Neid, for constraint, flickered over the doorway. There were other signs that I didn't recognize.

"These are used to mark targets," Hunter explained, holding the athame at some of the unfamiliar figures. "Do you still doubt that magick has been used against Afton?"

"No." Seeing these sigils, knowing they had been wrought with dark intent, was deeply upsetting. "But we still don't know whose magick this is."

"Don't we?" His voice was soft, dangerous. He held the athame to the sigil once more. "From which clan do you arise?" he asked.

The shape of a crystal flickered above the sigil.

"What is that?" I asked.

"The sign of the Burnhides," Hunter said. He didn't sound triumphant, just sad.

"Oh, no," I said. I felt hollow inside.

"This isn't real proof," Hunter said. "There are probably other Burnhides in the area besides David. Making magick is like handwriting—if you know someone's work, you can recognize it. I need to learn David's magickal signature. Then I'll have the proof I need."

I swallowed. "Great."

Hunter and I split up after leaving Afton's offices. Needing a break from the strain, I went home.

I walked in to find Mary K. sitting at the kitchen table, white-faced.

"What's wrong?" I asked quickly, thinking, Bakker.

"Aunt Eileen just called."

"What happened? Are they all right?"

She nodded, looking stricken. "Nobody was hurt, but those guys—or some of their buddies—came back last night. This morning they found the front of the house covered with spray paint."

"What did it say?"

"Aunt Eileen wouldn't tell me," said Mary K. "So I guess it was bad. They just got back from the police station."

I felt a surge of irrational guilt. If I hadn't gone to Practical Magick and then been with Hunter . . .

"I've never heard Aunt Eileen sound so shaken up," Mary K. went on. "She called here looking for Mom, and I could tell she'd been crying. She wants to put the house on the market."

"What? Oh, no! She can't be serious!"

Mary K. shook her head, her perfect bell of auburn hair brushing her shoulders. "They're tired of the Northeast. They think that in California, people will be more tolerant." Her voice trembled. "Aunt Eileen wants Mom to relist their house."

"That's crazy!" I said. "It's just three high school kids! Three idiots, three losers. Every town has them."

"Tell that to Aunt Eileen and Paula," Mary K. said. She got up and began taking clean dishes out of the dishwasher. "God, they were so excited about that house. I hate it that anyone is doing this to them!"

"I do, too," I said. And I can do something about it, I thought.

I glanced at my watch. I had about four hours before I had to be at Jenna's house for our circle. That would give me time to finish the protection charm. And to find a spell to teach those thugs a lesson they'd never forget.

18

Lost and Found

Fiona is dying.

The news of Linden's death broke her, I think. She'd been in pain before, but she had a core of toughness that kept the illness at bay. But in the last two years she has been . . . fading. Her hair, once so bright, is entirely white now, and her green eyes are sunk deep in her gaunt face. I see her agony, but I can't bear the thought of losing her, my dearest love, the only precious thing I have left.

This morning I broke the silence and sent a message to Giomanach. I didn't contact him directly, but I cast a spell that would open a door to him, that would let him know that we're alive. Now I'm living in terror that I've exposed him to the dark wave.

—Maghach

I was the first one to show up at Jenna's house. "This isn't like me," I said. "I'm never early." The truth was, I'd driven faster than I usually did. I felt weirdly edgy. Maybe because I was nervous about my decision to deliberately work a dark spell on the jerks who'd been harassing my aunt. Or maybe just because I was worried about going through another circle without connecting to my power.

Jenna took my coat. "All the others are running late. Ethan convinced them to go to a lecture at the Red Kill library with him. It's on sacred space and mythic time. I think it's being given by someone who studied shamanism."

"You didn't want to go?" I asked, following her into the Ruizes' comfortably shabby living room.

"With Matt? No thanks. I mean, I'm stuck in the same coven with him, but if I have a chance to avoid him, I take it."

"It must be awful to break up with someone after four years of being together," I said inadequately. Considering how I was pining over Cal, whom I had known barely three months, I could hardly imagine what Jenna was going through.

Jenna removed a large basset hound from the couch. "Go sleep in your own bed," she said. "We're having company." The dog padded off placidly, and Jenna turned to me. "Yeah. At first I just didn't know how to get through the days. Raven Meltzer!" She wrinkled her nose in disgust. "Of anyone he could have picked. I was so humiliated."

We sat down on the couch, and a big gray-and-white-striped cat jumped onto Jenna's lap, purring. She petted it absentmindedly. "We've been together since I was thirteen. I didn't know what to do without him. And everyone knew.

But now——" She shrugged. "It's amazing. I'm getting over it. I'm finding out that I'm different without Matt." She shook her head, and her fine, pale blond hair swished in a shining wave. "When I was with Matt, I was always checking in with him. I don't even know how I got into that habit. But there was nothing I did that Matt didn't know about."

The doorbell rang then, and I waited while Ethan, Sharon, Matt, and Robbie came into the house, all talking at once. "Sorry we're late," Robbie said, giving Jenna a casual hug. "We got hung up in traffic in Red Kill."

"Yeah, the place was packed," Matt said. "I had no idea that so many people even knew where the Red Kill library was."

I felt Hunter coming up the walk, and an unexpected sense of anticipation made me sit up straighter.

"My apologies, everyone," he said as he unzipped his jacket a minute later. He looked around, seeming pleased that everyone was there. "Since we're running late, let's get started. Jenna, what do you have for forming a circle?"

"Chalk, candles, incense, water," she answered.

"Perfect. Then if you'll get them and if everyone else will form a circle . . ."

Hunter quickly drew the circle and chanted an invocation to the Goddess and the God.

"I want to concentrate on things that have been lost," he said when we'd raised the energy of the circle. It was flowing among us so strongly that I could almost see it—a ribbon of light, linking and encompassing us in its strength. This time I felt more connected to it.

"Each of you, think of something lost that you want to be found," Hunter went on. "Don't say it aloud, but silently ask the energy of the circle to open a way inside you to find what's been lost."

What had I lost? My heart, was my immediate answer. But even to me that sounded too melodramatic to ask the energy of the circle to act on it.

My mind wandered, my connection to the circle weaker. I glanced at Hunter, wondering if he knew. His eyes were open, but whatever he was seeing wasn't in the room. He looked aeons away.

I closed my eyes, trying to find my connection again. Suddenly I was filled with a rush of emotion, a deep sense of loss, a yearning that I knew wasn't my own. I saw a man I didn't recognize, tall, with brown eyes and graying hair.

Father, something said within me. Father.

My eyes flew open. Somehow I knew I'd just seen Hunter's father. I had somehow picked up the images that he was experiencing in the circle.

Startled, Hunter's head whipped toward me. I flushed. I hadn't meant to invade his privacy in that way. I hoped he'd know that.

I felt him refocus, connecting to the rest of the group, and then he began taking the circle down. Once again we sat in a circle on the floor. Hunter avoided my eyes. He gave the others an apologetic look. "Would you please excuse us?" he asked. "Morgan, may I speak to you?"

Before I had a chance to answer, he was on his feet and steering me by my elbow to Jenna's kitchen.

"That was an abuse of power," he hissed at me. "You had no right!"

My mouth dropped open. "I didn't do it on purpose!"

Hunter's nostrils flared as he breathed in and out rapidly, trying to calm down. I couldn't tell if the two bright spots on his cheeks were anger or embarrassment.

I thought about how much I hated it when I felt he'd read my thoughts. He must feel awful, I realized. "I'm sorry. I truly, really, and totally have no idea how that happened."

He stared down at the tile floor. His breathing was returning to normal. "All right," he said shakily. "All right. I believe you."

"How could that have happened?" I asked. "I had a stray thought about you, and then I just . . . received all these images."

He nodded a few times, still not lifting his head. "We . . . we had a connection. That's all."

"That was your father, wasn't it?" I asked.

He looked at me, his green eyes glinting. "It was incredible," he half whispered. "I suddenly *knew,* clear as daylight, that I could call to my father, and he would hear me."

"You mean, you think he's alive?" Hunter's parents had disappeared when he was eight—more victims of the dark wave, the evil force that had destroyed Belwicket and other covens. Hunter, his brother, Linden, and their sister, Alwyn, had been taken in by their uncle Beck and aunt Shelagh. It had been hard, not knowing what had happened to his mother and father. No wonder it was what he focused on when thinking of something lost.

When Hunter looked at me, his eyes were full of pain. "Yes."

"Will you call to him?"

"I don't know. It's been so long since I've seen him—I

don't even know who I'd be calling. And I'm not sure he'd want to see what I've become."

"A Seeker?" I felt confused.

Hunter nodded. "We're not exactly popular among witches."

"You're the youngest member of the council. Wouldn't any Wiccan father be proud of that?"

"He's Woodbane," Hunter reminded me. "For all I know, he calls on the dark side, too."

"Don't you ever get tired of looking at the world that way?" I asked, feeling suddenly almost sorry for him. "This is your father! You haven't seen him in more than ten years. My God, if I could see my birth mother just once—"

"Ethan, quit it!" The sounds of Sharon's giddy laughter came through the kitchen door. Hunter gazed at it, as if he'd forgotten where we were.

"We'd better go back out there," he said.

I was reluctant to end this conversation. We were really talking to each other, not fighting, not having a lesson. But the others were waiting.

We went back into the living room, where the others instantly gathered around Hunter.

"I've been reading that book you told me about," Matt began. "And I don't get the part about the Four Watchtowers."

I watched for a few minutes as Hunter patiently answered their questions, in spite of all I knew he was feeling. His breadth of knowledge was impressive, and I knew he had much to teach me, including his ability to reach out to others and help them learn, even when he must be feeling so distressed.

Then it was time to leave. I got into Das Boot and sat for a few moments, letting the engine warm up. Christmas lights were already twinkling from most of the houses on Jenna's street. The house directly across from hers had a giant illuminated sleigh and reindeer spanning the width of the roof. I have got to start getting ready for Christmas, I reminded myself, resolving to talk to Mary K. tomorrow about possible gift ideas.

Das Boot was ready to roll, so I shifted into gear. Then I shifted back into park. I couldn't just drive off, I realized, not after Hunter had revealed himself to me that way. He'd been seriously shaken, and I didn't want to just leave him.

Shifting back into drive, I drove around the block so that the others wouldn't see me. I felt very protective of the conversation I was going to have with Hunter. It was private. I didn't want the high school gossip mill to start grinding.

I want to talk with you, I thought to Hunter. *Please come.*

Hunter walked up to my car a few moments later. I leaned over and opened the passenger door, and he got in. "What is it?" he asked.

"I think that if you know your father's alive, then you ought to contact him."

Hunter stared out through the windshield. "You think so?"

"Yes," I said firmly. "I know it's not quite the same thing, but I only found out that I was adopted a couple of months ago. I'm still trying to find out what the truth is. It drives me crazy not to know. And with your dad—if you don't contact him, it will just eat at you. You'll never stop wondering."

"I've wondered about him every day for the last ten years," Hunter said. "Wondering is nothing new."

"What are you scared of?" I asked.

He gave me an annoyed glance. "What is it with this country? Are all Americans amateur shrinks? You've got therapists on the radio and therapists on the telly, and every one of you speaks fluent psychobabble."

Then he shut his eyes and rubbed them with one hand. I wanted to hold his other hand.

"I'm sorry," he said. He blew out a breath. "I miss England," he said. "I never feel right here. Being a witch and a Seeker on top of that already make me an outsider, but here everything feels *off*. I'm never at home."

I hadn't realized that, and the insight made me feel a strange, new tenderness for him. "I'm sorry," I said. "That must be awful."

"I'm getting used to it. I've even gotten used to you, your forthrightness." He gave me a rueful smile. "You hit close to the bone, Morgan, more often than you realize." He sighed. "It's probably good for me."

"Probably," I agreed. "Now, what about your father?"

"I don't know," he said. "It's loaded. Both in an emotional way—I'm terrified that since the message I got was only from him, it means my mother is dead—and in the sense that I don't know what effect my contacting him will have on the dark wave. I could be opening a Pandora's box that I'll never be able to close. I have to think about it."

"I—I shouldn't be so pushy. I don't know how you feel. Not really."

His hand closed over mine. "You were being a friend, and I have precious few of those. Thank you."

I loved how his hand felt on mine, then wondered how I could feel that way so soon after Cal. And then I told myself I didn't owe Cal anything. Finally I decided it was too much for me to figure out, and I should just take what delight I could from the moment. "You're welcome," I said.

"It's late. I shouldn't keep you." Hunter took his hand away, and I felt a pang.

"It's okay," I said. I wanted so strongly to take his hand again that I actually slid my own hand under my thigh to keep it still.

He sounded exhausted. "We're still scheduled to work together tomorrow afternoon, right?"

I nodded. "I'm going to my aunt's house after church. I'll call you when I get home."

He got out of the car. "Get home safe, then." Hunter traced the rune Eolh in the air. "And sweet dreams."

19

Pursuit

I'm going to contact my father.

I'm terribly afraid. Not just of putting him and Mum in danger, nor of putting myself in danger. More than that, I'm afraid of how changed he'll look, how old. I'm afraid he'll tell me Mum is dead. I'm afraid he'll tell me that he's heard I'm a Seeker, and he's ashamed of me.

I want to ask Morgan if she'll stay with me while I do it.

—Giomanach

I didn't sleep well that night. My mind was whirling with thoughts of Aunt Eileen and Paula, of finding the right spell to help them, of David, of Cal, of Hunter. I'd never been as confused about anyone as I was about Hunter. I bounced from thinking he was the most insufferable male on the planet to seeing, beneath all that arrogance, one of the most complex and fascinating people I'd ever met. There was no neat way to sum up Hunter Niall or my feelings about him.

The next morning I got up early again. I left a note for my family, saying I'd be back in time for church. Then I went for a drive. I needed to think, and I didn't want to be at home when I did. I bought myself coffee, then headed along the river to a small sailing marina.

The marina was dead quiet, since it was the middle of December. Most of the boats had been pulled into dry dock and rested on pilings in a fenced yard. I got out of the car with my cup of hot coffee and walked along the waterfront. The air was bitterly cold, but that was okay. It would force me to make my decision quickly.

What was I going to do about Aunt Eileen and Paula? Every instinct told me that I had the power to protect them, but I knew the charm I'd made wouldn't be enough. If I wanted to be sure that those thugs never bothered them again, I'd have to take more direct action. How dangerous was that?

The wind whipped off the river in an icy gust, and I decided on procrastination: I'd go visit Aunt Eileen and Paula and see if they were serious about leaving. If they were, then I'd try the spell I'd found last night on the Internet.

Shaking with cold, I got back into Das Boot.

I arrived at Aunt Eileen and Paula's just in time to see a police cruiser pulling away. Oh, no, I thought. I was too late. My heart racing with dread, I ran toward the house.

Aunt Eileen opened the door seconds after I rang the bell. "Morgan! What are you doing up this early on a Sunday? I thought you and Mary K. were coming by later."

"I—I was worried about you two," I said honestly. "I just saw the police car pulling away and—"

She smiled and put a comforting arm around me. "Come on in," she said. "Have some breakfast with us, and we'll tell you all about our undercover triumph."

"Your what?"

Paula was in the kitchen, cooking eggs, spinach, and mushrooms in a skillet. "Morgan!" she said. "Care for some breakfast?"

"Sure," I said, pulling up a chair. "Now, what happened?"

Aunt Eileen gave me a sheepish glance. "I felt like an idiot after I got off the phone with your sister yesterday. I was totally giving in to hysteria and fear."

"And to those jerks," Paula added. "For the record, I was equally hysterical."

"We decided we couldn't give in to them," Aunt Eileen continued.

Paula set down three plates containing eggs. "Short version: We drove to a security store in Kingston and rented a couple of surveillance cameras. Then we came home and put them up. At about two o'clock this morning, the camera at the back of the house caught our vandals on tape and sounded a little alarm in our bedroom. We called the cops. They were too late to catch the kids in the act, but they took the tape."

"The cruiser that just left," Eileen finished, "came to tell us that all three are now in custody, and one of them has confessed. The DA thinks she can charge them with at least two other local hate crimes. And two of them are old enough to be tried as adults. What's more, two of our neighbors on the block have offered to testify to what they saw. The community is being really supportive, I'm happy to say."

"Wow!" I exclaimed, amazed. "That's fabulous!" I nearly collapsed with relief. They had solved their own problem without my help, without magick. The choice had been taken out of my hands.

Aunt Eileen sighed. "I'm glad we caught those kids, but I have to say this whole incident has really shaken me. I mean, you hear about gay bashing all the time, but it's just not the same as when you're actually experiencing it. It's totally terrifying."

"I know," I agreed. Then I couldn't help asking anxiously, "But . . . you're not going to move?"

"Nope," Paula promised. "We've decided to tough it out here—at least for now. You can't solve this kind of problem by running away from it."

"That is the best news! I am so thrilled," I told them. I got up and opened the fridge. "Oh, no," I groaned.

"What?" Aunt Eileen sounded worried. "What's the matter?"

I turned from the fridge, which was full of disgustingly healthy foods. "Don't you guys have any Diet Coke?"

After breakfast with Paula and Aunt Eileen, I helped them rearrange living room furniture; then I drove to church and met my family there. I made the effort because I wanted to make my parents happy—and because I felt badly in need of a nonmagickal, normal day.

After church the whole family opted out of our normal Widow's Vale Diner lunch so we could go back to Taunton for more unpacking. We got back to our house at three-thirty, and I decided to have a nice, long soak in the bathtub before calling Hunter.

The bath never happened. I'd just turned on the hot water

faucet when I felt Hunter and Sky approaching. With a sigh I turned off the bathwater and went downstairs. Now what?

I opened the front door and waited. They both looked grim.

"Yes?" I demanded. "Aren't we scheduled to meet later?"

"This couldn't wait," he said.

"Come in." I led them into the den. After shutting the door I asked, "Is it Stuart Afton?"

"He's the same," Hunter answered. He looked at Sky. "Tell her."

"Last night," Sky began, "Bree and Raven and I were out studying the constellations by the old Methodist cemetery. We saw David. He was performing a ritual. A ritual I recognized."

"So what was it?" I asked.

Sky glanced at Hunter. Then she met my gaze steadily. "He was letting blood as a preliminary ritual to a larger sacrifice that will be performed once the moon moves into a different quarter."

"Bloodletting?" I said. I looked back and forth between Sky and Hunter.

"It's a payoff," Hunter said. "For services rendered. It fits with the ritual markings I found in the field where you had first felt a dark presence. He needs to offer his own blood to call in the *taibhs*, the dark spirit. Remember, that's how I knew it wasn't Selene. She has enough power to call a *taibhs* without performing that particular rite."

I felt sick. "Well, I guess that's the proof you were looking for, then," I said to Hunter.

"It's proof that he's using dark magick," Hunter said. "It still doesn't connect him irrevocably to Stuart Afton. But that's just a formality now."

"David may not have bargained on or agreed to Stuart Afton having a stroke," Sky put in. "That's the kind of extra tithe that attaches itself when you deal with the blackness."

"In any case," Hunter said, "I've contacted the council, and they've told me to examine David formally."

There was something terrible in that sentence. "What does that mean?"

"It means that with the power vested in me by the council I am to ask David whether or not he's called on the dark energies," Hunter explained, not sounding like himself. "The procedure requires that two blood witches witness my examination of him."

I looked at him.

"It will be Sky and Alyce," he said, answering my unspoken question. "We're going to do it now, right away. There's no point in wasting any more time."

"I want to go, too," I said.

He shook his head, and Sky looked upset. "No. That's not necessary," he said. "I only came to tell you because I felt you needed to know."

"I'm coming," I said more strongly. "If David is innocent, that will come out in the examination. I want to be there to hear it. And if he's not . . ." I swallowed. "If he's not, I need to hear that, too."

Hunter and Sky looked at each other for a long moment, and I wondered if they were communicating telepathically. Finally Sky raised her eyebrows slightly. Hunter turned to me.

"You won't say anything, you won't do anything, you won't interfere in any way," he said warningly. I raised my chin but didn't say a word. "If you do," he went on, "I'll put a binding spell on you that will make Cal's look like wet tissue paper."

"Let's go," I said.

We drove to Red Kill in Hunter's car. My stomach was tight with tension, and I kept swallowing. I felt cold and achy and full of dread. As much as I wanted Hunter to be wrong, all the evidence pointed to David.

When the three of us walked into Practical Magick, Alyce looked up. She looked tired and ill, her face drawn and almost gray. As soon as I saw her, I felt her pain over what was about to happen. She, too, believed David was guilty, I realized.

"We need David," Hunter said quietly.

David emerged from the back room. "I'm here," he said, his voice perfectly calm. "And I know why you're here."

"Will you come with us, then?" Hunter asked.

David glanced at Alyce and said, "Yes. Just let me get my jacket. Alyce, can you get the keys for the door?"

"Of course," she said.

David disappeared into the back room to get his jacket. And then didn't reappear. We waited maybe a minute and a half before Hunter tore behind the counter and into the back room. Sky and I followed. The door that led outside from the back room was ajar.

"Dammit!" Hunter swore, going through the door to a weedy, overgrown lot outside. "I didn't think he'd bolt. Stupid, stupid, stupid!"

I wasn't sure if he was referring to David or to himself, but I was too freaked out to ask. Sky was scanning the trees at the end of the lot. "He's in there," she told Hunter.

The two of them set off at a lope across the snow-patched ground, and I followed, sick at heart. Alyce, wrapped in a lavender shawl, bustled after us.

It was dark and shadowy inside the area of evergreens where David had disappeared. The trees were tall enough to block out most of the fading daylight, and we found ourselves in a murky gray light, peering around shadowy trunks for any sign of David. I cast my senses and felt Sky, Alyce, and Hunter doing the same. It was strange to feel my power joined to theirs in this way.

My senses picked up hibernating animals, a few birds. Was Sky wrong? Had David come in here? Or was he somehow masking himself?

Sky suddenly whirled. "There!" she cried as a ball of witch fire flew straight toward Hunter.

Hunter raised a hand and murmured something, and the witch fire was deflected, bouncing away from an invisible shield and landing in a snowbank with a sizzle.

It seemed the witch fire had come from behind a tall blue spruce. Hunter moved toward it with a predator's quiet intensity.

Another ball of witch fire sped toward him, which he brushed off, not even bothering with the charm this time. I realized something in Hunter had changed. It was as if he was drawing power into him, taking in energies far beyond his own considerable powers, linked to the life force all around us. But it was even more than that.

Hearing my silent question, Sky said, "When he acts as Seeker, he can draw on the power of others on the council."

God, how much else did I not know? "Will the extra power protect him?"

"Yes and no. The act of drawing power itself will wear him out if he tries to use it for too long. But it will help him fight certain kinds of attacks."

"David Redstone of Clan Burnhide, I summon you to answer to the International Council of Witches. Athar of Kithic and Alyce of Starlocket appear as witnesses," Hunter stated in a cold, relentless voice. "You will stand forth now."

I heard David make a strange sound, as if he were in pain, and I wondered about the power of Hunter's words.

"Stand forth now!" Hunter repeated.

David staggered forward from behind the spruce, his eyes wild, pure animal terror driving him now.

The sapphire in Hunter's athame glowed with power. I watched as he traced a rectangle of blue light around David's body. David screamed and doubled over, trapped in the blue light. Hunter moved in quickly, and I saw the deceptively delicate silver chain, the *braigh*, appear in his hand.

Alyce put her hand to her mouth, her eyes full of anguish.

I couldn't watch but buried my face in Sky's shoulder as Hunter wrapped the silver chain around David's wrists. I heard David screaming and remembered Cal writhing in agony as Hunter bound his wrists.

"Let me go!" David was shouting. "I did nothing wrong!"

I opened my eyes. David was on his knees in the snow, his wrists bound by the silver chain. The flesh around the chain was already raised in angry red welts. Tears streamed from his eyes.

Hunter stood over him, stern and unyielding. "Tell us the truth," he said. "Did you summon a *taibhs* to get Stuart Afton to forgive your aunt's debt?"

"I did it for the people who lived above the store," David

insisted. "They would have been homeless."

Hunter pulled on the *braigh*, and David screamed in agony.

"Yes," David sobbed. "I made offerings to the *taibhs* in exchange for its help."

"Did you offer it Stuart Afton's life?"

"No, never!" Hunter pulled on the *braigh* again, but David didn't change his answer. "I just asked the *taibhs* to make him change his mind," he said. "I never wanted harm to come to him. I deliberately asked that no harm be done to anyone when I cast the spell."

"That was foolish." Hunter's voice was surprisingly gentle. "Don't you know that's the one request the blackness will never grant? It feeds on destruction, and all who seek out the darkness are powerless to control it."

David was sobbing.

Hunter turned to look at us. "Alyce of Starlocket, do you need to hear more?"

"No," Alyce choked out, weeping silently.

"Athar of Kithic? Are you convinced?"

"Yes," Sky said in an almost whisper.

Hunter looked at me then, an unspoken question in his eyes. I didn't answer, but my own tears were answer enough.

Hunter nodded and knelt next to David. I was surprised to see him put a hand on David's back and help him stand. Hunter seemed sad, tired, and old beyond his years. "Sky and I will take David to our house for safekeeping," he said quietly. "The council will decide what to do."

20

Dark and Bright

I put the braigh on David Redstone today. Morgan was there.
She saw the whole thing. I doubt she'll ever forgive me.
But I have to make her try, because I need her. Goddess, how
I need her.
I think I'm falling in love. And I'm frightened.
—Giomanach

Seeing David standing there in the snowy woods, tortured and ashamed, seeing the pain in Hunter's face caused by doing his job, made something snap in me. Without realizing what I was doing, I bolted. As I ran, I stumbled in the snow. Branches caught at my clothes. A birch twig tangled itself in my hair. I ran on, feeling my hair pull, hearing the snap of the twig. The tree flashed a current of pain. Everything that was alive was hurting, and I was part of the web, hurting and in turn causing pain.

I broke out of the woods and found myself behind an office building, its windows dark. Practical Magick was nowhere in sight. I had no idea where I was, and I didn't care. I kept running, my toes numb in my boots as they hit the tarmac. I was panting, my breath short, my chest aching. Then there were footsteps and a familiar presence behind me. Sky.

"Morgan, please stop!" she shouted.

I wondered if I could outrun her and realized that I was too worn out to try. I slowed to a walk, my heart pounding, and let her catch up with me.

She was panting, too. She waited until her breathing slowed before saying, "A formal questioning by a Seeker is never easy to witness."

"Easy?" I nearly shrieked. "I would have settled for non-horrific. I can't believe that Hunter *chooses* to do that."

Sky's jaw literally dropped. "Do you think he enjoyed that?"

I was still repulsed and sickened by what I'd seen. "He chose it," I said. "Hunter became a Seeker, knowing what he would be required to do. He's *good* at it."

There was long beat of silence, and then Sky said, "I'd slap you silly if I thought you knew what you were talking about."

Before I knew what I was doing I had shot out my hand, spinning off a ball of witch fire. Instantly Sky held up a finger, and the fire fizzled out like a Fourth of July sparkler.

"You're not the only blood witch here," she told me in a low, angry voice. "And while you may have more innate power than any witch I've seen, I've had a great deal more practice working it. So don't turn this into a fight, because you won't win."

I hadn't meant to send the witch fire at her. I was just so angry and sickened and exhausted that her threat was enough to make something inside me lash out. "I'm too tired to fight," I said.

"Fine, then get over yourself and listen for a minute. What Hunter does is harder on him that it is on anyone else."

"Then why does he do it?" I choked out the question. "Why?"

Sky thrust her hands into the pockets of her jacket. "In large part because of Linden's death. He still feels responsible. Being a Seeker is Hunter's atonement. He feels that if he can protect others from courting the dark, then maybe his brother's death won't be in vain. But it eats him alive whenever he has to do something like what he did to David."

The wind picked up, and I pulled my collar higher. "It sounds like he's punishing himself."

"I believe that's true," she admitted. "Even though the council acquitted him of all responsibility in Linden's death. Hunter's like a pit bull. He doesn't let go of anything—not the good or the bad. He'll be loyal to the death, but he'll also carry every grief with him to the grave."

We were drawing closer to another strip mall. There were neon lights, cars, people hurrying into stores. It seemed so strange that the normal world existed so close to the woods where David had been just bound by an ancient and terrible magick.

"I still don't see how Hunter can stand to be a Seeker," I said. "It's as if he's chosen to always be miserable."

Sky turned to face me. "There's another way to look at it, you know. Hunter's seen the destruction and grief caused by the dark side, and he's dedicated his life to fighting it. He's fighting the good fight, Morgan. How can you hate him for that?"

"I can't," I said quietly. "I don't."

"There's something else," she went on. "As the only surviving descendant of Belwicket, you must realize how vital it is that you help him in this fight. We can't let the dark wave win."

I shook my head, feeling dazed. "I thought I was finally okay with all of this—being a blood witch, being adopted, even dealing with Cal and what he did to me. Now there's this war against the dark side, too."

"Yes," Sky said. "And it's as dreadful and painful as any war ever fought. I'm sorry you're caught in it."

"My family doesn't even know the dark side exists."

"I wouldn't say that. They're Catholics, aren't they? The Church has a pretty well-defined notion of evil. They just give it different names than we do and use different means to deal with it. Darkness and evil have always been part of the world, Morgan."

"And I just lucked into getting close to it?"

Sky smiled. "Something like that. The only comfort is knowing you're not alone in the fight." She nodded toward a phone booth at the end of the strip mall. "I told Hunter to take David home. We'd better call someone if we're ever going to get home from here. How about Bree?"

I dug some change out of my pocket. "I'll call her."

Bree came and got us and drove us home. I went to sleep at once, and the next day I lay low at school. I avoided everyone in the coven, even avoided friends who weren't part of my Wiccan life. I was aching everywhere. I felt beaten, hurt, betrayed by my own birthright. I couldn't help thinking of that first circle with Cal. Wicca had been so beautiful to me. Now it was wound through with pain.

After school I drove Mary K. home and immediately shut myself in my room to do homework—calculus and history and English, all of it reassuringly mundane. I wanted nothing to do with magick. Mary K. poked her head in at one point, told me she was going out with her friend Darcy and that she'd be home in time for dinner.

It was my turn to cook, so at five-thirty I went down to the kitchen and started rummaging through the pantry and freezer. I found some ground beef, onions, canned tomatoes, garlic, a can of mild green chiles, and a box of cornbread mix.

I was putting diced onions into the cast-iron skillet when I sensed Hunter's presence. Dammit, I thought, what do you want now? Resigned, I turned off the flame beneath the pan.

Hunter was coming up the walk when I opened the door. He looked drained.

"I'm making dinner," I said. I turned around and went into the kitchen. I knew he was hurting, but I couldn't bring myself even to look at him. Despite what Sky had told me, despite what I knew in my own heart, all I could see right now was the Seeker.

He followed me into the kitchen. I turned the burner back on beneath the skillet and started chopping up the tomatoes.

"I came to see if you were all right," Hunter said. "I know yesterday was rough on you."

"It doesn't look like it was great for you, either." He moved as if he were badly beaten up.

"It's always hard," he said in a low voice. "And I didn't manage to deflect all the witch fire he shot at me."

I was surprised to realize how much the thought of him being hurt scared me. "Are you all right?" I asked.

"I'll heal."

I added the chilies and tomatoes to the pan and poured the cornbread mix into a bowl.

"I've got bad news," Hunter said. "I've heard from the council. They've passed sentence on David."

I dropped the wooden spoon I was holding. Hunter reached for it in the same instant that I did. He caught it and handed it to me.

"David must be bound and his magick stripped from him." Hunter's jaw trembled as he spoke, and I knew with certainty that this was harder on him than on anyone, except maybe, in this case, David. David had once told me that witches can lose their minds if they can't practice magick.

"So the council strips him?" I asked.

Hunter's face looked harsh beneath the kitchen's fluorescents. "I do. Tomorrow at sunset at my house. I'll need witnesses. Four of them—blood witches."

I stared at him, seeing the pain on his face, and knew what he wanted to ask me.

"No," I said, backing away from him. "You can't ask me to be part of that."

"Morgan," he said gently.

Suddenly I was crying, unable to hold it back anymore. "I hate this," I sobbed. "I hate it if having magick means I have to be part of this. I never asked for this. I'm tired and I hurt and I don't want to hurt anymore."

"I know," Hunter told me, his own voice breaking. His arms wrapped around me, and I let myself fall onto his chest. When I looked up, I saw that his eyes were wet with tears. "I'm so sorry, Morgan."

At that moment I remembered something Cal had told

me: that there is beauty and darkness in everything. Sorrow in joy, life in death, thorns on the rose. I knew then that I could not escape pain and torment any more than I could give up joy and beauty.

I clung to Hunter, sobbing, in the middle of my kitchen. He murmured nonsense words and stroked my hair gently. Finally my sobs quieted, and I pulled away. Wiping my eyes, I turned the heat off under the frying pan before it all burned.

Hunter drew a deep breath and brushed a tear from my cheek. "Look at us. Two kick-ass witches falling to pieces."

I reached for a tissue on the counter and blew my nose. "I must look like hell."

"No. You look like someone who has the courage to face even what breaks your heart, and I find you . . . beautiful."

Then his mouth found mine and we were kissing. At first the kiss was gentle, reassuring, but then something in me took over, and I pressed against him with an urgency and intensity that shook us both. It was as though there was something in Hunter I wanted with a hunger I barely recognized—something in him I needed the way I needed air to breathe. And clearly he felt that way, too.

When we pulled back, my mouth felt swollen, my eyes huge. "Oh," I said.

"Oh, indeed," he said softly.

We stood there for a long moment, looking at each other as if we were seeing each other for the first time. My heart was beating like crazy, and I was wondering what to say when I heard my dad's car pulling into the driveway.

"Well." Hunter ran a hand through his hair. "I'd better go."

"Yes."

I walked him to the door, and suddenly the reason for his

visit came rushing back. "Tomorrow is going to be terrible, isn't it?" I said.

"Yes." He waited, not looking at me.

"All right." I leaned my head against the door frame. "I'll be there." I wanted to cry again, and I said, "Oh, Goddess, is anything ever going to feel good again?"

"Yes." Hunter kissed me again, quickly. "It will. I promise. But not until after tomorrow."

On Tuesday at sunset we gathered at Hunter and Sky's house for the ceremony. Sky and Hunter were there, of course, and so was a skinny teenage boy who looked familiar. "Where do I know you from?" I asked him.

"Probably from the party at Practical Magick. I play guitar with The Fianna. That was a sweet night," he said sadly.

"You're Alyce's nephew."

He nodded and held out his hand. "Diarmuid." He shifted uneasily. "Lousy occasion to be formally introduced."

"Will Alyce be here?" I asked.

"Already is," he said in a grim tone. "She started crying the moment we walked through the door. She's upstairs with Sky now. Auntie Alyce always wants to believe the best of everyone. She still can't quite believe it—that David called on the dark side. He's her dear friend, you know."

When everyone had assembled, there were five of us in the living room: Hunter, Sky, Alyce, Diarmuid, and me. Wordlessly Hunter led us to the room at the back of the house.

Candles flickered on the altar and in each of the four corners of the room. Outside, wind swept through the ravine, sending a high keening sound into the room.

David knelt in the very center of the room, inside a pentagram of glowing sapphire light. He wore a simple white shirt and white pants. He was barefoot. His hands were bound behind him with rope, his head bowed. He looked fragile and frightened. I ached to hold him, to comfort him somehow. But I knew I couldn't get past the light.

Hunter gestured, and we each stood on one point of the pentagram, with Hunter at the top of it. I noticed a drum on the floor behind Sky. Alyce stood quietly, her eyes locked on David and filled with grief.

Hunter surrounded the pentagram in a circle of salt, tracing signs for each of the four directions and invoking the guardian of each.

"We call on the Goddess and the God," he began, "to be with us in this rite of justice. With the setting of the sun we take from David Redstone the magick that you gifted him.

"No more shall he wake a witch. No more shall he know your beauty or your power. No more shall he do harm. No more shall he be one of us.

"David Redstone, the International Council of Witches has met and passed judgment on you," Hunter went on in a still, neutral voice. "You called on a dark spirit, and as a result a man nearly died. For that you are to be punished by having your powers stripped from you. Do you understand?"

David lifted his head and nodded. His eyes were shut, as though he couldn't bear to keep them open.

"You must answer," Hunter said. "Do you understand the punishment that is now passed on you?"

"Yes." David's voice was barely audible.

Alyce bit back a cry of dismay, and I saw Diarmuid grasp her hand.

"Anger has no place here," Hunter cautioned us. "We are here for justice, not vengeance. Let us begin."

Sky began to beat a slow, solemn rhythm on the drum. The drumbeats seemed to go on forever. Gradually I noticed something shifting in the room. The drum was guiding us, subtly working on each one of us so that our breath aligned with it, our pulses followed it, and our energy joined and began to travel along the sapphire blue light of the pentagram as a line of blazing white.

I saw David hunch in on himself, as if trying to make himself small so that neither the blue light nor the white light could touch him.

The drum beat faster, more insistently, and the light intensified. The energy of five blood witches was fully intertwined now. The energy flowing around the pentagram crackled with power. We all held out our hands, drawing on the power, and I almost wept to feel my energy pouring out, familiar and strong.

Hunter stepped forward and touched the hilt of his athame to the pentagram. For a second the knife lit with blue and white light. The light continued to define the pentagram, but now Hunter walked around it, drawing his athame in a spiral around David, and the sapphire and white light blazed in a spiral as well.

I watched as our power flowed into the spiral and the spiral began to whirl around David. He whimpered as a transparent, smokelike image of a boy I recognized as himself appeared and vanished on the whirls of the spiral. Next came images of David in his robe, athame in hand, casting spells; David finding a wounded bird, making the sign of a healing rune over it and watching in delight as the bird flew from his hand; David charting the phases of the moon and its effect on the tides; David scrying with a crystal; David purifying Practical Magick with cedar and sage; David and another man facing each other in a circle and chanting in perfect harmony. All of it was leaving him, flying up the spiral like escaping spirits. And with each thing that left him, he sobbed with grief, a man watching everything he loved being destroyed. These were the experiences that had shaped him, that he used to define himself. They had formed the fabric of his life, and we were unraveling it.

When the very last of David's magick had vanished on the whirls of the spiral, Hunter held out the hilt of his athame, drawing the glowing spiral into it once again.

"David Redstone, witch of the Burnhides, is now ended," Hunter said gently. "The Goddess teaches us that every ending is also a beginning. May there be rebirth from this death."

The drumbeat finally stopped, and with it the sapphire light of the pentagram winked out. David lay collapsed on the floor, a hollow shell. I wanted to fall over, too, but I stayed upright, feeling if I moved, I would crack into a million brittle pieces.

Alyce bent down slowly and put her arms around David. "Goddess be with you," she murmured; then Diarmuid had to lead her out because she was weeping uncontrollably.

Sky watched silent and stricken as Hunter cut the bonds on David's wrists and gently helped him to his feet. "I'm going to give you some herbs to help you sleep," Hunter told David. The stern Seeker was gone from Hunter now, and he seemed only tender and sad. "Come with me," he said, taking David by the hand.

David let himself be led, walking with halting steps, like a lost child in a man's body.

Sky ran her hand through her hair and blew out a breath. "Are you all right?" she asked me as they left the room.

"It wasn't what I expected," I said. "I thought it would be more like the *braigh*."

"You mean, physical torture?"

I nodded. "This was gentler. And yet, much worse." I thought of how Selene had wanted to take my power for herself. Goddess, what would that have been like? It was unthinkable.

"I never want to do anything like it again." Sky walked to each corner of the room and extinguished the candles there but left the two on the altar lit. "Let's get out of here," she said with a shudder. "I'll come back in and do a purification ceremony in the morning."

Moving in slow motion, I followed her into the living room.

"We found out what happened, you know," Sky said. "The *taibhs* terrified Afton so badly that he wanted nothing to do with the store. That's why he forgave the debt. Then, later, the continued stress of the encounter led to the stroke. Receiving Alyce's muffins was what pushed him over the edge."

"You mean Alyce . . ." It was unbelievable.

"She had sent them as a thank-you. But dark forces work in devious ways, and so her kindness resulted in a terrible event." Sky put a finger to her lips. "She doesn't know, and I hope you won't tell her. It would hurt her too much."

I nodded. Then a thought occurred to me. "What happens to the store now?"

"Hunter spoke with Afton. He's getting better, but he wants nothing to do with Practical Magick. And the bookstore deal fell through, so the building has lost its value." Sky shrugged. "I think Alyce will probably have to pay off the debt, but Afton seems willing to work with her on the timing. She'll be able to keep the store running." She touched my shoulder comfortingly, and left the room.

I heard Hunter coming down the stairs and turned to look at him. "Morgan," he said. "You're still here." He looked exhausted and so much older than he had earlier that day. He came to stand before me. "Thank you. I know how hard that was for you."

I looked at him. He wasn't a monster. He had done what he had to, and through it all there'd been an undercurrent of compassion streaming from him, from Hunter to all of us.

"I have something for you." He reached into his pocket and took out a clear, faceted crystal.

"Quartz?" I guessed.

He gave me a look that made it clear that was the wrong answer.

"Oh, Hunter, please, I'm too worn out for guessing games."

"Tell me what it is," he said softly.

So I tried, thinking of the stones I'd learned, trying to fit a name to it: Zircon? Danburite? Diamond? Albite? It couldn't be moonstone. Frustrated, I sent my energy into the stone, asking it to yield its name to me. The answer it gave made no sense.

I gazed up at Hunter, baffled. "What it tells me is beryl, but that can't be right. Beryl is either aquamarine or emerald, and this is—"

"Morganite," he told me. "Your name stone, another form of beryl."

"Morganite?"

"It changes colors with the sunlight. At different times of day it will be white, lavender, pink, even pale blue. It's a powerful healing stone. And there's something else it can do." His hand closed around the stone. He looked at me, and his green eyes were as fathomless as the sea. "If a blood witch holds it and sends energy into it, it will reveal what is deepest in his heart."

Hunter opened his hand, and in the very center of the crystal I saw myself.

Book Six

SWEEP

Spellbound

Spellbound

SPEAK

Published by the Penguin Group

Penguin Group (USA) Inc., 345 Hudson Street, New York, New York 10014, U.S.A.

Penguin Group (Canada), 90 Eglinton Avenue East, Suite 700, Toronto, Ontario, Canada M4P 2Y3
(a division of Pearson Penguin Canada Inc.)

Penguin Books Ltd, 80 Strand, London WC2R 0RL, England

Penguin Ireland, 25 St Stephen's Green, Dublin 2, Ireland (a division of Penguin Books Ltd)

Penguin Group (Australia), 250 Camberwell Road, Camberwell, Victoria 3124, Australia
(a division of Pearson Australia Group Pty Ltd)

Penguin Books India Pvt Ltd, 11 Community Centre, Panchsheel Park, New Delhi - 110 017, India

Penguin Group (NZ), 67 Apollo Drive, Rosedale, North Shore 0632, New Zealand
(a division of Pearson New Zealand Ltd)

Penguin Books (South Africa) (Pty) Ltd, 24 Sturdee Avenue, Rosebank, Johannesburg 2196, South Africa

Registered Offices: Penguin Books Ltd, 80 Strand, London WC2R 0RL, England

Published by Puffin Books, a division of Penguin Young Readers Group, 2001
Published by Speak, an imprint of Penguin Group (USA) Inc., 2007
This omnibus edition published by Speak, an imprint of Penguin Group (USA) Inc., 2010

1 3 5 7 9 10 8 6 4 2

 Produced by 17th Street Productions,
an Alloy company
151 West 26th Street
New York, NY 10001

17th Street Productions and associated logos
are trademarks and/or registered trademarks of Alloy, Inc.

Speak ISBN 978-0-14-241021-9
This omnibus ISBN 978-0-14-241897-0

Printed in the United States of America

1

Kithic

Beltane, 1962, San Francisco

Today I met my future, and I'm dancing on sunlight!
There were I celebrated Beltane in the park downtown, and all
of us from Catspaw made beautiful magick right there in the
open while people watched. The sun was shining, we wore flowers in our hair, and we wove our ribbons around the fertility
pole and made music and raised a power that filled everything
with light. We had elderflower wine, and everything was so
open and beautiful. The Goddess was in me, her life force,
and I was awed by my own power.

I knew then that I was ready to be with a man—I'm seventeen and a woman. And as soon as I had that thought, I
looked up into someone's eyes. Stella Laban was giving him a
paper cup of wine, and he took it and sipped, and my knees
almost buckled at the sight of his lips.

Stella introduced us. His name is Patrick, and he's from Seattle. His coven is Waterwind. So he's Woodbane, like me, like all of Catspaw.

I couldn't stop looking at him. I noticed that his chestnut brown hair was shot through with gray, and he had laugh lines around his eyes. He was older than I thought, much older, maybe even fifty.

Then he smiled at me, and I felt my heart thud to a stop. Someone grabbed Stella around the waist, and she danced off, laughing. Patrick held out his hand, and without thinking I put mine in his and he led me away from the group. We sat on a boulder, the sun warm on my bare shoulders, and talked forever. When he stood up, I followed him to his car.

Now we're at his house, and he's sleeping, and I am so, so happy. When he wakes up, I'll say two things: I love you. Teach me everything.

—SB

I had been to Sharon Goodfine's house once before, with Bree Warren, back when Bree and I were best friends. Tonight Sharon was hosting Cirrus's usual Saturday-night circle, and I was curious to see how it would feel different from other circles we'd had. Each place had its own feeling, its own atmosphere. Every circle was different.

"Nice pad," said Robbie Gurevitch, my other best friend from childhood. He squinted at the landscape lighting, the manicured shrubs with their caps of snow, the white-painted brick of the colonial house. The landscaping alone probably cost more than what my dad makes in a year at IBM. Sharon's dad was an orthodontist with a bunch of famous clients. I'd heard a rumor that he'd straightened Justin Timberlake's teeth.

"Yep," I answered, pushing my hands into my pockets and starting up the walk. I'd gotten a ride with Robbie in his red Beetle, and I saw other cars I recognized, parked along the wide street. Jenna Ruiz was here. Matt Adler had come in his own car, of course, since he and Jenna were broken up. Ethan Sharp was here. Hunter was here, I noticed. I shivered inside my coat with a blend of excitement and dread. More cars were parked nearby, but I didn't recognize them and figured one of the neighbors was having a party.

On the porch Robbie stopped me as I started to ring the doorbell. I looked at him questioningly.

"You okay?" he asked quietly, his gray-blue eyes dark.

I opened my mouth to indignantly say, "Of course," but then I shut it again. I'd known Robbie too long and had been through too much with him to fob him off with white lies. He had been one of the first people I'd told about being a blood witch, about being adopted, about being Woodbane. Of the Seven Great Clans of Wicca, Woodbanes were the ones who sought power at all costs, the ones who worked with dark magick. When I'd found out about being a blood witch, I hadn't known my clan and had hoped that I was a Rowanwand, a Wyndenkell, a Brightendale, a Burnhide. Even a mischievous Leapvaughn or warlike Vikroth would have been fine. But no. I was Woodbane: tainted.

Robbie and Bree had saved my life three weeks ago, when Cal, the guy I'd loved, had tried to kill me. And Robbie's friendship had helped give me the strength to continue searching for the truth about my birth parents. He could read me well, and he knew I was feeling fragile right now.

So I just said, "Well, I'm hoping the circle will help."

He nodded, satisfied, and I rang the doorbell.

"Hi!" Sharon said, opening the door wide and ushering us in, the perfect hostess. I caught sight of Jenna and Ethan standing behind her, talking. "Dump your coats in the living room. I've set up a space in the media room. Hunter told me we'd have a real crowd tonight, and he was right." She pointed to a doorway on the far side of the large living room. Her fine, dark hair swirled around her shoulders as she turned to answer a question from Jenna. Her trademark gold bracelets jangled.

I was standing there, wondering how small the room must be if the seven members of Cirrus would crowd it, when Robbie caught my eye. "Media room?" he mouthed silently, shrugging out of his coat. I couldn't help smiling.

Then I felt a prickle of awareness at the back of my neck, and knowing what it meant, I looked around to see Hunter Niall coming purposefully toward me. The rest of the room faded, and I suddenly heard my own heartbeat loud in my ears. I was only vaguely aware of Robbie walking away to greet someone.

"You've been avoiding me," Hunter said softly in his English accent.

"Yes," I admitted, looking into his sea green eyes. I knew he'd called my house at least twice since the last time we'd seen each other, but I hadn't returned his calls.

He leaned back against the door frame. I was five-six, and

Hunter was a good seven inches taller than me. I hadn't seen him since a few days ago, when I'd had witnessed him stripping one of my friends of his magickal powers. He'd done it because it was his job. As a Seeker and the youngest member of the International Council of Witches, Hunter had been obligated to wrest David Redstone's power from him and to bind him magickally so that he couldn't use magick again for any reason. It had been like watching someone being tortured, and I'd had trouble sleeping since then.

But that wasn't all. Hunter and I had kissed the night before the ritual, and I'd felt a longing for him that astonished and disturbed me. Then, after the ritual, Hunter had given me a spelled crystal into which he'd put my image, through the sheer power of his feelings. We both knew there was something between us, something that might be incredibly powerful, but we hadn't explored it yet. I both wanted to and didn't want to. I was drawn to him, but what he had done still frightened me. Unable to sort out my own feelings, I'd resorted to a tried-and-true tactic: avoidance.

"I'm glad you came tonight," he said, and his voice seemed to smooth away some of my tension. "Morgan," he added, sounding uncharacteristically hesitant. "It was a hard thing you saw. It's a hard thing to be part of. It was the third one I've done, and it only gets harder each time. But the council decreed it, and it was necessary. You know what happened to Stuart Afton."

"Yes," I said quietly. Stuart Afton, a local businessman, was still recovering from the stroke David Redstone had caused by working a dark spell. Now David was in Ireland, at a hospice run by a Brightendale coven. He would live there for a long time, learning how to exist without magick.

"You know, some people join Wicca or are born into it, and it's more or less smooth sailing," Hunter went on. Ethan passed us on the way to the media room, and I heard the fizzy pop of someone opening a soda can. Hunter lowered his voice, and the two of us were alone in our conversation. "They study for years, they work magick, and it's all just a calm acknowledgment of the cycle, the circle, the life wheel."

I heard a burst of laughter from the media room. I glanced over Hunter's shoulder, catching a glimpse of a boy I almost recognized. He wasn't part of our coven, and I wondered why he was here.

Hunter was making me nervous, jumpy, as he often did—he had always affected me strongly, and I didn't understand our connection any more than I understood the surprising, even frightening attraction I had to him.

"Yes?" I said, trying to follow his thought.

"With you," he went on, "it hasn't been a smooth ride. Wicca and everything associated with it has been one huge trauma after another. Your birth mother, Belwicket, the dark wave, Cal, Selene, now David . . . You haven't had much of a chance to revel in magick's beauty, to appreciate the joy that comes from working a perfect spell, to experience the excitement of learning, finding out more and more. . . ."

I nodded, looking at him. My feelings about him had changed so radically, so fast. I'd hated him when I met him. Now he seemed so compelling and attractive and in tune with me. What was that about? Had he changed, or had I?

Hunter straightened his shoulders. "All I'm saying is, you've had a hard time, a hard autumn, and so far a hard winter. Magick can help you. I can help you—if you'll let me." Then he turned and went to the media room as I gazed after him, and a moment later the voices quieted, and I heard Hunter asking for attention.

I peeled off my coat, dropped it on a chair, and went to join the circle.

Sharon's plush media room was indeed crowded. Our coven, Cirrus, consisted of seven members: Hunter, our leader; me, Morgan Rowlands; Jenna; Matt; Sharon; Ethan; Robbie. But there were more than seven people in the room. Next to the big-screen TV, I caught sight of Robbie talking to Bree Warren. Bree—my ex–best friend, then for a while my enemy when we'd fought over Cal. What was she doing at Sharon's house, at our coven meeting? She was a member of Kithic, the rival coven that she'd formed with Raven Meltzer and Hunter's cousin, Sky Eventide.

"Morgan, have you met Simon?" a voice beside me said, and I turned to see Sky herself, motioning to the boy I'd thought I recognized. I realized I'd seen him at a party at Practical Magick, an occult store in the town of Red Kill. The store David Redstone had owned.

"Nice meeting you," Simon said to me.

I blinked. "You too." Turning to Sky, I asked, "What are you guys doing here?"

I was surprised to see a nervous look on Sky's face, which reminded me so much of Hunter's. They were both English; both tall, slender, incredibly blond, somewhat cool and standoffish. They were also both loyal, brave, dedicated to doing what was right. Sky seemed more at ease with people than Hunter did. But Hunter seemed stronger to me.

"Hunter and I have a suggestion," Sky said. "Let's get everyone together, and we'll fill you all in."

"Thank you all for coming," Hunter said, raising his voice. He took a sip of his ginger ale. "We have here two covens," he went on, gesturing around the room. "Cirrus, which has seven members, and Kithic, which has six." He pointed them out to us. "Kithic's leader, Sky Eventide. Bree Warren, Raven Meltzer, Thalia Cutter, Simon Bakehouse, and Alisa Soto."

There was a moment when we were all smiling and nodding at each other, all mystified.

"Hunter and I have been thinking about joining the two covens," said Sky, and I felt my eyebrows raise. When had this discussion happened? I wondered.

Across the room I caught Bree's eye, and she made an I-didn't-know-about-this-either face. Once Bree had been part of Cirrus. Once I had known all her thoughts as well as my own. Well, we were making progress: now we were speaking to each other without fighting, which was more than we'd done for months.

"Each coven is quite small," Hunter explained. "It divides our energy and our powers. If we join, Sky and I can share in the leadership, which will make us stronger."

"And the new coven will have thirteen members," said Sky. "In magick the number thirteen has special properties. A thirteen-member coven will have strength and power. It will make our magick more accessible, for lack of a better word."

"Join?" Jenna asked. Her light brown eyes flitted quickly to Raven, and I remembered her saying she could never be in the same coven as the girl who had so blatantly stolen

Matt away from her. Then her glance fell on Simon, and he looked back at her. I'd seen her talking to him at the Practical Magick party. Well, good for her, I thought. Maybe the lure of Simon would outweigh her feelings about Raven.

"Thirteen sounds really big," said Alisa, who looked young, maybe only fifteen. She had wavy golden brown hair, tan skin, and big dark eyes. "The smaller size is nicer because we know everyone and we can relax with them."

Hunter nodded. "I understand that," he said, and from the tone of his voice I knew he was about to flood her with logic, the way he had done with me so many times. "And I agree that part of a circle's appeal is its intimacy, the sense of closeness and support that we get from one another. But I assure you, after a couple months of working together, we'll appreciate the wider circle of support, the larger group of friends, the greater resource of strength."

Alisa nodded uncertainly.

"Do we get to vote on this?" asked Robbie.

"Yes," Sky said at once. "This is something Hunter and I have thought about a great deal. We share some of the same concerns that you might have. We do think it would be best for the two covens to merge, though, for us to join our energies and strengths. It's what we want to do, how we want to continue on our journey of discovery. But of course, we'd like to hear what the rest of you think."

We were all silent for a moment, everyone waiting for someone else to say something. Then I straightened up. "I think it's a good idea," I said. Until I spoke I wasn't sure what my reaction would be, but now I knew. "It makes sense for us to join together, to be allies, to be working together instead of working apart." Hunter's eyes sought mine, but I looked at the group. "Magick can be dark and dangerous sometimes," I added. "The more people we can count on, the better, in my opinion."

Twelve people looked at me. I had been shy and self-conscious for seventeen years, and I knew that my classmates, people who knew me well, were surprised at my offering an opinion so openly. But in the last month so much had happened that, frankly, I didn't have a lot of energy left to be self-conscious anymore.

"I agree," Bree said into the silence. I saw the warmth in her brown eyes, and suddenly we smiled at each other, almost as if it were old times.

Everyone started speaking then, and after another twenty minutes of discussion we voted and it was agreed: the two covens would merge. We would be thirteen members strong, and we would call ourselves Kithic. I hoped the end of Cirrus would help me cope with the traumatic end of Cal's and my relationship. And I tried not to be overwhelmed by all the new beginnings in my life.

We had what I thought of as a "baby" circle: we didn't actually go through the whole ritual, but we did stand in a circle, holding hands, while Hunter and Sky led us through some breathing exercises.

Then Hunter said, "As some of you have already discovered, Wicca has its frightening side." He cast a swift look in my direction. "It's not so surprising, perhaps, when you think that all of us have within us the capacity for both bright and dark. Wicca is part of the world, and the world can be a dark place, too. But one of the things this coven can do for you is support you and help you to conquer your personal fears. The fewer unexplored places you have within you, the easier it will be to connect with your own magick."

"We're going to go around the circle," Sky said, picking up where Hunter left off, "and each of us is going to tell the group one of our great fears. Thalia, you start."

Thalia was tall and earth-mothery looking, with long, ringlety hair and a pretty Madonna face (the saint, not the singer).

"I'm afraid of boats," she said, her cheeks turning slightly pink. "Every time I get in a boat, I panic, and I think a whale is going to come up under it and knock me into the sea and I'll drown. Even if it's just a rowboat on a duck pond."

I heard Matt stifle a snicker, and felt a twinge of irritation.

Robbie was next. He looked at Bree, then said, "I'm afraid I won't be patient enough to wait for the things I really want." Robbie and Bree had recently begun seeing each other, in a very cautious, uncommitted way. He was in love with her and wanted a real relationship, but so far she had shied away from anything more than fooling around.

I watched as Bree's gaze dropped from his, and I also noticed the interested gleam in Thalia's eyes. Weeks ago I had heard gossip that Thalia was hot for Robbie. If Bree's not careful, Thalia will steal Robbie from her, I thought.

Ethan spoke next, with none of his usual joking around. "I'm afraid I'll be weak and lose a really great person in my life." I guessed he was talking about his pot smoking. Around the time he and Sharon had started seeing each other, he'd more or less given up pot, in part because he knew she didn't like it when he smoked.

Sharon, who held Ethan's left hand, looked at him with

open affection. "I'm not," she said simply. Then she looked at the rest of us. "I'm terrified of dying," she said.

We kept going around the circle. Jenna was afraid she wouldn't be brave. Raven was afraid of being tied down. Matt was afraid no one would ever understand him. I thought of telling him he should start by trying to understand himself, but I realized this wasn't the right time or place.

"I'm afraid I'll never be able to have what I really want," Bree said in a small voice, looking at the floor.

"I'm afraid of unrequited love," Sky said, her dark eyes as enigmatic as ever.

"I'm afraid of fire," Simon said, and I jerked, startled. My birth parents had burned to death in a barn, and Cal had tried to kill me with fire when I'd refused to join the conspiracy he and his mother were part of. I, too, was afraid of fire.

"I'm afraid of my anger," Alisa said. That surprised me. She looked so sweet.

Then it was my turn. I opened my mouth, intending to say I was afraid of fire, but something stopped me. I felt Hunter's gaze on me, and it was as if he were shining a spotlight on the darkest recesses of my mind, urging me to dredge up my deepest fear.

"I'm afraid I'll never know who I am," I said, and as I said it, I knew it was true.

Hunter was last. In a clear voice he said, "I'm afraid of losing any more people I love."

My heart ached for him. His brother had died at the age of fifteen, murdered by a dark spirit called a *taibhs*. And his father and mother had disappeared ten years ago, driven into hiding by the dark wave, a cloud of evil and destruction that had wiped out many covens, including my own birth parents'. He had a younger sister, I knew, and it occurred to me that he must worry about her all the time.

Then I looked at him and found his gaze locked on me, and my skin prickled as if the air were suddenly full of electricity.

A moment later we dropped hands and it was over. I guessed a lot of people would stay to hang out, but I felt oddly antisocial, and I went to snag my coat. The events of the last week had shaken me more than I had admitted to anyone. As of the day before, school was out officially for winter break, and it was a huge relief finally to have hours of free time in front of me so that I could try to begin processing the myriad ways my life had changed in the last three months.

"Robbie?" I said, interrupting his conversation with Bree. They were huddled close, and I thought I heard Robbie cajoling and Bree playfully resisting.

"Oh, hey, Morgan," Robbie said, looking up reluctantly, and then Hunter's voice was at my ear, sending a shiver down my spine as he said, "Can I give you a ride home?"

Seeing the relief on Robbie's face, I nodded and said, "Yeah. Thanks."

Hunter put on his leather jacket and his hat, and I followed him out into the darkness.

2

Spin

August 7, 1968, San Francisco

I've been packing up Patrick's things. Last week we had his memorial service—all of Catspaw and some folks from Waterwind were there. I can't believe he's gone. Sometimes I'm sure he's not gone—that he's about to start up the stairs, he's about to call, he'll walk through the door, holding some new book, some new find.

My friend Nancy asked if it had bothered me that he was nearly forty years older than me. It never did. He was a beautiful man, no matter what his age. And even more important, he loved me, he shared his knowledge, he let me learn anything I could. My powers are ten times stronger now than they were when we first met.

Now Patrick's gone. The house is mine, all his things are

mine. I'm looking through his books and finding so many I never knew he had. There are books hundreds of years old that I can't even decipher. Books written in code. Spelled books that I can't even open. I'm going to ask Stella for help with these. Since she became Catspaw's leader, I've trusted her more and more.

Without Patrick here to distract me, so many things are becoming clearer. I'm not sure, but I think he worked with dark magick sometimes. I think some of the people who came here worked with darkness. At the time I didn't pay much attention to them. Now I think Patrick often had me spelled so I wouldn't question things. I guess I understand, but I wish he'd trusted me to accept what he was doing and not automatically condemn it.

I managed to open one book, breaking through its privacy charm with a counterspell that took me almost two hours to weave. Inside were things that Patrick never showed me: spells about calling on animals, spells for transporting your energy somewhere, spells to effect change from far away. Not dark magick per se, but proscribed nonetheless; the council says spells to manipulate should never be used lightly. No one in Catspaw would touch a book like this, even though they're Woodbane. But I would. Why shouldn't I learn all there is to know? If the knowledge exists, why should I blind myself to it?

This book is mine now. And I will study it.

—SB

There's something about being with someone in a car at night that makes you feel like you're the only people in the world. I had felt that way three weeks ago, when Cal kidnapped me, spelled me so I couldn't move, and drove me to his house. That night, alone in the car with Cal, it had been unspeakably bad: pure panic, fear, anger, desperation.

I felt differently tonight, with Hunter by my side. Recently, when it became clear that he might have to stay in Widow's Vale for a while, he'd bought a tiny, battered Honda to replace the rental car he'd been driving. The small space inside felt cozy, intimate.

"Thanks for backing us up about joining the two covens," he said, breaking the silence.

"I think it's a good idea. I'd rather know where everyone is and what they're doing."

He gave a short laugh and shook his head. "That's harsh," he said. "I hope someday soon you'll be able to trust other people again."

I tried not to flinch at the thought. I had trusted Cal, and it had almost cost me my life. I had trusted David, and he'd turned out to have a dark side, too. What was it about me that blinded me to evil? Was it my Woodbane blood?

And yet . . . "I trust you," I said honestly, uncomfortable with the feeling of vulnerability those words awoke in me.

Hunter glanced at me, his eyes an unfathomable shade of gray in the darkness. Without speaking he reached across the seat and took my hand. His skin was cool, and my fingers brushed against a callus on his palm. Holding hands with him felt daring, strange. Holding hands with Cal had been so natural, so welcome.

I was seventeen and had had only one boyfriend. I'd known since that remarkable kiss that Hunter and I had a definite connection, but he wasn't my boyfriend, and we'd never been on an official date.

I breathed deeply, willing my pulse to slow down. "I know magick is all about achieving clarity," I said. "But I feel so confused."

"Magick itself is about clarity," Hunter agreed. "But people aren't. Magick is perfect; people are imperfect. When you put the two together, it's bound to get cloudy sometimes. When it's just you and magick, how does it feel?"

I thought back to when I had worked spells, had circles by myself, scryed in fire, used my birth mother's tools. "It feels like heaven," I said quietly. "Like perfection."

"Right," Hunter said, squeezing my hand and turning the steering wheel with the other. His headlights sliced through the night on this winding road toward downtown Widow's Vale. "That's pure magick and only you. But as soon as you add other people into the mix, especially if they aren't totally clear themselves, you get confusion."

"It's not just magick," I said, looking out the window, trying to ignore the exciting feeling of his hand on mine. I didn't know how to put it—despite my two months with Cal, I was still a relative newcomer to the guy-girl thing. I thought that Hunter liked me, and I thought I liked him. But it was so different. Cal had been obvious and persistent in his pursuit of me. What kind of a person was I, liking Hunter, finding him attractive, when until just a few weeks ago I'd thought I was madly in love with Cal? Yet here Hunter was, holding my hand, taking me home, possibly kissing me later. A little shiver went down my spine.

Hunter zoomed around a tight corner, making me lean toward him.

Then he pulled his hand from mine and put it on the steering wheel.

"Whoa," I said, covering my disappointment. "Going a little fast, huh?"

"I can't help it," he said in his crisp English accent. "The brakes don't seem to be working."

"What?" Confused, I glanced over to see his jaw set, his face tense with concentration.

"The brakes aren't working," he repeated, and my eyes widened as I understood the words.

In alarm I looked ahead—we were going downhill, toward the curviest parts of this road, where signs recommended going no more than twenty miles an hour. The speedometer said fifty.

My heart thudded hard, once. "Crap. Downshift?" I said faintly, not wanting to distract him.

"Yes. But I don't want to make us skid. I could turn off the engine."

"You'd lose the steering," I murmured.

"Yes," he said grimly.

Time slowed. The facts—that the road was icy, that we were wearing seat belts, that the car was small and would crumple like a tin can, that my heart was thudding against my ribs, that my blood was like ice water in my veins—all these things registered as Hunter downshifted forcefully, making the engine buck and groan. The whole car shuddered. I gripped the door handle tightly, my foot pressing a nonexistent brake pedal on the floor. I'm too young to die, I thought. I don't want to die.

We were in third gear, going about forty miles an hour downhill. The engine whined, straining uselessly against the gravity and inertia that pulled the car forward, and we began to pick up speed again. I glanced at Hunter, hardly breathing. His face looked bleached in the dim dashboard light, as if he were carved from bone. I heard the squeal of the wheels and felt the sickening lurch of the car as we skidded around another curve, then another.

Hunter downshifted once more, and the whole car jumped with an annoyed sound. My back hit my seat, and the car seemed to dance sideways, like a spooked horse. Hunter grabbed the parking brake and slowly eased it upward. I didn't feel any effect. Then with a hard jerk Hunter popped it into place, and the car jolted again and started skidding sideways, toward a tree-lined ditch. If the car rolled, we would be crushed. I quit breathing and sat frozen.

He shifted into first gear and simultaneously turned into the skid so we did an endless, semicontrolled fishtail right in the middle of Picketts Road. Hunter let us skid, and when we had slowed enough, he cut the engine. The steering wheel locked, but it was okay—we were still headed into the spin, and finally we scraped to a noisy halt at the side of the road, not six inches from a massive, gnarled sycamore that would have flattened us if we'd hit it.

After the grinding screeches of the tortured engine and tires, the silence of the night was broken only by our shallow panting. I swallowed hard, feeling like my seat belt was the only thing holding me upright. My eyes felt huge as I searched Hunter's face.

"Are you all right?" he asked, his voice slightly shaky.

I nodded. "You?"

"Yes. That could have been bad."

"You have a knack for understatement," I said weakly. "That *was* bad, and it could have been deadly. What happened to the brakes?"

"Good question," Hunter said. He peered through his window at the dark woods.

I looked around, too. "Oh. We're near Riverdale Road," I said, recognizing this bend in the road. "We're about a mile and a half from my house. This isn't far from where I put Das Boot into a ditch."

Hunter unsnapped his seat belt. "Can we walk to your house?"

"Yeah."

Hunter locked the car where it sat neatly and quietly by the side of the road, as if it hadn't almost killed us. We started walking, and I didn't speak because I could tell Hunter was sending out his senses, and I realized he was searching for other presences nearby. And then it hit me: he wasn't sure the failure of the brakes had been an accident.

Without stopping to think, I flung out my own senses like a net, letting them infiltrate the woods, the night air, the dead grass beneath the snow.

But I felt nothing out of the ordinary. Apparently Hunter didn't, either, because his shoulders relaxed inside his coat, and his stride slowed. He came to a stop and put his hands on my shoulders, looking down at me.

"Are you sure you're all right?" he asked, his voice quiet.

"Yes." I nodded. "It was just scary, that's all." I swallowed. "Do you think that part of the road is spelled? It's so close to where I had my wreck. And Selene—"

"Is nowhere around here. We check every day, and she's gone," said Hunter. Selene Belltower was Cal's mother and the one who'd urged him to pursue me. She'd wanted me and my Woodbane power and my Woodbane coven tools under her control. Failing that, she'd wanted me dead and out of the way. Though she'd fled Widow's Vale weeks ago, I still felt my pulse race whenever I thought of her.

"When you had your wreck, you thought you saw head-lights behind you, right?" Hunter went on. "And you felt magick, didn't you?" He shook his head. "This felt simply mechanical—there just weren't any brakes. I'll call a tow truck from your house, if that's okay."

"Sure," I said, taking a deep breath and trying to unkink muscles still knotted with fear. "And I can give you a ride home."

"Thank you." He hesitated, and I wondered if he was going to kiss me. But he straightened again and took his hands away, and we began walking toward home.

The cold made us walk fast, and at some point Hunter took my hand in his and put them both in his pocket. The feeling of his skin against mine was wonderful, and I wished I could put my arms around him, under his coat. But I still felt unsure of myself with him—there was no way I could be that daring.

As if he'd read my thoughts, Hunter turned and caught my gaze. I blushed, ducked my head, and walked even faster. I was relieved when we turned onto my street.

My parents and my fourteen-year-old sister, Mary K., were watching a movie in the family room when we got home. Hunter blandly told them he'd had "a little car trouble," and they clucked and fretted while he called the tow service. When he hung up, I looked at the clock—it was a few minutes after eleven.

"Mom, is it okay if I take Hunter to his car and then to his house?" I asked.

Mom and Dad did the usual silent parent-communication thing with each other, then Mom nodded. "I guess so. But please drive extra carefully. I don't know what it is with you and cars, Morgan, but I'm starting to worry about you on the road."

I nodded, feeling a little guilty. My parents didn't know the half of it. Three weeks ago Robbie had saved my life. Unfortunately he had saved it by driving my car through the stone wall of Cal's pool house, where I'd been trapped. My parents (who thought I'd hit a light pole) had lent me some of the money to have the front end repaired.

"Okay," I agreed, and Hunter and I got our coats again and went out to Das Boot, my giant, submarine-like '71 Plymouth Valiant. Automatically I winced as I saw its shiny new front bumper, slate blue hood, and gray-spotted sides. I had to get it painted and soon. This rainbow look was killing me.

Inside my car it was freezing, and its old-fashioned vinyl seats didn't help any. We didn't speak as I drove back to Hunter's car to wait for the tow truck. Hunter seemed lost in thought.

After only a minute Widow's Vale's one tow truck came into view. I'd seen John Mitchell a few weeks before, when I had put Das Boot into the ditch. He flicked a glance at me as he bent to hook the tow chain up to Hunter's car.

"We lost the brakes," Hunter explained as John began to crank the car onto the bed of the truck.

"Hmmm," John said, and bent beneath the car to take a quick look. When he came up again, he said, "I don't see anything offhand," and spat onto the side of the road. "Besides the fact you don't seem to have any brake fluid."

"Really," said Hunter. His brows rose.

"Yeah," John replied, sounding almost bored. He gave Hunter a clipboard with a paper to sign. "Anyway, I'll bring it to Unser's and he'll fix you up."

"Right," said Hunter, rubbing his chin.

We got back in Das Boot and watched the tow truck take Hunter's car away. I started the engine and headed toward the edge of town, toward the little house he shared with Sky. "No brake fluid," I said. "Can that happen by itself?"

"It can, but it seems unlikely. I had the car tuned up last week, when I bought it," Hunter said. "If there was a leak, the mechanic should have caught it."

I felt a prickle of fear. "So what are you thinking, then?" I asked.

"I'm thinking we need some answers," Hunter said, looking out his window thoughtfully.

Ten minutes later I pulled up in front of his shabby rented house and saw Raven's battered black Peugeot parked out front.

"Are Raven and Sky getting along?" I asked.

"I think so," Hunter answered. "They're spending a lot of time together. I know Sky's a big girl, but I worry about her getting hurt."

I liked seeing this caring side of Hunter, and I turned to face him. "I didn't even know Sky was gay until she and I did our *tàth meànma*." Weeks ago Sky and I had done what I think of as a Wiccan mind meld. When our thoughts had been joined, I had been surprised to see that she felt such a strong desire for Raven, our resident gothy bad girl.

"I don't know that Sky *is* gay," Hunter said thoughtfully. "She's had relationships with guys before. I think she just likes who she likes, if you know what I mean."

I nodded. I had barely dipped my toes into plain vanilla heterosexual relationships—any variation seemed too mind-boggling to contemplate.

"Anyway," said Hunter, opening his car door and letting in the cold night air, "drive very carefully on your way home. Do you have a cell phone?"

"No."

"Then send me a witch message," he instructed. "If anything the slightest bit out of the ordinary happens, send me a message and I'll come right away. Promise?"

"Okay."

Hunter paused. "Maybe I should borrow Sky's car and follow you home."

I rolled my eyes, refusing to admit I was worried about the lonely drive home. "I'll be fine."

His eyes narrowed. "No, let me get Sky's keys."

"Would you stop? I've driven these roads a million times. I'll call you if I need you, but I'm sure I won't."

He sat back and pulled the door closed. The dome light blinked off.

"You are incredibly stubborn," he remarked conversationally.

I knew he meant well, so I swallowed my tart response. "It's just—I'm very self-reliant," I said self-consciously. "I've always been that way. I don't like owing other people."

He looked at me. "Because you're afraid they'll let you down?"

I shrugged. "Partly, I guess. I don't know." I looked out the window, not enjoying this conversation.

"Look," he said calmly, "I don't know what happened with the car. We don't think Cal and Selene are around, but in fact we don't know where they are or what they're doing. You could be in real danger."

What he said was true, but I felt reluctant to concede the point. "I'll be okay," I said, knowing I was being pointlessly stubborn and unable to stop myself.

Hunter sighed impatiently. "Morgan, I—"

"Look, I'll be fine. Now stop fussing and let me go home." Had I ever been so forthright with Cal? I had wanted so badly for Cal to find me attractive, felt I had fallen so far short of the kind of girl he would want. I had tried to be a more appealing Morgan for him, as stupid and clumsy as my attempts had been. With Hunter, I had never bothered. It felt very freeing to say whatever came to my lips because I wasn't worried about impressing him.

We stared at each other in a standoff. I couldn't help comparing his looks to Cal's. Cal had been golden, exotic, and astoundingly sexy. Hunter was more classical, like a Greek statue, all shapes and planes. His beauty was cool. Yet as I looked at him, the desire to touch him, to kiss and hold him, grew in me until it was almost overpowering.

He shifted in his seat, and I almost flinched when he brought a cool hand up to stroke my cheek. With that one touch I was mesmerized, and I sat very still.

"I'm sorry," he said, his voice low. "I'm afraid for you. I want you to be safe." He smiled wryly. "I can't apologize for worrying about you."

Slowly he leaned closer, his head blotting out the moonlight streaming through the windshield. Ever so gently his warm lips touched mine, and then we were kissing, kissing hard, and I felt completely exhilarated. When he pulled back, we were both breathing fast. He opened the door again, and I blinked in the glare from the dome light. He shook his head, as if to clear it, and seemed at a loss for words. I licked my lips and looked out the windshield, unable to meet his eyes.

"I'll talk to you tomorrow," he said softly. "Drive carefully."

"Okay," I managed. I watched him walk up to the front porch and wanted to call him back, to throw my arms around him and press against him. He turned then, and I wondered with embarrassment if he had picked up on my feelings. I stepped on the gas and sped off.

With witches, you never know.

3

Sharing

November 5, 1968

My mind is still reeling from all that I've seen in the past week.

It started when I found Patrick's Turneval Book of Shadows. That's when I discovered that Waterwind was only one of the covens that he'd belonged to. It was the one he had grown up with, back in Seattle, and it was just like Catspaw: Woodbanes who had renounced everything to do with the dark side. But since I started going through his Turneval stuff, I've seen a whole new side of him. What a waste: oh, Patrick, if only you had shared this with me, the way you shared everything else!

I wonder if he thought Turneval would horrify me. How

could he not know I'd be open to anything, anything he wanted to show me, teach me, any kind of power? He must have known. Maybe he was biding his time. Maybe he wanted to show me but died too soon.

I'll never know. I only know that I would've loved being in Turneval with him, loved for him to teach me all that it meant to be Woodbane.

On Samhain, instead of going to Catspaw's festivities, I went to a Turneval circle. We started by making circles of power and invoking the Goddess, just like at Catspaw. Then everything changed. The Turneval witches knew spells that opened us to the deepest magick, the magick contained in all the creatures and lives that are no longer part of this earth. For the first time I was aware of a universe of untapped resources, whole strata of energy and power and connection that I had never been taught. It was frightening and unbearably exciting. I'm too much of a novice to use this power, of course—I don't even fully know how to tap into it. But Hendrick Samuels, one of Turneval's elders, gave himself over to it, and he actually shape-shifted in front of us. Goddess, he shape-shifted! Covens talk about shape-shifting like it's the story of Goldilocks—but it's real, it's possible. Before my eyes I saw Hendrick assume the form of a mountain lion, and he was glorious. I have to get close to him so he'll share the secret with me.

This is what Patrick spent his life studying, what he hid

from me. It's what I was meant to do, what I should have been born to but wasn't. I see that now.

—SB

"Your folks don't mind you skipping church?" Bree's dark eyes were dimmed by the ribbon of steam coming from her coffee mug. We were in a coffee emporium in a strip mall off the main road. It was popular on Sunday mornings, and people surrounded us, drinking coffee, eating pastry, reading sections of newspaper.

I made a face and loaded my currant scone with butter. "They mind. Somehow they would be more comfortable about my being Wiccan if I also remained a good Catholic."

"And that's not possible?" Bree asked around a mouthful of bear claw.

I sighed. "It's hard."

Bree nodded, and we ate for a few minutes. I studied her covertly. While she was very familiar to me, still, we were both undeniably different people from who we had been three months ago, when Wicca and Cal came into both our lives. We were feeling our way back to being friends again. Things were still awkward between us sometimes, but it felt good to hang out and talk, anyway.

"I like a lot of things about Catholicism. I like the services and the music and seeing everyone," I said. "Feeling like I belong to something bigger than just my family. But it's hard to wrap my mind around some of it. Wicca just feels so much more natural to me." I shrugged. "Anyway, I just wanted to skip it this week. It doesn't mean that I'm never going back."

Bree nodded again and tugged her black top into place. As usual, she looked chic and beautiful, perfectly put together, though she was only wearing jeans and a sweater and no makeup. Usually I felt like a lumberjack around her, with my flat chest, strong nose, boring hair, and lame wardrobe. Today I was surprising myself by feeling strong beneath my looks, as if the witch inside might someday be attractive enough for the Morgan outside.

"How's Mary K.?" Bree asked.

I stirred my coffee. "She's been kind of down lately. Since the whole Bakker fiasco, it's like she's walking around waiting for a ton of bricks to fall on her." Bakker Blackburn, my sister's ex-boyfriend, had twice tried to use force to get her to have sex with him.

"That prick," said Bree. "You should put some awful spell on him. Give him Robbie's old acne." In October, in a fit of experimentation, I'd made a magick potion to clear up the terrible acne that had marred Robbie's looks for years. It had had some unexpected side effects, like correcting his bad vision so that he no longer needed his Coke-bottle glasses. Without the glasses and the acne, he turned out to be startlingly good-looking.

I laughed. "Now, you know we're not supposed to do things like that."

"Oh, like that would stop you," she said, and I laughed some more. It was true that I had either bent or flat-out broken quite a few of the unwritten Wiccan guidelines for responsible use of magick since I had first discovered my powers. But I was trying to be good.

"Speaking of Robbie," I said leadingly, raising my eyebrows.

Bree looked down at her plate. "Oh, Robbie," she said vaguely.

"Are you going to break his heart?" My voice was light, but we both knew I was serious.

"I hope not," she said, and tapped her finger against her plate. "I don't want to. The thing is—he's just throwing himself at me, heart, soul, and body."

"And the body you want," I guessed.

"The body I'm dying for," she admitted.

"You don't want anything else from him?" I said. "You know Robbie's a really good guy. He'd be a great boyfriend."

Bree groaned and dropped her face onto her hands. "How can you tell? We've known him since we were babies! I know him *too* well. He's like a pal, a brother."

"Except you want to jump him."

"Yeah. I mean, he's gorgeous. He's . . . fabulous. He makes me crazy."

"I don't believe it's only physical," I said. "He wouldn't tie you up in knots if there weren't some emotion going on, too."

"I know, I know," Bree muttered. "I don't know what to do. I've never had this problem before. Usually I know exactly what I want and how to get it."

"Well, good luck," I said, sighing. "So, relationships are heating up all over," I added. "Raven and Sky, Jenna and Simon . . ."

"Yeah," Bree said, cheering up. "Sky and Raven are freaking me out. I mean, Raven's a boyfriend machine."

"Maybe what she was looking for all along was a girl," I said, and we made dorky oh-my-gosh faces at each other.

"Could be. And you think Jenna and Simon?" Bree asked, taking a sip of her coffee.

"I think so. They seem to be interested in each other," I

reported. "I hope they do get together. Jenna deserves to be happy after Matt was such an ass to her." I stopped suddenly, remembering that Raven had tried to nail Matt primarily to get him to join her coven—the coven that Bree had also been a member of. The old Kithic.

For a moment Bree looked uncomfortable, as if she too were mulling over the convoluted events of the last month. "Everything changes, all the time," she finally said.

"Uh-huh."

"Anyway," Bree said, "what's with you and Hunter?"

I choked on my coffee and spent the next minute coughing gracelessly while Bree arched her perfect eyebrows at me.

"Uh," I finally said hoarsely. "Uh. I don't know, really."

She looked at me, and I shifted in my seat.

"It just seems that you guys set off sparks when you're together."

"Sometimes," I admitted.

"Do you still love Cal?"

Just hearing his name, especially spoken by Bree, made me wince. Bree had thought she was in love with him. They had slept together before Cal and I started going out, which, as I saw it now, Cal had done partly to drive a wedge between Bree and me so that I'd be all the more dependent on him. I still found it hard to stomach the fact that Cal and Bree had had sex, and he and I hadn't, despite how much I had loved him and thought he loved me.

"He tried to kill me," I said faintly, feeling like the coffee shop was too small.

Compassion crossed her face, and she reached across the

table to touch my hand. "I know," she said softly. "But I also know you really loved him. How do you feel about him now?"

I still love him, I thought. I am filled with rage and hatred toward him. He said he loved me, he said I was beautiful, he said he wanted to make love to me. He hurt me more than I can say. I miss him, and I hate myself for being so weak.

"I don't know," I finally said.

As I was opening my car door in the parking lot, out of the corner of my eye I saw a guy come out of the video store next door to the coffee place. I glanced up, and my heart stopped beating. He was looking down at a piece of paper in his hand, but I didn't need to see his face. I'd run my fingers through that raggedly shorn dark hair. . . . I'd kissed that wide, smooth chest. . . . I'd stared so many times at those long, powerful legs in their faded blue jeans. . . .

Then he looked up, and I saw that it wasn't Cal after all. It was a guy I'd never seen before, with palo blue eyes and bad skin. I stood there, stunned in the bright sunlight, while he gave me a funny look, then walked to his car and got in.

It felt like a full minute before my heartbeat returned to normal. I climbed into Das Boot and drove home. But the whole way, I couldn't help checking my rearview mirror to see if anyone was behind me.

Later that day the phone rang. I raced to answer it, knowing it was Hunter.

"Can I come over?" he asked when I picked up the receiver.

When I'd gotten back from seeing Bree, Mom, Dad, and

my sister were already home from church. I felt guilty about not having gone with them, so since then I had been trying to do good-daughter-type stuff around the house—shoveling the front walk, picking up my crap from the living room, unloading the dishwasher. Having Hunter over would kind of wreck my attempts at scoring points with my family.

"Yes," I said quickly. My heart kicked up a beat in response to his voice. "How will you get here?"

Silence. I almost laughed as I realized he hadn't thought about that.

"I'll borrow Sky's car," he said finally.

"Do you want me to come get you?" I asked.

"No. Are your parents there? Can we talk alone?"

"Yes, my parents are here, and we can talk alone if you want to stand out on the front porch with my whole family inside wondering what we're talking about."

He sounded irked. "Why can't we just go to your room?"

What planet did he come from? "I'm sorry, Your Highness, but I don't live by myself," I said. "I'm seventeen, not nineteen, and I live with my parents. And my parents don't think it's a good idea for boys to be in my room, because there's a bed in there!" Then of course the image of Hunter on my bed made my cheeks burn, and I was sorry I had ever opened my big mouth. What was wrong with me?

"Oh, right. Sorry—I forgot," he said. "But I need to speak to you alone. Can you meet me at the little public park that's by that big grocery store on Route 11?"

I thought. "Yes. Ten minutes."

He hung up without saying good-bye.

*　　*　　*

When I got there, Hunter was standing by Sky's car, waiting for me. He opened Das Boot's door and climbed into the front seat. He was in a tense, angry mood, and the funny thing was, I picked up on that just from waves of sensory stuff I got from him, not from the look on his face or his body language. It was as if he was projecting those feelings and I could just sense them. My witch powers were developing every day, and it was wonderful and a bit scary at the same time.

I waited for him to speak, looking out the windshield, catching the faintest hint of his clean, fresh smell.

"I talked to Bob Unser this morning," he said. "There wasn't any brake fluid in the car, but more than that, the actual brake lines had been severed, right by the fluid reservoir."

I turned to stare at him. "Severed?"

He nodded. "Not cut exactly, not as smooth as that. He couldn't say for sure that someone had cut them. But he did say that it was unusual since both brake lines looked fine when he checked the car last week. It didn't seem like they could simply wear through so quickly."

"Did you check the car for spells, magick?" I asked.

"Yes, of course," he said. "There wasn't anything, apart from the spells of protection I'd put on it."

"So what does that mean? Was this an accident, a person, a witch, what?"

"I don't know," he admitted. "I think it was a person rather than an accident. I think it was a witch because I just don't know that many nonwitches, and I certainly haven't got any nonwitch enemies."

"Could it have been Cal?" I forced myself to ask. "Or Selene?"

"They're the first ones I thought of, of course," he said matter-of-factly, and the hair on my arms rose. I remembered the guy I'd seen in the parking lot this morning—the one I'd thought was Cal.

"But I still don't think they're in the area," he added. "I run a sweep every day, checking this whole area for signs of them, and I haven't picked up on anything. Of course, I'm not as powerful as Selene," he said. "Just because I can't feel her doesn't mean she's truly gone. But I can't help thinking that I would pick up on something if they were still around."

"Like what?" I asked. My mouth felt suddenly dry.

"It's hard to say," Hunter said. "I mean, sometimes I do feel . . . something. But there are so many other things going on that I can't really delineate it." He frowned. "If you were stronger, we could work together, join our powers."

"I know," I said. I was too freaked to bristle at being called weak. "I'm just a newbie. But what about Sky?"

"Well, Sky and I have already joined our powers," he said. "But you have the potential to be stronger than either of us. That's why you must be studying and learning as much as you can. The faster we can get you up to speed, the faster you can help us, help the council. Maybe even join the council."

"Ha," I exclaimed. "There's no way I'm joining the council! Be a hall monitor for Wicca? No thanks!" Then I realized how that must have sounded to Hunter, who was a member of the council himself, and I wanted to take the words back. Too late.

Hunter pressed his lips together and stared out his window. No one else was around: it was a Sunday afternoon and not warm enough for kids to be on the playground. Silence filled my ears, and I sighed.

"I'm sorry," I said. "I didn't mean that. I know that what you do is more important than that. Much too important for me to contemplate doing it," I said honestly. "It's just I can hardly manage to dress myself these days, much less think about doing anything more. Everything is so . . . overwhelming right now."

"I understand," Hunter surprised me by saying. "You've been through a lot. And I know I'm putting a lot of pressure on you, and sometimes I forget how new this is to you. But a talent, a power like yours is rare—maybe once in a generation. I don't want to give you an inflated sense of your own importance, but you should realize that you are and will become an important person in the world of Wicca. There are two ways of dealing with it: You can become a hermit, shutting yourself away from people, studying and learning on your own. Or you can embrace your power and the responsibility it brings and accept the joys and heartbreaks associated with it."

I looked at my lap, feeling self-conscious.

"There's something I wanted to mention to you—a way of acquiring a lot of knowledge quickly. It's called a *tàth meànma brach*, and it's basically a supercharged *tàth meànma*."

"I don't understand," I said.

"You do a *tàth meànma* with a witch who knows a lot more than you, who's more learned and more experienced though not necessarily more powerful," Hunter explained.

"The two of you join very deeply and openly and in essence give each other all your knowledge. It would be as if you suddenly had a whole lifetime's worth of learning in a couple of hours."

"It sounds incredible," I said eagerly. "Of course I want to do it."

He gave me a warning look. "It's not something you should decide lightly. It's a big thing, both for you and the other witch. It can be painful and even dangerous. If one witch isn't ready or the two personalities are too dissimilar, the damage can be severe. I heard of one case where one of the witches went blind afterward."

"But I would know so much," I said. "It would be worth the risk."

"Don't decide right now," he went on. "I just wanted to let you know about it. It would increase your ability to protect yourself—the more knowledge you have, the better you'll be able to access your power. And part of the reason I'm telling you this is because you've already attracted the attention of some very powerful people: Selene and the rest of her Woodbane organization. The sooner you can protect yourself, the better."

I nodded. "I wish I knew where they were," I said. "I'm afraid to look over my shoulder. I keep expecting to see Cal or Selene."

"I feel the same way sometimes. Not about them specifically, but I've made enough enemies in my job as a Seeker to have an assortment of witches who would love to see me dead. Which, by the way, is something I've been thinking about in regard to the cut brake line. I'd be stupid if I didn't take every possibility into account." He shifted in his seat. "Really, all I'm trying to say is that we both have to be extra careful from now on. We need to strengthen the protection spells on your car and your house, and my car and house, and Sky's car. We have to be vigilant and prudent. I don't want anything to happen to . . . either of us."

For several minutes we sat quietly, thinking things through. I was worried, but Hunter's presence made me feel safer. Knowing he was in Widow's Vale made me feel protected. How long would I have that feeling? How long before he would have to leave?

"I don't know how much time I'll have here," he said, unnerving me with the accuracy of his response to my thoughts. "It could be another month, or it could be a year or more."

I hated the thought of his leaving and didn't want to examine why. Then his strong hand was brushing back a tendril of hair off my cheek, and my breath caught in my throat. We were alone in my car, and when he leaned closer to me, I could feel the warmth of his breath. I closed my eyes and let my head rest against my seat.

"While I'm here," he said softly, "I'll help and protect you in any way I can. But you need to be strong with or without me. Promise me you'll work toward that."

I nodded slightly, my eyes still closed, thinking, Just kiss me, kiss me.

Then he did, and his lips were warm on mine and I coiled my hand up to hold his neck. The barest wisp of Cal's image brushed across my consciousness and was gone, and I was drawn into Hunter's light, the pressure of his mouth, his breathing, the hard warmth of his chest as he pressed closer. I felt something else, too—a feathery touch deep inside me, like delicate wings brushing against my very heart. I knew without words, without doubt, that I was feeling Hunter's essence, that our souls were touching. And I thought, Oh, the beauty of Wicca.

4

Begin

May 2, 1969

My skin is shriveled, and my hair is sticky and stiff with salt. I soaked in the purifying bath for two hours, with handfuls of sea salt and surrounded by crystals and sage candles. But though I can dispel the negative energy from my body, I can't erase the images from my mind.

Last night I saw my first taibhs, and when I think of it, I start shaking. Every Catspaw child hears of them, of course, and we're told scary stories about evil taibhs that steal the souls of Wiccan children who don't listen to their parents and teachers. I never thought they really existed. I guess I thought they were just holdovers from the Dark Ages, along with witches riding brooms, black cats, warts on noses: nothing to do with us today, really.

But Turneval taught me differently last night. I had

dressed so carefully for the rite, wanting to outwitch, outbeauty, outpower every other woman there. They had promised me something special, something I deserved after my months of training and apprenticeship. Something I needed to go through before I could join Turneval as a full member.

Now, thinking back, I'm ashamed at how naive I was. I strode in, secure in my beauty, my strength and ruthlessness, only to find by the end of the evening that I was weak, untaught, and unworthy of Turneval's offering.

What happened wasn't my fault. I was just a witness. The ones leading the rite made mistakes in their limitations, in the writing of the spells, the circles of protection—it was the first time Timothy Cornell had called a taibhs, and he called it badly. And it killed him.

A taibhs! I still can't believe it. It was a being and not a being, a spirit and not a spirit: a dark gathering of power and hunger with a human face and hands and the appetite of a demon. I was standing there in the circle, all eager anticipation, and suddenly the room went cold, icy, like the north wind had joined us. Shivering, I looked around and saw the others had their heads bowed, their eyes closed. Then I saw it, taking form in the corner. It was like a miniature tornado, vapor and smoke boiling and coiling in on itself, becoming more solid. It wasn't supposed to do anything: we were just calling it for practice. But Timothy had done it wrong, and the thing turned on him, broke through our circles of protection, and there was nothing any of us could do.

Death by a taibhs is horrible to watch and sickening to

remember. I just want to blank it all out: Tim's screams, the wrenching of his soul from his body. I'm shaking now, just thinking of it. That idiot! He wasn't worthy to wield the power he was offered.

For the first time I understand why my parents, limited and dull as they were, chose to work the gentle kind of magick they did. They couldn't have controlled the dark forces any more than a child can hold back a flood by stuffing a rag in a dike.

Now I'm curled up on my bed, my wet hair flowing down my back like rain, and wondering which way I will choose: the safe, gentle, boring way of my parents or the way of Turneval, with its power and its evil twined together like a cord. Which path holds more terror for me?

—SB

"Open a window. This smell is making me sick," Mary K. complained.

I put down my paint roller and flung open one of my bedroom windows. Instantly frigid air rolled in, dispelling the sour, chemical smell of the wall paint. I stepped back to admire what my sister and I had already done. Two walls of my room were now a pale coffee-with-cream color. The other two walls were still covered by the childish pink stripes I was trying to obliterate. I grinned, already pleased with the transformation. I was changing, and my room was changing to keep up.

"You're only going to live here for another year," Mary K. pointed out, carefully edging a line by the ceiling. A paint-spattered bandanna covered her hair, and though she was in sweatpants and a ratty old sweater, she looked like a fresh-faced teen singer. "Unless you go to Vassar or SUNY New Paltz or something and just commute."

"Well, I don't have to decide about that for a while," I said.

"But why worry about your room now?" Mary K. asked.

"I can't take this pink anymore," I said, rolling a swath of paint over the wallpaper.

"Remember when I asked you if you'd had sex?" Mary K. suddenly said, almost making me drop my roller. "With Cal?"

There it was, the familiar wince and stomach clench I felt whenever that name was mentioned.

"Yeah?" I said warily.

"So, did you guys ever do it? After we talked?"

I took a breath and slowly released it to the count of ten. I focused on rolling a smooth, broad line of paint across the wall, feathering the edges and rolling over any drips. "No," I managed to say calmly. "No, we never did." A bad thought occurred to me. "You and Bakker . . ."

"No," she said. "That was why he always got so mad."

She was only fourteen, though a mature and curvy fourteen. I felt incredibly thankful that Bakker hadn't managed to push her further than she was ready to go.

I, on the other hand, was seventeen. I'd always assumed that Cal and I would make love someday, when I was ready—but the times he'd tried, I said no. I wasn't sure why, though now I wondered if my subconscious had picked up on the fact that I wasn't in a safe situation, that I couldn't trust Cal the way I would need to trust him to go to bed with him. Yet I had loved the other things we had done: the intense making out, how we had touched each other, the way magick had added a whole other dimension to our closeness. Now I would never know what it felt like to make love with Cal.

"How about Hunter?" Mary K. asked, looking down at me thoughtfully from her ladder.

"What about him?" I tried to sound careless, but I couldn't quite pull it off.

"Do you think you'll go to bed with him?"

"Mary K.," I said, feeling my cheeks heat up. "We're not even *dating*. Sometimes we don't even get along."

"That's the way it always starts," Mary K. said with fourteen-year-old wisdom.

We'd started early, so we finished the walls around lunchtime. While I cleaned up the painting equipment, Mary K. went down to the kitchen and made us some sandwiches. Recently she'd gotten into eating healthy food, so the sandwiches were peanut-butter and banana on seven-grain bread. Surprisingly, they were good.

I polished off my sandwich, then took a sip of Diet Coke. "Ah, that hits the spot," I said.

"All that artificial stuff is bad for you," Mary K. said, but her voice was listless. I regarded her with concern. It really was taking her a while to come out of her depression over Bakker.

"Hey. What are you doing this afternoon?" I asked, thinking maybe we could hit the mall, or go to a matinee movie, or do some other sisterly activity.

"Not much. I thought maybe I'd go to the three o'clock mass," she said.

I laughed, startled. "Church on a Monday? What's going on?" I asked. "You becoming a nun?"

Mary K. smiled slightly. "I just feel . . . you know, with everything going on—I just need extra help. Extra support. I can get that at church. I want to be more in touch with my faith."

I sipped my Diet Coke and couldn't think of anything constructive to say. In the silence I suddenly thought, Hunter, and then the phone rang.

I lunged for it. "Hey, Hunter," I said.

"I want to see you," Hunter said with his usual lack of greeting. "There's an antiques fair half an hour from here. I was wondering if you wanted to go."

Mary K. was looking at me, and I raised my eyebrows at her. "An antiques fair?" was my scintillating reply.

"Yes. It could be interesting. It's nearby, in Kaaterskill."

Mary K. was watching the expressions cross my face, and I pantomimed my jaw dropping. "Hunter, is this a date?" I asked for Mary K.'s benefit, and she sat up straighter, looking intrigued.

Silence. I smiled into the phone. "You know, this sort of sounds like a date," I pressed him. "I mean, are we meeting for business reasons?"

Mary K. started snickering quietly.

"We're two friends getting together," Hunter said, sounding very British. "I don't know why you feel compelled to label it."

"Anyone else coming?"

"Well, no."

"And you're not calling it a date?"

"Would you like to come or not?" he asked stiffly. I bit my lip to keep from laughing.

"I'll come," I said, and hung up. "I think Hunter just asked me out," I told Mary K.

"Wow," she said, grinning.

I skipped upstairs to take a shower, wondering how, when my life was so stressful and scary, I could feel so happy.

Hunter picked me up in Sky's car twenty minutes later. My wet hair hung in a long, heavy braid down my back. I offered him a Diet Coke and he shuddered; then we were on our way to Kaaterskill.

"Why did you care if this was a date or not?" he asked suddenly.

I was startled into an honest reply. "I wanted to know where we stand."

He glanced at me. He was really good-looking, and my brain was suddenly bombarded with images of how he had been when we were kissing, how intense and passionate he'd seemed. I looked out my window.

"And where do we stand?" he asked softly. "Do you want this to be a date?"

Now I was embarrassed. "Oh, I don't know."

Then Hunter took my hand in his and brought it to his mouth and kissed it, and my breathing went shallow.

"I want it to be what you want," he said, driving with one hand and not looking at me.

"I'll let you know when I figure it out," I said shakily.

The antiques fair took place in a huge warehouselike barn in the middle of rural New York. There weren't many people there—it was the last day. Everything looked kind of picked through, but still, I enjoyed the time with Hunter, the time without magick involved. My mood got even better when I found a little carved box that would be perfect for my mom and an old brass barometer that my dad would love. Two

Christmas gifts that I could cross off my list. I was woefully behind on my holiday shopping. Christmas was coming up fast, and I'd barely thought about it. Our coven was planning a Yule celebration, too, but fortunately that didn't involve any gift-giving.

I was engrossed in the contents of an old dentist's cabinet when Hunter called me over. "Look at these," he said, pointing to a selection of Amish-type quilts. I'd always liked Amish quilts, with their bright, solid colors and comforting geometry of design. The one Hunter was pointing to was unusual in that it had a circular motif.

"It's a pentacle," I said softly, touching the cotton with my fingertips. "A circle with a star inside." The background was black, with a nine-patch design in each corner in shades of teal, red, and purple. The large circle touched each of the four sides and was of purple cotton. A red five-pointed star filled the circle, and a nine-patch square was centered in the star. It was gorgeous.

I glanced at the middle-aged woman selling the quilts and cast my senses quickly to see if she was a witch. I picked up nothing. "Is it Wiccan?" I asked so only Hunter could hear.

He shook his head. "More likely just a Pennsylvania Dutch hex design. It's pretty, though."

"Beautiful." Again I ran my fingers gently across the cotton.

The next thing I knew, Hunter had pulled out his wallet and was counting out bills into the woman's hand, and she was smiling and thanking him. She took the small quilt, barely more than four feet square, and wrapped it in tissue before putting it into a brown paper bag.

We headed back to Hunter's car. "That's really beautiful," I said. "I'm glad you bought it. Where will you put it?"

We climbed into his car, and he turned to me and handed me the bag. "It's for you," he said. "I bought it because I wanted you to have it."

The air around us crackled, and I wondered if it was magick or attraction or something else. I took the bag and reached my hand inside to feel the cool folds of the quilt. "Are you sure?" I knew neither he nor Sky had much income—this quilt must have put a huge dent in his budget.

"Yes," he said. "I'm quite sure."

"Thank you," I said softly.

He started the car's engine, and we didn't say anything until he dropped me at my house. I climbed out of the car, feeling uncertain all over again. He got out, too, and coming around to the sidewalk, he kissed me, a soft, quick meeting of the lips. Then he climbed back in Sky's car and drove off before I could say good-bye.

5

Flicker

May 17, 1970

Spring has finally sprung in Wales. Here in Albertswyth the hills are a new bright green. The women of the village are on their hands and knees, setting plants in their gardens. Clyda and I have been walking over the hills and among the rocks, and she's been teaching me the local herb lore and the properties of the local stone, earth, water, and air. I've been here six months now, on one of life's detours.

Since I found out about Clyda Rockpel from one of Patrick's spelled books, I was determined to find her, to learn from her. It took two weeks of camping on her doorstep, eating bread and cheese, sleeping with my coat pulled over my head before she would speak to me. Now I'm her student, taking knowledge from her like a sea sponge absorbs ocean water.

She's deep, dark, terrifying sometimes, yet the glimmers of her power, the breadth of her learning, her strength and guile in dealing with the dark forces fill me with a giddy exhilaration. I want to know what she knows, have the power to do what she does, have control over what she controls. I want to become her.

—SB

On Tuesday, Mary K. and I once again spent the morning working on my room, touching up messy spots on the walls and painting the woodwork. In the afternoon I persuaded my sister to come shopping with Bree and me. The lure of hanging out with us had outweighed her disapproval of our destination: Practical Magick, an occult store up in Red Kill, ten miles north.

"The good thing about Christmas break," Bree said as she drove through downtown Widow's Vale, "is seeing all the poor saps who have to go to work."

"We're going to be poor working saps one day," I reminded her, watching people weaving in and out of the shops on Main Street. I picked at some speckles of paint on the back of my hand and adjusted the heater vent of Breezy, Bree's BMW.

"Not me," Bree said cheerfully. "I'm going to marry rich and be a lady who lunches."

"Gross!" Mary K. protested from the backseat.

Bree laughed. "Not PC enough for you?"

"Don't you want more than that?" Mary K. asked. "You could do anything you want."

"Well, I was kind of kidding," said Bree, not taking

offense. "I mean, I haven't figured out what my life calling is yet. But it wouldn't be the worst thing to be a housewife."

"Bree, please," I said, feeling a shade of our old familiarity. "You would last about two weeks. Then you'd go crazy and become an ax murderer."

She laughed. "Maybe so. Neither of you wants to be a housewife? It's a noble profession, you know."

I snorted. I had no concrete idea what to do with my life—I'd always thought vaguely about doing something with math or science—but I knew now without a doubt that the majority of my life would center on Wicca and my own studies in magick. Everything else was optional.

"No," said my sister. "I never want to get married."

Something in her tone made me crane around from the front seat to look at her. Her face looked drawn, almost haunted, in the gray winter light, and her eyes were sad. I glanced across at Bree and was touched by the instant understanding that passed between us.

"I hear you dumped Bakker in a big way," Bree said, looking at Mary K. in the rearview mirror. "Good for you. He's an ass."

Mary K. didn't say anything.

"You know who's cute in your class?" Bree went on. "That Hales kid. What's his name? Randy?"

"Just plain Rand," said Mary K.

"Yeah, him," said Bree. "He's adorable."

I rolled my eyes. Trust Bree to have scoped out the freshman boys.

Mary K. shrugged, and Bree decided not to press it. Then she pulled Breezy into a parking spot in front of Practical Magick, and we piled out into the chilly December air.

Mary K. looked at the storefront with only faintly disguised suspicion. Like my parents, she strongly disapproved of my involvement with Wicca, though I'd talked her into coming to a party here recently, and she'd enjoyed it.

"Relax," I said, taking her by the arm and pulling her into the store. "You're not going to have your soul sucked out just by looking at candles."

"What if Father Hotchkiss saw us?" she grumbled, naming our church's priest.

"Then we'd have to ask him what he was doing in a Wicca shop, wouldn't we?" I answered, grinning. Inside, I let go of my sister's arm and took a moment to get my bearings. I hadn't been to Practical Magick since I'd come with Hunter to confront David Redstone, the owner, about using dark magick. It had been profoundly horrible, and being in the store brought back the memories in a wave: Hunter questioning David; David's admission of guilt, wrenched from him against his will.

It hurt to associate those memories with this place, the place I had come to think of as my refuge, a lovely, scent-filled shop full of magickal books, essential oils, crystals, herbs, candles, and the deep, abiding peace of Wicca, permeating everything.

Looking up, I saw Alyce, a gentle sorrow still showing on her face. David had been a dear friend of hers. He had turned over the shop to her, a Brightendale blood witch, when he'd had his power stripped from him. She owned the shop now.

She walked toward me, and we embraced: I was taller than she, and I felt bony and immature next to her womanly roundness. We looked into each other's eyes for a moment, not needing to speak. Then I stepped back to include Bree and Mary K.

"Hi, Alyce," Bree said.

"Nice to see you, Bree," Alyce replied.

"You remember my sister, Mary K.?" I asked.

"Certainly," said Alyce, smiling warmly. "The one who was so taken with The Fianna." The Fianna was a Celtic band that Mary K. and I both loved. Alyce's nephew, Diarmuid, played in it. The only way I'd gotten Mary K. to come to the party here was by luring her with promises of The Fianna playing.

"Yes," said Mary K. shyly.

"We just got in a shipment of really interesting jewelry from a woman who works in Pennsylvania," Alyce said, leading Mary K. over to a glass case. "Come see."

I smiled as Mary K. was drawn to the jewelry. Bree moved down the aisle to examine a collection of altar cloths, and I was free to wander the side of the store that was floor-to-ceiling bookshelves. Soon Alyce joined me.

"How is Starlocket?" I asked. Starlocket was Selene Belltower's old coven. With her disappearance, Alyce had been asked to lead it.

"Going through transitions," Alyce said. "Some people have left, of course—those who'd been drawn to Selene's dark side. The rest of us are trying to heal and move forward. It's very challenging, leading a coven."

"I'm sure you're a wonderful leader," I said.

"Alyce?" I looked up as a man came toward us, holding up a box of black candles. "Do we put out all the stock at once or keep some in the back?" he asked.

"I usually put out as much as the shelves will hold," Alyce said. "Finn, come meet Morgan."

Finn looked like he was in his fifties; tall, and neither thin nor fat, but sturdy-looking. He had short, thick hair that was a faded red shot through with white. His eyes were hazel, his skin was fair, and he had faded freckles across his nose and cheeks. I sent out my senses without even deciding to and ran a quick scan. Blood witch. Probably Leapvaughn, I thought. They often had red hair. Then I saw the surprise in his eyes and shut down my senses, vaguely embarrassed, as though I'd been caught in the Wiccan equivalent of seeing someone's underwear.

"Hmmm," Finn said thoughtfully, holding out his large hand. "Pleased to meet you, Morgan." He gave Alyce an odd glance, as if she had introduced him to a questionable character.

Alyce smiled. "Morgan, this is Finn Foster. He's helping me in the shop," she explained. To Finn she added, "Morgan is a dedicated customer." She offered no other explanation, and with Finn's eyes on me I felt even more strongly that I had committed a faux pas.

"Who do you study with?" Finn asked.

"Um, right now a lot by myself, and some with Hunter Niall."

Finn blinked. "The Seeker?"

"Yes."

"You're Morgan Rowlands," Finn said, as if he'd just made a connection.

"Yes." I glanced at Alyce uncertainly, but she just smiled reassuringly.

Finn hesitated, as if debating whether to say something more, but then he just smiled and nodded. "Nice meeting you," he said. "Hope to see you again soon." He gave Alyce a glance and took the box of candles to the other side of the store. A moment later I heard Bree asking him about some clover oil. I looked for Mary K. and saw that she was holding some silver earrings up, looking at them in a small mirror.

"What was that about?" I asked Alyce, and she chuckled softly.

"I'm afraid you're a bit notorious," she said. "I'm sorry if you feel like a performing seal, but lots of people have already heard of your power, your heritage—not to mention what happened with Cal and Selene—and they're curious."

Ugh. I shifted uncomfortably.

Alyce reached past me to straighten some books on a shelf. "Has Hunter talked to you about your studies? About *tàth meànma brach?*"

"Yes," I answered, surprised by the change of subject.

"What do you think of the idea?" Her clear, blue-violet eyes searched mine.

"It sounded exciting," I said slowly. "I want to do it. What do you think about it?"

"I think it might be a good idea," she said, looking thoughtful. "Hunter's right—you need to learn as much as you can as fast as you can. For almost any other witch I would advise against it. It's hard, and I'm sure Hunter told you it can be dangerous. But you're an exceptional case. Of course, it's your decision alone. But you should consider it carefully."

"Would you do it with me?" I asked.

She looked deeply into my eyes. I had no idea how old she was—in her fifties?—but I saw a wealth of knowledge in her gaze. What she knew could help me, and I suddenly wanted her knowledge with a surprising hunger that I tried not to show.

"I'll think about it, my dear," she said quietly. "I'll talk to Hunter, and we can decide."

"Thank you," I whispered.

"Are you about ready?" Bree called down the aisle. Finn had already rung up her purchases; she held a small green bag with silver handles.

"Yes," I called back. "Where's Mary K.?"

"Right here," my sister said, emerging from the other aisle.

"Did you want those earrings you were looking at?" I asked, and she shook her head, her shiny auburn hair swinging around her shoulders. I wondered if she thought buying those earrings would be like taking witchcraft into the house and resolved to try to put her fears to rest on that point. Maybe I could surprise her with them for Christmas.

It was late afternoon when we headed home in Breezy. I was quiet and full of thought about the possibility of doing the *tàth meànma brach* with Alyce.

"Why do you like that store so much?" Mary K. asked from the backseat.

"Don't you think it's cool?" Bree asked. "Even if I wasn't into Wicca, I would still be into the candles and jewelry and incense and stuff."

"I guess." My sister sounded subdued, and I knew she was struggling with the conflict of liking anything that had to do with witchcraft while remaining true to her own religion and to my parents. She looked out her window, distant and withdrawn. None of us spoke for several miles, and I looked out my window at the rapidly darkening landscape, the rolling hills, the old farms, the snow clinging to everything. With a start I realized that Bree had taken her old route toward home and that we were in Cal's neighborhood. My heart sped up as we drew closer to the large stone house he had shared with his mother. I hadn't been past here since the night I'd almost died in the pool house, and my skin broke out in a clammy sweat at the memory.

"I'm sorry," Bree murmured as she realized where we were.

I swallowed and didn't say anything, my hand clenching the door handle tightly, my breathing fast and shallow. Relax, I told myself. Relax. They're gone. They're nowhere around. Hunter looks for them—scries for them every day—and he hasn't found them. They're gone. They won't hurt you.

As we passed, my eyes were irresistibly drawn to the house. It looked dark, abandoned, forbidding. I recalled the first floor, with its large kitchen, the huge living room with a fireplace where Cal and I had kissed on the sofa. Selene's hidden, spelled private library that I had found, where I had discovered Maeve's Book of Shadows. Cal's room that ran the length of the attic. His wide, low bed where we had kissed and touched each other. The pool house, where he had trapped me and tried to burn me to death . . .

I felt like I was choking and swallowed again, unable to move my eyes away. Then I stared hard as a flickering light, as if from a candle, passed in front of a dark window. Just one moment and it was gone, but I was sure I had seen it. Wildly I looked over at Bree for her reaction, but her eyes were on the road, her hands poised on the leather steering wheel. In the backseat Mary K. gazed out her window, unhappiness making her face seem younger, rounder.

"Did you—" I started to ask. I stopped. Was I sure I had seen it? I thought so. But what was the point of mentioning it? Mary K. would be upset and worried. Bree wouldn't know what to do, either. If only Hunter was here, I thought, and then grimaced as I realized what would be set in action if Hunter had seen it: a full-blown investigation, worry, trouble, fear.

And had I really seen it? A flickering candle in an abandoned house, at night, for just a moment? I leaned my head against the cold car window, my heart aching. Was this ordeal never going to be over? Would I ever relax again?

"Did we what?" Bree asked, glancing at me.

"Nothing," I mumbled. Surely it had been my imagination. Cal and Selene were gone. "Never mind."

6

The Lueg

March 18, 1971

At the age of twenty-seven, I have completed the Great Trial. It was four days ago, and I am only now able to hold a pen and sit up to write. Clyda thought I was ready, and I was so eager to do it that I didn't listen to the people who warned me not to.

The Great Trial. I have wondered how to describe it, and when my words get close, I want to cry. Twenty-seven is young—many people are never ready. Most people, when they do it, are older, have been preparing for years. But I insisted I was ready, and in the end Clyda agreed.

It took place on top of Windy Tor, past the Old Stones left by the Druids. Below me I could hear the waves crashing against rocks in a timeless rhythm. There was no moon, and it was as black as the end of the world. With me were Clyda and another Welsh witch, Scott Mattox. I was naked, sky clad, and we cast the circle and started the rite. At midnight Clyda held out the goblet. I stared at it, knowing I was scared. It was the Wine of Shadows: where she had gotten it, I don't know. If I passed the Great Trial, I would live. If I didn't pass, this wine would kill me. I took the goblet with a shaking hand and drank it.

Clyda and Scott sat nearby, staying to keep me from going over the edge of the cliff. I sat down, my lips numb, muttering all the spells of power and strength that I knew. Then the first needlelike tingles of pain started in my fingertips, and I cried out.

It was a long, long night.

And here I am, alive, on the other side. I am wasted by fasting, by vomiting, by a sharp-edged sickness in my gut that makes me wonder if they fed me glass. This morning I saw myself in the mirror and screamed at the dull-haired, hollow-eyed, greatly aged woman I beheld. Clyda says not to worry: my beauty will come back with my strength. What is it to her? She was never beautiful and has no idea how it feels to lose it.

Yet hollowed out as I am, like a tree struck by lightning, I can tell the difference. I was strong before, but now I'm a force of nature. I feel like wind, like rain, like lava in my strength. I'm in tune with the universe, my heart beating to its primordial, deeply held thrum. I'm made of magick, I'm walking magick, and I can cause death or life with a snap of my fingers.

Was the Great Trial worth this? The illness, the scream-ing agony, the clawed, ripped hands, the gouges in my thighs made when I was shrieking in terror and desperation and try-ing to feel anything normal, anything recognizable, even phys-ical pain? My brain was split open and put on display, my body was turned inside out. Yet in the destruction is the resur-rection, in the agony is the joy, in the terror is the hope. And now I've taken that terrible, mortal journey and I've come through it. And I'll be like a Goddess myself, and lesser beings will follow me. And I'll found a dynasty of witches that will amaze the world.

—SB

"So if your mother comes home, what should I do?" Hunter asked. "I mean, is she going to hit me with a cook-ing pan?"

I grinned. "Only if she's in a bad mood." It was Wednesday, my parents were at work, Mary K. was upstairs, and we were getting ready to study. "Anyway, I told you I could come to your place," I reminded him.

"Sky and Raven are at my place," he said. "I assume they wanted privacy."

"Really?" I asked with interest. "Are they getting serious?"

"I didn't come here to gossip," he said primly, and I wanted to smack him. I was trying to think of a clever reply when he looked around the kitchen restlessly.

"Let's go up to your room," he said, and I blinked.

"Uh," I began. Boys were so not allowed upstairs in our house.

"You said you'd made an altar," he said. "I want to see it. Your room is where you do most of your magick, right?" He stood up, pushing his hand through his pale hair, and I tried to gather my thoughts.

"Um." The only time Cal had ever been in my room was just for a minute, after Bree had almost broken my nose during a volleyball game at school. Even then my mom had gotten twitchy, despite the fact that I was a total invalid and hardly feeling romantic.

"Come on, Morgan," he coaxed. "We're working. I'll try not to jump you, if that's what you're afraid of."

My face burned with embarrassment, and I wondered what he would do to me if I zapped him with witch fire. I was almost willing to find out.

"Sorry," he said. "Let's start over. Please, may I see the altar you made in your room? If your parents come home unexpectedly, I'll do a quick look-over-there spell and get the hell out of here, okay? I don't want to get you in trouble."

"It's just that it's my parents' house," I said stiffly, standing up and leading the way toward the foyer. "I try to respect their rules when I can. But let's go up quickly. I want you to see it." I plodded up the stairs, intensely aware of his quiet tread behind me.

I was thankful that my room was no longer pink and stripy. Sea grass window shades replaced my frilly curtains, complementing my new café-au-lait-colored walls. The old cream-colored carpet had been pulled up, and I had a simple jute area rug instead. I loved my new room but stood nervously by my desk as Hunter looked around, taking it all in. I went to the closet and pulled out the old camp foot-locker that served as my altar, complete with violet linen cloth, candles, and four special objects that represented the four elements.

My single bed seemed to take on mythic proportions, almost filling the room, and I blushed furiously, trying to wipe the image of Hunter + bed out of my mind.

He looked at my altar.

"It's pretty basic," I muttered. "It's hard because I have to keep it hidden."

He nodded, then glanced up at me. "It's fine. Nice. Perfectly appropriate. I'm glad you made one." His voice was calm, reassuring. I pushed the altar back in my closet and artfully draped my bathrobe to cover it. Should we go back downstairs? I wondered, but as I came out of my closet, I saw that Hunter was sitting casually on my bed, his fingers playing with the smooth texture of my down comforter. With no warning I wanted to throw myself on him, press him down against the mattress, kiss him, be physically aggressive in a way I never had with Cal. And then of course as soon as that thought crossed my brain, I recoiled, knowing with certainty how attuned Hunter was to my every feeling. Oh, man.

But his face remained neutral, and he said, "Have you been memorizing the true names of things?"

"Sort of," I said, feeling guilty. I hadn't done much studying since the David incident, but before that I'd made a start on my memorization. I pulled out my desk chair and sat down in it, and at that moment Mary K. tapped lightly on the door and came in, not waiting for me to invite her. She stopped dead when she saw Hunter sitting on my bed, her mouth open in an almost comical O. She looked from him to me and back again, and even Hunter grinned at her expression, his normally serious face lighting up, making him look younger and lighthearted.

"We have to get a lock for that door," he said cheerfully, and I wanted to die. My sister's eyebrows rose, and she looked fascinated.

"I'm sorry," Mary K. said. "I just wanted to ask you about dinner—but I'll come back later."

"No, wait," I started to say, but she had already whirled out the door, closing it behind her with an audible click. I glanced back at Hunter to see him grinning again.

"I feel like a fox in a henhouse full of Catholic girls," he said, looking pleased. "This is doing wonders for my ego."

"Oh, like your ego needs help," I retorted, then wanted to bite my tongue.

But Hunter didn't take offense and instead said, "What names have you been studying?"

Huge, long freaking lists, I wanted to say. I took a deep breath and said, "Um, wildflowers and herbs of this geographic zone, ones that bloom in spring, summer, and fall and are dormant in winter. Ones that are poisonous. Plants that can counteract spells, either good or bad. Plants that neutralize energy." I named ten or eleven of them, starting with *maroc dath*—mayapple—then paused, hoping he was suitably impressed. Learning just the English or Latin names of hundreds of different plants would have been quite a feat, but I had also learned their true names, their magickal names, by which I could use them in spells, find them, increase or decrease their properties.

Hunter, however, looked underwhelmed. His green eyes were impassive. "And under what condition would you use *maroc dath* in a spell?"

I hesitated, something about his voice making me think carefully about his question. *Maroc dath, maroc dath*—I knew it as mayapple, a wild plant with a white flower that bloomed before the last frost of the year . . . used to clarify potions, to make a healing ointment, to . . .

Then I got it. *Maroc dath* wasn't mayapple. "I meant maroc *dant,*" I said with dignity. "*Maroc dant.* Mayapple." I tried to remember if *maroc dath* was something.

"So you're not studying spells in which you use menstrual blood," Hunter said, his eyes on mine. "*Maroc dath.* Menstrual blood, usually that of a virgin. Used primarily in dark rites, occasionally in fertility spells. That's not what you meant?"

Okay, now I wanted the earth to swallow me. I closed my eyes. "No," I said faintly. "That's not what I meant."

When I opened my eyes again, he was shaking his head. "What would happen if you did that in a spell?" he asked rhetorically. "What happens if you don't know all of this and therefore make errors in your spells?"

My first instinct was to throw a pillow at him. Then I remembered that he was trying to get me to learn so I would be protected. He was trying to help me. I remembered that I had told him I trusted him, and that it had been true.

With my next breath an awareness came over me, something unconnected to what Hunter and I were talking about, and my eyes widened and flew to his face.

"Do you feel it?" I whispered, and he nodded slightly, his whole body tense and still. I moved cautiously toward him, and he reached out his hand to clasp mine. Someone was scrying for me, someone was trying to find me. I sat next to Hunter on the bed, barely conscious of the warmth of his thigh against mine. As one, we closed our eyes and sent out our senses, dissolving the barriers between us and the world, reaching out toward our unseen spy as he or she reached out toward us.

I began to get a sense of a person, a person shape, an energy pattern—and in the next instant it was gone, snuffed as quickly as a candle, without even a wisp trail of smoke to lead me to it. I opened my eyes.

"Interesting," Hunter muttered. "Did you get an identity?"

I shook my head and untangled my fingers from his. He looked down at our hands as if he hadn't known they were joined.

"I have something to tell you," I said, and then I gave him the story of possibly seeing a candle in a window at Cal's house the day before.

"Why didn't you tell me immediately?" he asked, looking angry.

"It just happened last night," I began, defending myself. Then I stopped. He was right, of course. "I—I didn't know what to do," I offered awkwardly. "I figured I was making a big deal out of nothing, just being paranoid." I stood up, moved away from the bed, and pushed my hair over my shoulder.

"Morgan of course you should have told me," Hunter said. His jaw tensed. "Unless you have a good reason not to."

What was he trying to say? "Yes," I said sarcastically. "That's it. I'm in league with Cal and Selene, and I didn't want to tell you because when I *give* myself to the dark side, I *won't* want you to know about it."

Hunter looked like I had slapped him, and he stood quickly, so we were only inches apart and he was towering over me, bright spots of anger appearing on his fair cheeks.

His hands gripped my shoulders, and my eyes widened. I jerked away from him, slapping his hands away, and we stared at each other.

"Don't ever joke about that again," he said in a low voice. "That isn't funny. How can you even say something like that after what you saw David Redstone go through?"

I gasped, remembering, and to my horror, hot tears welled in my eyes. It *had* been stupid and appalling to throw that at Hunter after seeing it in reality. What had I been thinking?

Deliberately Hunter stepped back, away from me, and pushed his hand through his hair. A muscle in his jaw twitched, and I knew he was trying hard to control himself.

"I never lose my temper," he muttered, not looking at me. "My whole job, my whole life is about being calm and objective and rational." Then he glanced up, and his eyes were like green water, cool and clear and beautiful, and I felt caught by them, the fire of my anger doused. "What is it about you that gets under my skin? Why do you get to me?" He shook his head.

"We just rub each other the wrong way sometimes," I said clumsily, sinking back down into my desk chair.

"Is that what you think it is?" he asked cryptically. He sat down on my bed again, and I had no idea how to answer him. "All right," he said, "back to the candle. I believe that you saw something. Selene's house has been spelled inside and out with ward-evil, confusion, barrier spells, you name it. A member of the council and I worked for hours after the fire, trying to seal the house and dispel the negative energy from it. Obviously we didn't do enough."

"Do you think it's Cal, or Selene, back inside?" I asked.

Had that been Cal I saw in the window, Cal, so close?

"I don't know. I can't see how they could get in, after everything we did. But I can't dismiss the possibility. I'll have to check into it."

Of course he would. He was a Seeker. I realized then that I hadn't wanted to tell him in case it *had* been Cal I'd seen. Even after all that Cal had done, I didn't want Hunter to be seeking him. A vision of David Redstone, weeping and writhing as his power left him, rose up in my mind. I couldn't bear the thought of Cal suffering the same torment.

Hunter's face was serious and still. "Look," he said, standing up and reaching into his backpack. "Let's scry together, right now, joining our energy. Let's just see what happens." He took a purple silk bundle out of the backpack and unwrapped it. Inside was a large, dark, flattish stone. "This was my father's *lueg*," he said, his voice expressionless. "Have you scryed with a stone before?"

I shook my head. "Only with fire."

"Stones are as reliable as fire," he told me, sitting cross-legged on the floor. "Fire is harder to work with but offers more information. Come sit down."

I sat across from him, our knees touching, as if we were about to do *tàth meànma*. Leaning forward, I looked into the flat, polished face of the stone, feeling the familiar excitement of exploring something new in Wicca. My hair draped forward, brushing the stone. Quickly I gathered it at the base of my neck and with practiced gestures twisted it into a braid. I didn't bother securing the end but let it hang behind me.

"It seems like not too many girls have long hair anymore," Hunter said absently. "They all have short, layery . . ." He motioned with his hands, unable to come up with the vocabulary to describe modern do's.

"I know," I said. "I think about cutting it sometimes. But I hate fussing with a style. This way I never have to think about it."

"It's beautiful," Hunter said. "Don't cut it." Then he blinked and became businesslike, while I once again tried to get my bearings on the peaks and valleys of our interaction. "Right. Now, this is just the same as scrying with fire. You open yourself to the world, accept what knowledge the universe offers you, and try to not think: just be. Just like with fire."

"Got it," I said, still processing the fact that Hunter liked my hair.

"Good. Now, we're looking for Cal or Selene," Hunter said, his voice softening and fading.

We leaned toward each other, our heads almost touching, our hands joined lightly on the *lueg*. It was like looking into a black pool in a woods, I thought. Like looking down a well. As my breathing shifted and slowed and my consciousness expanded gently into the space around me, the *lueg* began to seem like a hole in the universe, an opening into incomprehensible wonders, answers, possibilities.

I could no longer feel anything physically: I was suspended in time, in space, and existed only because of my thoughts and my energy. I felt Hunter's life force near mine, felt his warmth, his presence, his intelligence, and nothing startled me. Everything was fine.

In the face of the stone I began to see swirls of gray mist, like striated clouds, and I released any expectations I'd had and simply watched to see what they would become. Then it was like watching a video or a moving photograph: I saw a person, walking toward me, as if looking into a camera. It was a middle-aged man, a handsome man, and he looked both surprised and alarmed and intensely curious. I'd seen him before, but I couldn't think where.

"Goddess," Hunter muttered, his breath suddenly coming sharp and fast. I felt my consciousness flare.

"Giomanach," said the man softly. His face was lined, his hair gray, his eyes brown. But there was something of Hunter in the shape of his jaw, the angle of his cheek.

"Dad," Hunter said, sounding strangled.

I gasped. Hunter hadn't seen either of his parents in ten years, and though we'd talked about the possibility of his trying to find them, as far as I knew, he'd done nothing about it yet. What was happening?

"Giomanach," said the man again. "You're grown. My son . . ." He looked away. In the background I could barely make out a house, painted white. I heard a seagull cry faintly and wondered where Hunter's father had been all this time, where he was now.

"Dad," Hunter said. I felt the coiled tension of his emotions; it almost caused me pain. "Linden—"

"I know," said the man, looking older and sadder. "I know. Beck told us how your brother died. It wasn't your fault. It was his own fate. Listen, my son—your mother—"

Then the picture changed as a dark presence washed across the face of the *lueg*. It was like a cloud, a purple-black vapor roiling across the *lueg*, and Hunter and I watched unspeaking as the dark wave focused and concentrated, blotting out his father's face, the whitewashed window.

With a jolt Hunter snapped back, straightening, his eyes

flicking open to stare widely at me, and I gazed at him, seeing his pale face as the grounding of my reality.

My temples were damp with sweat, and my hands were shaking. I rubbed my palms against my corduroys and tried to swallow but couldn't. I knew I had just seen the dark wave in the stone—the dark wave that had consumed my ancestors and almost every member of my ancestral coven almost twenty years before. The dark wave that we believed was somehow connected to Selene.

Hunter spoke first. "Do you think the dark wave took my father just then?" he asked, his voice hoarse.

"No!" I said strongly. He looked so lost. Without thinking I rose to my knees and clasped him in my arms, cradling his head against my chest. "I'm almost sure it didn't. It was more like it passed in front of the stone. Between us and him. I can't believe it, Hunter, that was your father. He's alive!"

"Yes," Hunter said. "I believe he is." He paused, then said. "I wonder what he was trying to tell me about Mum."

I was silent, unable to think of anything comforting to tell him.

"I've got to tell the council," he mumbled against my shirt.

After a few moments he pulled back slightly, and reached up to brush my damp hair away from my face. I looked in his eyes and couldn't read the emotions there. Cal's emotions had always seemed so transparent: desire, admiration, light-hearted flirtation. Hunter was still mostly unreadable to me.

Then I thought, To hell with it, and before either of us realized it, I bent down, put my hands on his shoulders, and pressed my lips against his, keeping my eyes open. I saw the flash of surprise, the sudden ignition of desire, and then his eyes drifted closed and he pulled me backward with him to the floor. I was on top of him, his chest against mine, our legs tangled together.

I don't know how long we lay against the hard floor, the unforgiving jute rug, kissing again and again, but finally I heard a furtive tap on my door and Mary K.'s quiet voice: "Mom just pulled up."

Flushed, breathing hard, I trotted downstairs and helped Mom unload groceries from her car, and ten minutes later when I went back to my room, Hunter was gone, and I had no idea how he had managed to leave without any of us noticing.

7

Circle of Three

November 8, 1973

Clyda fainted again yesterday. I found her at the bottom of the stairs. This is the third time in two weeks. Neither of us have mentioned it, but the fact is that she is old. She hasn't taken care of herself, she's worked too much magick with too few limitations, and she's dabbled too freely with the dark forces.

That's a mistake I never make. Yes, I'm part of Turneval, and yes, I call on the dark side. But never without protecting myself. Never without precautions. I don't drink from that cauldron without making sure it will be refilled.

At any rate, Clyda's health is Clyda's concern. She doesn't ask for or want my care, and now I need her less and less in my studies. Since the Great Trial, I can learn any-

thing easily; of course, the strength and the weakness of Wicca is that there's always more to be learned.

I just reread this entry and can't believe I'm yapping on about an old woman's health when just last night my life changed again. Clyda finally introduced me to some members of her coven, Amyranth. Even now my skin gets chilled, just writing the name. I won't lie: they terrify me, by reputation, by their very existence. And yet I'm so drawn to them and their mission. I have no doubt I was meant to be part of them. From birth I was marked to be in Amyranth, and to deny that would be lying to myself. Oh, I have to go—Clyda is calling.
—SB

There were only four other cars in the parking lot of St. Mary's when I pulled in to drop off Mary K. Probably thirty years ago, weekday-morning services were more attended, but nowadays it seemed amazing that Father Hotchkiss bothered to have them at all.

"You sure you want to go?" I asked Mary K. "Wouldn't you rather just go get coffee instead?"

My sister shook her head but made no move to get out of the car.

"What's going on, Mary K.?" I asked. "You seem so unhappy lately. Is it because of Bakker?"

Again she shook her head, looking out her window. "Not just Bakker," she said finally. "All guys. I mean, look at you and Cal. And Bree and all her boy toys. Guys are just . . ."

"Losers?" I suggested. "Jerks? Imbeciles?"

She didn't smile. "I just don't get it," she said. "It's just—I feel like I never want to date again. Never want to be vulnerable again. And I hate that. I don't want to go through my whole life alone."

I closed my mouth hard before I could say something stupid like, You're only fourteen, don't worry about it.

Instead I said, "I know how you feel."

She looked at me, troubled, and I nodded.

"I feel the same way sometimes. I mean, Cal was my first boyfriend, and look what a mistake that turned out to be. After that, how can I ever be sure of any guy again?"

"You can be sure of Hunter," she said. "He's a good guy."

"I think so. But then I think, Cal seemed like a good guy, too." I grimaced. "You know what the really sick thing is?"

"What?"

"I miss Cal," I admitted. "I felt like I knew him, like I understood him. Now I know he was lying to me, using me, setting me up. But it didn't feel that way at the time, so I don't remember it that way. I'm drawn to Hunter, really drawn to him, but I feel like I don't know him and never will."

We sat in Das Boot, feeling depressed. Instead of cheering her up, I had only brought myself down. "I'm sorry," I said. "I didn't mean to go off on my own problems."

"Want to come to church with me?" Mary K. asked with a touch of humor.

"No." I gave a tiny laugh. "Want to come to Practical Magick with me?"

"No. Well, I'd better go in. I'll walk home after. Thanks for the ride."

"Sure."

"And thanks for talking, too." She gave me a sweet smile. "You're a good sister."

"You are, too," I said. I loved her so much. She got out and walked up the church steps, and I put Das Boot in gear and headed north, to Red Kill and Practical Magick.

I'd come to Practical Magick looking for Christmas gifts, but once I got there, I realized I really wasn't in the mood to shop. I've got time, I told myself. I'd get those silver earrings for Mary K., and then everyone in my immediate family would be accounted for. That left my aunt Eileen and her girlfriend Paula, my aunt Margaret and her husband and kids, and Robbie . . . and after that I was in a gray area. Should I give Hunter a gift? It seemed almost too intimate for whatever our relationship was—but on the other hand, he'd bought me my beautiful hex quilt. And then what about Bree? Were we exchanging gifts this year or not? I sighed. Why did it all have to be so confusing?

A comforting voice interrupted my thoughts. "You look like you need to take your mind off your troubles. Come up and see my new apartment," Alyce suggested. After David's departure, she'd moved into one of the apartments upstairs from the store; it had been David's aunt Rosaline's apartment. David had inherited the shop—and Rosaline's considerable debts—when she'd died not long ago. Trying to find a way out of the debts was what had led him into his disastrous experiment with dark magick. Now that Alyce owned Practical Magick, she was paying back the money Rosaline had owed, on a long-term schedule.

Alyce told Finn where we'd be, and then we went out the front doors. "Since I'm running the shop, it makes sense to live close by, and it saves on rent," Alyce explained. Outside were three other doors, all in a line to the right of the store's glass double entrance. Alyce unlocked the door in the middle, and we went up a steep, narrow wooden staircase.

At the top of the stairs were two small, narrow apartments. Alyce led me through the door on the left. The living room was small and bare but freshly painted a warm cream color. Sitting on a surprisingly modern couch was Sky Eventide, reading a leather-bound book.

"Hey," I said. I hadn't seen her since last Saturday's circle.

"Hi," she answered, searching my face. I wondered if Hunter had told her about our vision of his father and about the dark wave.

"Sky and I have been working together," Alyce explained, stepping into the tiny windowless kitchen to make tea. I sat down on a large pillow on the floor.

"When you came in today, I thought maybe the three of us could have a circle," Alyce went on, getting out cups and saucers. "It'll help center you, Morgan. Also, you and Sky are both working with unanswered questions, and it could be helpful."

I thought about the two circles I had been to recently where my powers had been nonexistent and dreaded the idea of feeling that again.

"Yeah, okay," I said, taking the cup of tea that Alyce offered me.

Our circle was small, just the three of us, and somehow intensely *Alyce:* open, receptive, nurturing, strong, very womanly.

We stood, hands linked, in the middle of the living room. Pale winter sun streamed through the windows. Closing our eyes, we each chanted our personal power calls.

"An di allaigh, ne ullah," I began.

Sky and Alyce each quietly chanted to themselves: Alyce's was in English, while Sky's sounded more like mine, Celtic, old, incomprehensible. Three times we walked deasil around our central candle. By the third cycle I felt power flowing from Sky's fingers to mine, from my fingers to Alyce's. The power had a distinct and different quality: eternal, life enhancing.

Then Alyce invoked the four elements, the Goddess and the God, and said, "Lady and Lord, we are each on a personal quest. Please help us to be open to the answers that the universe provides. Please help us open our minds to the world's wisdom.

"My quest is as leader of Starlocket," Alyce went on. "Help me open my consciousness to receive the wisdom I need to guide the women and men of my coven. Help me understand why I have been chosen as leader. Help me fulfill my duties with love."

Then her blue-violet eyes were on Sky, and she nodded. Sky looked thoughtful, then said, "My quest is . . . whether I'll live up to my parents' heritage. Whether my magick will be as strong, as pure as theirs."

I looked at her, surprised to hear her doubt her own power and ability. She'd always struck me as arrogant, even overconfident, and I knew she had much more knowledge and spellcraft than I did. Now I saw that she had weaknesses, too.

Alyce looked at me, and I felt unprepared. This wasn't what I had come here for, and I had no ready statement. Which quest should I mention? I had so many unanswered questions: about Cal, Selene, Maeve's tools, my natural father, Hunter, Bree. . . . Where to begin?

"No, dear," Alyce said softly. "It's more than that."

Oh. Then I thought of the circle we'd had at Sharon's house, and it came to me. "My personal quest is about my own nature," I said, knowing it was true as the words left my mouth. "Am I more likely to lean toward evil because of my Woodbane blood? Will I have to fight it twice as hard as anyone else? How can I learn to recognize evil when I see it? Am I . . . can I escape the darkness?"

I felt rather than saw Alyce's approval that I had found the right questions, and Sky's piqued interest and slight alarm. We held hands for a moment longer, just standing there, and I felt the power flowing among the three of us, almost like an electric current. I am strong, I thought. And I have good friends. Hunter, Robbie, Bree, Alyce, even Sky—they would all stand by me and help me to make the right choices. For a moment I held that sure knowledge in my mind, and it gave me a sense of comfort and peace.

Then we walked widdershins three times, Alyce disbanded our circle, and we snuffed the candle.

"Thank you both," Alyce said. She began to put away her ritual cups. "Now my apartment will be blessed with good energy. And we've each found a question in our hearts that must be answered before we move forward."

"How do we find the answer?" Sky asked, sounding frustrated.

Alyce laughed and said gently, "That's part of the question, I'm afraid."

We stayed in Alyce's apartment for another half hour or so, just talking, enjoying one another's company. Then Alyce had to go back to the shop, so Sky and I reluctantly left.

"That was nice," Sky said as we came out onto the street.

"Yeah." I smiled, enjoying the moment of uncomplicated friendliness.

"Well, see you later." She walked down the street to where her car was parked.

As I started Das Boot, I thought about our circle. Oddly, I felt more afraid than I had before, now that I had openly acknowledged my greatest fear. I kept glancing over my shoulder the whole way home, as if expecting the dark wave to loom up in my rearview mirror.

Not really thinking, I started to take the road home that led past Cal's old house. At the last minute I realized what I was doing and swerved back into my lane, causing an angry honk from in back of me. I made an I'm-sorry kind of wave and took another route home. I didn't want to pass his house. Not today.

8

Attacked

Samhain, 1975

Last night my two-year apprenticeship with Amyranth ended. So much has changed in my life in the past five years. When I think back to who and what I was, it's like looking back at a different lifetime, a different person. Who I am now is so much more intense and fulfilling.

We're in northern Scotland now, and it's as bleak and forbidding a place as there is. The land is wild here, and I love it, even though I know I wasn't meant to live here. But here we are, and my bones are soaking up the power that seeps from the very rocks in this place.

Two years ago, when I was inducted into Amyranth, I'd heard only vague rumors of dark waves. Since then there have been three events that I know of, but I wasn't allowed to participate in them or know the details. Last night that changed.

The coven we took was Wyndenkell, and it was older than anyone knew. It had existed for at least 450 years. I can't imagine that. In America, most of our covens have existed for less than a hundred. The magick here is ancient and compelling, which is why we wanted it.

I'm bound not to describe the event, nor what we did to call the wave. But I will say that it was the most terrifying, exhilarating event I've ever witnessed. The sight of the huge, fierce wave, the purplish black color of a bruise, sweeping over the gathered circle—feeling its icy wind snatching the souls and power of the witches, feeling its energy being fused into me, like lightning—well, I'm a changed woman, a changed witch. I'm a daughter of Amyranth, and that fact alone gives my life meaning and joy.

Now the Wyndenkell coven's knowledge and magick are ours. As they should be.

—SB

"Now, this is a nice car," Hunter said, running his hand over Breezy's leather seats. "German engineering, fuel efficient."

My eyes narrowed. Was that a dig against Das Boot? It wasn't my car's fault that it was made before fuel economy became a desired trait. I tried to glare at Hunter, but I couldn't hold a grudge. It was just too beautiful a Friday, sunny, perfectly clear, and almost forty degrees. To have even a little break from the hellish winter we'd been having was a treat.

"Yeah, I like it," Bree said from the front seat. She navigated the on-ramp smoothly, and then we were on the highway, headed toward the nearby town of Greenport. Its downtown area had lots of cute shops and restaurants, and Bree had talked Robbie and me into an outing. After which I'd taken my nerve in both hands and called to invite Hunter to come, too. It wasn't exactly a date, but I was starting to feel more and more like we were a couple.

"Did you speak to the council about what we saw in the scrying stone?" I asked Hunter in a low voice.

He nodded. "I told Kennet Muir, my mentor. He promised the council would look into it. He warned me not to scry again, that it would only lead the dark wave to Mum and Dad. I know he's right, but . . ." He trailed off. I heard the impatience and frustration in his voice. I knew exactly how he felt. Even to know they were dead would in some ways be better than this constant state of limbo. I reached over and took his hand.

He turned to me, and we shared a look that seemed to melt my very soul. When had I ever felt so in tune with anyone?

"I know," he whispered, and I understood that he was saying he shared my feelings. My heart soared, and the bright day suddenly seemed almost too brilliant to bear.

Robbie turned around to look at me and Hunter. "Chip?" he offered, holding out the bag.

It was only ten-thirty in the morning, but I took a handful of barbecue-flavor potato chips and crunched them. With a particularly English look, Hunter declined. I hid a smile.

"Can I have a chip?" Bree asked.

Robbie fed one to her, watching her with an endearing combination of adoration and lust.

I ate another handful of chips and popped open a Diet

Coke. Hunter gazed at me steadily, and I tried very hard not to think about making out with him on the floor of my room. "Nature's perfect beverage," I said, holding up the can. He grimaced and looked away.

"What an amazing day," Bree said, stretching in her seat.

"Thanks to me and my weather charm," I said lightly.

Robbie and Hunter both looked at me in alarm. "You didn't," said Robbie.

"You didn't," said Hunter.

I was enjoying this. "Maybe I did, maybe I didn't."

Hunter looked upset. "You can't be serious!"

Cahn't, I thought. Cahn too.

"Have you learned nothing these past weeks?" he asked. "Weather-working is not something to be taken lightly. You have no idea of the consequences this could have. How could you possibly have toyed with improper magick in this way?"

I met Bree's eyes in the rearview mirror. Instantly a smile broke across her face; she alone could tell I was teasing. It felt so wonderful to be driving somewhere again with her. The last three months had been desolate without her. We had a long way to go toward rebuilding our relationship, but we were making progress, and it felt great.

"You don't understand what the council—" Hunter went on, really getting wound up.

"Relax, Hunter," I said, taking pity on him. "I was just kidding. I don't even know how to work weather magick."

"Wha—what?" he sputtered.

"I don't even know how to work weather magick," I repeated. "And I certainly have learned my lesson about the improper use of magick. Yes, sir. You won't catch me doing *that* again." I took a deep, satisfying swig of my Diet Coke.

Hunter drummed his fingers on his door handle and looked out the window. After a moment a reluctant grin crept across his face, and I felt a burst of delight.

"By the way," he said a few minutes later, "I went into Selene's house and checked it out, looking for the source of that candle you saw. I didn't find any trace of anything, neither a person nor any magick."

"What candle at Cal's?" Robbie asked.

"I thought I saw someone holding a flickering candle in the window of Cal's old house," I explained.

Robbie looked startled and alarmed. "Yikes."

"So you didn't see footprints or anything?" I asked Hunter.

"No. It's already dusty inside, and the dust was undisturbed," Hunter said. "I wanted to have another go at getting into Selene's hidden library, but once again I couldn't find the door." He shook his head in frustration. "She has incredibly strong magick, I'll say that for her."

"Hmmm," I said, thinking. I had been in that library only once, by accident, when I had found Maeve's Book of Shadows. I wondered if I could get into it again. The International Council of Witches would surely want to see what, if anything, was left in that room. But I just couldn't face it. I never wanted to go in that house again. I wanted to help Hunter but just couldn't bring myself to offer to do this.

"Hey, Bree, you'll be getting off at the next exit," said Robbie, who was navigating.

"Okay," said Bree.

We didn't talk much about magick after that. I started thinking about the circle I'd had with Sky and Alyce yesterday.

I knew I needed to learn more about my heritage, my birth parents, but I was at a loss as to where to begin. They'd died more than fifteen years before, and they'd known no one, had no close friends that I knew of, in America.

When I'd first found out that I was adopted, I'd read every newspaper article I'd found about the fire that killed my birth parents. I'd also found Maeve's Book of Shadows hidden in Selene's library (which probably should have tipped me off that Selene wasn't as open and giving as she seemed), and in the last few weeks I'd read it cover to cover. I'd even found secret passages detailing Maeve's passionate and tragic love affair with a man other than Angus, my birth father. I had Maeve's magickal tools, which she'd helped me to find through a vision.

But all that knowledge wasn't enough. It didn't fill in the gaping holes in my understanding of Maeve and Angus as *people*—and as Woodbane witches.

As I thought, the miles flew by, and then suddenly we were in Greenport, and Robbie was saying he was ready for lunch.

It was a happy, carefree day. We walked around, shopped, ate, laughed. I found a beautiful necklace of glass beads and twisted wire in a craft shop, and bought it to give Bree for Christmas, deciding on the spot to take the initiative. Someone had to be bold if we were going to put our friendship back together.

We all went home in the afternoon, and my aunt Eileen and her girlfriend Paula came over for dinner. Aunt Eileen, my mom's younger sister, is my favorite aunt, and I was glad to see them. I was even gladder to hear that they were settling into their new home. They'd recently moved to a house in the nearby town of Taunton, and at first they'd been harassed by a bunch of gay-bashing teenagers. Happily, those kids had been arrested, and the rest of the neighbors seemed to be going out of their way to make Aunt Eileen and Paula feel welcome.

At about eight-thirty I said my good nights to everyone and headed out to my car. Our coven was having its weekly circle a day early this week, because a couple of people had holiday obligations with their families on Saturday night. The circle would be at Hunter and Sky's house.

The beautiful day had flowed into an equally beautiful winter evening. I felt I hadn't seen the stars for ages, and I relished looking at them through Das Boot's windshield.

"Morgan."

In one second my heart stopped cold. I slammed on the brakes, and my car swerved to the right. When I recovered, I wheeled around and scanned the backseat frantically, then looked at the seat next to me, which was of course empty. That voice. Quickly I reached over and pushed down all the door locks and peered out into the darkness.

It had been Cal, Cal's voice, calling me, as he had done many times before. A witch message. *Where was he?* He was searching for me. Was he nearby? My heart pounded, and adrenaline flooded my body so that my hands were shaky on the steering wheel. Cal! Oh Goddess. Where was he? What did he want?

My next thought was that I had to get to Hunter. Hunter would know what to do.

I sat for a moment, willing my body to stop trembling. Then I put my car back in gear and pulled out again onto the road. I cast my senses out as strongly as I could. I drove carefully, trying to interpret the feelings and impressions I got, but there was no Cal anywhere in them: no voice, no image, no heartbeat.

Cal. The instantaneous tug of my heart horrified and angered me. For one moment, when I'd heard his voice, my heart had leaped in eager anticipation. How stupid *are* you? I asked myself furiously. How big an idiot?

With my senses still at their most alert, I turned down Hunter's street and parked along his dark, weedy curb. Still no inkling of Cal's presence. But could I be sure my senses were correct? I cast a fearful look around me, then ducked through the opening in the hedge and headed up the narrow path to Hunter and Sky's ramshackle house.

A few feet from the front stairs the sound of voices and laughter from around back stopped me, and I picked my way impatiently through the dead grass and clumps of old snow, down the sloping lawn to their back porch. Hunter, I thought. I need you. I had made a mistake in not telling Hunter about the candle in Cal's house. This I knew I had to tell him right away.

"Yo! Morganita," Robbie called, and I looked up to see him hanging over the side of the deck. The house had been built into the side of a steep hill, so in front there were only four steps to the porch, but in back the porch was on the second story, supported by long wood pilings. Dropping off sharply behind the house, the hill turned into a steep, rocky ravine that was wild and beautiful during the day, dark and ominous at night.

"Hey," I called. "Where's Hunter?" I heard Bree's voice, and Jenna's laugh, and smelled the spicy, comforting scent of clove and cinnamon and apples.

"Right here," Hunter called.

I looked up at him, sending him a message. I need to talk to you. I'm scared.

Frowning, he started down to meet me. I hurried up the stairs, comforted by the reality of his presence. How far could someone send a witch message? I wondered. Was it possible Cal had called me from, say, France? I wanted to believe it was.

The porch staircase was long and rickety, with two turns before the top. Hunter was halfway down, and when I was almost to him, our glances met: we were both feeling the first prickle of alarm, our senses processing the unnatural feelings of shakiness and sway in the staircase. Then Hunter was reaching out his hand to me in slow motion, and I reached back even as I heard the first, thundering crack of wood splitting and felt the steps fall away beneath my feet, leaving me to drop endlessly into darkness, away from the light and my friends.

I was unconscious barely a moment: when I opened my eyes, wood fragments were still settling around me, and dust tickled my nose. I hurt all over.

"Morgan! Morgan! Hunter!" It was hard to tell who was calling, but I sensed Hunter near me, trying to struggle into a sitting position beneath one of the porch's support beams.

"Here!" Hunter called back, sounding shaken. "Morgan?"

"Here," I said weakly, feeling like my chest had been crushed, like I would never have enough breath in my lungs again. I tried to turn my head to look at the porch, but I must have rolled far down into the ravine, because I couldn't see the top.

"Hang on—I'll come get you," said Hunter, and I saw that

he was about eight feet above me. Then Robbie, Matt, and Sky were leaning over the edge of the ravine with flashlights and a long rope. Holding the rope, Hunter edged his way toward me, and I grabbed his hand. Together we climbed up the rocky slope, and by the time I reached the top and sat down on the edge, I was trembling all over. I saw that the porch was still attached to the house, but the corner where the stairs had been sagged frighteningly, and the stairs themselves were in pieces. Our coven members stood on the lawn in a frightened group. It looked as if only Hunter and I had fallen when the stairs collapsed.

"Are you guys all right?" Bree asked. I saw fear and concern in her eyes.

I nodded. "Nothing feels broken. I must have landed on something soft," I said.

"That was me, I think. But I'm all right, more or less," Hunter added. He put a hand to his side and winced. "Just a few scrapes and bruises."

Sky put her arm around my waist and helped me around to the front of the house and inside.

"What happened?" Matt asked, following us. "Was the wood rotten?"

The coven members gathered around, going over what had just happened. As soon as they'd seen the stairs collapsing, they had crowded back through the kitchen door. I was so glad no one else had been hurt.

Sky left the kitchen, and Bree led me to a chair. "That was terrifying," she said. "Seeing you and Hunter go down." She shook her head.

"Here. I found some kava kava tea," said Jenna, pressing a warm mug into my hand.

I nodded and took it from her. "Thanks." I sipped the herb tea, hoping it would take effect soon. What a night it had been already, between hearing Cal's voice and then having this accident.

A few minutes later Sky came back in. "Hunter's looking at the porch," she reported. "Now let's get you cleaned up." She fetched a small basket of supplies from the bathroom and started washing my cuts and bruises. "Arnica," she said, holding out a small vial. "Good for trauma."

I was letting the pills dissolve under my tongue when Hunter limped in, his face grim. He had scrapes on his cheek, and his sweater was ripped and bloody on one side. For myself, I knew I'd have bruises on my back and legs, but that was pretty much it.

"The posts were sawed," Hunter announced, throwing down the coil of rope.

"What?" Robbie exclaimed. He, Bree, and Jenna were hovering by my chair. Matt, Raven, Sharon, and Ethan were standing at the back door, looking out at what was left of the porch. Thalia, Alisa, and Simon hadn't arrived yet.

I stared at Hunter in alarm, and Cal's voice echoed in my head again. "Sawed with a saw, or spelled to break?" I asked.

"Looked like a saw," Hunter said as Jenna gave him a mug of the same tea I was drinking. "I didn't sense any magick. I'll have a closer look tomorrow, in the daylight."

He looked at me: we needed to talk. This was the second time we had almost been killed when we were together. It couldn't be coincidence.

"Maybe we should call the police," said Jenna.

Hunter shook his head. "They'd think we're subversive Wiccan weirdos who are being persecuted by the neighbors," he said dryly. "I'd rather not bring them into this."

"Okay, everybody, I'm going to lead the circle tonight," Sky announced, getting everyone's attention. "We'll start in a few minutes. Why don't the rest of you come to the circle room and start getting settled in while Morgan and Hunter finish their tea?"

They all trooped out. Robbie cast a worried glance over his shoulder at me as he left.

Alone, Hunter and I sat in silence for a moment.

"Neither of these accidents looked like magick," Hunter said at last. He breathed in the steam from his mug. "But as I said, I just can't think of any enemies I might have who aren't witches."

"What about someone who used to be a witch?" I asked, thinking of how David had been stripped of his magick. David was in Ireland, but Hunter must know other witches whose magick was bound.

"That's a thought," Hunter agreed, "although I pretty much know the location of the ones I've had to work against, and none of them are anywhere nearby." He put down his mug. "I'd better get cleaned up," he said, wincing as he stretched his arm. Automatically I followed him to the downstairs bathroom.

He snapped on the light. The room was small, unrenovated, with old-fashioned white tiles. It was scrupulously clean, and he started rummaging in the medicine cabinet. I perched on the edge of the tub. "I have something to tell you," I said.

He turned to look at me. "That sounds ominous." With careful movements he stripped off his dark, ripped sweater and the torn T-shirt underneath. Then he was wearing only his jeans, and I was trying not to stare at his naked, muscled chest. He was much fairer than Cal, his skin a smooth ivory color, and he had more chest hair than Cal. It was a golden brown and stretched from beneath his collarbone down in a V to where it disappeared into his pants, at eye level to where I was sitting. My mouth went dry, and I tried to focus on the large scrapes that sullenly oozed blood along his side.

When I dragged my eyes up to his face, he was looking at me with an almost glittering awareness. Wordlessly he handed me a wet washcloth, then held his arm away from his side.

Oh, I thought, standing up and starting to wash away the blood and dirt. My fingers tingled where they touched him. He turned for me, and I saw his back had been scraped as well, though not as badly. His skin was smooth, and he had pale freckles across both shoulders. I remembered that he was half Woodbane. He and Cal had the same father.

"Do you have a Woodbane athame?" I asked. "The birthmark?"

"I do, actually," he said. "Do you?"

"Yes." I dropped the washcloth in the sink and reached for the antibiotic ointment.

"I'll show you mine if you show me yours," he said with a wolfish smile.

Mine was under my left arm, on my side. Since I couldn't see his, I could only assume it was somewhere under his pants. My mind couldn't even begin to go there, so I said nothing.

"Don't you want to know where mine is?" he asked teasingly, and I could feel my blush starting at my neck and working its way upward. He leaned over me and brushed my hair over my shoulder, then traced my jawline with one finger. I remembered the way he felt, pressed against me, and most of my coherent thoughts fled.

"No," I said unconvincingly, lost in his eyes.

"I want to know where yours is," he breathed, his mouth close to mine.

The idea of his hands under my shirt, roaming over my skin, almost made my knees buckle. "Uh," I said, trying to talk myself out of whipping off my shirt right there. Focus. Come on, Morgan.

"Cal called me tonight," I blurted.

His hand fell away from my cheek. *"What?"* His voice reverberated loudly off the tiles.

"On my way over here. He sent me a witch message. I heard it in my head."

Hunter stared at me. "Why didn't you tell me right away?"

I just looked at him, and then he realized what had happened as soon as I got here.

"Right. I'm sorry. Well, what did he say? Could you tell where he was? Do you know where he is? Tell me everything." Moments before he had been playful and flirtatious; now he was intense, all business.

"There's nothing much to say," I explained. "I was driving here, and suddenly I heard Cal say, 'Morgan.' That's all. I was totally freaked and sent my senses out to find him but didn't feel him anywhere. I mean, I didn't feel a thing. And that was all he said."

"Do you know where he is?" Hunter demanded, holding my shoulders. "Tell me the truth."

"What do you mean? I *am* telling you the truth! I don't know where he is." I stared at him in bafflement. How could he think I might lie about something so important to both of us?

"Cal! That bastard," Hunter snapped, letting go of me. His hands clenched into fists, and the bathroom seemed too small to hold his rage. "Are you sure he didn't say anything else?"

"I'm positive. I already told you." I returned his glare. "Why are you treating me like a criminal? I didn't do anything wrong."

A muscle in his jaw flickered. But he didn't reply directly. Instead he shot questions at me like bullets. "Did you feel at all different? Is there a period of time you don't remember? Anything that feels confusing or odd?"

I realized what he was getting at. "Wouldn't I know if he'd put a spell on me?"

"No," Hunter said disdainfully. "He's a piss-poor witch, but he knows more than you do." He looked deeply into my eyes, as if he would see the spell reflected there. Then he turned away. I felt embarrassed and angry. Hunter was hurting my feelings, and I felt myself closing off to him. Especially when he wheeled back to me and added, "You're not holding anything back from me, are you? You're not feeling some idiotic urge to protect him because he's such a bloody stud and you still want him even after he tried to kill you?"

My mouth fell open, and my hand had shot up to slap him when it hit me: he was jealous. Jealous of my past with Cal. I stood there with my hand in the air as I tried to process this.

"Goddess, that bastard!" Hunter said. "If he's here, if I find him . . ."

Then what? I wondered. You'll kill him? I couldn't believe Hunter, cool, reserved Hunter had turned into this furious person I barely recognized in a matter of seconds. It frightened me.

"Hey, are you lot almost done in there?" Sky called from the other room.

"Yes," I called back, wanting to get away from Hunter. I wondered why on earth I had thought telling him would make me feel better or safer.

"This is one of the most useful rituals there is," said Sky almost half an hour later. I was finding that Sky's circle was different from any circle I'd attended: the fact was that whoever was leading a circle naturally imbued it with their aura, their power, and their whole persona. It was fascinating to see how different leaders cast different circles. So far I liked Sky's circle.

"I'd like to teach you how to deflect negative energy," said Sky. "This isn't something to use if you're under attack or in real trouble. It's more like something gentle and constant to surround yourself with in order to reduce negativity in your life and increase your positive energy."

I glanced at Hunter, thinking, He could use some positive energy right about now. His anger seemed less intense, but I could tell he was still brooding.

"It uses runes as its base," Sky explained. She took a small red velvet pouch from her belt and knelt. "Everyone sit down and come closer." Opening the pouch, she dumped its contents onto the wooden floor. Rune tiles spilled out, really pretty ones, made of different-colored stones. I had a rune set at home that I'd bought at Practical Magick, but mine was only fired clay. "There are so many different tools a witch can use. Incense, herbs, oils, runes or other symbols, crystals and gems, metals, candles." She grinned up at us as we crowded around her like kindergartners. "Witches are very practical. We use whatever we can find. Today we're using runes."

With deft fingers she organized the runes into three rows, each tile in line according to its place in the elder futhark, the traditional runic alphabet. We all knew the runes by heart at this point, and I could hear the coven members quietly identifying them.

"First we need Eolh, for protection," said Sky, pulling it out of line. "What's another name for Eolh?"

"Algiz," I said automatically.

"And Wynn," she said, placing the Wynn tile next to Eolh. "For happiness and harmony. Another name for it?"

Simon said, "Wunjo."

"Uine," said Robbie, and Sky nodded. I liked how she was involving everyone—she wasn't just lecturing, but including what little knowledge we had.

"Sigel, for sun, life, energy," said Sky, placing it by the other to form a triangle.

"Sowilo," said Thalia, looking pleased that she knew.

"Sugil," Bree added.

Sky grinned. "You guys are good. One more. Ur, for strength." She placed the tile for Ur so that the four symbols together made a diamond shape.

"Uruz or Uraz," said Raven, and her eyes met Sky's for a moment of private communion.

"Right. Now," Sky went on. "You can write these runes on a piece of paper, scratch them into an old slate or stone, carve them into a candle, or what have you. But use *these* four runes in *this* order. Put the written runes in your personal space, your bedroom, your car, even your school locker. When you see them, tap them with a finger and repeat, "Eolh, Wynn, Sigel, Ur. Come to me from where you are. Guide the things I do or say, and let your wisdom come this way."

She sat back. "You can also circle your hand, palm down, three times deasil over the runes to help increase their power." She showed us. "That's all there is to it. It's not big magick or especially beautiful magick, but it's very useful magick."

"I think it's beautiful," said Alisa, looking young and sincere. "All magick is beautiful."

"No," I said, sounding more abrupt than I had meant to. "It isn't."

People looked at me, and I felt self-conscious. Hunter and Sky nodded, and I knew they understood. We three had seen magick that was dark and ugly. It existed; it was all around us.

That night I found myself driving behind Bree on the way home from Hunter and Sky's. I felt shaken and upset, not to mentioned bruised and achy: hearing Cal's voice, the frightening fall I'd had, Hunter's awful reaction to hearing about Cal. Was Cal nearby? Just thinking about it terrified me. It was all too much. I just wanted to go home and get in bed and hold my kitten, Dagda.

Bree had taken the short route home, down Gallows Road. There were lots of twists and turns, but it took less time than going on main streets. Bree had always been the more daring driver of the two of us, and despite my trying to keep up, within minutes I lost sight of her in the darkness.

Suddenly I was overwhelmed with the feeling of being completely alone on a dark road.

Without warning, my headlights flashed on something on the road ahead. I caught a blurry glimpse of something—a deer?—barely in time to slam on my brakes. As Das Boot screeched heavily to a halt, my eyes focused, and my mouth opened in a wordless, "Oh." My headlights shone on a figure who was walking toward my car, hands upraised.

Cal.

9

Cal

Lammas, 1976

I'm fairly well settled into the house now that Clyda's gone.
Her death three months ago was a surprise to everyone but me.
She'd been sick, getting frailer and weaker. I think it was the
dark wave in Madrid that really took it out of her. Really,
she had no business traveling at her age. But it's difficult for
some people to acknowledge their weaknesses.

I was in Ireland last week and met two interesting witches.
One was a gorgeous boy, just old enough to shave, whose power is
already frightening and strong and worth watching. I took
Ciaran to bed for a night, and he was charmingly youthful,
enthusiastic, and surprisingly skilled. I'm smiling even now,
thinking about it.

But it's Daniel Niall who's haunting my thoughts, and
the irony of this can't escape me. Daniel is a Woodbane from

England who came to one of Amyranth's gatherings in Shannon. I could see he was uncomfortable, had come out of curiosity and found us not to his liking. For some reason that made him even more attractive to me. He doesn't have Ciaran's harsh, raw beauty, but he is good-looking, with strong, masculine features, and when he looked into my eyes and smiled shyly, my heart missed a beat. Sweet Daniel. He's deeply good, honest, from one of those Woodbane covens that renounced evil ages ago. It's oddly endearing and also a challenge: how much more satisfying to seduce an angel than a villain?

—SB

At once I felt a wash of cold fear sweep over me from head to foot, and my hands clenched the steering wheel. Cal gestured with one hand, and Das Boot's engine died quietly and the headlights winked out. Automatically I began to use my magesight, the enhanced vision I'd been able to call on since shortly after I learned I was a blood witch.

Cal came closer, and I wrenched my door open and jumped out, determined to be standing during any meeting we had. When I saw his face, my breath left me, not in a whoosh but in a quiet trail, like a vine of smoke in the cold night air. Oh Goddess, had I forgotten his face? No—not when he haunted my dreams and my waking thoughts. But I had forgotten his impact on me, the sweet longing I felt when our eyes met, despite my fear.

Then of course came the remembered anger and a fierce rush of self-protective instinct.

"What are you doing here?" I demanded, trying to make my voice strong. But in the darkness I sounded harsh and afraid.

"Morgan," he said, and his voice crept along all my nerves, like honey. I had missed his voice. I hardened my heart and stared at him.

"Last time I saw you, you were trying to kill me," I said, striving for a flippancy I was too scared to pull off.

"I was trying to save you," he said earnestly, and came so close, I could see he wasn't an apparition, wasn't a ghost, but a real person in a real body that I had touched and kissed. "Believe me—if Selene had gotten her hands on you, death would have been far better. Morgan, I know now that I was wrong, but I was crazy with fear, and I did what I thought was best. Forgive me."

I couldn't speak. How did he do it? Even now, when I knew I should just jump in my car and drive away as fast as I could, my heart was whispering, Believe him.

"I love you more now than ever," Cal said. "I've come back to be with you. I told Selene I wouldn't help her anymore."

"You're telling me you've broken away from your mother?" I said. Emotion made my voice harsh, raw. "Give me one good reason I should believe you."

Wordlessly Cal opened his jacket. Underneath he wore a flannel shirt, and he unbuttoned the top three buttons and pulled it open so that I could see his chest. Instantly Hunter's naked chest flashed into my mind. Oh God, I thought with a tinge of hysteria.

Then I saw the blackened, burned-looking patch of skin

directly over Cal's heart. I focused my magesight on it so that I could see clearly, despite the darkness. It was in the shape of a hand.

"Selene did that to me," Cal said, and remembered pain thrummed in his voice. "When I told her I chose you over her."

Goddess. I swallowed hard. And then, without allowing myself to think about what I was risking, I put out my hand and touched my fingers to his cheek. I had to know the truth.

His eyes flared open as he realized what I was doing, but he stood still. I pushed through the outer layers of his consciousness, feeling his resistance, feeling him will himself to accept my invasion. For the first time with Cal, I was controlling the joining of our minds. I would see what I wanted to see, not simply what he wanted to show me.

Then I was inside, and Cal was all around me. I saw my face, but the way he saw it, with a sort of glow around it that made me beautiful, unearthly. I was shaken to sense how much he wanted me.

I saw Hunter striding down the street in Red Kill, and felt an ugly burst of hatred and violence from Cal that rocked me.

I saw a steep hillside below me, dotted with small stucco houses with red roofs, that stretched down to a sparkling blue bay. I felt a breeze blowing against my cheeks. In the distance a red bridge stretched from one headland to another, and I realized I was seeing San Francisco, where I'd never been. It was beautiful, but it wasn't what I needed to see, so I kept searching.

Then I saw Selene.

She was looking directly at me, and I had to fight a strong

impulse to hide my face, though I knew I was only seeing Cal's memory. She wasn't looking at me but at him. The expression in her eyes was cold fury.

"You can't go," she said. "I won't allow it."

"I am going," Cal said, and I felt his defiance, his fear, his resolve.

Selene's beautiful face twisted into a snarl of rage. "You idiot," she said. Then her hand was snaking toward him, so fast, it was just a blur, and I felt a searing pain as she touched Cal's flesh. Her hand felt deathly cold, as if it were made of liquid nitrogen, but then a wisp of smoke rose up in front of my eyes, and I smelled charred flesh. I cringed and gasped, twisting with Cal as he sought to escape the agony.

Then she took her hand away, and it was over, except for the memory of the pain.

"That was just the barest taste of what I can do," she said in a voice like iron. "I could have taken your heart as easily as plucking a cherry out of a bowl. I didn't because you are my son, and I know this foolishness will pass. But now you've experienced what I can do to those who cross me."

And she turned and strode away.

I let my hand drop, shaken, but Cal grabbed it. "Morgan, I need you. I need your love and your strength. Together we're strong enough to fight Selene, to win against her."

"No, we're not!" I cried. I snatched my hand away. "Are you insane? Selene could crush both of us and five other witches besides. I don't even know if she *can* be stopped."

"She can!" Cal said, coming closer still. He looked thinner than when I had seen him last, and his perpetual golden tan had faded slightly. I wondered if he had been eating, where he had been staying, and then told myself I didn't give a damn. "Selene can be stopped. The two of us, and your mother's coven tools, will be enough to stop her cold. I'm sure of it. Just tell me you'll work with me. Morgan, tell me you still love me." His voice dropped to a raspy whisper. "Tell me I haven't killed your love for me."

With a sense of shame I recognized that I cared for him, cared about him, that despite everything I didn't, couldn't hate him. But I couldn't say I still loved him, either, and there was no way I would agree to help him go up against Selene.

"There's no way we can be together now," I said, and the image of myself pressed against Hunter, kissing him fiercely, flashed into my mind.

"I know what I did to you was terrible," Cal said. "At first I was just trying to get next to your power. I admit that. But then I fell for you. Fell for your strength and beauty, your honesty and humility. Every time I saw you was a revelation, and now I can't live without you. I don't want to live without you. I want to be with you forever."

He looked so sincere, his face contorted with pain. I didn't know what to say: a thousand thoughts flew through my head like sparks flying upward from a fire. I recoiled from his presence even as part of me ached for his words to be true. I was scared of him and also afraid that what he was saying was real, that no one would ever love me so much again.

"All I ask is that you give me another chance," he pleaded in a tone that threatened to break my heart. "I was so horribly wrong—I thought I could have you and give Selene what she wanted, too, but I couldn't. Please give me a chance to make it up to you, a chance to redeem myself.

Morgan, please. I love you." He stepped closer still, and I could feel his breath, as cold as the night air, brushing against my cheek. "I don't want Selene to hurt you. Morgan, she wants to kill you. Now that she knows you'll never join her, she needs you dead so she can have your tools." He shook his head. "I can't let her do that."

"Where is she?" I asked shakily.

"I don't know," he said. "We were in San Francisco, but she's not there anymore. She's not far. I pick up on her sometimes. At least four members of her coven are with her. They're coming for you, Morgan. You have to let me protect you."

"Why should I trust you?" I demanded, trying to shut out the pain that seared my heart. "You tried to kill me once— why should I believe you won't just do it again?"

"Do you remember how good we were together?" Cal whispered, and I shivered. "Do you remember how we touched, how we kissed, how we joined our minds? It was so good, so right. You know it was real; you know I'm telling you the truth now. Please, Morgan . . ."

Part of me was no longer listening, my senses attuned to another vibration, another image. I looked down the road. "Hunter," I said before I thought.

Cal wheeled and looked down the road. I thought I could see the faintest stripe of light on the tree trunks. Headlights.

For an endless moment Cal and I looked at each other. He was just as breathtaking as he'd always been, with a new layer of vulnerability that he'd never had but that made him even more appealing. He was Cal, my first love, the one who'd opened new worlds to me.

"If you call me, I'll come," he said so softly, I could barely hear him.

"Wait!" I said. "Where are you staying? Where can I find you?"

He just smiled, and then he was running easily toward the woods that lined the road, and he faded between the trees like a wraith. I blinked, and he was completely gone, with no trace of ever having been there.

The headlights caught me in their glare, and I understood how a deer or rabbit could be pinned by them in terror. I stood by Das Boot, waiting for Hunter to stop.

"Morgan," he said, getting out of his car. Illogically, even after the scene in the bathroom, I felt almost like weeping with relief to see him. "Are you all right? Did something happen?"

My tongue pressed against my lips. Hunter was a Seeker. He had gone ballistic at the thought that Cal had even contacted me. If I told him I had just *seen* Cal, that Cal was nearby somewhere, Hunter wouldn't stop until he found Cal. And when he found him . . .

Hunter and Cal hated each other, had tried to kill each other. It was only luck that they *hadn't* killed each other. If Hunter found Cal now, one of them would die. That thought was completely unacceptable to me. I didn't know what to do about Cal, didn't know what to do about the knowledge that Selene was coming. All I knew was that I had to keep Hunter and Cal apart until I figured something out.

"I'm okay," I said, making my voice strong and sure. I chose my words carefully, knowing that he'd sense it if I lied outright. "I thought I almost hit a deer just now and stopped, but it's gone."

Hunter glanced at the woods, then he frowned slightly. "I sense something. . . ." he said, half to himself. He stood still for a moment, a listening expression on his face. Then he shook his head. "Whatever it was, it's gone now."

I kept my face blank.

He looked back at me. "I got an odd feeling about you," he said. "Like . . . panic."

I nodded, hoping he couldn't tell I was lying. "I thought I was going to crash. It's been kind of . . . an eventful day. I guess I freaked."

Hunter's frown cleared, and he looked contrite. "Are you sure you're okay?" he asked.

"Yeah." I started to get back in my car and prayed desperately that it would start, that Cal hadn't permanently disabled the engine. I couldn't believe I was lying so blithely to Hunter, Hunter who I had acknowledged was just about the only person I could trust. But I wasn't lying for me—I was trying to save Cal. And Hunter. I had to save them from each other.

Hunter leaned in the open doorway, bending to be at eye level with me. "Morgan—I'm sorry about the way I behaved earlier, in the bathroom. It's just—I'm upset about my father. I want to reach him and I can't. And I'm afraid for you. I feel that I need to protect you, and it kills me that I can't be with you all the time, making sure you're safe."

I nodded. "And that's why you want me to do the *tàth meànma brach*," I said.

"Yes." He paused. "Are you sore from the fall?"

"Yeah. I bet we'll both feel awful tomorrow. Especially you."

He laughed, and I turned my key. Das Boot's engine turned over at once.

"I'm going to get home now," I said unnecessarily. Quickly Hunter leaned in and kissed me, and then he stood back and shut my car door.

Had Cal seen that? I thought in panic. Oh Goddess, I hoped not. It would only infuriate him more. I drove off, looking back at Hunter in the mirror until I went around the next bend and I couldn't see him anymore. All I wanted to do was go home, curl up, and cry.

10

Open

December 13, 1977

The mysteries of Amyranth can't hold a candle to the mysteries of love. What is it about Daniel Niall that makes me so crazy? Has he spelled me to love him? No—that's ludicrous. Noble, honest Daniel would never do such a thing. No, I love him for himself, and it's so out of character for me that I can't stop questioning it.

Why is he so compelling? How is he different from other men I've had? Like every other man, he's given in to me—no one has ever told me no, and Daniel is no exception. Yet I sense an inner wall that I can't breach. There's something within him that my love, my power, my beauty hasn't touched. What is it?

I know he loves me, and I know he wishes he didn't. I enjoy making him realize how much he wants me. I take pleasure *in watching him try to resist and being unable to. And then I make his compliance worth his while. But what is he holding back?*

At any rate, Daniel is here and there working on various studies—he's very academic; he wants to understand everything, know the history of everything. A real book witch. It takes him away from me often. Which is a good thing, because his presence severely curtails my Amyranth activities. I'm now doing more and more within the group and less with Turneval. The Unnamed Elders have begun teaching me the deeper magick of Amyranth, and it's more draining and exciting than anything I've imagined. I'm lost within it, drunk with it, immersed in it—and the only thing that pulls me out is the chance of spending time with Daniel. This makes me laugh.

—SB

That night I dreamed that Selene took on the form of a giant bird and snatched me off the school playing field, where, ludicrously, I was playing hockey with Hunter and Bree and Robbie. They stood on the grass, waving their hockey sticks helplessly, and I watched them get smaller and smaller as Selene bore me away. She took me to a giant nest perched on top of a mountain, and I looked down and saw Cal in the nest, and before my eyes he turned into a baby bird and gazed up at me with his sharp predator's beak gaping wide to engulf me. Then I woke up, drenched with sweat, and it was morning.

I spent the morning trying not to think about Cal. Three

times I found myself picking up the phone to call Hunter, and three times I put the cordless handset back in its cradle. I felt too conflicted about what I would say.

"What's the matter, Morgan?" my mom asked as I prowled through the kitchen for the fourth time. "You seem so restless."

I forced myself to smile. "I don't know. Maybe I just need to go for a drive or something."

I grabbed my coat and car keys and headed out to Das Boot, not sure what my destination was. Then my senses tingled, and I knew Hunter was nearby. I felt a surge of elation and alarm as I saw him pull up in front of the house.

I walked over to his car, willing myself to seem calm, normal. He rolled down his window and peered out at me.

"We need to talk. Can I drive you somewhere?" he asked.

"Uh—I was just going for a drive," I mumbled. "I'm not really sure where."

"How about Red Kill?" he suggested. "I need to pick up some essential oils at Practical Magick. And you need to talk to Alyce."

So I climbed into his car and off we went.

"This morning Sky and I examined the porch supports more carefully," Hunter said as he drove. "They'd definitely been sawed, and we couldn't find any trace of magick."

"So what are you thinking?" I asked.

"I don't know," he said, tapping his fingers against the steering wheel.

I thought: Had it been Cal? Had he been trying to kill both me and Hunter at the same time? Had he cut Hunter's brake line as well? But why would he do it mechanically instead of with magick? Was I being a complete and total idiot by not telling Hunter that I'd seen Cal? I was so confused.

Alyce fed us lunch in her small apartment. I hadn't realized I was hungry until I smelled the beef stew that was filling the rooms with its rich scent. Hunter and I fell on it, and Alyce watched us, smiling. She sat at the table with us, not eating but sipping from a mug of tea.

"I've been considering your request for a *tàth meànma brach*," she said as I took a second slice of bread. "It's a serious thing, and I've given it a great deal of thought."

I nodded, my heart sinking at her tone. She was going to say no. I saw a glance pass between her and Hunter and felt my appetite fade away.

"You know, it can be very difficult," Alyce went on. "It would be very draining, both physically and emotionally, for both of us."

I nodded. I had asked too much.

"But I understand why you want to do this, why you asked me, and why Hunter also thinks it's a good idea," Alyce said. "And I've come to agree. I think that you're a target of Selene's group, and I think you need more protection than others can provide for you. The best kind of protection comes from within, and by joining with me and learning what I know, you will be much stronger, much more capable of defending yourself."

I looked at her with hope. "Does that mean—"

"You'll need to free yourself of as many mental distractions as you can," Alyce said gently. "And there are some ritual preparations you'll need to make. Hunter and Sky can help you with them. Let's do it soon—the sooner the better. Tomorrow evening."

Back in Hunter's car, on our way to my house, I could hardly sit still. The idea of being able to absorb all of Alyce's considerable learning, all in one day, was exhilarating and nerve-racking.

"Thank you for speaking to Alyce for me," I said. "Encouraging her to do the *tàth meànma brach*."

"It was her decision." He sounded remote, and I felt a surge of frustration about our relationship. It struck me for the first time that Hunter and I were similar, and that was why we clashed so much. With Cal it had been clear, easy— he had been the pursuer and I the pursued, and that had worked well with my shyness and insecurity. But both Hunter and I would be more comfortable if the other person were taking charge. At this point I had to assume there was some reason why we had kissed each other, and not just once or twice. Hunter wasn't the kind of person who would do that lightly, and neither was I. So what were we doing? Were we falling in love?

I have to lay myself on the line, I realized with a flash of perfect clarity. If I want to go deeper with him, I have to open myself to him and trust that he doesn't want to hurt me. And I do want to go deeper with him.

But first . . . but first I had to tell him about Cal. It was too huge a secret between us. Nor was it my secret to keep. Hunter was in danger from Cal as much, maybe even more than I was. I would have to tell him and hope that he wouldn't let his emotions overtake his good sense.

I swallowed hard. Do it, I told myself. Do it!

"I saw Cal last night," I said quietly.

Next to me Hunter went rigid, his hands clenching the steering wheel. He glanced quickly right and left, then swung the car onto a dirt road that I hadn't even seen. We bumped over rocks and frozen mud before coming to a halt about twenty feet off the main road.

"When?" Hunter demanded, turning off the engine and facing me. He unclipped his seat belt and leaned toward me. "When?" he repeated. "Was it when I saw you on the road?"

"Yes," I admitted. "It wasn't a deer I saw. It was Cal. He was standing in the road, and he held up his hand and my car went dead."

"What happened? What did he do to you?"

"Nothing. We just talked," I said. "He said he came back to Widow's Vale to be with me. He told me he's broken away from Selene."

"And you believed that load of crap?" Hunter exclaimed. His eyes blazed.

My chin came up. "Yes." His contemptuous tone made me feel small, hurt. "I did *tàth meànma* with him. He's telling the truth."

"Goddess." Hunter spat out the word. "How could you be so bloody stupid? You've done *tàth meànma* with him before, and he still managed to fool you."

"But I controlled it this time!" I cried.

"You *think* you did. Why did you lie to me?" His eyes narrowed. "He *has* put a spell on you!"

Remembering how it had felt when Cal had put a spell on me made me shiver. "No. I just—I had just told you about his witch message, and you freaked out, and I thought if I told you he was right there, you guys would—would fight, and it made me sick to think about."

"You're damn right I freaked out!" Hunter said, raising his voice. "Good God, Morgan, we've been looking for Cal and Selene for three weeks now! And all of a sudden you say, guess what? I know where he is! I mean, what the hell kind of game are you playing?"

I hated the way he was looking at me, as if he were questioning his trust of me—if he had ever trusted me at all, and to my horror, I started crying. I don't cry easily in front of people, and I would have given up a lot to have not cried then, but everything crashed down on me all at once, and I crumbled.

"I'm not playing games!" I said, dashing my tears away. "I'm just confused, just human! I loved Cal, and I don't want you two to kill each other!"

"You're not *just* human, Morgan," Hunter said. "You're a witch. You have to start living up to that fact. What do you mean, you loved Cal? What has that got to do with anything? He tried to kill you! Are you stupid? Are you blind?"

"It wasn't all his fault!" I yelled, seeing the blazing fury in Hunter's eyes. "You know that, Hunter. He grew up with Selene for eighteen years. What would you have been like in that situation?" I took a couple of quick, hard breaths, trying to get hold of myself. "I'm not blind. Maybe I am stupid. Mostly I'm just confused and scared and tempted."

He narrowed his eyes, seizing on my words like a snake does a rat. "Tempted? Tempted by what? The dark side? Or by Cal? Is that it? Are you saying you still love him?"

"No! Yes! Stop twisting my words! All I'm saying is that I

loved him, and I thought he loved me, and I haven't forgotten that!" I shouted. "He introduced me to magick. He made me feel beautiful!" I abruptly shut up, breathing hard.

Heavy silence filled the car. I sensed Hunter striving to rein in his anger. What am I doing? I thought miserably.

Then his face softened. I felt his hand at my neck, brushing my hair back, stroking my skin. My breath caught in my throat, and I turned to him.

"I'm sorry," I whispered. My skin felt like it was on fire where his fingers passed over it.

"What do you want? I know you were happy with Cal, and I want you to be happy with me. But I'm not Cal, and I never will be," he said, his face close to mine. His voice was soft. "If you want me, then tell me. I need you to tell me."

My eyes widened. Cal had always been almost forceful, the one who decided, cajoled, seduced. Why was Hunter asking me to make myself vulnerable?

As if reading my thoughts, he said, "Morgan, I can tell you and show you what I want. But if *you* don't know what you want, I don't want to go there. *You* need to know what you want, and you need to be able to tell me and show me." His eyes were wide, vulnerable, his lips were warm and close to mine.

Oh my God, I thought.

"It's not enough for you to let me want you," he went on. "I need you to actually want me back and to be able to show me that. I need to be wanted, too. Do you see what I mean?"

I nodded slowly, processing a hundred thoughts.

"Can you give me that?"

My eyes felt huge as I wondered if I could—if I was brave enough. I didn't speak.

"Right, then." He pulled back, my body saying, no, no, and then he started the car, carefully backed up, and we went back to Widow's Vale. In front of my house he stopped and turned to look at me again.

"I have to look for Cal," he said. "You know that, don't you?"

I nodded reluctantly. "Don't hurt him," I said in a near whisper.

"I can't promise that," he told me. "But I'll try. Will you think about what I said?"

I nodded again.

Hunter took my chin in his hand and kissed me hard and fast on the mouth, not once but again and again, hungrily, and I made a little sound and opened my mouth to him. Finally he pulled back, breathing hard, and we looked at each other. He put the car into gear again. I climbed out in a daze and headed up my front walk.

11

The Graveyard

Beltane, 1979

I've been married for less than twenty-four hours, and already my new husband is threatening to leave me—he thinks the ceremony was all my doing, it wasn't what he expected, I didn't respect his wishes, etc. He'll be all right. He needs to calm down, to relax, to get over his fears. Then we can talk, and he'll see that everything is all right, everything is fine, and we were meant to be together.

Why did I marry Daniel Niall? Because I couldn't help myself. Because I wanted him too much to let him go. Because I needed to be the one he wanted, the one he would live with and come home to. My mother would have approved of this match. Anyone who actually knows me thinks I'm crazy. At any rate, Daniel and I were married last night, and for me it was beautiful, powerful, primal. When we stood, sky clad, under *the ripe, full moon, with Turneval chanting around us, the heady scent of herbs burning, the warmth of the bonfire toasting our skin—I felt like the Goddess herself, full of life, fertile. For me it was so natural that we embrace, open our mouths and kiss, that I press myself against him. And how could he not respond? We were naked, I was seducing him, it was a full moon. Of course he responded. But he found his physical response (so public, so witnessed) to be unbearable. For Daniel it was humiliation, abasement.*

How will I reconcile these two areas of my life? How can I keep my work with Amyranth a secret? How can I protect Daniel from Amyranth?

I'll have to solve the problems as they come.

—SB

On Sunday, I once again skipped church and tried to ignore my mother's disapproving looks. She and my dad tried to talk me into meeting them for lunch at the Widow's Vale Diner afterward, but I was fasting to purify my body for my upcoming *tàth meànma brach* with Alyce, so I declined. Instead, I stayed in my room, meditating. Alyce had recommended that I spend at least three hours meditating on the day of the ritual to cleanse my spirit and my psyche of negative patterns and clutter, for lack of a better word.

By eleven o'clock, I was starving. My stomach cried out for Diet Coke and a Pop-Tart, but I resisted, feeling virtuous.

At noon I'd just pulled out my altar when Hunter called. He told me in a neutral way that he'd gone to Cal and Selene's old house and one or two other places to see if he could find Cal, but he'd had no luck. "I know he's been there—I can feel traces of him," Hunter said. "But everywhere I go, he's moved on, and I can't tell where he's gone. I didn't think he was skilled enough to hide his trail from me once I'd picked up a trace of him, but he seems to be."

I decided it was time to change the subject. "I can't believe the *tàth meànma brach* is tonight," I said. "I'm kind of nervous. Should I be?"

"Yes," Hunter said. "But come over to my house at three, and we'll help you get ready. You've got to drink the tea, then take the ritual bath so that you'll be fully cleansed. And you'll need to wear a green linen robe—Sky's got one. Tell your mum and dad you're having dinner with us and you won't be home until fairly late."

"Okay," I said, feeling scared and uncertain.

His voice softened. "You'll be all right, Morgan," he said. "You're strong. Stronger than you know."

After we said good-bye and hung up, I went back to my room. I opened a spell book that Alyce had loaned me and began to read through the purification spell she'd marked, but my stomach kept distracting me. All of a sudden, when I was trying so hard not to think about food, I had a realization: my brain was still incredibly cluttered with Cal. I thought about him, wondered about him, dreamed about him.

Then I realized I had to talk to him, find out once and for all where we stood. I had to put all my feelings toward him to rest or I would never be able to move forward, and I couldn't take part in the *tàth meànma brach*. I had to get closure somehow, put an end to all my confusion about him.

I knew I was doing something that could be dangerous. But I also knew I had to do it. Before I could change my mind, I drove over to the old Methodist cemetery, the place where my former coven, Cirrus, had celebrated Samhain. The place where Cal had kissed me for the first time.

It was another clear, cold day, sunny with a wintry brightness and almost no wind. Sitting on the old tombstone we had once used as our altar, I felt almost shaky with nervousness and adrenaline and lack of food. Would Cal come? Would he try to hurt me again? There was no way to know except by calling him. Closing my eyes, trying to ignore the rumbling of my stomach, I sent a witch message to him. *Cal. Come to me, Cal.* Then I sat back and waited.

Before, when I had called Cal, he had usually come within minutes. This time the wait seemed endless. My butt had turned numb on the cold stone before he appeared, gliding silently between the overgrown juniper trees. My eyes registered his appearance, and I was glad it was broad daylight and that I wasn't alone on a dark road.

"Morgan." His voice was soft as a breeze, and I felt it rather than heard it. He walked toward me with no sound, as if the dried leaves underfoot were silenced. I was drawn to his beautiful face, which was both guarded and hopeful.

"Thanks for coming," I said, and I suddenly knew without a doubt that he'd been waiting, scanning the area, making sure I was alone. The last time we were in this place, he had overpowered me and kidnapped me in my car. This time, despite some lingering fear, I felt stronger, more prepared. This time, too, I was ready to call Hunter at a moment's notice.

"I was so glad to hear from you," he said, coming to stand in front of me. He reached out and put his hands on my knees, and I drew back from the familiarity. "There's so much I need to talk to you about. So much I need to tell you, to share with you. But I didn't know how much Gìomanach had influenced you." He spat Hunter's coven name, and I frowned.

"Cal, I need to know," I said, getting to the point. "Have you really broken away from Selene? Do you really want to stop her?"

He again put his hands on my knees. They felt warm through my jeans, against my cold flesh. "Yes," he said, leaning close. "I'm finished with Selene. She's my mother, and I always had a son's loyalty to her. That's not hard to believe, is it? But now I see that what she does is wrong, that it's wrong for her to call on the dark side. I don't want any part of it. I choose you, Morgan. I love you."

I pushed his hands off my knees. His brow darkened.

"I remember when you didn't push me away," he said. "I remember when you couldn't get enough of me."

"Cal," I began, and then my anger pushed ahead of my compassion. "That was before you tried to kill me," I said, my voice strong.

"I was trying to save you!" he insisted.

"You were trying to control me!" I countered. "You put binding spells on me! If you had been honest about what Selene wanted, I could have made my own decision about what to do and how to protect myself. But you didn't give me that chance. You wanted all the power; you wanted to decide what was best." As soon as I said that, I realized it was true, and I realized that I had never absolutely trusted Cal, never.

"Morgan," he began, sounding infuriatingly reasonable, "you had just discovered Wicca. Of course I was trying to guide you, to teach you. It's one of the responsibilities of being an initiated witch. I know so much more than you—

you saw what happened with Robbie's spell. You were a danger to yourself and others."

My mouth opened in fury, and he went on, "Which doesn't mean I don't love you more than you can imagine. I do, Morgan, I do. I love you so much. You complete me. You're my *mùirn beatha dàn*, my soul's other half. We're supposed to be together. We're supposed to make magick together. Our powers could be more awesome than anything anyone's ever seen. But we have to do it together."

I swallowed. This was so hard. Why did it still hurt so much, after all Cal had done to me? "No, Cal. We're not going to be together. We're not *mùirn beatha dàns*."

"That's what you think now," he said. "But you're wrong."

I looked deeply into his golden eyes and saw a spark of what looked like madness. Goddess! My blood turned to ice, and I felt incredibly stupid, meeting him here alone.

"Morgan, I love you," Cal said cajolingly. He stepped closer to me, his eyes hooded in the look that had never before failed to make me melt inside. "Please be mine."

My breath became more shallow as I wondered how to extricate myself from this. This Cal wasn't the Cal I had known. Had that person ever existed? I couldn't tell. All I knew was that now, here, I had to get away from him. He frightened me. He *repulsed* me.

Just like that, like extinguishing a candle with my fingertips, my leftover love for him died. I felt it in my heart, as if a dark shard of glass had been pulled out, leaving a bleeding wound. My throat closed and I wanted to cry, to mourn for the death of the naive Morgan who had once been so incredibly happy with this falsehood.

"No, Cal," I said. "I can't."

His face darkened, and he looked at me. "Morgan, you're not thinking clearly," he said, a tone of warning in his voice. "This is me. I love you. We're lovers."

"We were *never* lovers," I said. "And I don't love you."

"Morgan, listen to me," Cal said.

"You're too late, Sgàth," said Hunter's voice, cold and hard, and Cal and I both jumped. How had he come up without our feeling it?

"There's nothing for you to hunt here, Gìomanach," Cal spat. "No lives for you to destroy, no magick you can strip away."

I felt a wave of power welling up from Cal, and I scrambled off the tombstone. I had once been caught between Cal and Hunter during a battle. I didn't want to go through it again.

"Hunter, why are you here?" I asked.

"I felt something dark here. I came to investigate," he said tightly, not taking his eyes off Cal. "It's my job. It was you who cut the brakes in my car, wasn't it, Sgàth? You who sawed through the stair supports."

"That's right." Cal grinned at Hunter, a feral baring of teeth. "Don't you wonder what else is waiting for you?"

"Why didn't you use magick?" Hunter pressed. "Is it because without Selene, you have nothing of your own? No power? No will?"

Cal's eyes narrowed, and his hands clenched. "I didn't use magick because I didn't want to waste it on you. I am much stronger than you will ever be."

"Only when you're with Morgan," Hunter said coldly. "Not on your own. You're nothing on your own. Morgan knows that. That's why she's here."

I started to say it was *not*, but Cal turned on me. "You! You lured me here, to turn me in to him."

"I wanted to talk to you!" I cried. "I had no idea Hunter would be here."

Hunter turned his implacable gaze on me. "How could you go behind my back after all we've talked about?" he asked in a cold, measured voice. "How could you still love *him?*" He flung out his hand at Cal.

"I don't love him!" I screamed, and in the same instant Cal threw up his hands and began to chant a spell. The language he used was unfamiliar, ugly, full of guttural sounds.

Hunter let out a low growl. I sucked in my breath as I saw that his athame was in his hand, the single sapphire in its hilt flashing as it caught the late winter sun. Stepping back, I saw how he and Cal were facing each other, saw the violence ready to erupt. Damn them! I couldn't go through this again, not Cal and Hunter trying to kill each other, myself frozen, an athame leaving my hand and sailing through the intense cold. . . .

No. That was another time, another place. Another Morgan. I felt power rise inside me like a storm. I had to put an end to this. I had to.

"*Clathna berrin, ne ith rah.*" The ancient Celtic words poured from my lips, and I spat them into the daylight. Hunter and Cal both spun to look at me, their eyes wide. "*Clathna ter, ne fearth ullna stàth,*" I said, my voice growing stronger. "*Morach bis, mea cern, cern mea.*" I knew exactly what I was doing but couldn't tell where it was coming from or how I knew it. I snapped my arms open wide, to encompass both of them, and watched with a strange, fierce joy as their knees buckled and they sank, one at a time, to the ground. "*Clathna berrin, ne ith rah!*" I shouted, and then they were on their hands and knees, helpless against the force of my will.

Goddess, I thought. I felt like I was outside myself, watching this strange, frightening being who controlled the gravity of a world with her fingertips. My right hand outstretched to keep Cal in place, I slowly moved toward Hunter.

He didn't speak, but when I saw the blazing fury in his eyes, I knew I couldn't release him yet. I pointed at him. "Stand up," I commanded. When I raised my hand, he was able to stand, like a puppet. "Get in my car."

Stumbling like an automaton, Hunter headed for Das Boot. I walked backward, following him, keeping Cal under my power. Hunter climbed clumsily into the passenger seat, and I fished out my keys with my left hand. Then I drew some sigils in the sky, sigils I didn't remember learning, that would keep Cal in place until we were well away.

Then I leaped into the driver's seat, jammed the keys into the ignition, stomped on the gas, and got the hell out of there.

I released Hunter after I had parked in front of his house and felt the sudden tightening of his muscles as he took control of them again.

I was afraid to look at him, scared even to think about what I'd done. It was as if I'd been taken over by my power, as if the magick had controlled me instead of the other way around. Or was I just trying to make excuses for having done something unforgivable?

I felt the burning fury of Hunter's gaze on me. He slammed the car door and walked unsteadily up to his house. I felt weak and headachy from lack of food and too much magick, but I knew I needed to talk to Hunter. I got out of Das Boot and followed him into the house.

Inside, Sky looked up as I came in, and seeing my troubled

expression, she pointed wordlessly up the stairs. I'd been upstairs once before but hadn't really taken in any details. Now I looked into one room: it was Sky's, or at least I hoped it was since there was a black bra draped across the bed. I walked past a small bathroom with black-and-white tile flooring and then came to the only other room and knew it must be Hunter's bedroom. The door was ajar, and I pushed it open without knocking: daring Morgan.

He lay across his bed, staring at the ceiling, still wearing his leather jacket and his boots.

"Get out," he said without looking at me.

I didn't know what to say. There was nothing I could say right now. Instead I dropped my coat onto the floor and walked to the bed, which was just a full-size mattress and box spring stacked on the floor, neatly made up with a threadbare down comforter.

Hunter tensed and looked at me in disbelief as I lowered myself next to him. I thought he was going to push me right off the bed onto the floor, but he didn't move, and hesitantly I edged closer to him till I was lying by his side. I put my head on his shoulder and curled myself up next to him, with my arm draped over his chest and my leg across his. His body was rigid. I closed my eyes and tried to sink into him. "I'm so sorry," I murmured, praying that he would let me stay long enough to really apologize. "I'm so sorry. I didn't know what else to do. I didn't know what was going to happen. I just couldn't bear to see you hurt each other—or worse. I'm sorry."

It was a long time before he relaxed at all and longer still before his hand came up to stroke my hair and hold me close to him. It was starting to get dark outside, it was late, and I hadn't yet drunk the special herb tea I was supposed to drink before my *tàth meànma brach*. But I lay there with Hunter slowly stroking my hair, feeling like I had found a special sort of refuge, a safe haven completely different from what I had experienced with Cal. I didn't know if Hunter would ever be able to forgive me; I had never been able to truly forgive Cal for doing the same thing to me. But I hoped that somehow Hunter was a bigger person than I was, a better person, and would find a way not to hold this against me forever.

It was then I realized how incredibly important his opinion of me was, how much his feelings mattered to me, how desperately I wanted him to care for me, admire me, the way I cared for and admired him.

Finally I took a deep breath and said, "I love you. I want you. This is right."

And Hunter said, "Yes," and he kissed me, and it was as if a universe unfolded within me. I felt infinite, timeless, and when I opened my eyes and looked at Hunter, he was outlined in a blaze of golden light, as if he were the sun itself.

Magick.

12

The *Brach*

Daniel is in England again. He's been gone two weeks, and I'm not sure when he'll be back. He always comes back, though. The temptation is strong to cast a summoning spell on him, pulling him to me sooner, but I have resisted, and there's a satisfaction in knowing that he always comes back because he can't help himself and not because I forced him to.

Is this marriage? This isn't my parents' marriage, quiet and sedate and tandem. When Daniel and I are together, we are shouting, arguing, fighting, and despising each other, and then we are grappling, falling to the bed, making love with intense passion that has as much to do with hate as it does with love. And then in the aftermath I see his beauty once again, not just his physical beauty, but his inner sweetness, the good-

ness inside him. I love and appreciate that, even as it clashes so harshly with what is inside me.

We have moments of calm and gentleness, during which we're holding hands and kissing sweetly. Then Amyranth raises its head or his studies call him away, and we are again two angry cats tied in a burlap bag and thrown into a river: desperate, clawing, fighting, trying only to survive no matter the cost. And he goes away and I immerse myself in Amyranth, and I know I could never give it up. Then I miss Daniel and he comes back, and the cycle starts again.

Is this marriage? It is my marriage.

—SB

I'm not sure how long I lay with Hunter. Eventually his even breathing told me he was asleep. I didn't think he had forgiven me just because I had told him I loved him and he had kissed me. Was I fickle, to love someone else so soon after Cal? Was I setting myself up for another heartbreak? Did Hunter love me? I felt he did. But I had no idea whether we had a future, where our relationship would lead us, how long it would last. These questions would have to wait: now it was time, past time, for me to prepare for the *tàth meànma brach*.

Moving quietly, I uncoiled myself and left the room. Holding my shoes in one hand, I went downstairs. Sky was in the kitchen, reading the newspaper and drinking something hot and steaming in a mug. She looked at me expectantly.

"I'll explain it all later," I told her, feeling very tired.

"It's late," she said after a moment. "Almost five o'clock.

I'll fix you your special tea." She made me a huge pot of it, and I started drinking it obediently. It tasted like licorice and wood and chamomile and things I couldn't identify.

"What does this tea do?" I asked, finishing the mug.

"Well . . . ," said Sky.

I found out before she finished speaking. The secret of the herbal tea was that it was a system cleanser and basically finished off the effects of the fasting and the water drinking. I doubled over as I felt my stomach cramp. Sky, trying not to smirk, pointed to the downstairs bathroom.

In between bouts of, ahem, gut emptying, I meditated and talked to Sky. I told her what had happened with Cal, and she listened with surprising compassion. I wondered—hoped—that my binding spell had worn off and he wasn't still stuck in the cemetery in the cold. It must have. Where was he now? How angry was he? Had he felt my love for him die, the way I had?

Sky asked at some point, "How are you feeling?"

"Empty," I said bleakly, and she laughed.

"You'll be glad of it later," she said. "Trust me. I've seen people do a *brach* without cleaning out their systems and fasting, and they truly regretted it."

I sniffed the air. "What's that?"

"Lasagna," Sky admitted. "It's almost seven."

"Oh, Jesus," I moaned, feeling hollow and starving and exhausted.

"Here," Sky said briskly, holding out a bundle of pale green linen. "This is for you. I've drawn you a bath upstairs and put in some purifying herbs and oils and things. Have a good soak in the tub, and you'll feel better. Afterward put this on, with nothing underneath. Also, no knickers, no jewelry, no nail polish, nothing in your hair. All right?"

I nodded and headed up the stairs. Hunter was in the upstairs bathroom, putting out a rough, unbleached towel. I had showered here once before, but now it felt bizarrely intimate, taking a bath in his house—especially so soon after we had been kissing on his bed. I felt myself blush, and he gave me an unreadable look and left the room, closing the door behind him.

The bathroom looked lovely, very romantic, with all the lights off and candles burning everywhere. Steam rose from the water in the claw-foot tub, and there were violet petals floating on it, and rosemary, and eucalyptus. I shimmied out of my clothes and sank blissfully into the hot water. I don't know how long I lay there, my eyes closed, inhaling the fragrant steam and feeling the tension draining away. There was a fine grit of salt lining the bottom of the tub, and I rubbed it into my skin, knowing it would help purify me and dispel negative energy.

I felt Sky coming closer, and then she tapped on the door and said, "Ten minutes. Alyce will be here soon."

Quickly I grabbed the homemade soap and a washcloth and scrubbed myself all over. Then I shampooed my hair. I ran fresh water and rinsed myself off well, then rubbed hard with the rough towel until I was dry. I felt like a goddess; clean, light, pure, almost ethereal. The horrible events of the day receded, and I felt ready for anything, as if I could wave my hand and rearrange the stars in the sky.

I untangled my long, damp hair with a wooden comb I found, then put on the green robe. At last I floated downstairs barefoot to find Alyce, Sky, and Hunter waiting for me in the circle room. I paused uncertainly in the doorway, and the first thought I had was, Hunter knows I'm naked under this.

But nothing in his face betrayed that knowledge, and then Alyce was walking toward me, her hands outstretched, and we hugged. She was wearing a lavender robe very similar to mine, and her hair was down for once, silver and flowing halfway down her back. She looked serene, and I was so grateful to her for doing this.

Sky and Hunter both came forward and hugged each of us, and I was acutely aware of how his lean body felt against mine. I noticed that he had already started drawing circles of power on the floor. There were three: a white one of chalk, then one made of salt, and then an inner one of a golden powder that smelled spicy, like saffron. Thirteen white pillar candles ringed the outer circle, and Alyce and I walked through the circle openings. We sat cross-legged on the floor, facing each other, smiling into each other's eyes as Hunter closed the circles and chanted spells of protection.

"Morgan of Kithic and Alyce of Starlocket, do you agree to enter knowingly and willingly into a *tàth meànma brach* here tonight?" asked Sky formally.

"Yes," I said, and nervousness bubbled up inside me. Was I really ready? Could I accept Alyce's knowledge? Or would I end up going blind, like that witch Hunter had told me about?

"Yes," Alyce said.

"Then let's begin," said Hunter. He and Sky drew back from the circles and sat leaning against cushions by a far wall. I got the impression they were like spotters who would jump in and help us if anything weird happened.

Alyce reached out with her hands and put them on my shoulders, and I did the same to her. We leaned our heads over until our foreheads touched lightly, our eyes still open. Her shoulders felt warm and smooth and round under my hands; I wondered if mine felt bony, raw, under hers.

Then, to my amazement, she started chanting my own personal power spell, the one that had come to me weeks ago.

"An di allaigh an di aigh
An di allaigh an di ne ullah
An di ullah be nith rah
Cair di na ulla nith rah
Cair feal ti theo nith rah
An di allaigh an di aigh."

My voice joined hers, and we sang it together, the ancient rhythm flowing through our blood like a heartbeat. My heart lifted as we sang, and I saw joy on Alyce's face, making her beautiful, her violet-blue eyes full of wisdom and comfort. We sang, two women, joined by power, by Wicca, by joy, by trust. And slowly, gently, I became aware that the barriers between our minds were dissolving.

The next thing I was aware of was that my eyes were closed—or if they weren't closed, I was no longer seeing things around me, was no longer conscious of where I was. For a moment I wondered with panic if I were blind, but then I lost myself in wonder. Alyce and I were floating, joined, in a sort of nether space where we could simultaneously see everything and nothing. In my mind Alyce held out her hands and smiled at me, saying, "Come."

My muscles tensed as I seemed to be drawn toward an electrified wormhole, and Alyce said, "Relax, let it come," and I tried to release every bit of resistance I had. And then . . . and then I was inside Alyce's mind: I was Alyce, and she was me, and we were joined. I took in a sharp breath as waves and waves of knowledge swept toward me, cresting and peaking and lapping against my brain.

"Let it come," Alyce murmured, and again I realized I had tensed up and again I tried to release the tension and the fear and open myself to receive whatever she gave. Reams of sigils and characters and signs and spells crashed into me, chants and ancient alphabets and books of learning. Plants and crystals and stones and metals and their properties. I heard a high-pitched whimpering sound and wondered if it was me. I knew I was in pain: I felt like I wore a helmet of metal spikes that were slowly driving into my skull. But stronger than the pain was my joy at the beauty around me.

Oh, oh, I thought, unable to form words. Flowers spun toward me through the darkness, flowers and spiked woody branches and the scents of bitter smoke, and suddenly it was all too intense, and bile rose in my throat, and I was glad I had nothing in me to throw up.

I saw a younger, brown haired Alyce wearing a crown of laurel leaves as she danced around a maypole as a teenager. I saw the shame of failed spells, charms gone wrong, a panicked mind blanking before a teacher's stern rebuke. I felt flames of desire licking at her skin, but the man she desired faded away before I saw who he had been, and something in me knew he had died, and that Alyce had been with him when he had.

A cat passed me, a tortoiseshell cat she had loved profoundly, a cat who had comforted her in grief and calmed her in fear. Her deep affection for David Redstone, her anguish and disbelief at his betrayal swirled through me like a hurricane, leaving me gasping. Then more spells and more knowledge and more pages and pages of book learning: spells of protection, of ward evil, of illusion, of strength. Spells to stay awake, to heal, to help in learning, to help in childbirth, to comfort the ailing, the grieving, the ones left behind when someone dies.

And scents: throughout it all the scents roiled through me, making me gag and then inhale deeply, following a tantalizing scent of flowers and incense. There was smoke and burned flesh and oils gone bad; there was food offered to the Goddess, food shared with friends, food used in rituals. There was the metallic tang of blood, coppery and sharp, that made my stomach burn, and wretched odors of sickness, of unhealed flesh, of rot, and I was panting, wanting to run away.

"Let it come," Alyce whispered, and her voice cracked.

I wanted to say something, say it was too much, to slow it down, to give me time, that I was drowning, but no words came out that I could hear, and then more of Alyce's knowing came at me, swept toward me. Her deep, personal self-knowledge flowed over me like a warm river, and I let myself go into it, into the power that is itself a form of magick, the power of womanhood, of creation. I felt Alyce's deep ties to the earth, to the moon's cycles. I saw how strong women are, how much we can bear, how we can draw on the earth's deep power.

I felt a smile on my face, my eyes closed, joy welling up inside me. Alyce was me, and I was her, and we were together. It was beautiful magick, made more beautiful as I realized that as much as Alyce was sending toward me, she was also receiving from me. I saw her surprise, even her awe at my powers, the powers I was slowly discovering and becoming comfortable with. Eagerly she fed on my mind, and I was delighted by how exciting she found the breadth of my strength, the depth of my power, my magick that stretched back a thousand years within my clan. She shared my sorrow over Cal and rejoiced with me in the discovery of my love for Hunter. She saw all the questions I had about my birth parents, how I longed to have known them. Gladly I gave to her, opened myself to her thoughts, shared my heritage and my life

And it was in opening my mind to share with Alyce that I saw myself: saw how strong I could be if I realized my potential; saw the dangerously thin line between good and evil that I would walk my whole life; saw myself as a child, as I was now, as a woman in the future. My strength would be beautiful, awe-inspiring, if only I could find a way to make myself whole. I needed answers. Dimly I became aware of warm tears on my cheeks, their saltiness running into my mouth.

Slowly, gradually, we began to separate into two beings again, our one joined whole pulled into two, like mitosis. The separation was as jarring and uncomfortable as the joining had been, and I mourned the loss of Alyce in my consciousness and felt her mourn the loss of me. We pulled apart, our hands slipping from each other's shoulders. Then my spine straightened, and I frowned, my eyes snapping open.

I looked at Alyce and saw that she, too, was aware of a third presence: there was Morgan, and Alyce, and some unnamed force that was intruding, reaching toward me, sending dark tendrils of influence into my mind.

"Selene," I gasped, and Alyce was already there, throwing up blocks against the dark magick that had crept around us like a bog wisp, like smoke, like a poisonous gas. The ward-evil spell came to me easily, remembered and retrieved, and without effort I said the words and drew the sigils and put up my own blocks against what I sensed coming toward me. Alyce and I knew each other, had each other's learning and essence, and I called on knowledge only minutes old to protect myself against Selene, scrying to find me, reaching out to control me.

She was gone in an instant.

When I opened my eyes again, the world had settled into relative normalcy: I was sitting on the wooden floor of Sky and Hunter's house, and they were kneeling close, outside the circles, watching us. Alyce was opposite me, opening her eyes and taking a deep breath.

"What was that?" Sky asked.

"Selene," I answered.

"Selene," Alyce said at the same time. "Looking for Morgan."

"Why would she need to look for me?" I asked.

"It's more getting in touch with your mind," Alyce explained. "Seeing where you are magickally. Even trying to control you from a great distance."

"But she's gone now, right?" said Hunter. When I nodded, he asked, "How did it go? How do you both feel?"

My eyes met Alyce's. I ran a mental inventory. "Uh, I feel strange," I said, and then I fainted.

13

Charred

November 12, 1980

Another day, another fight with Daniel. His constant antagonism is exhausting. He hates Amyranth and everything about it, and of course he only knows a tiny, tiny part of it. If he knew anything like the whole story, he would leave me forever. Which is completely unacceptable. I've been trying to come to terms with this dilemma since I met him, and I still don't have an answer. He refuses to see the beauty of Amyranth's cause. I've rejected his attempts to show me the beauty of goody-two-shoes scholarship and boiling up garlic-and-ginger tisanes to help clear up coughs.

Why am I unable to let him go? No man has ever held this much sway over me, not even Patrick. I want to give Daniel up, I've tried, but I get only as far as wishing him gone before I start aching desperately to have him back. I simply love him, want him. The irony of this doesn't escape me.

When we're good together, we're really, truly good, and we both feel a joy, a completeness that can't be matched or denied. Lately, though, it seems like the good times are fewer and further between—we have truly irreconcilable differences.

If I bend Daniel's will to my own through magick, how much would he be diminished? How much would I?

—SB

When I woke up on Monday, I felt awful. I had dim memories of Hunter driving me home in Das Boot, with Sky following in her car. He had whispered some quick words in my ear on my front porch, and I was able to walk and talk and look halfway normal for my parents before I stumbled upstairs into bed with all my clothes on. How did I get out of the robe and back into my clothes? Ugh. I'd think about that later.

"Morgan?" Mary K. poked her head around the bathroom door. "You okay? It's almost ten o'clock."

"Mpf," I mumbled. Dagda, my gray kitten, padded in after her and leaped up onto my bedspread. He had grown so much in just a few weeks. Purring, he stomped his way up the comforter toward me, and I reached out to kiss his little triangular head and rub his ears. He collapsed, exhausted, and closed his eyes. I knew how he felt.

In fact, I knew how Mary K. felt as well. I opened my eyes again to see my sister regarding herself in the mirror. I could sense her feelings with more accuracy and immediacy than just sisterly intuition. Mary K. was sad and kind of lost. I frowned, wondering how I could help her. Then she turned around. "I guess I'll go over to Jaycee's. Maybe we can get her sister to take us to the mall. I've still got to get some Christmas presents."

"I'd take you," I said, "but I don't think I can get out of bed."

"Are you coming down with something?" she asked.

Not exactly, but . . . "Probably just a cold." I sniffled experimentally.

"Well, can I get you anything before I leave?"

I thought about food, and my stomach recoiled. "Do we have any ginger ale?"

"Yeah. You want some?"

"Sure."

I was able to keep the ginger ale down. I didn't feel sick, exactly, just drained and fuzzy. Other aftereffects of the *brach* were apparent as well. It was similar to what I'd felt after my first circle with Cal and Cirrus, but magnified by a factor of ten. My senses seemed even more heightened than they had that time: I could make out distinct threads in the jeans hanging over my desk chair; I saw tiny motes of dust caught in the new paint on my walls. Later in the morning I heard a bizarre crunching sound coming from downstairs, as if a hundred-pound termite was eating the basement. It turned out to be Dagda working on his kibble. I felt my lungs absorbing oxygen from every breath; felt my blood cells flowing through my veins, suspended in plasma; felt how each square inch of my skin interpreted and analyzed air or fabric or whatever touched it.

I felt magick everywhere, flowing around me, flowing out of me, in the air, in anything organic, in the sleeping trees outside, in Dagda, in anything that I touched.

I assumed this hyperawareness would fade gradually. It had better. It was wonderful, but if I were this sensitive all the time, I'd lose my mind.

A golden brownish maple leaf drifted past my window. It came to rest for an instant on the sill, and I gazed meditatively at it, marveling at the complex network of tiny veins that spread across its surface. I almost thought I could make out a face in the intersecting lines—a wide, firm mouth, straight nose, two golden eyes. . . .

Goddess. Cal.

In the next instant the leaf was caught in a gust of wind and danced away.

I lay there in bed, breathing deeply, trying to regain my lost peace. But it was hard, because although after yesterday I no longer feared Cal the way I had, every thought of Cal led to a thought of Selene and to the sure knowledge that she was still searching for me, still plotting to destroy me.

Gradually I became aware of something nagging at the edge of my consciousness. My quest. My search for more knowledge about my birth parents, my heritage. I hadn't done anything about it yet, but now, with the new clarity I had achieved as a result of the brach, I saw how much I needed to. Only then would I be whole; only then would my power be fully accessible to me; only then would it be truly mine. And only then would I have a hope against Selene.

Eventually I struggled to my feet and changed into clean clothes, dismissing a shower as unnecessary. I brushed my hair and my teeth and felt I'd done enough grooming for one day. After I flopped back onto my bed, I sensed Hunter coming up my front walk. I groaned, wanting to see him but knowing I could never make it downstairs to open the door.

"Hunter, just come in," I whispered, sending him a witch message.

Moments later I heard the front door snick open, then Hunter calling, "Morgan?"

"I'm upstairs," I managed to call. "You can come up." I wondered if I now had a spell in the recesses of my brain that would keep my mom from unexpectedly coming home from work.

His footsteps were light on the stairs, and then he was peering around my door. "Is it okay for me to be here?" he asked.

I smiled, pleased that he'd asked. "No one's here but me," I said.

"Right," said Hunter, coming in. "If we feel someone coming home, I'll jump out the window." He stood, tall and lean and newly familiar, and looked down at me. His hair was messy from his hat, and it stood up in pale gold spikes.

"Okay," I said. Cautiously I put out my senses and felt his awareness that I'd done so.

"How are you feeling?" he asked.

"Crappy. Weak. But really, really magicky." I couldn't help grinning.

He groaned theatrically. "Now I'm frightened. Please, please," he said. "I'm begging you. Please do not do anything with your new magick just yet. Do not cast spells. Do not run around town throwing witch fire at anyone. Promise me."

"It's like you don't trust my judgment or something," I said. He came to sit on the end of my bed and put one hand on my comforter-covered leg. I started to feel better.

"Oh," he said, rolling his eyes. "So you actually think you use judgment sometimes?"

I kicked him, and then we were grinning at each other, and I felt much better.

"That was an amazing *brach* last night," he said. "Very intense."

"It was," I agreed. "How's Alyce? Have you talked to her?"

He nodded. "Sky is with her, and another witch from Starlocket, too. She feels about like you do. She's excited, though. She got a lot from you."

"I got a lot from her," I said slowly. "I haven't begun to process it."

"It will take you a long time," Hunter predicted. Absently he rubbed my leg, below the knee, and I looked at his eyes, wondering how to say what I needed to.

"I'm so sorry about yesterday," I said, and his eyes darkened. I swallowed. "It was just—I couldn't go through that again. The last time—on the cliff—when I thought you were dead, that I had killed you. I just—couldn't go through that. I couldn't have you two fighting—trying to kill each other. Never again."

His face was still, watchful.

"I'm so sorry I put the binding spell on you," I said. "I know how horrible that feels. I've never forgiven Cal for doing it to me. Now I've done it to you. But I just didn't know how else to get out of there and to take you with me. I'm so sorry," I ended miserably.

"Cal needs to come in," Hunter said quietly. "He needs to answer to the council. And because of who I am and where I am, it will be me who has to bring him in."

I nodded, trying to accept that.

Hunter stroked my knee, and I felt a trembly sensation start at his fingertips and move up to the pit of my stomach. He was quiet for a long while, and I reached out and held his hand.

"Yule is tomorrow," he said finally.

"That's right. I lost track of the days. I hope I'll be up to celebrating by then."

"I think you will," he said with a smile.

"There's something else I need to do tomorrow," I said. "If I can move."

"What's that?"

"I need to go to Meshomah Falls." That was the town where my birth parents had briefly lived—and where they had died. "I want to find the place where the barn burned down."

"Why?" he asked.

"To learn," I said. "There's so much I don't know. Who set the fire? Why? I need to find out. I feel like I won't be whole until I do. That's what I learned from the *brach*."

Hunter looked at me for a long moment. "It's dangerous, you know," he said. "With Cal roaming about and Selene on her way."

I didn't say anything.

Then he nodded. "All right," he said. "I'll pick you up at ten, shall I?"

God, I loved him.

Hunter drove, because I was still a little shaky on Tuesday. He didn't bring up the subject of Cal, except to tell me that he still hadn't been able to locate him. "I wonder if he's got someone helping him," Hunter said, rubbing his chin, and I thought of Selene and felt a flash of dread. Was she here now? No. She couldn't be. I wasn't ready.

Then Hunter took my hand without speaking, and I felt his strength flowing into me, calming me. I am with you, he was saying without words. And I felt suddenly better, lighter.

I'd been to Meshomah Falls once before, and it felt familiar to me now. I directed Hunter to the outskirts of town. There was an old field there, tan and dry from the winter cold. I got out of the car and walked to the middle of it. I still felt weak, drained, as if I were getting over the flu.

Maeve's coven tools were in the trunk of the car, but I left them there. I didn't need them yet. Hunter came to stand next to me.

"Okay. Let's find the old barn site," he said.

I stood still, my arms slightly out by my sides, and shut down all thoughts, all feelings, all expectations. Soon I no longer felt the winter sun on my face or the wind in my hair. But I could see where the barn had been, see what it had looked like and what the site looked like now. I followed it in my mind, tracing how to get there from here. When it was clear, I opened my eyes, feeling vaguely nauseated.

"Okay, I got it," I said, and swallowed. I headed back to the car and the Diet Coke that was waiting there.

"Are you sure you're up to this?" Hunter asked as I swigged soda and held the cold can against my forehead.

"I have to do it," I said. "I just . . . I have to."

He nodded and started the car. "Yes, I think you're right. Tonight at the Yule circle we'll send you some restoring energy."

"Take the next left," I said, already feeling better.

*   *   *

We found it almost fifteen minutes later, after getting lost a couple of times. Like Widow's Vale, this area was hilly and rocky, the narrow roads lined with skeletal trees and bushes. In the springtime it would be beautiful and in the summer unbelievably lush and green. I hoped Maeve had found a small measure of happiness here, at least for a short while.

"There it is," I said, pointing suddenly. I recognized a twisted spruce as one that I'd seen in my mind's eye. "In there."

Hunter pulled the car to the side of the road and peered skeptically past the tree line. We got out, and I quickly jumped the old-fashioned slat fence. Hunter followed. I strode forward through the dead clumps of frozen grass, sending out my senses and looking alertly at everything. There was almost nothing alive around here, no birds, no animals hibernating in nests or trees, no deer or rabbits watching quietly nearby.

"Hmmm," said Hunter, slowing down and scanning the area. "What do you feel?"

I swallowed. "I feel like we're close to something really bad."

I slowed my pace and started looking more closely at the ground. Suddenly I halted, as if an invisible hand had pressed my chest and stopped me cold. I looked closer, focusing sharply on the ground between the clumps of grass. I didn't even know what to look for, but then I saw it: the rippled, broken back-bone of a large brick foundation. The barn had once stood here.

I stepped back, as if it were poison ivy. Hunter came up next to me, looking uncomfortable and edgy.

"Now what?" he asked.

"I get my tools," I said.

I made Hunter turn around while I wiggled out of my clothes and put on Maeve's robe. No one but my mother, my sister, and my gynecologist had seen me naked, and I was going to keep it that way. At least for the immediately foreseeable future.

"Okay, I'm ready," I said, and Hunter turned to look at me.

"How do you want to do this?" he said. "I don't have my robe or tools with me."

"I'm thinking meditation," I answered. "Together, the two of us, with my tools."

Hunter thought about it and nodded. By picking our way through the years of overgrowth, we found two walls of the former foundation. Gauging our position from the angle of the crumbling bricks, we sat in what had been the center of the barn. I held Maeve's athame in my left hand, her wand in my right. Between Hunter and me I placed several crystals and two bloodstones. We drew a circle of power around us with a stick and then closed our eyes. I took a deep breath, tried to release tension, and lost myself in nothingness.

The inside of the barn was dark. Angus and I stood in the middle of the building, hearing running footsteps around the out-side. I was muttering spells under my breath, spells I hadn't used in two years. My magick felt dull, blunted, an unhoned blade no longer useful. Beside me I felt Angus's fear, his hopelessness. Why are you wasting energy on feelings? I wanted to scream.

My eyes adjusted to the blackness inside the barn. The scents of old hay, animals from long ago, ancient leather filled my nose, and I wanted to sneeze. Still I chanted, drawing power to me: "An di allaigh an di aigh . . ." I reached out with my senses, probing, but they recoiled on me. It was as if we were trapped in a cage made of crystal—a cage that reflected our power back at us rather than letting it out to do its work.

The first sharp scent of smoke came to me. Angus gripped my hand tightly, and I shook him off, feeling sudden anger at the way he'd loved me all these years—years when he'd known that I didn't love him. Why hadn't he demanded more from me? Why hadn't he left me? Then maybe he wouldn't be here now, dying with me.

Smoke. I heard the hungry crackling of the fire as it lapped the base of the barn, as it whipped down the sides, hurrying to meet itself, to make a full circle of flames. The barn was old, dry, the wood half rotted: perfect kindling. Ciaran had known.

"Our child." Angus's voice was full of pain.

"She's safe," I said, feeling guilt weighing on me, further weakening my powers. "She will always be safe." The small windows, high on the barn walls, glowed pinkly, and I knew it was from fire, not from dawn. No one would find us. Ciaran's magick would make sure of that. No one would call the fire department until it was much too late. Already the building was filling with smoke, hovering by the ceiling, swirling on itself, thickening.

Maybe it wasn't too late. Maybe I could find a way out. I still had my power, rusty though it might be. "An di allaigh an di aigh . . . ," I began once again.

But at my words, the cage of magick around us seemed to tighten, to contract, glittering as it pressed in on us. I coughed and inhaled smoke. And then I knew there was no hope.

It had come to this. Ciaran was going to be my death. He had shown me what love was, what it could be, and now he would show me my death. I felt sharp regret that Angus would die here, too. I tried to console myself with the fact that it had been his choice. He had always chosen to be with me.

I wondered what Ciaran was doing outside: if he was still watching, making sure we didn't escape; if he was weaving magick all around us, spells of death and binding, panic and fear. I felt panic's claws scraping at my mind, but I refused to let it in. I tried to keep calm, to call power to me. I thought about my baby, my beautiful baby, with her fine, fuzzy infant hair the color of my mother's. Her tilted, brown eyes, so like her father's. The most perfect baby ever born, with a thousand years of Belwicket magick in her veins, in her blood.

She would be safe from this kind of danger. Safe from her heritage. I had made sure of that.

It was hard to breathe, and I dropped to my knees. Angus was coughing, trying to breathe through his shirt, pulled up to cover his nose and mouth. I had mended that shirt this morning, sewed on a button.

Ciaran. Even here, now, I couldn't help remembering how he'd made me feel when we'd first met. It had been so clear we were meant to be together. So clear that we were mùirn beatha dàns. But he was married to another and a father. And I chose Angus. Poor Angus. Then Ciaran chose the darkness, over me.

I felt light-headed. Sweat was beading on my forehead, in my hair; soot was stinging my eyes. Angus was coughing nonstop. I took his hand as I sank into the fine dust on the barn floor, feeling the heat pressing in from all sides. I no longer chanted. It was no use. Ciaran had always been stronger than I—he had gone through the Great Trial.

I had never had a chance.

14

Bait

November 1981

I'm pregnant. It's a bizarre physiological experience, like being taken over by an alien that I can't control. Every cell in my body is changing. It's thrilling and terrifying: much like being part of Amyranth.

Daniel, of course, is furious. These past six months he's always furious with me, so there's nothing new there. We'd agreed not to have children because our marriage has seemed so rocky. By myself, I decided I wanted to have part of Daniel always, wanted to have something permanent that was partly me and partly him. So I used magick to override his conception block. It was easy.

So Daniel's thrown a fit and hightailed it back to England. I've settled in San Francisco because of the strong Amyranth presence here. What is it about England that *pulls him back so strongly? This is the third time in three months that he's gone back. For me, my home is where Amyranth is. Daniel's sentimental loyalty seems naive and misplaced.*

He'll be back soon. He always comes back. And the mirror shows me that pregnant, I am more beautiful than ever. When he sees me glowing, carrying our child, it will be a new start for us. I can feel it.

—SB

When I opened my eyes, tears were streaming down my face. Hunter was watching me, looking calm and alert. He reached toward me and brushed some tears away with his hand.

"Did you see any of that?" I asked, my throat tight and full of pain.

"Some," he said, helping me stand. We were both chilled through, and I wanted to be gone from this place, far away from these feelings. I looked down at the broken foundations and could still smell the ancient ash, the charred boards. I could hear the snap of the windows as they broke one by one from the heat. The smell of skin and hair, burning. They had been dead by then.

"The images I got were confused," said Hunter. He pulled me to him as we walked back to the car, and by the time I had changed out of my robe and was sitting in the passenger seat, I was crying hard, my hands over my face. Hunter hugged me, his arms around me, his hands stroking my hair.

"It was Ciaran," I finally got out. "The love of my mother's life. He killed her and Angus."

"Why?"

"I don't know," I said, frustrated. "Because he couldn't have her? Because she rejected him when she found out he was married? Because she chose Angus? I don't know."

I rested my head against Hunter's chest, feeling how lean and hard he was through his coat. I knew that he understood pain because of what had happened to his parents. Maybe someday, I'd be able to help Hunter as he was helping me now. Suddenly his fingers stilled against my back and tension entered his body. I raised my head and closed my eyes.

"Selene," I whispered, already throwing up the magick blocks I had learned from Alyce. I quickly erected wall after wall around me, sealing my mind off from outside influences, surrounding myself and Hunter with ward-evil spells, protection spells, spells of concealment and strength. It took only instants, and I felt Selene's increased pressure as she tried to get through, tried to get into my mind. My hand gripped Hunter's, and our powers joined—I felt his strength shoring up mine and was grateful.

Just like that, it was over. I no longer felt any other presence. Slowly Hunter and I let each other go, and I felt a pang of regret at losing that particular closeness.

"She wants you badly," Hunter said grimly, sitting back in his seat. "That's the second time she's tried to get into your mind. She must be closer than I thought. Dammit! We've searched everywhere for her—I scry every day. But I haven't been able to pick up on anything." He thought for a moment, drumming his fingers on the steering wheel. "I'm calling in help from the council." He started the car and turned on the heater.

"Will they really be able to help?" I asked, wrapping my arms around myself. I felt overwhelmed, sad, and weary.

"I hope so," Hunter answered me. "Selene is working up to something, and it's going to happen soon. I feel it." He glanced over at me and put his hand on my leg. I was starting to thaw but still felt nauseated. I hoped I wouldn't have to ask Hunter to pull over so I could barf.

"Recline your seat," he suggested as I sipped the rest of my Diet Coke. "Are you sure you should be drinking that? We could stop and get a nice cup of tea somewhere."

"Coke settles your stomach," I said. "Everyone knows that." I put the can in the cup holder, then pulled the lever that reclined my seat.

"Better?" Hunter asked.

"Um," I said. My eyes felt heavy, and I let myself sink into a lovely lack of consciousness where there was no pain. The next thing I knew the car had stopped and Hunter was gently rubbing my shoulder.

"Home again, home again, jiggity jig," he said.

We were parked in front of my house. Through my window I saw that the day had turned ugly, with dark, heavy clouds rolling in from the West. It looked like snow was on the way. My watch said it was four o'clock.

I reached for the handle to straighten my seat but was caught by the expression in Hunter's eyes. All at once he seemed like the most beautiful thing I had ever seen, and I smiled at him. His eyes flared slightly, and he leaned down. I curled my arms around his neck and held him to me as our mouths met. Eagerly I kissed him, wanting to join with him, wanting to show him how I felt about him, how much I appreciated him. His breathing quickened as he held me closer, and it was thrilling to know how much he wanted me, too.

Slowly he pulled back, and our breathing gradually returned to normal.

"We need to talk about what you saw," he said quietly, stroking one finger along my jaw.

I nodded. "Maybe you could come in for a while? We could hang out in the den. My mom will more or less leave us alone in there."

He grinned at me, and we walked up to my front door. Before I could unlock it, it opened, and my mom looked at me kind of wild-eyed.

"Morgan! Thank goodness you're home! Do you know where Mary K. is? Is she with you?" She looked past me as if expecting to see my sister walking up the driveway.

"No," I answered, feeling a jolt of alarm. "I saw her this morning. She said she was going to Jaycee's."

"They haven't seen her all day," my mom said, the lines around her mouth deepening. "I came home early, and there was a message from Jaycee asking why Mary K. had stood her up."

Mom stepped aside and motioned us to come in. I was thinking about possibilities, my brain firing fast, battling the weariness I'd had since Sunday.

"Did she leave a note? What does her room look like?" I asked.

"No note anywhere, and her room is fine, like she just left," said my mom. "Her bicycle is here." Her voice sounded strained. I knew what she was thinking: Bakker.

"Let me call Bakker's house," I said, shrugging out of my coat. I headed for the kitchen, looked up Bakker's number, and dialed it. Maybe his family would know where he had gone. Maybe Mary K., showing incredibly poor judgment, had gone over there to watch TV or something.

His mother answered, and I asked to speak to Bakker. To my relief, he was home, and soon said a cautious, "Hello?"

"Bakker, it's Morgan Rowlands," I said briskly. "Where's Mary K.?"

"Huh?" he said, instantly defensive. "How would I know?"

"Look, is she there? Just let me talk to her."

"Are you kidding? Thanks to you, she'll never speak to me again. I haven't seen her since school let out."

"It's *your* fault she won't speak to you," I said scathingly. "If I find out she's there and you're lying to me—"

"She's not here. Go screw yourself." Click.

I looked up to see Mom and Hunter watching me. "Apparently she's not with Bakker," I said. I tapped my finger against my lips, thinking. Mary K. had been so different lately. She'd been going to church so often, praying and reading the Bible. I felt a pang of guilt, thinking of all the times I'd tried to talk to her but hadn't pushed her to open up to me. She might be in real trouble now, and maybe I could have prevented it.

"Maybe she just went shopping or something," I said, not believing it. "Or maybe she went to an afternoon service at church. But why would she stand up Jaycee?"

"She wouldn't," said Mom, and I felt her tension, felt how close she was to panicking. "She would never do that. You know how conscientious she is."

I looked at Hunter and saw that he was thinking the same thing I was: that we should scry to find Mary K., and that we couldn't do it in front of my mom.

"Okay," I said, reaching for my coat. "Tell you what. Hunter and I will go and look at the coffee shop and church, maybe Darcy's house, and some of the shops downtown.

We'll call you in an hour with an update, but I'm sure we'll find her. She probably just forgot to leave a note. I'm sure she's okay, and there's a simple explanation."

"Okay," my mom said after a moment. "I'm probably over-reacting. It's just so unlike her to take off like this." She bit her lip. "I already called Dad. He's on his way home. He said he'd take a look around the Taunton mall, see if she's there."

"It'll be okay. We'll call you." Hunter and I went out the front door and started down the walk toward his car. I felt like I'd been in that car all day and didn't want to get back in it. Just as we reached the sidewalk, our next-door neighbor, Mrs. DiNapoli, walked over from her house.

"Hi, Morgan," she said, drawing her coat around her. "Is your mother home?" She smiled and held out a glass measuring cup. "I need to borrow—"

"Sugar?" I asked.

"Flour," she said. "Harry's aunt and uncle are coming to dinner, and I'm making a roux. Do you think your folks have any flour?"

"Um, probably," I said as Hunter smiled at Mrs. DiNapoli and opened the driver's-side door. "Mom's inside—you can ask her. We were just on our way out."

"Okay." She headed up our driveway as I turned to get in. "That was some car earlier," Mrs. DiNapoli called back. "Whose was it?"

"What do you mean?" I asked.

"That Jaguar Mary K. got into earlier."

I froze. "You saw Mary K. getting into a Jaguar?" I'm so stupid, I thought. Why didn't I ask any of the neighbors if they had seen anything?

Mrs. DiNapoli laughed. "Yes, a beautiful green one."

Selene drove a green Jaguar. I looked at Hunter, and again our thoughts were in accord. He nodded at me briefly, then slid behind the wheel and started the engine.

"I'm not sure whose it was," I said. "How long ago was this?"

Our neighbor shrugged. "Two hours, at least. I'm not sure."

"Okay, thanks, Mrs. DiNapoli." I climbed into the passenger seat and Hunter took off, heading out of town. We knew where we needed to start looking.

Cal's old house.

15

Trap

April 1982

Be careful what you wish for, they say. Because you may get it.

I've gotten what I wished for, and the Goddess must be laughing. Daniel's come home, after being gone almost three months. The baby is due in June, and I look big and vibrant and fertile, like the Goddess herself. It's been interesting to see how pregnancy affects my magick: I'm more powerful in some ways, but there are some unpredictable side effects. Some spells fall apart, some have unexpected results. Nothing can be counted on. It's funny, for the most part. However, for the last seven months I've haven't been able to do my part for Amyranth. They've been understanding, though—they know I'll soon present them with a perfect Amyranth baby, one literally born to do their work.

It's hard for me to put the next words down. I've found out the reason Daniel goes to England so much: he has a girl-friend there. He actually told me this himself. I was sure he was joking—what woman, witch or human, can compete with me? But as he droned on and the words started sinking in, I went through being amused, then horrified, then furious. This other woman, whom he won't name, and he have known each other for years and had a childhood romance. But their affair only started six months ago—right after I conceived my baby. I'm shocked beyond words. The idea that Daniel could keep such a secret from me is unbelievable. It means his powers are stronger than I knew, and how is that possible?

I'm thinking about what to do next. That this other woman has to be found and eliminated goes without saying. Daniel says their affair is over. Pathetically, he wept when he told me. What a worm! He came back to me for the sake of the baby we're having, but he won't sleep with me and says he won't pre-tend we're a couple anymore. This won't do at all. He's going to be mine or no one's. I have to break his will, bind him to me. Now I must go—I have research to do and people to consult.

—SB

Hunter pulled over while we were still a mile from Cal's. He cut the engine and turned to me.

"Why are you stopping?" I said urgently. "Let's go! If she has Mary K.—"

"I know, and we'll get there. But first, send Sky and Alyce a witch message," he said. "I'd send it, but yours will be stronger.

Tell them to contact the council and get reinforcements to Selene's as fast as they can. It will take a couple of hours at least, but maybe they can get here in time to help us."

"Should I ask Sky and Alyce to meet us there now?" I asked. "We could all join our powers. . . ."

He shook his head. "They aren't equipped for this battle," he said gently. "Neither are you, if it comes to that. But this is about you, about what Selene wants from you."

"I'll be strong enough," I said, not at all sure that was true. "If she's done anything to Mary K.—"

"What's important is that you use your own powers," Hunter said, looking at me intently. "Use your powers, coupled with Alyce's knowledge. Feel the power within you. Know it absolutely. Selene is going to try to use illusion and fear to break you down. Don't let it work."

I looked into his eyes, feeling dread. "All right," I said shakily.

He started the engine. Five minutes later he was turning down the street that led to the huge stone house where Cal and Selene had worked their magick.

Darkness was all around us. It was barely five o'clock but wintertime, and the sun had sunk below the horizon, obscured by ominous-looking clouds. I could feel that soon the sky would open and start dumping snow and ice.

Mary K., I thought as Hunter parked down the street, out of sight of the big house. My sweet sister. Although we shared no blood, I felt we had always been sisters in spirit: destined to be related to each other, to love each other as family. In some ways she was so much savvier than I—she knew what to wear, who to hang out with, how to flirt and be cheerful and charming. But in some ways she was so naive. She trusted most people. She believed that her faith would protect her. She believed that if she was good enough, everything would work out. I knew better than that.

"Pop the trunk," I told Hunter, and he did. I knew I would need every ounce of power I could possibly have: I was still feeling the draining effects of the *tàth meànma brach*. Without more than a moment's awkward hesitation I stripped off my coat, sweatshirt, and undershirt and put on my mother's robe, the thin emerald green silk instantly warming me in the cold night air. I felt my cheeks heat with a blush as I unsnapped my jeans and pushed them and my underwear down. Of course then I realized I still wore my sneaks and socks and had to kneel and get out of them to get out of my pants.

Then I stood, feeling completely comfortable in the robe and nothing else even though it was winter in upstate New York. Like a Wiccan force field, I thought, picking up Maeve's wand and athame.

"I wish I'd had time to collect my own robe," Hunter said, frowning. He pulled out his athame. Thus armed, we began to move quietly toward the house.

We were immediately aware of a darkness of magick all around. Keeping to the shadows of the hedge that surrounded the property, I cast out my senses and felt a miasma of black magick emanating from the house, from the stones themselves. The green Jaguar sat in the circular driveway, and to my eyes it seemed to glow and pulse, almost as if it were radioactive. I realized that I was terrified and tried to release my fears.

In unspoken agreement we paused, and together we wrapped ourselves in cloaks of illusion, of vagueness, of shadows. With no effort I pulled spells out of Alyce's memory and called them to me, as familiar to me as Dagda. Under any other circumstances I would have felt thrilled with my new ability, but now I merely fretted. To any lesser witch we would certainly be undetectable, but would these spells work on Selene? She was so powerful that I doubted it.

We looked at the house, with its gaping black windows, its air of recent neglect. Dried leaves had blown onto the porch and steps and remained unswept.

"How did she get in?" I whispered. "The house was spelled against her."

"The council did its best," Hunter replied softly. "But Selene has powers and connections we don't fully understand. The question is, how can *we* get in? The front door will be a trap."

I crouched down for a moment, examining the house. Then an idea came to me, and I stood up. "Come with me."

Without waiting for his response, I strode along the hedge until we reached a break in the tall shrubbery to the right of the house. We crunched across dead grass, around to the back, where a narrow metal staircase led up to the third-floor attic. Cal's old room. I started climbing, my bare feet making hardly any sound.

"We spelled all the entrances," Hunter reminded me quietly.

"I know. But you can break your spells; you made them. And I don't think Selene will expect us to come in this way." The whole time I climbed, I was feeling with my senses, searching for my sister, for Selene's presence, trying to get through the spells of privacy that cloaked the house. I could feel nothing except an aching, bone-deep weariness, the faint edges of nausea around the rim of my consciousness, and the seeping of tendrils of dark magick writhing in the air all around me.

At the top of the narrow staircase was a small wooden door. Cal used to use it to get from his room to the backyard and to the pool beyond. I stopped for a moment, pressed my hand against my brow, closed my eyes, and concentrated.

It wasn't as if everything suddenly popped out at me in neon colors. But as I thought, willing magick to show itself to me, the layers of the spells on the door slowly and faintly began to glimmer. I was vaguely aware of Hunter, next to me, becoming very still and alert as the sigils and markings of spells shone with a slight sheen around the door frame. I saw the oldest markings, those of Cal himself, spelling the door so that it would open only to his command. I can't say how I knew these spells were his, how I knew what they were and how he had made them. It was more like seeing a daisy and thinking, Daisy. It was clear and instantaneous.

It was also clear that Cal's spells had been mostly obliterated, I guessed by the International Council of Witches. Their spells were complicated and gleamed brightly. I didn't know the council members well enough to recognize their handiwork but felt that I saw traces of Hunter's handwriting, his personality in the spells. Again I could never have explained it or proved it. I just knew.

Overlying everything were dark, spiky spells of illusion and repulsion that I recognized as Selene's handiwork. She had used an ancient alphabet and an archaic set of characters, and just seeing the spells written there brought forth a wave of fear that I tried to dismiss. Selene's work glowed the brightest: she had cast these spells recently.

"All right," breathed Hunter next to me. I kept the spells in sight as he began slowly and laboriously dismantling them, layer by layer, saying the words that unknit the spells, dispersing their energy and power. My head was beginning to ache with a sharp, piercing pain at my temples as I strove to concentrate. The cold wind seemed to intensify, and it buffeted us as we stood on that narrow staircase outside the attic of the stone house.

At last the spells were taken apart, and then it was simple for Hunter to magickally undo the mechanical lock of the door. It swung open silently, and with a glance at each other, Hunter and I stepped through.

Inside, Cal's room was as he'd left it that night he'd tried to kill me. With a quick scan I saw he had taken some of his books, and probably some clothes, since his dresser drawers were pulled askew. But it didn't appear that he'd been staying here.

The room was startlingly familiar, and it brought an unwelcome ache to my heart to see the place where Cirrus had had circles, the chair where I'd opened my birthday presents from Cal, the bed where we had lain and kissed for hours.

As noiselessly as possible, we did a quick search of Cal's room. I held my athame before me and on virtually every surface turned up runes, sigils, other markings: the magick Cal had worked in this room. But other than the marks, and some dangerous tools and talismans, we found nothing, no sign of Mary K. or of Cal's or Selene's whereabouts.

"This way," Hunter said, his voice no louder than a whisper, and motioned toward the door that led to the rest of the house. When he opened the door, I almost recoiled. Now I could sense Selene, feel her dark presence. She had been working black magick in this house: its bitter and acrid aura clung to everything. It felt like the very air was contaminated, and I was afraid.

Gently Hunter brushed his hand against my hair, my cheek. "Remember," he whispered. "Fear is one of her weapons. Don't give in to it. Trust your instincts."

My instincts? I thought, panicked. We both knew how reliable *those* had been in the past. But I knew that was the wrong answer, so I just nodded, and we started down the narrow back staircase to the second floor. Maeve's wand felt slim and powerful in my left hand, and the athame felt as protective as a shield. But I still felt vulnerable as I crept downstairs and was glad Hunter was beside me.

Cal's room took up the entire attic, and on the second floor were five bedrooms and four bathrooms. Here, as upstairs, the dusty floors were undisturbed until our feet traced patterns on them. To a rational mind, that meant that no person had walked here since the house had been shut. But witchcraft is not bound by laws of rationality.

Searching as a witch was different than searching as a person. I used my eyes and ears, but more important, I used my senses, my intuition, my Wiccan instinct that warned me when danger was near and what form it would take. Between me, my tools, and Hunter, we made short work of the second floor. None of the rooms looked touched, but more telling, none of the rooms *felt* touched. I didn't detect Selene's unmistakable aura in any of the bedrooms: she hadn't been to the second floor.

The only time I felt anything at all was when I paused before an open window in the last bedroom. I felt a faint chill there, as if I stood beneath an AC vent, but the window curtains were motionless, and then I picked up on it: Cal. Cal had been here; he'd stood here with a lit candle not long ago. The day Bree, Mary K., and I had come back from Practical

Magick and I had seen him. His traces lingered here still.

Hunter came to stand by me. Our eyes met, and he nodded. He felt it, too. Taking my elbow, he led me to the main staircase, the wide, ornately carved steps leading to the first floor. The rich carpet looked dull, dusty, and my nose tickled as our feet stirred motes into the chill, silent air.

Selene's presence felt stronger with every step. In my hand, the hilt of the ancient Belwicket athame seemed to grow warm. Then I knew: Selene was in her library, the hidden library that I had seen only once, a lifetime ago, when I had discovered Maeve's Book of Shadows on Selene's shelves. When Hunter had come here, he hadn't even been able to find the concealed door. In fact, the council witches themselves hadn't been able to break the spells that guarded Selene's secret lair.

Today would be different. Today we would get into the hidden library because today Selene wanted us to. She had taken my sister to try to make me come here. In an instant I saw the whole plan: Selene had been trying to get into my mind and had been thwarted by my ability to block her. Had she then turned to my sister? Mary K. had been withdrawn and sad for weeks—was Selene working on her mind even then?

Since she had first met me, Selene had been courting me, through her son. She had commanded Cal to get close to me, and he had. She had wanted him to make me love him, and he had. She had wanted him to convince me to join their side, to ally my magick and Maeve's coven tools with theirs. This I had refused. Since then she had wanted two things: my compliance or death and Maeve's tools. And now here I was, in her house, at her bidding, just as she had planned.

Today we would finish what had been set in motion the day we met. With a sudden, chilling certainty I knew that

Selene intended for only one of us to survive this encounter: her. By the end of the day she wanted me dead and she wanted Maeve's tools. No doubt she also wanted Hunter dead. Mary K. probably didn't matter much to her, but as a witness, she would have to die as well.

I almost sagged against the stair rail as these thoughts flashed like lightning across my mind. If I were a full, initiated witch, I would be quaking in my boots at the idea of facing Selene Belltower. If I had the entire council standing behind me, wands raised, I would still feel a cold and desperate terror. As it was, there was only me and Hunter, and I was just a barefoot, talented amateur from a small town.

I gulped and looked at Hunter, my eyes wide and filling with hopeless tears. Jesus, get me out of this, I thought in panic. Please, God. Hunter watched me, his eyes narrowed, and then he reached out and gripped my shoulder hard, so hard, I winced. "Don't be afraid," he whispered fiercely.

Yeah, right, I wanted to scream. Every cell in my body wanted to turn, run, and get the hell out of here. Only the image of my innocent sister, trustingly getting into Selene's car, kept me in place. I felt nausea rise in the back of my throat, and I wanted to sit down and start crying, right there on the steps.

"Morgan, come." Selene's voice spoke in my mind.

My eyes widened, and I looked at Hunter. His face showed me that he hadn't heard it.

"Selene," I whispered. "She knows I'm here."

Hunter's face hardened. Leaning over, he put his mouth close to mine. "We can do this, love. You can do this."

I tried to focus, but I couldn't stop thinking that I might die today. A deep despair started in the pit of my stomach, as if I had swallowed a cold stone the size of my fist.

But there was nothing to be done. Mary K. was here. She was my sister, and she needed me now. Hunter was by my side as I took a step downward, my bare feet making no sound on the thick carpet. When we reached the bottom of the steps, the parquet floor was cold and dust covered. Here, at last, were signs of disturbance. I saw dim outlines of footprints, swept mostly away by something soft and heavy—the bottom of a cape? A blanket?

I turned and headed down the hallway toward the large kitchen. Halfway down the hall I stopped and looked to my right. The door had to be around here somewhere, I knew. The door to Selene's library.

16

Selene

June 1982

Praise the Goddess. I finally had my baby boy. He is a big, perfect baby, with fine dark hair like mine and odd, slate-colored eyes that will no doubt change color later. Norris Hathaway and Helen Ford attended as midwives and were absolute lifesavers during labor. Labor! Goddess, I had no idea. I felt I was being rent in two, torn apart, giving birth to an entire world. I tried to be strong but I admit I screamed and cried. Then my son crowned, and Norris reached down to twist out his shoulders. I looked down to see my son emerge into the light, and my tears of pain turned to tears of joy. It was the most incredible magick I've ever made.

His naming ceremony will be next week. I've decided on Calhoun: warrior. His Amyranth name is Sgàth, which means darkness. It's a sweet darkness, like his hair.

Daniel didn't come to the birth: a sign of his weakness. He

slouches around, mooning over England and his whore there, which makes me despise him, though I can't stop wanting him. He seems pleased with his son, less pleased with me. Now that our baby is here, flesh and blood, beautiful and perfect, perhaps Daniel will find happiness with me. It would be best for him if he did.

Now that I've had the baby, I'm hungry to get back to work with Amyranth. They were in Wales and then in Germany in the past several months, and I was gnashing my teeth with envy. The Germany trip yielded some ancient books on darkness that I can't wait to see—I can already taste them. It will be intensely fulfilling for me to watch Calhoun grow up within the arms of Amyranth, their son as well as mine. He will be my instrument, my weapon.

—SB

Selene wasn't going to make it *too* easy: it took Hunter and me several minutes to find even the dim outlines of the concealed door. Finally I managed to come up with one of Alyce's revealing spells and, using my athame, detected the barest fingernail-thin line in the hallway wall.

"Ah," Hunter breathed. "Well done."

I stood by, concentrating, lending my power to Hunter while he carefully, slowly, and methodically dismantled the concealment and closure spells. I felt Selene's magick as bursts of pain that needled into every part of my body, but I thought about Mary K., and I tried to ignore them.

It felt like hours later that Hunter passed his hand down the wall and I heard the faint snick of the latch opening. The door, barely taller than Hunter's head, swung open.

The next instant I clamped my mouth shut as darkness and evil surged through the doorway like a flood tide, coming to suck us under and into the room. Instinctively I stepped back, throwing up ward-evil spells and spells of protection on top of the ones Hunter and I had already placed on ourselves. Then I heard the soft, dark velvet of Selene's laughter, from inside the library, and I forced myself to take a step forward, across the threshold, into her lair.

It was dark in the room. The only light present was coming from several black pillar candles on wrought-iron holders taller than me. I remembered the layout from the only other time I had been here: it was a big room, with a high ceiling. Bookshelves lined the walls, connected by brass railings and small ladders on wheels. There was a deep leather couch, several glass display cases, Selene's huge walnut desk, a library table with a globe, and several book stands holding enormous, ancient, crumbling tomes. And everywhere in the room, in every book and cushion and rug, was Selene's magick, her dark magick, her forbidden spells and experiments and concoctions. The needlelike pains intensified as I scanned the room for Mary K.

Hunter moved behind me, coming into the room. I sensed danger coming from him, a deep, controlled anger at Selene's obvious misuse of magick.

"Morgan!" Mary K.'s soft, young voice came from a dark corner of the room. I cast out my senses and detected my sister huddled against the far wall. Sweeping the room for signs of Selene, I walked quickly to Mary K. and knelt down beside her.

"Are you okay?" I murmured, and she leaned forward, pressing her face against me.

"I don't know why I'm here," she said. Her voice was thick, as if she'd just woken from a deep sleep. "I don't know what's going on."

I was ashamed to tell her she had been merely bait, intended to lure me here. I was ashamed to admit that she was in terrible danger because of me and my Wiccan heritage. Instead I said, "It'll be okay. We'll get you out of here. Just hold on, okay?"

She nodded and slumped back down. Just in touching her I had felt that she was spelled—not strongly, but enough to make her lax and docile. Rage sparked deep in my stomach, and I stood. Hunter was still close to the door, and I saw he had prudently wedged a small wooden trunk in its opening.

Where was Selene? I'd heard her laugh. Of course, it could have been an illusion, a glamor. I was panicking: would I be locked in and trapped here? Would Selene set me on fire? Would I burn to death after all? My breathing quickened, and I peered into the darkest shadows of the room.

"Selene will try to scare you," Hunter had said. "Don't be fooled." Easier said than done. I stepped closer to one of the pillar candles and focused on it. Light, I thought. Fire. There were candles in holders on the walls, and around the room were candelabras filled with tall black tapers. One by one I lit them with my mind, sparking them into life, into existence, and the shadows lessened and the room grew brighter.

"Very good," said Selene's voice. "But then, you're a fire fairy. Like Bradhadair."

Bradhadair had been Maeve's Wiccan name, the name

given her by her coven. It had been in her Book of Shadows, and probably no one else alive today knew about it. I swung toward the sound of Selene's voice and saw her appear in front of one of the bookcases, stepping out from a deep shadow into the light. She was as beautiful as ever, with her sun-streaked dark hair and strange golden eyes, so like Cal's. This was his mother. She had made him what he was.

Like me, Selene wore only her witch's robe, which was a deep crimson silk embroidered all over with symbols I recognized as the same ancient alphabet she'd used for the door spell. It had been taught to Alyce only so she could recognize it and neutralize it: it was inherently evil, and the letters could be used only for dark magick. Because Alyce had learned it, I knew it, too.

"Morgan, thank you for coming," Selene said. Out of the corner of my eye I saw Hunter circling the room, trying to put Selene between me and him. "I'm truly sorry I had to resort to these means. I assure you I've caused no harm to your sister. But once I realized you wouldn't respond to an ordinary invitation, well, I had to get creative." She gave me a charming, rueful smile and seemed like the most attractive person I'd ever seen. "Please forgive me."

I regarded her. Once I had admired her intensely, envied her knowledge and power and skill. Now I knew better.

"No," I said clearly, and her eyes narrowed.

"It's over, Selene," Hunter said in a voice like ice. "You've had a long run, but your days with Amyranth are done."

Amyranth? What's that? I wondered.

"Morgan?" Selene asked, ignoring Hunter.

"No," I repeated. "I don't forgive you."

"You don't understand," she said patiently. "You don't

know enough to realize what you're doing. Hunter here is simply weak and misguided, and who cares? He isn't worth anything to anyone. But you, my dear. You have potential I can't ignore." She smiled again, but it was creepy this time, like a skeleton baring its teeth. "I offer you the chance to be more powerful than you could possibly imagine," she went on. I could hear the sibilant swish of her robe as she moved closer to me. "You are one of the few witches I've met who's worthy of being one of us. You could add to our greatness instead of draining us. You—and your coven tools."

My fists instinctively tightened on my wand and athame, and I tried to release the tension in my body. I had to stay loose and calm, to let the magick flow.

"No," I said again, and my senses picked up the instantaneous flare of anger from Selene. She quickly clamped it down, but the fact that I even felt it meant she wasn't as much in control of herself as she needed to be. I took a deep breath and went against every instinct that I had: I tried to relax, to open myself up, to stop protecting myself. I released anger, fear, distrust, my desire for revenge: I kept thinking, Magick is openness, trust, love. Magick is beauty. Magick is strength and forgiveness. I am made of magick. I thought how I felt after my *tàth meànma brach*, how I felt that magick was everywhere, in everything, in every molecule. If magick surrounded me, it was mine for the taking. I could access it. I could use it. I had the power of the world at my fingertips if I chose to let it in.

I chose to.

The next moment found me doubled over, gasping, as a wave of searing, biting pain hit me. I gagged, choking on the horrible cramping agony, and then I was on my hands and knees on the floor, sucking in breath and feeling like I was being turned inside out.

"Morgan!" Hunter said, but I was only barely aware of him. Every nerve in my body was being flayed, every sense I had was occupied with the exquisite, soul-consuming torture. My hands, still gripping the tools, clawed into the carpet as an invisible ax cleaved my belly in two. In disbelief I stared at myself, expecting to see guts and blood spewing from my body, but I was whole, unchanged on the outside. And yet I was gasping, writhing on the ground as my insides were eaten by acid.

It was an illusion. I knew it intellectually. But my body didn't know it. Between spasms I glanced up at Selene. She was smiling, a small, secret smile that showed me she enjoyed causing me agony.

"Morgan, you're stronger than that!" Hunter snapped, and his words seeped into my consciousness. "Get up! She can't do this to you!"

She's a playground bully, I thought, my breath coming in fast, shallow pants. When I had bound Cal and Hunter, had knocked them to the ground, I had felt the dark, shameful pleasure of controlling another person. That's what Selene was feeling now.

It was an illusion. Everything in me thought I was dying. But I was more than just my thoughts, more than just my feelings, more than my body. I was Morgan of Kithic and of Belwicket, and I had a thousand years of Woodbane strength inside me.

I feel no pain, I thought. I feel no panic.

Slowly I rose back up to my hands and knees, my mouth parched, sweat popping out on my forehead. My hair dragged on the ground, my hands were claws around my tools. *My* tools. They were not Maeve's. Not any longer.

I feel no pain, I thought fiercely. I am fine. Everything in my life is perfect, whole, and complete. I am strength. I am power. I am magick.

Then I was standing tall, my back straight, my hands at my sides. I looked calmly at Selene and for one fraction of a second saw disbelief in her eyes. More than disbelief. I saw the barest hint of fear.

Whirling, she turned to face Hunter and threw out her hand. I saw no witch fire, but Hunter immediately raised his hands and drew sigils in the air. His chest heaved as he pulled in breath, and though I couldn't actually see anything, I knew that Selene was trying to do to him what she had done to me and that he was resisting it. I had never seen so much of his power, not even when he was putting the *braigh* on David Redstone, and it was awesome.

But it wasn't enough for us to resist Selene. We had to actually vanquish her. We had to render her powerless somehow. I searched Alyce's data banks, concealed within my brain, and began to sift through the encyclopedias of knowledge she had acquired in her lifetime.

How do you fight darkness with light? I asked myself. In the same way that sunlight dispels a shadow, came the unhelpful answer. I almost screamed with frustration—I needed something practical, something concrete. Not mumbo jumbo.

The edge of my senses picked up a slight breathing sound—Mary K. She sat, as motionless as a doll, her open eyes unseeing, in the shadows of the corner. Without thinking, I quickly called up spells of distraction, of turn-away. If Selene looked at Mary K., I wanted her to shift focus slightly, to see nothing, to not remember my sister's presence.

Hunter and Selene were facing each other, and suddenly

Hunter surprised me by snatching up a crystal globe from a shelf and humming it at Selene. Her eyes widened and she stepped sideways, but the globe hit her shoulder with an audible thunk. In the next instant she flung out her hand and an athame flew across the room, straight at Hunter. It reminded me too much of that awful night weeks ago, and I flinched, but Hunter deflected the knife easily, and it glanced off a lamp and fell to the ground.

What could I do? I had no experience at things whizzing through the air—I had never practiced controlling physical things like that. In this battle I would need to use magick and magick alone. I would need to use my truth.

I saw Hunter pull out his *braigh*, the silver chain that was spelled to prevent its wearer from making magick. Coupled with some spells, it was enough to stop most witches.

But Selene merely glanced at Hunter with contempt, dismissing his threat and turning to me. Walking quickly across the room, she said, "Morgan, stop this foolishness. Call off your watchdog. You have it in you to be one of the greatest witches of all time: you are a true Woodbane, pure and ancient. Don't deny your heritage any longer. Join us, my dear."

"No, Selene," I said. Inside me, I consciously opened the door to my magick and with a deep, indrawn breath allowed it to flow. The first strains of a power chant began to thread their way into my mind.

Her beautiful face hardened, and I once again realized what I was up against. Hunter had said that Selene had been wanted by the council for years—that she had been implicated in countless deaths. Clinging to calmness, I nevertheless wished every member of the council would suddenly burst through the open door, capes waving, wands brandished, spells spouting from their lips. Coming here alone had been desperate. It had been crazy. Worse, it had been stupid.

Hunter began moving on Selene. His lips were moving, his eyes intent, and I knew he was starting the binding spells he used as a Seeker. Seeming bored, Selene barely waved a hand at him, and he stopped still, blinking. Then he started forward again, and again she stopped him.

With my mind I reached out, closed my eyes, and tried to see what I felt was there. I saw that Selene was putting up blocks and that Hunter was working through the blocks—but not as quickly as she was able to put them up. I also saw the first thin ribbons of my power spell coming to me, floating toward me on the winds of my heritage. I reached out for them, but Selene interrupted me.

"Morgan, don't you want to know the truth about how your mother died?"

17

Shift

Yule, 1982

    The house is decorated with yew boughs and holly, winter-green and mistletoe. Red candles burn and catch Cal's eyes, now golden, like mine. This is his first Yule, and he loves it.

    I found out that Daniel's whore in England had a baby, a boy, a month ago. It's Daniel's. She named him Giomanach. Daniel must be shielding her, because I haven't been able to find her, this Fiona, and get rid of her. Now I'm going to ask Amyranth to help me. It's hard to describe the feelings I have. It's so painful to admit to humiliation, despair, fury. If I were truly strong, I would strike Daniel dead. In my fantasies I've done that a thousand times—I've put his head on a spike in my front yard, cut out his heart, and mailed it to dear Fiona. I would scry to see her opening the box, seeing his heart. I would laugh.

Except that this is Daniel. I don't understand why I feel about him the way I do. Goddess help me, I can't stop loving him. If my love for him could be cut out from me, I would take up an athame and do it. If my need for him could be burned out, I would sear myself with witch fire or candle fire or an athame heated red hot in flame.

The fact that I still love him, despite his betrayal, despite the fact that he had a bastard with another woman, is like a sickness. I asked him how it had happened; were they both such poor witches that they couldn't even weave a contraceptive spell? He snapped at me and said no, the child was an accident, conceived of honest emotion. Unlike Calhoun, who had been my decision alone. He stormed out, into the wet San Francisco fog. He'll be back. It'll be against his will, but he always returns.

The joy in my life right now consists of one being, one perfection who delights me. Cal at six months is surpassing all my hopes and expectations. He has wisdom in his baby eyes, a hunger for knowledge I recognize. He's a beautiful child and easy: calm-tempered yet determined, willful yet heartbreakingly sweet. To see his face light up when I come in makes everything else worthwhile. So this Yule is a time of darkness and light, for me as well as the Goddess.

—SB

I blinked and snapped my head to look at Selene. She will use anything against you, I thought. Even your dead mother. This is why you needed to know yourself. And you do.

At once Selene seemed pathetic, like an ant, like an insect, and I felt all-powerful. In my mind the ancient ribbons of power, the crystalline tune that contained the true name of magick itself, intensified.

"I know exactly how my mother died," I answered evenly, and saw her flicker of surprise. "She and Angus were burned to death by Ciaran, her *mùirn beatha dàn*."

I felt rather than saw Selene sending out fast, dark tendrils of magick, and before they reached me, I put up a block around myself so I remained untouched inside it, free of her anger. I felt the urge to laugh at how easy it was.

But Selene was older than I, much more educated than I, and in the end she knew how to fight better than I did. "You're seeing only what Hunter wants you to see," she said with a frightening intensity. She moved closer to me still, her eyes glowing like a tiger's, lit from within. "He has been controlling you these past weeks. Can't you see that? Look at him."

For some stupid reason I actually did flick a glance toward Hunter. "Don't listen to her!" he gasped, walking toward me with halting movements.

Before my eyes, the Hunter I had come to know changed: the bones of his face grew heavier, his jaw sharper, his mouth more cruel. His eyes sank into shadow. His skin was mottled with odd white striations. His mouth twisted in a hungry leer, and even his teeth seemed sharper, more pointed, more animal-like. He looked like an evil caricature of himself.

In my split second of uncertainty, of dismay, Selene struck.

"An nahl nath rac!" she cried, and shot a bolt of crackly blue lightning toward Hunter. It hit his throat and he gagged, his eyes wide, and sank to his knees.

"Hunter!" I yelled. He still looked different, evil, and I knew Selene was doing it, but I couldn't help feeling repelled. I felt intense guilt and shame. I was supposed to trust myself, my own instincts, but the problem was, my instincts had been wrong before.

Now Selene was muttering dark spells as she advanced on me, and involuntarily I took a step back. All at once panic came crashing down on me: I had screwed up. I had made a good start but had lost it. Now Hunter was down, Mary K. was vulnerable, and I was going to die.

I felt the first prickles of Selene's spells as they flitted around me like biting insects. Tiny stings bit my skin, making me writhe, and gray mist swirled at the edges of my vision. I realized she was going to wrap me in a cloud of pain and smother me. And I couldn't stop her.

"Not my daughter."

I heard the Irish-accented voice clearly in my head, its sweet inflection not hiding the steel underneath the words. I recognized it instantly as Maeve, my birth mother. "Not *my* daughter," she said again in my mind.

I gulped in a breath. I couldn't let Selene win. Hunter was curled on the floor, motionless. I couldn't even see Mary K.; the gray mist had closed in so that I could see only Selene, glowing in front of me as if she contained a fire within her. In my mind I stretched out my hand to seize power, to draw it to me. I tried to forget everything, to concentrate only on my own spells of protection and binding. I am made of magick, I told myself. All of magick is mine for the taking. Again and again I repeated these words until they seemed part of my song, my chant that calls power. Ancient words, recognizable but unknown, came to my lips, and I flung out my arms and twirled in a circle, barely feeling my hair flying out in waves behind me.

"*Menach bis,*" I muttered, feeling the words coming to me in a voice that I didn't recognize, a man's voice. Could it be Angus? "*Allaigh nith rah. Feard, burn, torse, menach bis.*" I swirled faster in my circle of one, weaving this spell, this one perfect spell that would protect me, stop Selene, help Hunter, and keep Mary K. safe. To me it was like seeing a perfect geometric shape forming in space: the lines of the spell, its forms, its intersections and boundaries and limitations. It was a shape made of light, of energy, of music, and I saw it forming around me in the room, being woven by the words that spilled from my mouth.

And as the shape formed, I saw another shape come into focus in the background, behind Selene. Cal. He stepped through the door, into the library, and Selene's head turned toward him.

"Mother." His voice was clear, strong, but I couldn't read his intentions from his tone. Had he come to help me? Or to help Selene kill me?

No time to stop and ask. I saw myself as if from outside, dressed in Maeve's green silk robe, its hem rippling around my bare ankles like seawater as I turned. Magick crackled all around me, glowing like fireflies, floating in the air: a dandelion flower of magick that had burst and was seeding itself everywhere. Motes of power began to draw themselves around Selene. Inside me was a fierce pride, an exhilaration in my strength and the ecstasy of weaving this spell. With my ancient words I gathered the motes around Selene; I began to encase her in them, as if I were sealing her inside.

Dimly I realized what I was doing. Dimly I recognized the cage of ice and light as I wove it around Selene. It was the same as the cage that had imprisoned Maeve and Angus. But I had no time, no energy to spare for wondering what this meant, where this knowledge had come from. I was caught in the magick. It consumed me.

It was the most beautiful and the most terrifying thing I had ever seen. It was like the beauty of a star's death when it goes nova: exhilarating and devastating. The awe inside me welled up and spilled out of my eyes as tears: purifying salt crystals in and of themselves.

"No!" Selene bellowed suddenly, a horrible, gut-wrenching howl of fury and darkness. "No!" The crystal cage around her shattered, and she loomed within it, dark and malevolent and cloaked with blackness.

I didn't have the experience to duck or swerve or throw up a block. I saw the boiling cloud of dark vapor spinning away from Selene, churning toward me, and I knew that in a moment I would experience the soul being sucked from my body. All I could do was watch.

And then a dark form blocked my sight, and like a high-speed camera, my mind snapped image after image but gave me no time to process what happened. Cal surged forward, his eyes burning and hollow as he blocked Selene's attack on me. I stepped back, eyes wide, mouth open in shock as Cal absorbed the dark vapor; it surrounded him, fell upon him, and then he was sinking to the ground, his eyes already unseeing as his soul left his body.

Now I knew. He had come to help me.

Selene was on him in an instant, screaming, falling onto his chest, beating him, trying to force life back into him as I watched stupidly and without comprehension.

"Sgàth!" she shrieked, barely sounding human. "Sgàth!

Come back!" I had never heard a banshee, but that's what she sounded like, an inhuman keening and wailing that seemed to have the agony of the world in it. Her son was dead, and she had killed him.

When Hunter staggered to me and grabbed my hand, I could only stare at him. He looked like himself again, pale and ill, but the Hunter I knew.

"Now," he croaked, his voice sounding charred. "Now." ·

It all came back to me again, my brain began to function, and Hunter and I took advantage of Selene's grief and joined our powers to bind her.

Feeling cold, I gathered my magick and wove it tightly once more, a beautiful cage. Hunter stepped forward and snapped the silver *braigh* onto Selene's wrists, catching her unguarded as she held Cal's face and wept over him. She screamed again, the chain already burning her flesh. I shrank back at the horror of it: Cal's dead body, Selene's grief, her endless screaming as she thrashed, trying to get the *braigh* off.

Then she paused for an instant, her eyes rolling back into her head, and began a deep guttural chant. I saw the silver chain begin to crumble and dissolve. "Morgan!" Hunter yelled, and quickly I dropped my beautiful cage of light and magick over her.

It was like watching a black moth slowly smothering inside a glass. Within a minute Selene's rage was burning out: her screams were quieting, her thrashing had stilled; she lay coiled inside my spell as if trying to hide from the pain.

When I met Hunter's eyes, he looked horrified, shaken, yet there was an acknowledgment on his face that at last he had accomplished his goal. He was breathing hard, sweat beading his pale face, and he met my eyes. "Let's get out of here," he said shakily. "This place is evil."

But I was frozen, staring at Cal. Beautiful Cal, whom I had kissed and loved so much. Kneeling, I reached out to touch his face. Hunter didn't try to stop me.

I shuddered and shrank back—Cal's skin was already cooling. Suddenly racking sobs began to burst through my chest. I wept for Cal: for the brief illusion of love that I'd cherished so deeply, for the way he'd given his own life for mine, for what he could have been if Selene hadn't warped him.

What happened then is hard to explain. Hunter shouted suddenly and I whirled, tears still raining down my cheeks, to see Selene standing, her wrists held in front of her. I could see the blisters, but the silver *braigh* was gone. Her golden eyes seemed to burn through us. Then she sank down, collapsing on the Oriental carpet with her eyes closed. Her mouth opened, and a vaporous stream floated out, like smoke.

Hunter shouted again and threw out his arm to push me back. We watched as the vapor streamed upward and seemed to disappear through the one library window. Then it was gone, and Selene was still and ashen. Hunter stepped quickly to her and put his fingers against her throat. When he looked up, his eyes reflected his shock. "She's dead."

"Goddess," I breathed. I had helped kill Selene—and Cal, too. I was a murderer. How could Hunter and I be standing in a room with two corpses? It was incomprehensible.

"What was that smoke?" My voice was thin and shaky.

"I don't know. I've never seen anything like it before." He looked worried.

"Morgan?" came Mary K.'s voice, and I shook off my

paralysis and hurried to her. She was sitting up, blinking, and then she stood to brush off her clothes. She looked around her as if she were waking from a dream, and maybe she was. "What's going on? Where are we?"

"It's all right, Mary K.," said Hunter in his still-raspy voice. He came and took her arm so that we braced her on either side. "Everything's all right now. Let's get you out of here."

By keeping his body close to her, Hunter managed to steer Mary K. out of the room without her seeing Selene's or Cal's bodies. I followed them, forcing myself not to look back. When we were in the hall, Hunter spelled the library door so that it couldn't be shut again. Then we went outside, into the darkness, the biting cold of winter pressing in on us.

As we came down the stone steps, Sky pulled up in her car, followed by a gray sedan. A stout man with graying hair climbed out, and Hunter moved to speak to him: he had to be the closest council member.

I sat on the broad stone steps in my gown. I couldn't think about what had just happened. I couldn't process it. All I could do was hold Mary K.'s hand and start to think up what I would tell my parents. Every version I could think of started with, "It's because I'm a witch."